Wicked Lies

by

KERRY BARNES

To Robert Wood, my editor and teacher.

Deryl Easton my friend and sanity check.

Other books by Kerry Barnes.

The Vincent's trilogy -

Ruthless

Ruby's Palace

Raw Justice

The Raven's Saga -

Cruel Secrets

Acknowledgements

A huge thank you to all my family and friends, whose encouragement spurs me on every day. Without their support, I would have given up by now. I also want to thank my Facebook friends and dedicated fans, whose kind words and fantastic reviews make all the difference.

Wicked Lies

CHAPTER ONE

September 2017, Montego Bay, Jamaica

The steel drums played somewhere in the distance, the sun beat down on her deeply sun-creamed body, and just as she was about to doze off, she heard the clink of two glasses. From under her large straw hat, Kelly removed her sunglasses, as she eyed the extremely fit-looking man before her. He was rippled with muscles and the sun had given his caramel skin a shiny reddish tone. His hair was longer now and cane rolled, and his green eyes looked almost dazzling in the bright sun. She giggled and took the drink from him, so he could sit down before the hot sand burned the soles of his feet.

"Keffa, I think I could see meself living here. I've never been anywhere so hot and beautiful."

His chuckle was deep and raspy. "That's 'cos you ain't been anywhere outside of London. See, what did I tell you? Getting away for a bit, every so often, does the world of good. Ya know, just me and you, no business, no phone calls, just pure relaxation."

He lay back on the sunbed and reached out to hold her hand. She felt safe with her hand in his, with him by her side. He was right about one thing, though. This was so tranquil and maybe she had neglected him too much lately. In fact, when she looked back over the past year, she had really started to take him for granted. Taking on the businesses was exhausting, but she had a reputation to keep up and a manor to run. Perhaps Keffa had taken a back seat, and yet, here he was, still by her side.

Keffa watched as her eyes closed, and she lay there, totally at peace. He loved every inch of her, and he had done from the day she turned up at his flat with a mouth like a sewer but a heart of gold. It was wrong then to admit his feelings because she was only fifteen years old, but now, as a woman of twenty-two, she was mature and even more beautiful.

"Kelly, let me rub more of that sun cream on you. You don't want to ruin this evening, walking around like a lobster."

She rolled over onto her front and enjoyed his big strong hands massaging the cream into her skin. She had missed him, his touch and his sexy voice, whispering sweet words into her ears. This was special, and she was going to make sure it remained that way.

He stared down at her scarred back and winced as the cream gathered in the deep grooves. Those scars didn't bother him. It was the thought of what she'd gone through as a child that made him sad. Leisurely, she sat up, grabbed his oily hands, and led him back to their villa. He didn't say a word but followed.

This holiday had all the makings of a perfect wedding, and one day, he would bring her back and wed her on the very same beach, with the steel drums in the distance, the waves lapping against the white sand, and the smell of coconut and mango. This was where his mother was born, Montego Bay, Jamaica, and one day, they would return to England from here with the same surname. But for now, he would just enjoy the fresh romance that was a long time coming.

They picked up speed across the burning sand and rushed into the entrance of their grand villa, one of a few in the Half Moon complex.

So big was the place that it came with a maid. Aiesha popped her head from around the kitchen door and smiled to herself. The sight of a couple so obviously in love melted her heart.

At the foot of the stairs, Keffa scooped Kelly into his arms and laughed as her oversized straw hat fell on the floor. As if he was holding a baby, he carried her to their room and laid her on the bed. She lowered her eyes and smiled. He then saw the soft sweet girl and not the hardened woman she had so sadly become. He loved her all the same but had yearned to see her innocent eyes look at him with affection. And there it was, that look she had the day he'd rescued her from her father's clutches, the day she tilted her gaze and said, "You came for me, Keffa."

He replied, "I will always have your back."

Earlier that day, Aiesha had made their bed, as soon as they had gone out, and added a sweet, romantic touch by sprinkling red petals over the white sheets. It couldn't be more perfect. Kelly was the most beautiful she had ever felt because he made her feel that way, with his gentle touch and soft kisses which tempted her into complete submission.

Autumn 2016, Otford, Kent

It had been two months since their mother had gone and left Malakai to fend for his three sisters. At first, he thought she had gone to a party, as she often did, and was sleeping off a hangover somewhere. But, as the days turned into weeks, he realised, finally, she wasn't coming back. He was close to the girls because their mother's ways had left him no choice but to parent them. Star was the youngest and then there was Tilly, aged seven, named after their grandmother, someone they

11

had never met. The eldest sister was Saskia, who, at nearly sixteen, was as wild as an untamed pony. They called her Sassy for short and it was a name which suited her personality. She loved Malakai, but she was at times unruly, and he struggled to keep her in line. It wasn't as if their hippy mother was any good anyway; she was away with the fairies most days, stoned out of her box, and promising them the world. Her idea of being a good mother was making daisy chains and chanting with her legs crossed, calling in the good spirits and blessing the house with peace and harmony. He had watched her switch from a smartly dressed woman to a leather jacket biker and then finally to a hippy, as if she had a multitude of personalities all contained inside her tiny mind.

They had originally lived in London in a two-up two-down. It was good back then because Malakai had friends and neighbours he could call upon, especially if they ran out of food. The old lady who lived next door was a sweet old girl and she often made them a fat juicy meat pie and lamb stew. It was not until Malakai was older that he realised what the kind dear was doing. She would make a huge pot and then call, offering her leftovers, saying, "Malik, I've cooked too much again, any good to ya?" Most people, except his mother, referred to him as Malik. Every other day, the old lady would donate something delicious for them. Therefore, they never went hungry. Malik would pop into her house and offer to do housework or fix anything, just to pay her back in kind, because he had no money to offer her.

Jean, their mother, wasn't disliked by their neighbours: there was nothing to dislike. To the outsider, or those who didn't know her, she was just a sweet woman, with a pretty, innocent face and four kids to manage. She was polite and always wore a smile, yet all that friendliness never paid the bills or put a new school uniform on the back of any one of his sisters. Her attitude was so far removed from the real world, well, so she led everyone to believe. They had lived on a rough estate where it was dog eat dog. There could be a serious punch-up going on right under Jean's nose, and she would casually walk past, as if she were seeing something else from another planet and therefore not in her orbit. Malik would get so frustrated with her, and over the years, he took on the role as father to his sisters. He made sure they got up and had breakfast and then walked them to school, while Jean lay in bed. She wasn't cruel to her children, in so far as she ever hit them, but her constant disregard for their welfare infuriated Malik, and so, rather than relentlessly shout at her, he took charge.

In one of her new phases, Jean wanted to live in the country to be in touch with nature, and when her father left the cottage to her, she upped sticks and moved in, completely neglecting the state of the place. It had been left standing empty for two years before she took it on. The property was situated in an idyllic setting in a beautiful part of Kent called Otford. Her hippy mates came with their camper vans and helped her move the furniture. They stayed for weeks, having the time of their lives in the new back garden. Malik was run ragged, trying to settle the girls into their bedroom and making sure the house was fit to live in. Jean hadn't really considered the upheaval it would cause and just thought about the long rambling garden and the open-air parties she could have – and she did. They had moved in the summer, and for the most part, he could see the attraction. A huge bonfire was constantly burning, the oddly assorted chairs were arranged in a semicircle, and there were no neighbours to complain about the out of tune guitars and the continual singing and chanting. They cooked sausages, drank home-made wine, and smoked pot – the adults, of course, not the children.

It all ended abruptly one afternoon. Malik was inside the house upstairs, washing down the damp walls of his sisters' bedroom. The mould was growing up to the ceiling and stank to high heaven. He poured every cleaning product he could find into a bowl of hot water and scrubbed until his hands were stinging and the back of his throat burned. The constant whine from the ongoing party was pricking his nerves, and as he went to shout out of the window, he noticed a man dressed in a long hippy shirt slovenly sitting on a deck chair opposite his mother. He was laughing and pulling on a fat joint. Sassy was dancing beside him, and her two little sisters were at the end of the garden playing with a stray cat. He watched the man hand Sassy the joint. In a fit of rage, Malik dropped the bowl, ran frantically down the stairs, just managing to snatch the joint from Sassy, and then threw it on the fire. The man, livid at what he perceived as gross effrontery, jumped to his feet to shout at Malik, but before he could open his mouth, Malik pulled his fist back and punched him hard in the stomach. As he bent over in agony, Malik swiftly kicked him in the head knocking him to the ground, an inch away from the fire. The others were up on their feet and pulled the man away before his long hair caught alight.

Malik was shaking with anger and his chest heaved in and out. Sassy was wide-eyed and shocked; she knew from school that her brother could ruck, if need be, but she'd never seen him take down a grown man. Jean leaped from her seat and grabbed Malik by the shoulders; it was probably the first time she had ever shouted at him.

"What the hell do you think you're doing, Malakai?" Her eyes glared into his, searching for an answer.

Malik shook free of her and screamed back, "I'm doing what you should be doing! That man was gonna give Sassy a joint. Are you bleedin' blind?"

Jean rolled her eyes. "Lighten up, Malakai. A little weed never hurt anyone. You should try it, son, as it might do you some good."

Her voice was calm, which irritated Malik even more, and with a quick movement, he slapped her face. "You ain't fucking fit to be a muvver. You're like a cement life jacket, no good to anyone."

The dynamics had changed. He was now the one in charge, removing that task from his mother. "You lot, get ya fucking stuff and clear off!"

Another man, his mother's boyfriend, called Dennis, walked over to them and pulled Jean away. Then he poked a finger into Malik's chest. "You, son, need to apologise to your mother. There was no need to get violent and this is your mother's home. You would be wise to remember that."

Malik looked at the others all staring at him, as if he was a nobody — not Jean's son but a misfit who shouldn't be opening his mouth. Instantly, he jumped back, pulled a long piece of wood from the fire and dared Dennis. "Touch me again, ya fucking wanker, and I'll smash the life out of ya. Now, I've told ya once, I won't tell ya again, so all of ya, piss off!"

Dennis observed the fury in his eyes, and he decided the boy was not messing about.

The group left without a word and Malik returned to the bedroom. His main concern was for the girls, not for his mother or her loony friends.

Sassy edged into the bedroom sheepishly. "Malik, I wasn't gonna smoke it, ya know."

Malik whirled around and stared at his sister. What he saw in front of him was no longer an adolescent child but instead a young woman and an attractive one at that. Tall for fifteen, she was in the early throes of femininity with all the attendant signs. It wouldn't be long before this was evident to every male around Otford. Her dishevelled ginger curls and piercing green eyes gave her a striking look. She was cheeky and was always mouthing off, yet today, she was speechless. Her

15

brother had stood up and protected his family. She knew smoking pot was wrong, and although she took the joint, she did not intend to smoke it. She also knew that one of the men had touched her up, and she wasn't too comfortable in their company. Although she liked the open-air fires, the sausages, and the giggles, she still had concerns that one day one of her mother's friends may do more than pinch her backside. Her brother was her safety net, the one she respected. He was her idol, and she knew she was very lucky to have him looking after them all.

"Sassy, you shouldn't 'ave taken it, not even touched the shit!"

Sassy inclined her head; she felt ashamed and wanted nothing more than to please her brother. They argued and bickered, but she also knew in her heart that without him they would have probably died.

"All right, Malik, I'm sorry. What ya doing, anyway?"

Malik picked up the bowl. "Cleaning this black shit off the walls. It stinks in 'ere. It's damp and gonna make you sick, if we don't get it dried out before the winter. Fucking muvver, she's too busy being a hippy to sort anything out. Sass, this room is cold and it's only October. What's it gonna be like come winter?"

Sassy shuddered. "Is mum's room cold, too?"

Malik shook his head. "Nah, there's no damp, either. That's a good point. I'm gonna swap you all over. Star has asthma, and there's no way she can sleep in here during the winter. It's been three weeks and she's wheezing. It must be this poxy room."

Sassy sat drearily on the lumpy old bed. "It's creepy an' all. I can hear all the animals of a night. It keeps me up. Tilly shits herself and

16

jumps in bed with me! Why did mum have to move? At least our old house was warm."

Malik laughed. "Well, Sass, it was stuck between two houses. This monster is open to all weathers, get what I mean? The stupid woman! She probably never even checked the inside, before she decided to move. Jesus, I know she's our mum, but, Sass, I'm beginning to hate her."

Sassy chewed the inside of her mouth. "Malik ...?"

Malik turned his head to the side. "What is it, Sass?" His voice was calm.

"I heard mum the other day saying to Dennis that she wished she was totally free and didn't have children. She never wanted us, Malik. That's bad, ain't it?"

"Sass, I've always known it. She should have stopped after she'd 'ad me, instead of bringing you girls into this shit life. Well, never mind, we're 'ere, and one day, we'll have our own lives."

Sassy's eyes shone and with a wide smile she jumped up. "Yep, when I grow up, I'm gonna be a model and wear all those fancy clothes." She tilted her head to the side and gave a fake model pose, pouting her lips. Malik laughed. "And a fine one, too. But there's one problem. Just make sure ya don't open ya mouth and speak!"

"And what's wrong with the way I speak?"

Malik shook his head. "Have you not heard yourself? Ya sound like a pikey!"

"Oh, shut up, ya cunt. There ain't nuffin wrong with the way I talk."

Malik rolled his eyes, yet he really admired his sister; she was mouthy but funny too.

"D'ya think we should try and find our farver?"

Malik sighed. "Which one? 'Cos it's my guess none of us has the same! I mean, look at you! You're ginger, me, I'm mousy, Tilly's got the jet-black hair, and as for little Star, well, she's got white curls! We're a complete joke, really. We look like an advert for the United Colors of Benetton. All we need is a black brother and we'll be complete!"

Sassy gave a hearty laugh. "Yeah, still, I don't care. We are family, we might be a tent short of a circus, but we're lucky, Malik, really lucky."

"How d'ya work that out, you divvy?"

Sassy turned to leave the bedroom, but then, as she glanced back, her face softened. "'Cos, Mal, we have you."

Malik, as young as he was, knew she meant it. It was true; without him, they would be so much worse off. He cursed his mother — and his father, whoever he was. He looked out of the window to see the last of the camper vans loaded up and driven away. His mother was with Dennis, standing in the garden, with a knitted shawl wrapped around her shoulders. She did look sweet and unassuming, but underneath her light-hearted, happy-go-lucky front, she was a waste of space. Malik decided then that he didn't care for his mother at all. Star was fighting for her mother's attention, but Jean was more interested in her hippy gang and her drippy boyfriend. Malik continued to watch as Star was showing Jean the kitten she'd found, but Jean was more concerned by being hugged and comforted by Dennis. It was a sorrowful sight, seeing his youngest sister, with her huge eyes, looking up at her mother and then slowly slipping away whilst looking back with a sadness which had now spread across her round baby face. Malik wanted to run back down the stairs to the garden and hug Star and slap his mother again. Instead, he sighed, and pragmatically he took control and set about swapping the bedrooms' contents over. If his mother was too busy fucking every hippy in sight and not taking care of her kids, then he would look after them instead. He shouted for Sassy to help, which she was only too happy to do. Her mother's room was cleaner, warmer, and let in more light. It was the biggest of the three upstairs bedrooms and faced the front of the house. Malik realised that the back wall facing the garden was damp and a serious concern that his mother had completely overlooked. He was happy to remain in his room, even though it too was at the back, but he couldn't countenance the thought of his sisters sleeping with the mould and the smell.

By the time the sun went down, Malik had completely moved his mother's belongings and bed into the back room. He made it look cosy and even put a side lamp on to enhance the homely feel. The front bedroom was less cramped, and the girls had a little more room now to walk around between the bunk beds and the single bed occupied by Sassy. She didn't mind sharing a room with her younger sisters, and if the truth be told, she really enjoyed their company. She was no iron maiden; she liked to think of herself as their friend as well as their sister, although she wouldn't take any bullshit off them. She wasn't that soft! However, she didn't bully her little sisters; although she teased them, she was never unkind. Well, she hoped she wasn't, anyway.

Malik had done a good job, and in doing so, he was also making a clear statement – if she, his mother, wasn't up to caring for his siblings, then he would.

Jean had drunk far too much wine and spent the evening in the garden with Dennis, keeping the fire well fuelled. When it was time

19

for her to go to bed, she staggered up the stairs, with Dennis behind her steering the way. Malik had made sure the girls were tucked up in bed and the door shut. After hearing his mother climbing the stairs, he left his room to join her on the landing. She gave him a disapproving glare and turned to go to her room.

"Er, no, muvver, you're in the back room. I've swapped the rooms over. You don't need all that space and the girls do." His voice was firm and very mature, much to the shock of Dennis, who stood upright and raised his eyebrow.

"Listen, son, you can't just throw your weight around like you're the man of the house. You're just a fucking kid and you should have respect for your mother."

Sassy heard the voices and bounded from her bed to join her brother. She felt even more confident, knowing Malik was there for her rather than her mother. "Oi, wanker, *he* is the man of the house. You ain't, Dennis. You're just another one of me muvver's fellas, so shut ya fucking mouth."

Malik was laughing inside at his sister's choice of words. Jean was still staggering, with her head nodding all over the place. She stumbled, trying to grab Sassy, and then she fell into a crumpled heap onto the floor. It was all Malik could do but just stare at her, shaking his head. She looked pathetic, and it was at this point, his dislike turned to disgust.

Dennis tried to get Jean to her feet but was embarrassed because deep down he knew Malik was right. He never wanted a serious relationship with Jean; she was a good fuck, but that was all. He wasn't about to take on a woman with four kids — and bloody mouthy ones at that. He'd tried to put Malik in his place, only so he and his mates could

20

have a free ride and use their country cottage as a place to party and smoke dope.

Sassy was standing with her hands on her hips and her hair wildly sticking in all directions. "And another thing, Dennis. If you want a fucking fight, then you'll 'ave one, 'cos I don't like being touched up by your pervy mate. I just might go to the Ol' Bill. I might be a kid, but I know that ain't right."

Dennis looked from Sassy to Malik; his eyebrows snapped together, and his mouth went dry. He had underestimated them; they were young, but they were also clued-up and fierce. He knew exactly who Sassy was on about: it was his own brother, Jake. His ogling at Sassy had been unsubtle and noted by Dennis. Looking at the kid now, he knew she meant it.

He nodded to Malik. "I'll put your mother to bed and be off, all right?"

Malik gave him a sarcastic smile. "Yeah, mate, you do just that."

Dennis was considering the eyes of an adult not a teenager. For a second, he shuddered; if looks could kill, he was a dead man. He lifted Jean, carried the dead weight into the back room, and laid her on the immaculately made bed. He was somewhat surprised that Malik had not just dumped her belongings there; instead, he had made the room neat and tidy. Jean was never that way inclined; she was, in the main, slovenly and never house proud. She got away with a lot because of her pretty face and slim toned figure. Dennis, however, liked the natural look, although he realised that Jean had taken the hippy thing to a whole other level. She was more natural than she should be; she didn't bathe too often or even shave her armpits or her legs for that matter, and to cap it all, there was never a can of deodorant in the house. Dennis looked down at Jean snoring and decided there was no point in ever returning; this woman would never stand up to Malik. She was too weak and liked the pipe too much. He backed out of the room and jumped when he came face-to-face with Malik. "Good luck, boy, you're going to need it. I'll be gone, and I won't be back."

Malik gave him a sarcastic smile. "I couldn't give a shit what ya think. Just fuck off!"

As Dennis clambered down the stairs, Malik turned to find his little sisters peering out of the bedroom. Tilly looked terrified and Star's bottom lip quivered. He gave them a huge smile and they breathed a sigh of relief; they ran to him, putting their arms around his legs.

"Come on, back to bed," he said, as he helped them inside their shabby sheets. To his surprise, he heard a rustling under the bed. Tilly was on the top bunk and leaned over. She watched Malik, as he searched underneath for what he thought might be a rat. Then, he felt the soft fur and grabbed the wriggling animal and retrieved it from its hiding place. It was the kitten that Star had found. It was too young to be away from its mother, and so he had to explain to his sister that what she did was not right, and he would have to return the animal to where she had found it. Her lip quivered again, and her eyes instantly filled with water.

"Hey, it's okay, Star, you can have him when he's old enough, but for now, he needs his muvver."

He studied her distraught face and thought about his words – "but for now, he needs his muvver." The kitten was like her; she needed her mother, as she was only a baby. Another nerve pricked, and the hate began to increase. He didn't see Jean as their mother; well, how could he? In his head, he called her Jean; he couldn't bring himself to call her mum.

With a rotten dry mouth and a head like cotton wool, Jean lay in the cold damp room trying to recall yesterday's events, and then it hit her. Malik was his father's son all right. That mean glare and almost imperious posture was him all over. She knew the day would come when her son would show his father's traits and brandishing that long piece of wood to take on any man didn't really shock her. It would be inevitable that he would turn out to be a handful. He had his father's expression which would have the toughest of men shitting themselves. If she was honest, he scared her. If only she'd just had an abortion. In fact, what would her life have been with no kids? *Well, probably a damn sight better than this,* she thought.

Across the landing, she could hear Sassy playing with the youngest two; she had them in fits of giggles, and the sound was grating on Jean's nerves. She could handle them, if she was stoned, but nursing a hangover, with no weed or any pills to ease the pain, it only intensified their shrieking. She was about to tell them to shut the noise up, but then the vision of her son's aggressive-looking face made her quickly bite her lip. She had to face facts: he was of an age whereby she couldn't get away with anything, and yesterday's antics had made that very clear. Slowly, she eased herself into an upright position and felt the bare floorboards under her feet. She peered down at the bruise on her knee, where she'd taken a tumble, and noticed her unshaven legs. Pulling the tatty old dressing gown from the end of the bed, she wrapped it around her body and tried to stretch, but the headache made her wince. Looking around the small room, she swallowed back the bitter taste. Malakai had taken the right piss moving her into the back room. Yet she had to accept it; there was no argument. Shuffling herself out of the bedroom and into the bathroom, she slammed the door shut and the house fell quiet; the children must have heard her. The old mirror in the bathroom was the same one she had peered into all those years ago, and yet what stared back was not the attractive teenager but a well-worn woman. She blinked a few times to focus and noticed the crow's feet and lines around her mouth. Her once thick wavy hair was dull and thin. She really had let herself go.

So much had changed in those years. If only she could turn the clock back, if only she had listened to her father. There were so many *if onlys*. But the biggest regret was accepting that visiting order to Brixton prison, agreeing to the chapel visit, and handing the chaplain the two litres of vodka. All for what? It had been just a quick shag at the back of the chapel with a villain who had no intention of making a life with her when he got out. Was it the thrill or the thought of a future life with money and status? She sighed heavily and turned on the taps. The cool water on her face sobered her thoughts. Enough was enough. She was going to tidy herself up and find a way to get the life she deserved. The only man she had really loved was now out of prison, and she knew exactly how to win over his affections; besides, the hippy life wasn't really her thing — but it had been fun for a while.

The day he realised his mother wasn't coming home was the day he became a man; he'd had plenty of practice, having to be grown up for so long. His childhood was taken away from him at such a young age. The only solace he had was at school: here he could be a child. He respected his teachers; they were strict, but this was something he admired.

It was the end of October 2016 when Jean left the cottage and her family. She did not return. Malik made sure they all went to school, so that the social services didn't ask any questions; he needed to keep his nose clean. They had used up all the food in the freezer and the washing powder, so now he was left with nothing. Luckily, he had milk to warm up and feed the little ones' bellies, ready for school. They were entitled to free school dinners and he told them to eat as much as they could.

Even Star, as young as she was, understood she was never to say their mother wasn't at home. Malik told her she was looking after her sick friend and she would be back soon. Tilly was the quiet, nervous one. She knew her mother wasn't coming back and turned to Sassy and Malik, as if they were her parents.

Winter had arrived three weeks ago and was at its worst. Malik tried his best to keep the house warm. He used the axe he found in the shed to chop branches. His skinny arms were now bulking out and his tiny chest was broad like a man's. The food had dwindled away, and they were left penniless. Star was shivering and snivelling so much that Malik had no choice but to put another log on the fire; it spat and hissed due to the damp, but it would be a while before any heat could be gained from it. The logs should have dried out, but the harsh winter had made it very hard for them all. He recalled bringing in some logs a few days ago; the girls had screamed, and he'd looked at them with astonishment until he saw one monster of a spider crawling along the floor.

Malakai wrapped Star in his sheepskin coat and plonked her in front of the open fire. "Now, then, you get yaself warm, and stop bleedin' snivelling. So, ya wet the bed. It's no big deal, right?"

Sniffing back another tear, she peered up and nodded. "I didn't mean to, Malik."

She was only five and too young to understand. Yet, at almost seventeen, Malik was in over his head, even though he was trying his utmost to hang on to his family. No way would he let the social services know that they were alone. He had contemplated it, but then he'd heard of stories of kids going into care, being separated, and even suffering from child abuse. Therefore, he dismissed the idea completely.

Sassy came heavy-footed down the stairs, rubbing her eyes. "What's happened now?" she asked, with her hands on her hips and glaring at Star.

Malik was rubbing Star's little blue legs. "Nothing, Sass. She's had another accident, that's all."

Sassy shook her head. "We ain't got no clean sheets, or any washing powder."

Star snivelled again. "It's all right, Star," soothed Malik, pulling a sour face at Sassy.

"I've got an idea," blurted Sassy.

Malik nodded. "Oh, yeah? What's that, then?"

"Well, when we take the short cut to school, there's a launderette. There are always people shoving sheets and shit in the machines, and guess what? They fuck off and don't come back for a while. I noticed the other day, only 'cos when you walk past it, the heat hits ya. Well, I'm gonna go in and nick the sheets. Besides, that lot around 'ere are stinking rich. They won't mind."

Malik raised his eyebrow. "Nah, you won't, Sass. If ya got caught, we'll all get nabbed by the social services. You wait 'ere with the girls. I'm gonna go and 'ave a butchers. Where's that big stripy laundry bag, the one that muvver kept her clothes in?"

Sassy thought for a moment and ran up the stairs. They rarely ventured into her room; it was too cold, and besides that, Malik had already stripped her bed for the blankets. There, on the floor, was the bag. Sassy tipped the contents on the bed and ran back downstairs. "'Ere ya go."

Malik jumped up and took the bag. "Sass, listen to me. Make sure the fire doesn't burn out, keep the girls warm, and if by nightfall, I ain't back, then I guess the next knock at the door will be the police and social services. Don't fight or argue, just do as they say."

Realisation hit her in the face. "No, Malik, don't do it. What if ya get caught? Look, we can find another way."

Malik shrugged his shoulders. "Sass, look at Star. She's freezing and fucking wheezing, and Tilly has a stinking cold. Damn our bleedin' muvver."

Sassy looked over at her youngest sister and her heart sank. He was right: Star was struggling. Sassy nodded for him to go, and as she opened the front door, an icy wind blew in. She shivered. Star tried to smile, but she was tired, and her eyes were glazed over. Sassy felt like crying, seeing Star so poorly. It just wasn't fair. She hurried over and scooped Star onto her lap and cuddled her.

"It's gonna be all right, Star. Malik will see to it. Now, you keep warm, and I'll sing us a song."

Star, as young as she was, was so tiny she looked more like a three-year-old. Her big eyes were so trusting that she nodded without question.

"Twinkle, twinkle, little star, how I wonder what you are,

All wrapped up in Malik's coat,

You look like a nanny goat ...."

CHAPTER TWO

Malik stepped outside and glanced back at the partially hidden cottage. The trees in the front garden were hundreds of years old and towered over the rooftop. Yes, it was a beautiful property from the outside and in an attractive location, but inside, it was a different matter. The house lacked a damp-proof course and there was no central heating. He marched along the windy path to the gate, trying to dodge the cold dew on the bushes, which were so overgrown, their branches had spread across to the path like giant tentacles. A fog clouded his view and he smiled; this would help if he needed a fast escape route. The launderette was busy, just as Sassy had said. He wandered in and noticed two old women and a young man; so, three people, and yet there were four tumble dryers hurtling round and one left idle with nothing in it. The young man pulled his washing from the machine, and Malik's attention focused on the sheets and a quilt. Before he left, the guy placed them in the dryer. Next, the two women did the same. He was now alone and with four tumble dryers to choose from. He glanced around the room to see if there were any cameras: there was not one.

Quickly, he opened the dryers and took the contents from each, hoping fervently he wouldn't get caught. In the corner of the room were two laundry bags, so he helped himself, and by the time he'd filled both and the one he'd brought with him, he was out of breath and unsure how the hell he would carry them home. But with the vision of his little sisters freezing, and the conviction that his need was greater than those whose clothes he had stolen from, he mustered enough strength to flip the bags over and onto his back and run as fast as he could. The fog and the biting cold wind made his lungs ache. He was chilled to the bone because his coat was still wrapped around his little sister. Just as he turned a corner, he noticed a delivery van, with its back doors wide open and no one in sight. The delivery driver must be in the big house with the long drive. He looked up at the enormous house, and then, quick as a flash, he hid behind the van door and peered in. There were shopping bags all labelled up, there for the taking. Again, he reasoned, his family's needs were probably greater than theirs, so he snatched two and ran. No one called out, so he knew he was safe. He just had to get home but struggled with all the weight over his shoulders and the handles cutting into his fingers. *A small price to pay*, he thought. Finally, fighting for breath and weak at the knees, he arrived totally knackered, but with so much adrenaline pumping through his body, he honestly forgot about his tired state, as he saw the front door open and his big sister run out to help him with his bags. He slammed the door shut behind him, took a long, slow breath, and leaned against the wall. But he had a big smile on his face as he did so.

"What happened? Did ya get chased?"

Malik shook his head. "Nah. That lot is so fucking heavy, I can't breathe."

Sassy laughed. "Thank fuck for that."

Malik rolled his eyes. He didn't like to hear his sister swearing so much; she was only a kid.

"Get it all into the kitchen. I wanna see what we've got," urged Malik.

Sassy was peering into the shopping bags and could feel her mouth salivating and her stomach rumbling; she was so hungry. The only food she'd had was during the week at school, and if there were rolls with lunch, she pocketed them, too, for her sisters to have for tea. However, it was the weekend, and there was nothing except what awaited them inside the bags.

Sassy impatiently poured the contents over the floor and Malik grabbed the other bag and did the same. Their eyes were wide, and excitedly, they went through the offerings.

"This is great, Malik. This will do us for a week."

Malik nodded, but those words hit him, as if he'd been given a rabbit punch. The clock was ticking, and with only a week's supply, he would have to find another way to fill the freezer and pay the bills.

"Look, a big bag of pasta and tinned tomatoes. That's bolognaise for three days," she laughed. The two joints of meat and bacon were put in the freezer and the rest of the food was shoved in the rickety old fridge. The kitchen faced north, which would normally be no bad thing, but the back of the house felt as though they had walked into a giant fridge themselves. A stone floor and old-fashioned wooden cabinets didn't make the room any more inviting. In the corner was a log burner, which would be a bonus, but Malik was relying on the few logs they had left to keep the living room warm.

"Sassy, get Tilly up. Tell her to bring her blankets down to the living room. It's too cold up there. From now on, we're gonna sleep in there. I'm gonna keep the fire going."

He studied Star carefully, who was looking very pasty-faced. She was trembling in this cold, lifeless room. He emptied the laundry bags, not really remembering what he'd snatched, but was over the moon when he found soft brushed cotton sheets, two expensive quilts, and a pair of designer jeans and a jumper, obviously from the young man in the launderette.

Tilly appeared, looking just as ill as her younger sister. With her sunken eyes and pale face, they didn't need a doctor to discover she was coming down with the flu. Malik swallowed hard. He was doing his best, but it wasn't good enough; both the youngest girls were in serious need of medicines and professional help. He contemplated calling the social services; this just wasn't fair on his sisters. They needed a warm home with good food, not stale bread and scraps. Tilly tiptoed over to Malik with her thumb in her mouth and holding her comforter, and which, in truth, resembled a dirty old rag. She hugged his leg. "Malik, I thought you had left us. I was frightened. Ya won't leave us, will ya? Ya won't do what mummy did?"

That honest and heartfelt plea from Tilly was all he needed to realise that he was the man in this house. It would be he and he alone who would look after his siblings. There would be no question of handing them over to the authorities: they were his family, his responsibility now.

"Tilly, get on the sofa with Star and wrap this quilt around you." They had never had a quilt, only old hippy crochet blankets. Instantly, the girls felt the heat and huddled together, and very gradually, the colour returned to their cheeks.

"Right, let's cook sausages and 'ave hotdogs."

Tilly's eyes lit up with excitement, and she wrapped her tiny arms around her sister. Malik, however, felt sick with sadness: to see his sisters get excited over a fucking sausage was the pits.

"Sass, cook them, will ya? I'm gonna pop out. I won't be long. Make sure you all stay in 'ere and keep warm."

"Where ya going, Mal?" Her voice was pitched with concern. She hadn't considered how worried she would be if he didn't return, until now. They were all in this sad existence together.

"Look, Sass, I've gotta get some food together. You just stay 'ere and wait, and keep warm, and I'll be back." Sassy nodded.

The fog was slowly lifting, as Malik left the house. He was now much warmer, having his coat on his back this time. He had to think, and think quickly, of ways to support his family. The open delivery van gave him an idea. He headed for the large superstore, to suss out how the deliveries worked, and then he was going to make a plan, the beginnings of which were forming in his mind.

The superstore was actually only about a ten-minute walk from the cottage. As usual, it was a hive of activity, and it was at this point, Malik cottoned on that the local people were loaded. The cars in the car park were mostly fairly new and quite a few were top-of-the-range vehicles. As far as he could see, the customers were not just popping bread and potatoes into their baskets but loading up trollies with expensive meats, cheeses, and wines. It was so different from their local supermarket in the East End of London, where he'd once lived. He hadn't bothered to take in his surroundings before – there had been no need – but things had changed radically. It was a daunting experience for him: he was the provider, and his siblings were literally putting their lives in his hands. After wandering around the huge building, he found himself at the back where the deliveries were made. Two large Eddie Stobart trucks were parked with their back doors open, facing the warehouse. He sat on the wall by the dumpster bins and watched the fork lift trucks whirl around as they moved their pallets into the cavernous building.

Kimi Wade was ordered to take the out-of-date food to the bins by her manager, Cordelia Sharp. She rolled her eyes and huffed. "Kimama, I am warning you. If you slacken off one more time, then you'll have a written warning," spat Cordelia in her hoity-toity voice.

Kimi bit her lip. *Fucking stuck-up madam*, she thought. Kimi had moved with her parents closer to Sevenoaks because she was getting out of hand back in London. Her father had sold up and moved as soon as she got caught smoking a joint. She was expelled from school just before her exams and that was that. All her father could do was to move her away from the local gang and to find her a job, to keep her away from trouble. She hated the job, yet it was the only money she would get now. Her stepmother refused to give her any pocket money, and what she said went, as far as her father was concerned. He was so smitten with her that he refused to let Kimi get in the way, so she was stuck in this supermarket loading shelves.

Kimi looked at the big trays of meats and tutted. All those huge joints of lamb, priced at almost twenty quid, going to the dump seemed a wicked waste. Tossing her long dyed black hair away from her eyes, she bagged all the meat up and took her time waltzing over to the bins. There, out of the corner of her eye, was a teenager; he was just sitting on the wall, and she nodded in his direction. It was unusual to see anyone of her age around here, and he looked a little cheeky bugger – *right up my street*, she thought.

"All right?" she shouted to him.

In his own world, Malik forthwith snapped out of his gaze and looked her over. He could see she was pretty, although she had on way too much make-up for his liking, but, nevertheless, she had a friendly face. He smiled back.

"What ya doing?" she asked, as she skipped over to him.

Malik was uneasy; he had to keep his wits about him. "Er, nuffin, really, just sitting mindin' me own business, like."

Kimi, thinking he was being sarcastic, said, "All right, I was just being friendly, suit yaself." With that, she turned away to empty the meat into the bins.

He watched, as she pulled from the bags, one at a time, the legs of lamb. Realising they were going to waste and he could use them, if they were cooked thoroughly, he smiled to himself. They would be fine, even if they were a day or so past their sell-by date.

"Er, sorry, I didn't mean to be funny, I was just ..."

Kimi smiled his way. "Ah, that's all right. Me name's Kimi. So, are you from around 'ere, then?"

Malik nodded. "Yeah, not far. So, what ya doing, Kimi?"

She laughed. "Throwing away half the store, by the look of it. It's a piss-take, really, ya know. I mean, look at me. Do I look like I should be filling a bin?"

Malik was amused by the girl. She was full of life, with plenty of cheek to go with it. She put him in mind of a chubbier version of Cheryl Cole. He raised his eyebrow and Kimi noticed how attractive he was. He wasn't fashionably dressed, and his hair wasn't trendy, but his cocky smirk was enough for her to think he was a looker.

"Nah, not really. So, that's ya job, then, is it?"

She giggled. "Well, I fill the poxy shelves and empty the crap. A really cool job, eh?"

Malik jumped off the wall and strolled over to her. "Any chance I can 'ave those joints? Me dogs will love 'em."

Kimi stopped hurling them into the dumpster and gestured for him to have the other bag. "Yeah, 'course, mate. There are loads inside, and they've got beef, too." She pointed to the back of the store.

"Yeah? So, do they always chuck out stuff, or did they order too many?"

Kimi giggled again. "Cor, blimey, mate, you really don't come from around 'ere. I'm guessing you're from the East End, like meself."

At once, Malik felt more comfortable. He'd noticed when joining his new school, the kids were better spoken, but Kimi was like him.

"What's ya name?" she asked brazenly.

"Malik. So, Kimi, do they always lob food away?"

She nodded. "Yeah, anything past its sell-by date, they throw. Everyone that comes in 'ere is too posh to look at discounted stuff. Even the toys. If the box is damaged, it's thrown out."

Malik's mind was registering it all, and he knew then he could feed his sisters. "I bet the toys get snapped up, though?"

Kimi frowned. "A bit old for toys, ain't ya?"

Malik blushed and tilted his head. "I've got little sisters. I was just thinking about them, that's all."

Kimi pulled out a packet of cigarettes. "'Ere, Malik, want one? It's me break."

He shook his head. "I don't smoke."

Cordelia was on her period and so not in the best of moods. She noticed Kimama missing – again – and headed for the back of the store. Her shriek made Malik jump. "Kimama, it's not your break yet! You've enough to do before you can take your lunch hour!"

"Kimama?" questioned Malik, cheekily, but with a gentle smile on his face, all the same.

Kimi stubbed her cigarette out and winked at Malik. "Yeah, me real mum named me Kimama. Its Native American for butterfly, but everyone, apart from that snooty bitch, calls me Kimi. I best be off. I've nearly had all me warnings! Will I see ya again, Malik?"

He grinned. "Yeah, I'll be back." That cheeky grin had Kimi wishing she could get to know him more. There was something behind the mystery lad which intrigued her. She was bored and in need of a distraction from her suffocated life.

He gripped tightly the plastic bag containing the meat, and as soon as she was out of sight, he wandered around the bins, and sure enough, there, piled up behind the blue dumpster, were two heavy-duty black bags filled with toys, including genuine Barbie dolls, and lots of short story books for very young children. He wasted no time in grabbing both bags and heading home. Once again, he'd taken more than he could comfortably carry, but nothing was going to stop him. He was sweating under the coat, and his hands were aching, gripping the bags. *Only half a mile to go.* He thought about Christmas and how over the years it had been a dull, bleak experience. His mother never really did much over the festive period. She made cakes and cooked a turkey, and the girls got a few bits and pieces but no toys to speak of. The more he thought about Jean, the angrier he became. He had no idea what else was in the bags, but he could see dolls and pink things. It was enough to know he was doing the right thing by breaking his back to get home.

Once he put the key in the door, Sassy was there, ready to help him with all his bags. She feasted her eyes on them and clapped her hands. "What ya got there, Mal?"

He winked. "Sass, I think I've got the girls their Christmas presents. Shush, I'll sneak them upstairs."

After they'd moved all the perishable food into the kitchen and stored it away, Sassy followed her brother into his cold, damp bedroom and watched as he emptied the other bags onto the bed. Straight away, she put her hands to her mouth, to stop the excited squeal from leaving. It was a kid's fantasy: there were dolls, play dough, games, puzzles, books and teddies. Then he emptied the next bag. When all the boxes of chocolates and skin care products fell out, his face lit up in amazement. They were, as Kimi had said, perfect except for the dented or torn boxes.

"Jesus, Malik, where did ya nick that lot?"

He sat down, looking at his hands shaking from the weight of the bags. "I didn't, Sass. I got them from the back of the superstore and there's more. This bird called Kimi reckons they are always throwing gear away. I'm going back tomorrow or maybe even tonight. She's chucking out beef. With a few more trips, I reckon I'll have the freezer full up. We definitely won't starve now."

Sassy looked at her brother's indented and bruised hands. Her heart went out to him. He was only a kid himself, really. She knew that he was too young for this way of life, but like Malik, she was also aware that she had to grow up quickly, if they were going to survive.

Tilly and Star were huddled up together in the warm living room. Malik joined them, with one of the boxes of chocolates. Their crestfallen faces soon transformed when they saw the tray of posh delights and they giggled with excitement. Malik knew then that how they had been raised wasn't right; children should have treats not beansprouts and raw carrot. He smiled to himself, thinking about the toys he could give them for Christmas and how excited they would be.

Sassy cooked her spag boll, and although it was nothing special, it was warm and filling. The little ones were ravenous, and after stuffing their faces, they dozed off to sleep listening to Sassy telling them some mad fairy story. Malik returned to his bedroom and shivered; it was bitterly cold. He dragged his blankets and pillow back down the stairs and made up a bed by the fire. Sassy had already made her bed up on the other sofa. For the moment, the only room to be heated would be the living room.

Sunday, Malik was up at the crack of dawn; he hurriedly got himself dressed and put more logs on the fire. He was worried about his youngest sister; her coughs were still causing her a problem.

A thick frost covered the ground, and although it looked pretty, it was freezing. At the end of the long rambling back garden, beyond the rickety wooden fence, was a wooded area. He knew he was not supposed to go there chopping down trees, but he had no choice. At this time of the morning, no one would notice. As he climbed the back fence, his eyes scanned the fallen trees for a decent-sized branch. There was nothing in the immediate vicinity, so he wandered further into the woods to find what he needed.

The axe was getting blunt, and as he swung hard at a log on the ground, the bluntness caused a pain to shoot up his arm. Again, he tried to take a chunk out of the wood, but it was no use. In his desperation to find firewood, Malik didn't notice a man with his dog and took one last attempt to split the log. At this point, the man shouted, "Oi, what do you think you're doing?" His voice was deep and intimidating. Malik looked up and he had a split second to make a choice: stand still, and brazen it out with the geezer, or scarper. He decided not to argue but run. As he turned towards where he'd come from, a dog appeared from behind and attacked him, sinking its razor-sharp teeth deep into his arm. Malik screamed in terror as the dog literally dragged him to the ground and then launched another bite, this time into his hand. Terrified the dog would rip his right hand off, his only means of supporting his family, he let out a blood-curdling, agonising shriek. In the distance, he heard the man shout out for the dog to stop and instantly the beast let go. Malik was struggling to get to his feet and the pain was increasing. One arm was becoming so badly bruised that he couldn't grip his hand and blood was now pouring onto the ground.

The sturdily built man in his sixties, dressed in a green Barbour coat, and carrying a twelve-bore shotgun empty, open, and over the crook of his arm, hurried over to Malik. "Christ, boy, let me see," he said, as he tried to help Malik to his feet. Stein, the dog, had never bitten anyone before; he was a Rottweiler and would retrieve any pheasants that his master shot. Malik was teary eyed and white as a sheet, and it was all he could do to stand upright.

"Let me help you, son. I'm really sorry. Stein has never done that before. I need to get you to hospital. Come with me."

Malik was terrified he was going to lose his hand. He could see the blood and feel the pain, but he couldn't look too closely, for fear of seeing the real damage. In his state of panic and confusion, he couldn't think quickly enough, totally on autopilot, and so he allowed the stranger to hold his good arm to enable him to walk over to a Range Rover parked just in the lay-by.

"I'm Cyril Reardon. I own this land. So, who are you?"

Malik was still dazed; he managed just one word. "Malakai," he whispered.

Cyril helped him onto the front passenger seat and shut Stein in the back. He took a closer look at the boy's hand and shuddered; it was a nasty bite and would need stitches. He glanced at his dog that still had blood around his mouth and cursed his luck. He loved the dog; in fact, he loved the dog more than he loved most people, and so he was worried that this kid would have his pride and joy put down. He wouldn't blame him, either, but he thought maybe he could settle outside the justice system. It would not look good in court, especially since that was the last place he would want to be. Courts, police stations, and prisons gave Cyril a bitter taste in his mouth.

Malik swooned; the blood was still pouring and covering his clothes as well as the interior of the man's Range Rover.

"Right, Malakai, I'll get you to hospital. Don't worry, son, everything will be all right." He rubbed Malik's shoulders. All Malik wanted was for the blood and deep throbbing pain to stop. As they hurried to the hospital, Cyril used his mobile phone and called Dr Seeton-Jones, an old friend.

"Hey, ol' buddy, are you in the hospital? It's Cyril."

Malik couldn't hear the man's voice on the end of the phone.

"Cheers, me ol' mucker. I have a boy with me. He's had a nasty dog bite. Can you see to him right away?"

Cyril put his phone away and tapped the boy's knee. "Right, Malakai, me mate, a brilliant surgeon, will see to you. He'll be

41

expecting us, so we don't have to bugger about. Bloody hospitals, I fucking hate 'em."

Malik was grateful. The thought of waiting in A&E for hours turned his stomach.

"Thanks, mister."

Cyril recognised the accent and guessed that Malakai wasn't from the Sevenoaks area. He sounded more like he was from his own manor.

"So, what were you doing in me woods?" His voice softened.

Malik tried to think up a story, but his mind was on the pain. "I just needed a few logs for me fire."

Cyril sniffed. "So why don't your parents order them? We've a local delivery service, ya know."

"Our heating has only just gone up the creek, so it was just to warm the place."

There was silence as Cyril carefully thought about how he would broach the situation regarding his dog being put in the frame. He knew very well that it was the doctor's job to question a dog bite, and, if necessary, to call the police in, if the bite was bad enough to consider having the dog destroyed.

"Malakai, what are you going to tell the doctor about the dog?"

Malik shrugged his shoulders; at first, he didn't grasp what Cyril was getting at, but then it hit him. Cyril could be done for this.

"What do you want me to say, Mr Reardon?"

Cyril inspected the boy's face. In that moment of silence, there was an unspoken understanding.

"You could say a stray dog attacked you in the woods?"

Malik nodded. "Then, that's what I'll say …" He paused and took a breath to carry on, but Cyril interrupted him.

"Malakai, what help would you like from me?"

Malik frowned; the man used the word "help", as if he knew Malik needed something. "I dunno. Maybe, one day, you could return the favour, and, by the way, you can call me Malik."

Cyril saw the look in Malik's eyes. He was a child on the outside but inside he was a man, and yet there was something else. Cyril bit down hard on his bottom lip and inwardly shuddered.

✺*✺

Dr Seeton-Jones was there outside the A&E department, waiting, and as soon as Cyril's car pulled up, he helped Malik inside. "Good to see you, Cyril. I was just saying to Stephanie that we hadn't seen you for a while. Why don't you pop over next weekend? We can have one of her afternoon teas. It will be good fun, my dear chap."

Malik summed Cyril up, there and then. He was a lord, with plenty of money and rich friends. One day this lord would help him; he would keep that favour close to his heart.

Little did he know that Cyril was no lord at all; he was, in fact, a semi-retired old-school gangster with as much finesse as a bulldozer sliding off a mud bank. Yet, he did have money, and the locals found him to be amusing, to say the least. The fact that he was stinking rich gave him kudos, and so he quickly eased into the fellowship of the community.

Whilst Malik was being stitched up and sorted out, Cyril waited in the car. The pain killers gave Malik so much relief, he felt like a new person. The drive home was peaceful. Malik relaxed, as the comforting feeling of the analgesic medication fuzzed his brain. Without thinking, he asked Cyril to stop right outside the cottage.

Cyril observed the cold and damp-looking dwelling; he knew it well, as his old pal Marcus River had once lived there.

"You live there?" He pointed to the house.

Malik was struggling to open the door, and so Cyril hopped out to help, feeling so responsible. Malik leaned forward and allowed Cyril to take his good hand and arm and ease him from the seat.

"Yeah, I do. Thanks for the ride, Mister Reardon."

"So, are you Marcus River's grandson, then?"

Malik didn't know his grandfather's first name, only his grandmother's, because Tilly was named after her. "Well, I s'pose so. Me last name is River, and this was me granny's house. She left it to me muvver, so we moved in."

Cyril appeared uncomfortable. "So, are you Jean's son?"

Malik nodded. "Yeah." He had to think quickly in case the lord asked about his mother's whereabouts. "Yeah, me muvver's gone away for the weekend to visit a sick friend."

Cyril stared at the boy, perhaps for longer than he should.

"Thanks again for the lift." He hurried away and returned to the safety of his home, away from prying eyes and questions.

CHAPTER THREE

Cyril hurried back to his house; the mansion was well set back and not visible from the main road. It was a huge place which he had acquired through a poker game.

He parked the car haphazardly on the drive and opened the rear door for Stein to get down. Frank, the other Rottweiler, was under the weather, so Cyril had left him dozing in the kitchen, much to the annoyance of the housekeeper, Mary, who, even after three years, Cyril still insisted on calling Maggie.

As he entered the house, Mary was there in a flash, moaning about the mess he'd left in the bathroom. "Lord Fuckwit, I am talking to you!" she yelled, as he marched past her. She frowned; that was odd. He usually had a moan back; it was a bit of banter really. A woman in her early sixties, Mary had continued with her employment as housekeeper when Cyril took over the place. It took some time to get used to, since her previous employer, Lord Chambers, was the real deal.

"What's up with you, Cyril? You look like ya found a penny and lost a pound."

Cyril spun around. "Maggie, order up a load of firewood, will ya."

"It ain't firework night, ya silly ol' sod." Mary had given up correcting him when he called her Maggie.

"Nah, I want a load delivered down at the old cottage," he said calmly, with a deadpan face.

"What for? The old man's dead … and his missus. I think the place is empty."

"Maggie, be a good girl, will ya, and fucking get on the phone and 'ave it delivered today!"

Mary knew that tone was not banter, or one to be argued with, so she hurried to the kitchen and did exactly as she was told. Cyril was as daft as a brush when it came to being regarded as a proper lord. She knew only too well that he was a gangster, and although she found her new employer a bit of a handful and missed the real lord of the manor, she had definitely warmed to Cyril. She also knew that there were times when she should not question him or ever open her mouth about what went on in his house. People came and went, and business was discussed, but it was his business, not hers. He paid her well enough and she could not complain. She was beholden to him too. He had paid for her to fly to Australia when her sister became sick, and there was no way she could have afforded it herself. Therefore, when she mentioned it to him, he had the airline tickets, the spending money, and the hotel all arranged. All she had to do was pack her bags.

Cyril sat in his armchair, looking out of the huge windows across the landscape, in deep thought. Mary joined him with a pot of tea. "The logs are on their way. Er, are you all right, Cyril?"

He turned his head to face her and his eyes were glazed over. She'd never seen him look emotional or vulnerable. He slowly nodded. "Yeah, Maggs, I am. It's just that I had a run-in with this kid Malakai and he says he's Jean's son."

Mary rested herself opposite Cyril, attempting to gauge his expression. "Jean?"

He nodded. "Marcus River's daughter. I knew her years ago. A right little fucker, she was. She was selling her fanny to buy pot. I knew her father, see, years back. He worked for me, but then he moved with his wife, Tilly, a right sweet girl she was, into the cottage. I s'pose they'd had enough of Jean. She was always bringing trouble to the door, and what with Marcus and his business, he couldn't afford to 'ave the Ol' Bill sniffing around, so he jacked it all in to live a quiet life."

Mary smiled compassionately. "Well, I guess she changed her ways and settled down."

His face registered with indignation, he replied. "Never! That one wouldn't know how to settle down. I remember the last time I saw her. She was pregnant and swanning around like some stoned hippy. I felt sorry for Marcus. He was a good bloke an' all. I don't know, Maggie, the boy looked so much like someone I once knew."

Mary was on the edge of her seat, wanting to know more. "Who?"

"Ya know my Kelly? Well, I call her my Kelly, but she's the daughter of Eddie Raven. He's dead now, of course."

Mary nodded. "Funny, 'cos I call her your Kelly as well. Lovely girl, she is. It seems to me that she looks up to you as her dad."

Cyril laughed. "Yeah, she does, love her heart. Anyway, her father, Eddie Raven, was having prison visits from Jean. He boasted that he had permission by the prison chaplain to have them in the chapel. Well, need I say more——?"

"What, they turned Catholic?"

Almost spitting his tea out, Cyril laughed, "Gawd, girl, think about it. Raven was a sex addict. He paid Jean to turn up with no knickers, ready for a fuck. It's like a conjugal visit."

"What, d'ya reckon Eddie is the boy's father?"

"The boy's a fucking ringer, to tell the truth. His hair is that mousy brown, but his skin is dark, and his eyes are green. In fact, he's like Kelly. He's her double, but younger. I would say he's about sixteen, or, maybe, seventeen at most."

"Are ya gonna say something to Kelly?"

He sighed. "I dunno. It might all be a coincidence. Anyway, it's really none of me business, so you, Maggs, keep ya mouth shut, yeah?"

Mary nodded. "Of course."

✖*✖

Malik and Sassy were trying to think of a way to keep the house warm. He had played down the extent of his injuries because his sisters had enough to worry about. The diesel engine purring outside, though, startled Sassy. A log lorry had just pulled up, reversing into the overgrown drive, and two men were unloading the wood into the front garden.

She ran to the window and shouted at Malik. "Oi, look, some divvy's unloading logs to the wrong house."

Malik jumped from his seat and peered out of the window and stared as the log pile grew. The supply would last them the whole winter. "I think the old geezer that took me to the hospital arranged it. Maybe it's his way of compensating me."

Sassy giggled, "Ya best let his dog bite you again, then, as he might deliver a fucking central heating system next time."

Malik laughed at his sister. She had such a way with words, spitting them out before she tasted them.

As soon as the men left, Malik and Sassy carried some of the split logs inside and stoked up the fire. There were also enough to get the kitchen burner going. By the time it was dark, most of the house was warm and cosy. Malik cooked one of the lamb joints and Sassy roasted the potatoes. Star was awake, and at last she was breathing without the awful wheezing sound.

With a glance around the room, Sassy sighed; her little sisters were rosy-cheeked and smiling, as they tucked into the crispy potatoes. She was pleased with her successful efforts at cooking. She then looked at her brother who was struggling with his hand but hadn't even moaned.

Later, Malik and Sassy took it in turns to read the girls *Big Bad Bun* by Jeanne Willis and Tony Ross, which they'd discovered among all the discarded goodies Malik had brought home. There were so many books, it seemed a shame to wait until Christmas. Sassy volunteered to wash up. She knew her brother was in pain and needed his sleep. Before she had finished, he'd crashed out, curled in a ball, under the tattiest of bedclothes. Sassy would have whinged the place down, if it were her. She watched him with the pain etched across his face; even as he slept, his features held a look of torment for all to see. She noticed his skin was sickly and there were beads of sweat, regardless of the cold in the air, along his forehead. This was no life for them; it was a cruel world, all because Jean had left them to fend for themselves. A sudden unexpected tear trickled down her nose, and instantly, she wiped it away and held back the sniff that would have woken him up. Her rising frustration pushed her to take drastic action and one that she would regret. Yet, all she could think of was that she needed to remove some of the burden, which was dragging down the family, away from her brother's shoulders.

The next morning, Sassy was up earlier than the others. She had spent more than enough time in the bathroom, the coldest place in the house, getting ready for school. By the time Malik arose from his makeshift bed, Sassy was ready and heating the milk for the girls to have lumpy porridge.

"You look different, Sass, what ya done?" asked Malik, in between jaw-breaking yawns.

Sassy tilted her head. "Nuffin. I've just tried to straighten me hair, is all."

She hid her face away, afraid he would notice the thin layer of her mother's old lipstick, which she'd found in the bathroom.

Three weeks later

Malik had done as he promised his sisters. Food was on the table, and most of the house was warm, thanks to the donation of logs which were also used now to fuel the log burner in the kitchen. But the other part of his plan – money to pay bills – was a real concern.

The little ones had cosy quilts and Star stopped wetting the bed. He, however, kept his pain to himself. The healing from the dog bite was a slow process and made carrying anything a chore. Luckily, the school didn't ask questions, when Sassy took in the note from the hospital. She had a few more ideas of her own, and when Tilly and Star had holes in their school uniform, she went through the lost property

52

box and pinched replacement jumpers and skirts. The school was full of well-to-do pupils, so they didn't miss the odd jumper here and there. The girls never mentioned their mother; as young as they were, they understood what was going on, and so they just did as they were told.

As Christmas approached, the air turned bitterly cold and the food was dwindling away. The girls were at school and Malik decided to return to the superstore and see if there were any more goodies being thrown into the dumpster. The superstore was busier than ever, but it wasn't the inside he was interested in, it was the bins. He wandered around the back and hurried over to the dumpster, before anyone saw him. Not that he was doing anything wrong. He sat as he had done before, dangling his legs off the wall and waited. He hoped Kimi was working today; he quite liked her smart-aleck face and forward attitude. He was in luck; after a few minutes, she appeared looking flustered and hadn't noticed him until he whistled, and then a generous grin crossed her face, lighting up her heavily made-up eyes.

"Long time, no see, Malik," she said, acting coyly for show.

He jumped from the wall and walked towards her, with his half-smile and a twinkle in his eye. "Hello, sweetness." Kimi blushed; he had just come across as more confident, almost cocky even. She noticed he had a bounce in his step and his hair was brushed back. She liked long hair; it was rare these days to see a boy with it below his ears. She noticed how the hair fell in gentle waves around his eyes.

"So, what are you doing 'ere?" She hoped he would say he was there to see her.

"Me dogs are hungry. Are there any joints going spare?" His voice had a real husk to it which made his appeal seem all the more alluring. Kimi was no sweet innocent virgin, and back in London, she had a reputation for screwing around. Malik, however, was a virgin. He hadn't had time for girls, being too busy looking after his family, even when his mother was at home. He was attracted to Kimi, though; she had a cute tight body with large breasts and plump lips. Her long hair was fashionable and tied up in a pineapple bun and her round cheeks had rather charming dimples when she smiled.

"Yeah, I've got a few bags inside. They're all yours for a kiss," she giggled.

Malik was taken aback. He'd never met a girl so open and upfront, but he still liked her.

"Oh, yeah, well, come 'ere, then," he said, as he tugged her shirt and pulled her close. She bit her lip and gazed into his green smouldering eyes. His half-grin turned her on, and she leaned into him and kissed his lips. He may have been a virgin, but he knew how to kiss. Their lips were a perfect match, as far as she was concerned. Malik enjoyed it too, but he had work to do; he needed to get food on the table and find a way to earn some money. The first bill since his mother had gone had arrived on the mat. He guessed it was for the electric, and that soon, others would follow.

"You're a good kisser, Malik. I could get used to that," she winked.

Unable to resist, he pulled her close again and landed her the most passionate kiss she had ever experienced. She melted in his arms. "Oh, I've died and gone to 'eaven!"

Malik said nothing but raised his eyebrow and ran a finger down her cheek. Goosebumps covered her skin. No fella had ever got to her like that. His eyes had narrowed to stare intensely into hers, and his neat straight white teeth, as he bit his bottom lip, together with his husky voice, sent a tingle up her spine.

She hurried back and collected the bags of meat and put them on the ground in front of him. "There ya go, Malik. That should feed them for a month." She tried to look innocent and sweet, but he knew she wasn't. He picked them up and went to walk away.

"Malik, fancy going out sometime?"

He paused and then slowly he nodded. "Yeah, I've just gotta get some stuff sorted out. I'll be back next week, though."

Kimi was gutted; she didn't want to wait – she couldn't – because he was so gorgeous, and she wanted him now.

"I've got some right good gear tomorrow to throw out," she lied.

He cocked his head to the side. "Oh yeah, what?"

"Er, turkeys, toys, hams …" She was trying to think of the things he would be interested in.

He laughed. "Well, it sounds like I'll be back tomorrow then, sweetness."

Kimi was just about to run to him and kiss him again when two men jumped over the wall and landed almost in front of Malik. He saw the look of fear on Kimi's face and frowned at the two men.

They were bigger than Malik, roughly twenty-five years old, and dressed in dirty black trousers, holey T-shirts, and Dealer boots. The fatter of the two looked Malik up and down. "What ya fucking doing wiv me meat, boy!" His gypsy accent was raised and threatening.

The other gypsy laughed and shook his head. "Ya don't wanna be taking what's ours, unless ya wanna fucking fight on ya hands."

Malik held on to the bags and sized both the men up. Kimi nervously bit her nails. She knew exactly who the two gypsies were. They had collected meat from the dumpster every week and were nasty with their mouths. Kimi never argued with them and had always left the bags and wandered back into the store. "That's his meat, it's first come, first served!" she declared, now with her hands on her hips, hoping they would leave Malik and her alone.

The bigger gypsy laughed. "Cor, divvy gal, ya wanna mind ya fucking business, 'cos if I say that's me meat, then that's me meat."

The smaller gypsy stepped forward to take the bags from Malik but received a rude awakening. Malik stepped back and nodded his head. "Like she said, first come, first fucking served, but if ya wanna fight, then go for it."

Kimi was shocked; she hadn't realised that this shy sexy teenager was unafraid of anything. The two gypsies were twice the size of him, being big ugly oafs.

"D'ya 'ear that, Tommy boy? This fucking chav's gonna fight us for it. May me muvver lay free boiled eggs, the kid thinks he's gonna dance on me top lip."

The other gypsy laughed, and his big beer belly wobbled. "So, Zaac, boy, give the mush a fair fight."

Malik stood still, staring at both men; he didn't even blink, but he glared with such conviction that the bigger gypsy, Tommy, was worried.

"If you so much as raise your fucking hand to him, then I'm gonna call the police!" shouted Kimi.

Zaac stepped back; they didn't want the police on their backs over a few bags of old meat. However, it was Malik who stopped her. "No, Kimi, don't do that. If this pikey wants to fight for the meat, then a fight he shall have." He turned from Kimi to Zaac. "If I beat ya, then I get the meat, and if ya beat me, then it's all yours."

Tommy laughed again. "Go on then, Zaac, fair fight, bash the mush and then let's go." He looked at Malik. "But I warn ya, boy, once you're fucked up, I don't wanna see your skinny arse around 'ere again. Got it, mush?"

Malik laughed. "And fucking likewise."

Tommy flicked his head towards the wall. "Over there, then. I don't want no cunt getting involved," he snarled at Kimi.

The pikeys climbed over the wall, out of Kimi's sight. They were followed by Malik, who was still holding his bags of meat.

Kimi didn't know whether to follow them and watch or call the police. She thought it better to stay put and perhaps call an ambulance. The two gypsies were real men, who were more than capable of killing Malik. He was still just a kid, in comparison.

The bank on the other side of the wall was steep but the gully was wide. Tommy sat like a sack of potatoes on the grass mound and watched as Zaac took off his coat, revealing his torn T-shirt and fat belly. Malik, however, noticed his big arms, and he knew that if he received a punch hard enough, he would probably be out cold. He needed that food for his sisters, and no one, no matter how big they were, was going to stop him. Removing his coat, he looked down at his bruised and scarred hand that was still partially swollen from the dog bite. Without any warning, Zaac lunged at him. But Malik realised that the man was slow; he saw the punch coming and ducked, and with his left hand, he swung and caught Zaac on the chin, which was enough for him to falter. The gypsy was enraged; no way could he let a skinny runt like this kid hurt him. He had a reputation to live up to. He swung his clenched fist but again he missed. Malik was dancing around him like a kangaroo on speed. Two punches caught Zaac in the ribs and he doubled over. The kid might be skinnier than him, but he could throw a nasty left hook.

Zaac was still missing with his punches and getting hurt; he needed to land a good blow, or it would be all over. "Ya cunt, I'll fucking smash the life outta ya!" he hollered.

Malik said nothing, but in a full body lunge, he punched Zaac on the side of the head. Then, he stepped back, as the lump of a man fell to the ground. He took a few deep breaths and waited for Zaac to get to his feet, shake his hand, and let him go on his way with his well-earned meat. Instead, though, he felt a hard whack at the nape of his neck, which took the wind out of him. As he staggered towards the wall, Tommy grabbed his shoulders, spun him round, and punched him in the face, and followed this up with crafty kicks to the ribs and legs. Malik was coughing and spluttering; he doubled over, when Tommy pulled Zaac to his feet and the two of them climbed back over the wall. Malik tried to catch his breath, but the kicking had almost crippled him. He knew his ribs were broken because it hurt to breathe, and yet he'd been through worse from that dog. Once he was back upright, he saw the bags had gone. In disgust and now seriously angry, he too climbed the wall. That was when he saw Kimi running towards him.

"Oh my God, I thought they'd killed ya." She helped him climb down.

He shook his head. "I won that fight fair and square, but then the other fat bastard gave me a right sly dig and caught me unawares. Well, they ain't getting away with it."

Kimi was trying to look at the swollen lump under his eye. "Don't you go up to that gypsy site, or they'll kill ya. Besides, Malik, I've got loads more meat inside. Ya can 'ave it, babe."

Malik stared for a second. "Nah, Kimi, they shouldn't 'ave done that. I mean, a fair fight is a fair fight. They took a right fucking liberty and I ain't taking too kindly to that. Where's their site?"

Kimi pointed straight ahead of her. "A mile or so up towards West Kingsdown, but ya best take all ya family and a shotgun, 'cos otherwise, you'll be needing a body bag."

"Listen, sweetness, don't you worry about me. I'm gonna be all right. I will see ya tomorrow, yeah, for me turkeys." He winked, kissed her on the cheek, and began to walk away.

"Oi, Malik, don't go!" she called after him.

He turned and smiled. "Nah, babe, I'm gonna go and get what's mine, from the gypo site, so you save the rest for me, for when I come back."

Kimi was still shaking when Cordelia called her back inside. She felt sick with nerves. The two gypsies were gross, nasty, loud, and crude. She hated them; they always had something disgusting to say to her. *As if she would ever give them a second look*, she thought. Her mind was on Malik and how handsome he was, and he was hard too. She liked a bad boy and Malik came with the good looks and a likeable arrogance. She just prayed he would come back the next day and not get eaten alive by those stinking travellers.

Malik was raging, as he marched ahead. As far as he was concerned, the men had really taken the piss, and looking at the size of their bellies, he needed the meat more than they did. Blinded by fury, he stormed towards the campsite totally unperturbed by what may face him. He would fight any one of them, one-to-one. He approached the site and noticed about eight caravans spread out in a huge field. Inspecting them more closely, he could see that they had been there for some time, since the fences enclosed the garden areas. There were dogs running loose, dusty and thin, and of all shapes and sizes. Two chickens ran past him. Straight ahead, a fire was blazing, with men sitting on old chairs, drinking and laughing. Malik had never been on a gypsy site before and was struck by life in a different world. He could make out Tommy, the man who had given him the sly dig, sitting among the oldies. Malik's anger was focused on smashing the living shit out of the fat ugly gypo. Without even a thought about the consequences, he marched straight up to the fire, dragged a burning stick, and plunged it in the ground like a Native American declaring war. The other men were stunned and stared on in total amazement.

"Ya fat 'orrible cunt! I won that fucking fight with your pal, fair and fucking square, so I want me meat!" he yelled.

Tommy rose to his feet, pulled his trousers up around his waist, and looked awkwardly at the other men, who were staring at him and waiting for a reaction. "Fuck off, divvy boy, before I shove that stick up your arse and spit-roast ya on me fire."

Malik didn't look at the other men; instead, he glared at Tommy. "I beat ya fucking mate, and you, ya crafty bastard, hit me on the sly. Well, ya want a fucking fight, I'll give ya one!"

Sitting next to Tommy was an older gypsy; he was a big man with a thick gold earring and hands like shovels. His hair was wavy and long, like his sideburns. He was the main man and went by the name of Noah. He remained seated with his huge meaty arms folded. "Who are ya, boy?" he asked, in a deep voice.

The whites of Malik's eyes were almost red with anger, which made the green stand out. "Me name's Malakai River, and I've come for what's rightfully mine, and that cunt has, as I see it, stolen from me, and I want it back."

Noah was shocked that a bit of a kid had the balls to march onto his site and start throwing his skinny weight around, and in such a fearless fashion too.

"And who did ya beat fair and square, boy?" asked Noah.

Tommy jumped in before Malik could answer. "Fuck off, kid! Zaac knocked you spark out. I saw him. Now, ya best be gone before I fucking skin ya alive, ya cunt!"

Noah lifted himself off the chair and towered above Tommy. Malik swallowed hard; the man was a monster. He had never seen a man so big. But Malik didn't move; he was going to stand his ground, come what may. Noah marched around the fire and grabbed Malik's face, tilting it into the light. "Oh yeah, Tommy, I can see Zaac really beat the fuck outta the kid. Go and get Zaac 'ere, now." He let go of Malik, who still didn't flinch. "I wanna see for meself who got a fucking beating."

Before Tommy could react, one of the other gypsies, a younger kid around eighteen, left to go in search of Zaac. He was gone a minute whilst Malik and Tommy stared each other out. Noah was amused by the kid and his gumption. When Zaac appeared, his head was down, hiding the marks on his face. Noah grabbed Zaac by the arm and then pulled his head back by his hair. Malik turned to see the state of Zaac's

61

face and grinned; he hadn't realised he'd made such a mess. The gypsy's two eyes were swollen and purple, his lip was split, and his nose looked red and twisted.

Noah threw his head back and laughed. "Fuck me! I think Malakai River gave Zaac a proper pasting. Ya sly bollocks, Tommy. I should bash you meself. Well, Malakai River, you won that fight, fucking too right, fair and square." He laughed again. "Get the boy's meat, and you, Zaac, have gone right down in my book, fucking beaten by a lanky kid. It took two of ya to do it, so shame on you."

While Zaac trudged off to get the bags, Tommy kept quiet. No one argued with Noah — not if they wanted to live.

"So, Malakai, where are you from, boy? Ya got travelling blood in ya?"

"Nah, I'm just 'ere to collect what's mine. I'm no one, from nowhere."

The bag of meat was handed to Malik by the younger gypsy with a kind smile.

"Ta, mate," Malik said, as he turned to walk away.

"Oi, boy, wait up! I wanna talk!" called Noah.

Malik stopped and turned around. "Look, mister, I don't want no trouble. I just want what's mine."

Noah nodded. "Yeah, right an' all, boy. I don't need to know who you are, or ya fucking business, but d'ya wanna earn a few quid, 'cos you, boy, are probably worth ya weight in gold?"

Malik shrugged his shoulders; he needed money, but he didn't want to get caught up with a load of wayward pikeys.

"If you can break a face like Zaac's, then you can fucking box. D'ya fancy prizefighting? There's a few hundred quid in it for ya." He grinned, showing his gold teeth.

Malik ran his fingers through his hair, took a deep breath, and nodded. "I'll think about it." He stared at his swollen hand. "I can't just yet. I got bitten by a Rottweiler, so me hand's still healing." He paused, and then he said, "But, in a week or so, yeah, I might be up for it."

Noah looked at the boy's hand and his stomach churned; those scars were nasty. "I'll tell ya something, Malakai River, you've impressed me. Not many men would front us out, the way you did. Who is ya ol' man?"

Malik shrugged again. "I dunno."

Noah nodded. "All right, son, you come back next week, or when ya get your hand fixed. Come and see me and we'll talk." He patted the young man's back and watched as Malakai walked away with a confident stride.

Fearless fucker, he thought. Noah was a fighter and had been all his life. Not a man to date had beaten him in a fight, but he was knocking on a bit, and with no son of his own to pass on his legacy, he watched Malakai walk away, and something inside touched him. Maybe it was the undaunted look in Malakai's eyes, or the arrogant cloak he wore, which stirred Noah. The one thing he was sure of was that the boy had more guts than anyone he had ever met.

He returned to the fire and scowled at Tommy. "I'll tell ya now, mush, you may have just trodden on the wrong pair of shoes. Mark me words. That Malakai comes from someone who just might come for you. 'Cos in all my days, I ain't seen a boy that small that could larrup anyone that fucking hard and then wanna take on more over a bit of grub."

Tommy was embarrassed and dared not argue with Noah. He lowered his head in shame and thought long and hard. He concluded that Noah was probably right and decided there was no need for retribution. Maybe Malakai River did have family members who were as hard as him, and although he'd given the boy a crafty punch, he also saw just how fast and fierce the kid really was.

Noah asked Tommy to leave his seat by the fire. He wanted to talk business with his old friend, Johnnie O'Connell, a gypsy from the London site. Johnnie was down visiting his brother and was enjoying a beer at the fireside. He didn't like bullies at all, even though his own son, Levi, and his nephew, Farley, were prime examples and had caused him considerable embarrassment. They had taken serious liberties with his niece Kizzy and dabbled with the notorious Vincent family. Another nephew, Billy O'Connell, was also involved, but he died on the spot from a heart attack due to the stressful circumstances. In a way, his was a less painful death, for Noah beat Levi and Farley O'Connell so savagely with his bare hands that both ended up on a cold slab. Johnnie felt as though a weight had been lifted off his shoulders and shook Noah's hand at the time.

Ravaged by shame, Tommy slouched his shoulders and quietly walked away. The others followed, knowing there was serious talking to be done between Johnnie and Noah.

Johnnie O'Connell was a prizefighter in his younger day, and still now, no one from his site messed with him. He and Noah had a mutual respect. They followed the old gypsy ways and kept to their own.

"I see your Kizzy was down at the grave when I was visiting me sisters, gawd bless 'em. She's a good gal, your Kizzy. Ya know, your own sister's grave is always covered in flowers. I reckon she has them delivered 'cos they're always fresh."

Johnnie smiled. "Ah, yeah, she's a good gal. Kizzy and Jack Vincent have been engaged for a while now. I like the boy, Jack. He looks after Kizzy and she wants for nuffin." Johnnie took a swig of his beer; he drank slowly, not one for getting drunk. He just savoured the old ways, where he could sit around a fire and take part in man talk while enjoying the company of the older gypsies. They weren't full of bullshit like the youngsters Tommy and Zaac.

"Yeah," acknowledged Noah, "I've a lot of respect for the lad. He's got a good 'ead on his shoulders, and I 'ear he's got his own club in the East End now."

"The boy's done good and that's a fact. He's keen to help lads from poorer families with fuck all chance of making it in the boxing world without his help."

Noah nodded in appreciation. "Johnnie, me and you are getting old, and all I knows is the fighting game. You've got your scrap metal, and, well, I've got nuffin."

Johnnie sat up straight. "I'm listening, go on."

"That kid, Malakai River, I wanna train him to fight, 'cos, judging by the state of Zaac's face, Malakai has got it in 'im. Fucking 'ell, mush, the boy is reckless. I've only ever seen a look like that before, and that was in Jack's eyes, the day he beat Ocean. Cor, now, that's a boy that can fight, if ever I saw one."

Johnnie smiled. "Yeah, though, Jack's hung his boxing belt up for now. He's more into running the clubs and pampering my Kizzy. He works hard, mind you. If Malakai is gonna be your fighter, then Jack will let him use the gym. Not that he owes me a favour, but the boy treats family with respect. It's this thing they have, and I'll tell ya, some of us travellers could take a leaf outta their book. Those Vincents are tighter than a duck's arse."

"You don't 'ave to tell me, Johnnie. I've seen those Vincents in action, remember. Anyway, I'm thinking of getting this Malakai trained up. I wanna see him smash a few names and earn meself a retirement fund," mused Noah, as he swigged the last remains of his beer.

The fire was dying down and the cold was making its way into their bones. It was time to go back inside, for as tough as they were in being used to the inclement weather, their warm caravans were more appealing.

They stretched their legs and shook hands, but just as Noah walked away, Johnnie called him back. "'Ere, did the lad say his name's Malakai River?" asked Johnnie, in deep thought.

"Yeah, why, do ya know the River family, 'cos I ain't 'eard of 'em?"

Johnnie stared across the field and tilted his head. "Come to think of it, I know, well knew, a man years ago. His name was Marcus River, an old villain, from the East End. If I remember, he moved down 'ere somewhere. He would be an ol' man now, though. He might be the boy's grandfather. And it's my guess, the lad would get that fire in his belly from him, 'cos if I recall rightly, he was a dangerous bastard. But, hey, listen, don't get too attached to the boy. He looks lost, and I reckon, one day, he's gonna find his way."

CHAPTER FOUR

As soon as Malik got inside the house, he shivered. The fire had gone out, and there was a chill starting to creep in. The girls would be coming home from school, and little Star couldn't afford to get cold, as her asthma was at its worst during the winter. He got to work in the living room, lighting the tinder and then piling on the logs. He did the same in the kitchen until the fire was roaring and the house was warming up. The milkman, a rarity these days, had parked the milk float on the corner of the road, and so Malik was able to pinch some eggs, milk, bread, and potatoes. He wasn't greedy; he'd only taken what he needed. He'd learned over the last few months how to be doubly vigilant and was getting good at pinching. That little heist would see them all right for the next few days.

The front door opened and in came the two little ones, followed by Sassy, who gasped when she saw Malik's bruised eye. "What the fuck's 'appened to you, Mal?" She peeled off her coat and walked towards him to get a closer look. "Cor, that's nasty! Who did this? I swear, I will—"

Malik put his hands up. "Leave off, Sass, it's nothing. You should see the other fella!"

She laughed. "He best 'ave a black eye, 'cos I'll fucking give 'im one, if he ain't."

Malik rolled his eyes. Trust Sassy to be so fiery. It suited her, though, with her wild red hair and scowling eyes.

He looked down at Tilly. "What are you smiling at, cheeky chops?"

Tilly was twisting on her foot, so typical of a seven-year-old. "We broke up today, and I've got a present for ya, Malik." She giggled, hiding behind her back the calendar she had made.

"Me, too!" squealed Star.

"Oh yeah, is it for Christmas?" he asked, with a soft tone.

Their eyes were wide with excitement. "Yeah, but you can have it now," replied Tilly.

Malik shook his head. "No, I can wait until Christmas." His heart sank, and he prayed that the electric would still be on so that he could cook the turkey promised to him by Kimi. He had no idea about bills, only that every so often his mother would send him to the shop with the bill and cash to pay for it. He left the girls in the living room to warm up with a glass of chocolate milk while he studied the letter. It informed him that he had two weeks to pay the amount shown but the letter was dated a week ago. Christmas was next week. He racked his brains, trying to think of how he could raise the money. As he gazed out of the window, he noticed how dirty many of the cars were. It was the time of year when the roads were covered with salt and the resultant black mess coated the cars. He could offer a car cleaning service. There were plenty of cars dotted around, parked up outside the big posh houses. He decided to search the cupboards for a bucket and cleaning fluid but found nothing suitable. He then went into the garage where there were all kinds of car cleaning products, including car shampoo.

It was too dark outside to start cleaning cars, but tomorrow, he would go in search of a few quid and earn it honestly.

Sassy was up first. She stretched, farted, and then clambered off the sofa and threw another log on the glowing remnants. The air had a nip to it, but it would soon be warm again. Malik was curled in a ball on the floor where the light from the fire left a warm glow on his face. His eyes were still swollen, and Sassy felt an anger in the pit of her stomach. If she got her hands on whoever had hurt Malik, then she would plunge them with a knife. She didn't give a shit; no one hurt her brother. Almost at once, she sat back down with a cramped feeling deep in her stomach. She cursed fucking periods. Venturing upstairs was horrible; it was so cold and damp, and the toilet seat was like sitting on a block of ice. The shower that trickled out took an age to heat up and the towels were thin and shabby. Still, she couldn't really complain. Malik was doing his best to keep them safe and warm. She'd been using her mother's pile of sanitary towels and was now down to the last one. She had to think of another way. Then, she had an idea. Her mother's clothes, which were no good to anyone, could be cut up into rags and used for now. She slowly opened the door to her mother's bedroom and went to the small lopsided wardrobe. Jean's long Afghan coat was still hanging there; she wore it every day in winter for its warmth. Sassy shuddered at the thought of her mother and how cruel she was in leaving her little sisters alone in a damp house with no money or food. She didn't cry because she missed her mother, she cried because she loved her siblings, and their present situation was so sad and so unfair. As if all the anxiety over the last few months had hit her at once, she began to sob. Sitting on her mother's cold mattress, she broke down and cried like she had never wept before. But seeing her brother drag food home for them, his hand almost ripped off by a dog, and now afflicted with the black eye, it was definitely the worst point of her life so far. He was sad, she could see it in his eyes. This was no life for him, breaking his back to keep them together. *One day, Jean, you will pay for this.*

Malik got up and heard a whimpering sound coming from upstairs, so he peeled back the thick duvet that covered him and the two little ones, huddled together, who were warm and sound asleep. His heart melted: they resembled two cherubs from a holy picture in the church. He covered them up again and then turned to find Sassy's makeshift bed empty. He ran up the stairs and saw his mother's room ajar and his sister sitting on the bed.

"Sass, what's the matter?" He sat beside her and put an arm around her shoulders.

She stopped crying instantly and straightened up. "I'm all right, Mal. I'm just fucking annoyed, that's all. I know I shouldn't hate me muvver, but I fucking do, Malik. Cor, I wanna smash her in the face. It ain't right, ya know. I mean, who fucks off and leaves their babies behind? It's all right for me, 'cos, well, me and her never saw eye to eye, but those two, Star and Tilly, they're helpless babies."

She wiped the snot with the back of her hand and sniffed back a tear.

"Are you all right, though, sis? I mean, there's nothing else worrying ya, is there?"

Sassy thought about the sanitary towels but shook her head. "Nah, Mal, I'm fine."

He looked at his sister's wild hair and her milky face with the speckled freckles and wished he had the money for her to have all the fashionable clothes that girls of her age would naturally expect. Instead, she only had the cast-offs her mother had left behind and her school

70

uniform, which was now frayed around the edges. He admired her spirit, and he was glad she could stick up for herself, or school would have been such a ruthless place for her.

"Sass, I'm gonna try and get some money together washing cars. I've gotta pay the electric bill before they cut us off. Can you stay 'ere? I'll go an' try an' earn a few quid. I'm then setting off to the dumpster. I've a turkey on order."

She forced a smile. "Yeah, no worries, I'll keep the girls amused."

Malik washed his face, climbed into the only pair of jeans he had, and left with the bucket, the car shampoo, and a few old rags. He flexed his bad hand, loosening up the tension. The weather was bitterly cold, and as he looked to the skies, he noticed how white it appeared. That's all he needed, more fucking snow. The first car in the lane was a new Jag which looked a bit neglected as the white paint was covered in black slush compared to the virgin white lawn. He tapped on the door of the big house and smiled to himself. The house was impressive: a large wreath hung from the door and even the steps leading up to it were pristine. In contrast, the car appeared anything but perfect, covered in all that crap. A woman came to the door. She was probably in her early twenties, dressed out in designer gear, and attractively made-up. She looked Malik up and down, before saying, "Can I help you?" Her voice was soft in tone; it was hard to determine the accent, but she was well-spoken.

Malik pointed to her car. "I was thinking maybe you would like your beautiful car as clean as your lovely house." He winked at her which took the woman aback. *Wow, he's a charmer*, she thought.

With a smile and a nod, she replied, "Well, I suppose you make a good case for cleaning my car, so how much?"

Malik hadn't thought that far. He merely shrugged. "How much do you wanna pay?"

The lady checked him over and noticed how his good looks and cheeky smile, all but the black eye, didn't match his well-worn clothes and tatty trainers. She was in a good mood, her business was making big money, her boyfriend had booked a week on a cruise ship, and she was convinced he was going to propose.

"If you can get that beast gleaming white, I'll pay you twenty-five pounds. If you give me your bucket, I'll fill it with warm water for you."

Malik was surprised; that was so much more than he expected, he almost chewed her hand off for the money. "Can I use your garden tap to rinse off?"

She nodded. "You'll need to unfasten the wraps around the tap first, though, as they are there because of the cold weather. Would you like a nice hot cocoa before you start? I'm having one myself."

She watched out of the window at the young man scrubbing away, buffing, and polishing. He was meticulous, and he had done as she asked. But then she noticed him keep rubbing his right hand. He drank the hot chocolate and devoured the biscuits, as if he was ravenous. She gazed around her room filled with luxuries all ready for Christmas, and here was someone in the freezing cold who was washing her car for a few quid. She opened her purse which contained a wad of notes and counted out one hundred pounds. Once Malik had finished, he tapped on the door and handed back the cup and plate. "Thanks for the drink and biscuits. It was very kind of ya. Are ya happy with the car?"

The posh lady felt a lump in her throat; he reminded her of Oliver Twist. "May I ask why you are cleaning cars? Are you saving up for anything special?"

Malik rubbed his hands together. "I wanna give me family a special Christmas. Ya know, turkey, all the trimmings, and a Christmas cake."

The lady felt her eyes fill up. She wasn't born to money; in fact, far from it, as she'd originally come from a council estate and worked hard to get to where she was in life. She had more than enough, and so turkey and Christmas cake were not things she gave much thought to. She was having Christmas dinner in London with friends at a well-known extravagant hotel. "Oh, lovely …" She paused. "Look, would you mind doing a few odd jobs for me? I'll pay you a decent amount. Only, I hate lifting things, and you seem like a strong lad."

Malik nodded. "Yeah, what do ya want done, Mrs, er …?"

"Oh, call me Penelope, and you are …?"

"Malakai."

Penelope led him through the house. He had never been inside a house like it. Everywhere was immaculately decorated and the place exuded wealth. The kitchen was as big as his house, and the lounge was like a palace, with all the white leather sofas and fur cushions. Penelope noticed how he was admiring her home.

"Cor, it's a lovely place you have here, Penelope. You must work hard, eh?"

Penelope never expected him to say a thing like that, and she warmed to him instantly. "Yes, Malakai, I have worked hard. You know, some people think I've got a rich husband, but I'm proud to say it's all mine, with no man involved."

Malik laughed. "Right an' all, so good on ya."

She was amused by his words, as if they came from a grown man, and yet he was just a boy – maybe only seventeen years old. She was only twenty-two herself, but her past had forced her to grow up so fast that, somewhere along the way, she had left her youth behind. She felt her flesh chill from nowhere because it was as if she had met him before somewhere or had stared into those same eyes.

She took him into the back garden where the trees hung heavy and the snow-covered leaves had piled up in every corner from the wind. The summer furniture was left out and even the barbecue wasn't covered.

"None of me business, Penelope, but shouldn't all that garden stuff be put away? It'll get ruined in all the bad weather, you know."

Penelope shivered as she gazed across the garden. "My sentiments exactly. There's a log cabin over there. Do you think you could put all the furniture away and bag up those leaves for me?"

Malik smiled. "Yeah, of course, no problem. Look, you're shivering. You get back inside and leave all this to me."

She returned his smile and went into the kitchen. She actually felt quite bemused by the boy's visit. He was very different from anyone she had met. It wasn't just his appearance – and those eyes – which interested her. It was the revered manner in which he addressed her and the concern for her well-being out there, shivering in her garden. No one had ever treated her like that, that was for sure.

As she watched Malakai get to work, Penelope decided she would also have a clear-out. Her wardrobe was now full to the brim, and she knew she wouldn't have the room for her new winter collection, so she opened two laundry bags and filled them to the top. As she tried to lift them, she realised they were too heavy. It would have to be another job for the young man.

He worked tirelessly, and by eleven o'clock, he had the furniture neatly put away in the log cabin and the leaves in the garden waste bins. Stretching his back, which ached from all the bending down, he stood on the patio and admired the beautiful landscaped garden and his work – there was not a leaf in sight.

Penelope ushered Malik inside and offered him another hot drink. "Well, you've saved me a hard job there. One more for you, if that's okay? I have two heavy bags upstairs. I can't carry them. Strong mind I might have but muscles I haven't," she laughed. Malik regarded the woman. She had an open, fresh face and a sweetness in her eyes. He removed his old trainers and admired all the large photos, some in colour, some black and white, showing models with amazing hair styles, as he followed her up the wide staircase to the landing where she had dragged the two bags. The top of each bag was open, too stuffed full to zip up.

"What do ya want to do with them?" He assumed they were going to the launderette.

For a second, his eyes caught her attention, and she stared for longer than she should have. He winked and gave her a smile that made her heart race. She had to look away: he was stirring an odd feeling in the pit of her stomach. The small age gap shouldn't have been a problem, for, after all, there was probably only a difference of five years, but she was used to dating men much older than herself.

"Oh, er, yes, I will dump them off at the charity shop."

Malik noticed the soft pink jumper sticking out of the top of one of the bags.

Without thinking, he said, "Can I have 'em? I've got a sister about your size, and well, she——"

Before he could finish, Penelope touched his shoulder. "Yes, of course, you can. They are all clean, and, to be honest, I haven't worn half of them. You are more than welcome, and now let me sort out your money." She guessed right away he was desperate, and she knew exactly how that felt. After shaking off the thoughts of her past, she needed to turn away from him, before she was sucked into those hypnotic green eyes.

Malik put his hands up. "Nah, this is payment enough. Honestly, I can't take any more money."

Penelope frowned. "I insist. Those clothes were going to be thrown away, and I was worrying about the garden furniture, so I feel better about giving you an honest day's pay."

Malik shrugged his shoulders. "If you insist, then, I won't say no!"

Penelope handed him a rolled-up wad of notes. He held the cash in his hand and his mouth fell open. "I can't——"

But Penelope stopped him. "You can, and you will. I want you and your family to have a good Christmas. I'll be offended, if you don't take it."

Malik, on impulse, kissed her on the cheek, which left her dumbfounded. She watched him struggle down the drive with the two heavy bags, as if the morning had been a dream. She had shared a happy time with a teenager, who, she realised, was far more than that: a stranger he may be, yet he was like an angel, a charming man in a child's body. Those eyes would stay in her mind for a long time.

The short walk home was both agonising and heart-warming. The bags were heavy and killing his hand, yet he had money and could put a smile on Sassy's face. He thought about Sassy, and for some reason, an anxious feeling gripped him. She was not herself; he'd noticed she was more sullen than normal and had taken to biting her nails and staring off into space. At first, he'd put it down to their mother leaving, but there was something more to it. Some time ago, she had returned from school with a bag containing basics: bread, butter, cheese, and toilet rolls. When he asked where she had found the money for them, she'd lowered her face and told him the school had paid her for cleaning the art room at lunchtime. Sick with waves of pain and relentless sweating from the dog bite, he never questioned it. The uneasy feeling in his stomach caused him to stop at the garden gate and to take a deep breath. How did she get the money to buy a carrier bag full of food? And it wasn't just the one time either. The school surely wouldn't pay a pupil for cleaning a classroom. He took a big breath and then exhaled slowly, as he considered fronting her out over it, but first he would hide the bags in the shed and bring them out at Christmas – it would be Sassy's big surprise. Maybe the new clothes would lift her spirits.

Inside, the kids were singing Christmas carols, and Sassy was getting grumpy when their words became muddled. Then Malik heard her say, "How are we gonna make any money, if you two keep getting it wrong?"

"What's all this about, Sass?"

Star, with her rosy cheeks, spoke first. "We're going singing at the doors, and Sassy said they will give us money."

Malik shot her a glance. "No, Sass, it's not safe. Besides, look, I've got us some money. I'm off to pay the electric. You don't leave the house, right?"

Sassy was still in her nightdress and wearing her thick knee-high socks. She pursed her lips. "But I wanna help, Mal."

His mouth curved into a smile. "Sass, you are helping! You are looking after the girls, while I get what we need, so stay inside in the warm, and I'll be back."

She didn't argue; she had made a promise to herself to do as he said. Her little moneymaking secret was just that – a secret – and now that they had broken up from school for the Christmas holiday, she wouldn't be able to make any money. She needed to find another way, but it seemed carol-singing was a no-no.

He first retrieved a laundry bag, and then he headed down to the supermarket, hoping that the two gypsies, Tommy and Zaac, had heeded Noah's words and kept away. The store was overly busy, and so, as before, he snuck around the corner and waited. It was an hour before Kimi appeared, but it was well worth the wait. She looked sexier than ever, dressed in a short red santa dress and wearing a hat to match. He gave her his most enticing smile, not that he was aware he could, but she noticed just the same. She giggled and hurried over.

"Oh, Malik, I thought you'd never come."

She was nose to nose and comfortable being so close. Her thoughts would often wander to him during her days at the store, and her heart raced whenever she thought about that kiss they'd had. Now, here he was. She planted her lips on his, and then she ran her hands up inside his coat, feeling his toned muscles. He certainly didn't resist: he liked the feeling and felt himself getting aroused.

"Cor, Kimi, what ya doing to me, girl?" he gasped, as he took a deep breath.

"Ya like it, don't ya?" she chuckled.

"Yeah, but how can I walk home with this rod sticking out of me trousers!"

She laughed and dragged him behind the dumpsters. "You don't have to, babe. I'll sort that out for ya."

She kneeled down and unzipped him. He looked to the sky and almost gasped when he felt his manhood suddenly engulfed in a warm soft void. He'd never had oral sex and was not going to stop her now, the feeling euphoric and so intense. Before he knew it, he'd shot his load and his knees buckled.

Kimi wiped her mouth and stood up. "Happy Christmas, Malik." She gave him a kiss on his cheek and looked up at him with so much admiration and pride. He was a one-off, and it occurred to her just then how lucky she was for him to appear in her life.

Malik, meanwhile, was just reeling from a feeling which was indescribable. He looked down at this lovely young woman, kissed her hair, which smelled of orange blossom, and held her close until he got his senses – and his heart rate – back to normality. "I wasn't expecting that," he whispered in her ear.

"Well, guess what? I wasn't expecting you to walk into my life, so there we have it. Two surprises. Oh, before I forget, I've a few goodies put aside. The trouble is, you might have to wait until it gets dark, 'cos I found a trolley out the back. It's loaded already. No one noticed because they're all temp Christmas staff. None of 'em have a clue. Gormless pricks they are."

Malik was nodding and laughing at her quick tongue and air of excitement. He looked to the sky again: it was almost dark. The nights had well and truly drawn in. "I'd say in about twenty minutes, it's gonna be completely dark."

Kimi kissed him again and pranced away before the wicked witch, Cordelia, screamed at her.

Malik waited patiently, and then, as the blackness crept over him, she appeared, dragging a big trolley. It was a wooden box on four wheels with a long metal handle that steered it. It wasn't a modern piece of equipment but ideal for him. She hurried to the dumpster and beckoned him over.

"Listen, Malik, you go now. Get this outta sight before they catch me, and I'll see you tomorrow, yeah?"

Eagerly, he nodded and grabbed the metal arm to tug the trolley up the hill. He didn't bother to have a peep in the heavy-duty bags; instead, he hurried away before anyone saw him. It was a hard slog up the hill to his cottage, but when he unloaded all the bags, he realised that there was no way they could have been carried home. Once he pushed the front door open and started to drag everything inside, Sassy appeared excitedly and willingly helped him. "What the fuck have ya gone an' got this time?"

Malik laughed. "Well, I ain't been collecting dead bodies. Listen, keep the little 'uns in there, just in case there are toys here. I brought back a lot of stuff before, though, if ya remember. We can wrap these up for their Christmas presents as well, yeah?"

Sassy nodded and hurried back to Tilly and Star who were engrossed in a puzzle game at the kitchen table. As before, Malik left the bags containing all the food down in the hallway for the moment.

They were filled with meats, a turkey, all the trimmings including pigs in blankets, a gammon, and an assortment of cheeses. His mouth watered: it would be like a real posh Christmas dinner. He then hauled the remaining bags upstairs to his bedroom. As he tipped out the first one, he gave a whoop of excitement as he cast an eye over all the goodies. There were chocolates, sweets, toys, kids' slippers, and nightwear. He frowned, when he noticed the age shown on the clothes, which were for children aged five and seven. How could Kimi have known that they would fit his two little sisters? He assumed she'd guessed. His eyes filled up when he saw children's Christmas jumpers and two beautiful pink jackets. The next bag contained decorations including a small light-up tree, baubles, and paper chains. A tear trickled down his cheek. The final bag contained numerous items, including thick chunky jumpers for a man, and a box with trainers, his size too. Right at the very bottom was a make-up bag filled with stuff, and it was not cheap shit either, and there was also a pair of pyjamas to fit Sassy. He sat back and wondered. How could Kimi know what to give him? He could see that this wasn't a coincidence. He would ask her tomorrow. Meanwhile, he needed to go and sort out the bags he'd left downstairs and give Sassy a hand in the kitchen.

After putting the food away, he turned to Sassy. "We're gonna have the best Christmas ever, you see."

Sassy was excited. What a difference just a few hours could make to all their lives. Malik had come up trumps once again. They spent the evening decorating the living room and making it cosy with the Christmas lights and pretty multicoloured baubles on the tree. Star was arranging the paper chain awkwardly at the bottom and Tilly was meticulously hanging the tinsel. She was the one who liked everything in order.

Sassy was fidgeting and kept going to the toilet, the old rags leaving her sore. Malik watched her white sickly face, and after the tenth trip to the bathroom, he said, "What's up, Sass, are you ill?"

Her face went crimson with embarrassment and she averted her eyes to the floor. It was not a sight he was used to. Sassy was never one for being self-conscious or ashamed in any way. Then it dawned on him – women's problems. "D'ya need women's stuff, Sass?"

She looked out of the corner of her eye and nodded. He jumped to his feet and grabbed his coat. The local chemist was a two-minute walk away and he still had change from the electric bill. He had lost his pride already, so purchasing sanitary wear was nothing to him. He bought six months' worth, knowing he never wanted his sister to suffer in that way again. As he left the shop, he took a deep breath. *Damn you, Jean.*

Once he was back inside the comfort of his festive home, he went into the bathroom and placed the packets beside the toilet. Sassy ran up behind him and whispered, "Thanks, Mal."

He peered inside his mother's bedroom and saw the scissors and the rags and swallowed hard – the poor cow. His sister had never even bothered him with it. He detested his mother more now than ever. If she showed her face here again, he would bury her in the back garden. No wonder Sassy was so down; she may have been really suffering with girl problems and he couldn't help. That was a mother's job.

CHAPTER FIVE

Malik missed Kimi the next day. He had waited but she didn't show up. He checked the dumpster and found a couple of Christmas cakes, the boxes having been battered, but the cakes were fine. He noticed two bottles of brandy and snatched them too. Walking away, he felt gutted that he'd been unable to wish her a happy Christmas.

Christmas Eve arrived almost in a heartbeat, and the kids were excited. It stemmed from the contagious expectation from the other school children. His family weren't used to presents as such. If they were lucky, they might receive the odd second-hand doll or handmade poncho but nothing to get too excited over. They didn't know any different, except when they went to school and the children spoke of the wonderful toys they'd been given.

Tilly asked if she could hang a sock out for Father Christmas. Star rolled hers down and proudly held it out in front of her. "D'ya fink he will come this year?" asked Tilly wistfully.

Malik felt a deep sadness: for years now, his younger siblings had been unable to experience what most children throughout the universe would see as a right. Their lives with their mother hadn't been great at all, really. It was all wrong; his little sisters should have been expecting a present like the other kids and not wondering whether Father Christmas would remember them or not. Malik swallowed back the emotion lodged in his throat. "I'll tell you what. How about you take the pillowcases off your pillows and hang them out? Maybe, he'll fill them with something, but first, you have to go to sleep. Is that a deal?"

Star clapped her hands together. "Yes!" she squealed. "Malik, mummy said that when she was having me, she looked out of the back window and saw a bright star, and so she called me Star."

Sassy laughed. "Yeah, well, if she had looked out of the front window, she would have called you Tesco."

Malik chuckled. "Well, it's a special name for a special girl."

Tilly looked down in silence. She was the more thoughtful, quiet one, out of his sisters. "I suppose she didn't think of anything special for me, as my name is old-fashioned, and the girls in my school laugh at me."

Sassy looked at Malik and frowned. She appeared puzzled. "What's up, Sass?" he asked.

"Malik, do you know Tilly's real name? Only, I'm sure she ain't really Tilly. I remember when we started school and muvver telling the teacher it's easier to call her Tilly because we couldn't pronounce her actual name."

Malik nodded. "Yeah, of course I do. It's Chantilly Magenta, as in Chantilly lace and Magenta, the colour purple. It's like the colours of the sunset."

Tilly looked up and stared. She wanted to believe them because it sounded so pretty. "Really, Malik? Only, I've always been called Tilly, after our grandmother."

Malik smiled at her, with her earnest features and inquisitive, expressive eyes. "Yes, she was called Tilly, but our muvver …" he almost choked, when he said those words, "she liked fancy names. So, yours, really, is Chantilly, and before you go back to school, I'll show you how to write it, and I'll tell your teacher you want to be called it from now on. How about that?"

Tilly almost cried with excitement, as she threw herself at Malik and thrust her arms around his chest, squeezing him so tightly. "I do love you so much, Malik!"

He hugged her back. "Yep, and I love you too, Chantilly River. Now, you two monkeys get into bed and go to sleep, and let's see what Santa brings you in the morning."

During the night, Malik sneaked out to the shed where he'd hidden Sassy's surprise. The bags were heavy as he hauled them up the stairs. From the two laundry bags he'd been given by Penelope, he retrieved top quality rig-outs, all with designer labels. Carefully, he hung each garment on a hanger and placed them in Sassy's wardrobe, and then, once he was done, he tied a tinsel bow around the handle. Pleased with his efforts, he then filled the pillowcases with dolls, games, books, and sweets and quietly arranged them under the tree in the living room, being very careful not to wake the girls.

When the bright sun shone through the living room window, Tilly and Star quickly rose from their beds, giggling with excitement. "He's been, Malik, look, he's been!" They squealed so much, they woke Sassy. She stretched and sat upright and watched her sisters pull their presents from the pillowcases which was a new experience for them. Malik's eyes lit up at the sight of the two children who were so overcome with pleasure. He glanced over at Sassy and winked. Under the tree was a pillowcase for her. "Santa's left you a parcel, Sass."

In a flash, she leaped from her bed and retrieved the pillowcase and pulled out the make-up bag full of cosmetics. He left the girls to enjoy themselves whilst he went to start up the oven. They would have the best meal ever. Sassy joined him. "Ah, Malik, I wish I had something for you."

He turned to face her. "Helping me with those two little 'uns is quite enough, Sass. Oh, I forgot. You have a present upstairs, so why don't you go and look in your bedroom."

Sassy gave him her famous one-eyed frown. She ran from the kitchen and hurried up the stairs two at a time. Just as Malik was filling a saucepan with water, he heard a high-pitched shriek, followed by, "Oh my God, Oh my God …"

He smiled to himself and began peeling the potatoes. He'd found a way to keep his family together, but this was just the start. They would never go without, not all the time he had a mouth to speak with and a pair of hands with which to work.

After they had eaten their fill, the two youngest dozed off on the sofa, and Sassy sat with an odd expression plastered on her face.

"Are you okay, Sass?"

"Yeah, I think I just ate too much, and now my stomach hurts."

His eyes narrowed, as he could see the colour drain from her face, but before he could ask any more, she'd risen from her seat and headed upstairs, but not before Malik noticed the blood on the back of her nightdress.

"Jeez!" he yelled, as he ran up the stairs after her.

Sassy had shut herself in the bathroom and tried to hold back the screams. The cramp in her stomach was unbearable; she'd never experienced period pains of this intensity and assumed this one was just going on for longer than normal. Then, she felt a warm sensation and looked down to find blood trickling down her legs, her sanitary towel too heavy, and now, with the flood of blood, totally ineffective. She whipped it away and into the toilet. Her mind was in a panic and Malik's voice echoed somewhere in the distance. She couldn't let him in; he mustn't see her like this, but the pain was there again, and this time it took her breath away. He banged furiously at the door. "Sass, open up! What's happening? Let me help you!"

The waves of immense pain engulfed her once more and she lay there helpless until it subsided. Taking a deep breath, she pulled herself up from the floor, and putting her modesty aside, she unlocked the door. Malik grabbed both her arms before she collapsed and helped ease her to the floor. His eyes scanned the small bathroom. He saw the blood on the tiles; it was also running down her legs, but it was the deathly look in her eyes that made him panic. "Sassy, what's happening?" he said, as he held her head and stroked away the wet stray hairs from her face.

"It's my period, it's just heavy and ..." She stopped and lifted her knees, to try to ease the next wave of pain. "Malik, it hurts so bad. I've never had it like this."

Malik flicked his eyes around the room, looking for something to cool her burning face. As he gently removed his arm holding her head, he jumped up, snatched a towel, and ran it under the cold tap. "Here, Sass, put this at the back of your neck. You're fucking burning up!"

Sassy was breathing heavily and groaning in pain. He watched in horror, as she writhed around the floor and lay there in agony.

"This ain't normal. I must get you to the hospital. Surely, it ain't right?"

"No, Malik, I'll be all right. It's just a painful time of the month. Please, leave me. I'll be okay. I just need to get outta this mess."

Malik looked down at the nightdress, which, by now, was completely bright red. "Christ, Sass, no one bleeds this much!"

Through her blue lips and in a breathless voice, she replied stoically, "Lucky I ain't in a fucking shark tank, eh."

"Let's get you in the bath. Maybe the bleeding will stop and the pain will ease."

In the midst of another wave of agony, Sassy let out a scream. She was now in a squat position with only her toes supporting her entire body. A further cry escaped her mouth, sending Malik into a panic.

"Sass, I'm gonna get help. You stay here. I need to get someone."

Just as he went to leave, she grabbed his trousers. "No, Malik, please, please—" At that precise moment, she stopped talking. With a look of pure horror, she felt something slide between her legs.

He crouched down beside her, grabbing her arm. "What, Sass, what is it?"

A hot tear trickled down her face and she was finally able to relax her shoulders in exhaustion. She unravelled from her tightly curled position and sat back against the bath. She had splayed her legs to make herself more comfortable and was now able to control her heart rate and her breathing. The look of intense pain on her face a moment ago disappeared almost as quickly as it had arrived. It was easy to see why. Malik's expression said it all, as he witnessed a brutal event whereby the forces of nature had overridden his sister's bodily functions.

Quickly, she masked the mess by pulling the cold towel from her neck and placing it over her lap.

Unable to face her brother, she turned away. But he knew the score, and he gently sat next to her, sliding his arm across her shoulders. "Sis, it's gonna be all right. Let's run that bath, eh, and get you cleaned up. I'm gonna find some tablets and make you a nice cup of cocoa." He knew he had to leave the bathroom, so she could flush the blood and tissue down the toilet and not endure further embarrassment.

Malik returned to find Sassy wrapped in her mother's old bathrobe and the bathroom spotless. The bath was steaming, and he had to wonder if the last hour hadn't been a dream, but his sister's lack of eye contact cemented the notion that it was no illusion. She had been to hell and back, and questions were tearing around his brain as to when, who … and fucking why.

Realising the horrendous ordeal she'd gone through, he decided he would only broach the subject once she was well enough, although, inside, he was ready to rip someone's head off.

She took the hot drink and the paracetamol, still unable to look him in the eyes.

"I am, er … I'm sorry, Mal." Her usual brash tone was a mere dampened whisper.

"I know, Sass, I know. You get that cocoa down ya neck and call me if ya need anything." He grabbed her hand and squeezed it.

Another hot tear trickled down her cheeks; it wasn't for her pain or the humiliation, but the kindness which Malik had shown towards her.

As he looked in his mother's room, he felt an overwhelming urge to smash it to pieces, to launch every last one of her belongings into the fire. She should have been here, to help Sassy, not leave and have him see to something he should never have been privy to. And poor Sassy. The one time when she really needed her mother, she had to face a miscarriage alone in a cold bathroom, with nothing but a wet towel to cool her burning skin, and even worse, to have suffered the humiliation of her brother witnessing it. This day would be embedded in his head forever — *you will pay one day, Jean*.

He paced the room, as he tried to rid himself of the image of the mess on the floor and his sister's face contorted in agony. Then the questions attacked his mind again. He wanted to know everything and then nothing at all. He was angry but not with Sassy — no, it was with the unforgiving world.

An hour later and Sassy slowly descended the stairs. Malik was on the edge of the armchair. He wanted to raise the subject, but he knew he had to be careful, not wanting to make her feel worse.

"You okay, Sass?"

She nodded, with her head still looking to the floor.

"Did he hurt ya, Sass? I mean, was ya raped?" Those words made him feel sick.

She shook her head and blinked back a tear. "I'm so sorry, Malik, I just wanted to help. You couldn't do it all, ya hand was fucked, you looked tired, I couldn't let ya fight for us alone, so I needed to help."

Malik cocked his head to the side in disbelief. "What are you saying, Sass? What did you *do*?" His voice was now firmer, and the tension in the air was so intense, it almost seemed tangible.

She had started, so now she had to tell him. Even if he threw her out, well, then it would be one less mouth to feed in the family. She was a burden and he didn't need it. "I slept with a boy at school, for money, for food … I, er, I didn't clean the art room." She waited for the backlash, the torrent of swear words. But instead there was only silence. Slowly, she lifted her head to see her brother look over towards her, his face showing fat tears streaming down his face. But there was something else as well: compassion. He stood then and held his arms open for her to fall into. She sobbed from relief and he cried with her and for her.

"Never again, Sass. You will never need to do that again. You put it outta ya head and you let me take care of us. You need to be a kid, like ya s'posed to be, and this never happened, okay? You're not a woman yet, and just you tell yaself that one day you will be, and you'll be a fine one, too."

"Ya don't think I'm disgusting, do ya?"

"Aw, Sassy, I could never think that of ya. You are fucking brave, reckless, and, yes, a stupid girl at times, but you're not disgusting. You did what you did, to help us. It was wrong, but it was done with a good heart. Does anyone else know? I mean, has he told the other boys or …?"

She let out a soft half-suppressed laugh. "Nah, it's not what you're thinking, all the boys lined up at the back of the bike sheds with a tenner in their hands."

She was right: he did have a disturbing vision of exactly that.

She sat back on the sofa and looked to check the two little ones were asleep. Malik returned to the armchair and waited for her to tell him what happened.

91

"This boy at school, well, he's liked me for ages. He's older than me, so seeing that I'm a bit weird to some of them, he won't make us official, like. I mean, he doesn't want to be seen around the school with me, in case his mates take the piss."

"You what, Sass, you ain't ugly!"

She sniggered. "Fuck off, Malik, I ain't blind. There's a poxy mirror in the bathroom that says I am, what with ginger hair and milky-white skin. Anyway, I like him, and I would love to be popular and have him on me arm waltzing around the playground, but it was never going to happen. So, one afternoon when the boys had football, he hates footie, we bunked off and spent some time alone, you know, kissing and talking. He wanted to take it further, and as much as I really like him, I'm not really like that, but then I thought, me and him could have a deal. I would sleep with him, if he paid me, and I would keep our little secret quiet."

Malik screwed his nose up. "What d'ya mean, 'keep our little secret quiet'?"

"He was a virgin, and me too, but him and his mates all pretended they weren't, so there you have it."

"So, tell me, Sassy, if he had been your official boyfriend, would you have slept with him at some point anyway?"

Her face lit up. "Yeah, I guess so. I liked him a lot, Malik, but what can I offer as a girlfriend?"

A sudden feeling of relief enveloped him, and he laughed, causing the little ones to stir. "Sass, you've a lot to offer, you just don't know it yet. One day, Sass, you'll grow into yaself, and you watch. All the boys will wish they had you on their arm, but they'll have your big brother vetting them first," he winked.

∽* споров

Two weeks had passed, and Malik noticed just how much Sassy had changed. The new clothes and make-up transformed his scruffy mouthy sibling into a more tranquil girl. She was right, she could be a model; with her hair tamed and a bit of slap on her face, she looked a lot older for one thing and extremely attractive. He realised that she had pride in herself and it gave her confidence. The little ones were happy, and Star seemed so much healthier. There were no signs of her asthma. Malik then realised that it was due to the change in their diet since their mother had left the cottage. By the time they returned to school, they looked fatter and content. Sassy had not only taken time with her appearance, but she had also made her sisters look neat and tidy, tying their hair in ponytails and making sure they were clean.

∽*∾

Malik stood at the entrance to the campsite; he'd made the decision to try bare-knuckle prizefighting. He had thought hard about it and decided that he could make some money, for even though he had done well so far at school, he felt that he had no choice but to leave. Reading Shakespeare wasn't putting bread on the table. Maybe, one day, he could go back to studying, so he could realise a dream of wearing a suit and driving a Jag like Penelope's.

The site was quiet, apart from a few cockerels crowing and two terriers having a tear up. He had no idea where the big gypsy lived. As he wandered over to the caravans, he noticed just beyond them a couple of men dragging straw bales. Once he was close enough, he could see they were making a walled square. "What ya doing?" called out Malik.

One of the men turned to face him, his face a sorry sight. His nose was twisted at an odd angle, and it looked as though the left side was caved in with no cheek bone. Even worse, one of his eyes was missing. Malik swallowed hard, as the vision made him feel queasy.

"Who are you, a gavver?" shouted the other gypsy, who was a big man with red hair that stood out against his ivory skin. The pair looked like characters out of the film *The Hills Have Eyes*.

"I'm looking for Noah! Me name's Malakai River."

The ginger-haired gypsy dropped the bale and walked towards him. "Cor, fuck me, bruv. I was expecting a lump of a fella. Are you really Malakai River? 'Cos Noah reckons you're the next Kent champion." He looked Malik up and down. "I can't see it meself, mind ya. I reckon you'll get mullered."

The other man, with the wrecked face, laughed. "Yeah, too much of a pretty boy to fight."

Malik didn't like his tone, and his response was fast and furious. "Looks like you ain't done too well in a fight. Don't tell me, the other man came off worse."

The ginger-haired man laughed. "Me name's Vinnie Joe. Pleased ta meet ya, Malakai River." He put out his fat hand to shake Malakai's.

Malik took it and nodded. He then turned to the ugly gypsy. "Sorry, mate, I didn't mean to be nasty, that weren't fair. So, what's ya name?" asked Malik, as he offered his hand.

The ugly gypsy took his hand, shook it, and tried to smile, but his muscles seemed to bulge in all directions, as if he had no control over his facial expressions. "Ocean," he replied.

94

"So, what ya doing?" Malik asked again.

Vinnie Joe smiled. "This 'ere, me boy, is the ring. We've got a fight on Saturday. A couple of the London lads are having a decent wager and some off the south Kent site. Up for it?"

Malik sat on a bale and gazed around. The field was surrounded by tall trees, so the action couldn't be seen from the surrounding roads. He smiled to himself. Saturday was two days away. Unsure of how it all worked, he asked Vinnie Joe. "How do I put meself up for it?"

Vinnie Joe laughed. "Cor, bruv, don't tell me you ain't fought before in a ring. May my muvver drop down dead. Ya'll get poggered."

Just then, from behind them, came a deep and familiar voice. "Malakai River! Good to see ya!" greeted Noah. The weather was still bitterly cold, and yet, there he stood, in a vest, black trousers, and braces. Malik then saw the actual size of the man's arms, which were as big as oak tree trunks. He had scars too, big scars. Malik reckoned that they probably came from men who were not hard enough to bring him down with their fists; instead, they took to a tool.

"How's ya hand, boy?" he asked, as he lifted Malik's arm to get a closer look.

"Good."

"It looks all right, boy."

Noah glanced with approval at what was shaping up to become a straw bale arena. "Now then, Malakai, are you up for a match on Saturday? I can fix you up with the Albanian."

Malik nodded. "How much will I be paid?"

The men stared at Noah in silence, waiting. Noah rubbed his bristly chin and smoothed down his unruly sideburns before he said, "I'll tell ya what. Afore I decides, I wanna see ya spa. Vinnie Joe, go and fetch ya pads. Spa with Malakai, and I'll do me sums, yeah?"

Vinnie Joe wouldn't argue, not with Noah, so he hurried down the hill to his caravan where his two brothers, Bobby Lea and Callum, were tucking into a fry-up, courtesy of Lou-Ann, their mother.

"'Ere, boys, d'ya wanna watch this Malakai River spa with me? I'll tell ya, I think Noah's lost the plot. The kid's a skinny runt. No way, he's gonna beat the Albanian."

The two lads jumped from their seats, both the image of Vinnie Joe, with their red hair and white faces. Callum, the eldest brother, laughed, "Cor, I wanna see this next fucking champion that Noah's got lined up, the silly old cunt."

Lou-Ann turned to face her boys. "Now then, don't you go disrespecting our Noah, 'cos if he 'ears ya, you'll be sparring with him, and it won't be a pretty sight, so watch ya mooi."

All three left their caravan and headed up the hill. Vinnie Joe could fight and had only lost a few, including his last one to an Albanian called Albi because no one could pronounce his name.

Malik was calm. He was rarely nervous; the only time he felt worried or sick was if the girls were in trouble. He didn't care much about himself.

Vinnie Joe was twice the size of him and stood like a gorilla holding the pads. It didn't faze Malik, though. He took off his coat and jumped in the ring. Callum and Bobby Lea sat on the bales, whilst Noah stood, rolling his tobacco. Without warning, Malik launched into action. His punches were so swift, Vinnie Joe got himself tied up in knots.

"Stop!" shouted Noah. "Give me the pads, Vinnie Joe, ya fucking pussy!"

Not even out of breath, Malik stood solid, with Noah's approving look of respect. "Do ya best, boy. I wanna feel those punches. So, no fannying around. If ya miss the pads and hit me, well, boy, that's my fault, got it?"

Malik nodded and began throwing hard and fast jabs. Noah was turning the pad, shouting, "Right hook, upper cut, left jab." Malik responded faster and harder than Noah expected. Then the big man held his hands up. "All right, son, enough."

The three spectators were open-mouthed; the kid could fight, and even they began to think he would take out the Albanian.

"A grand, boy," said Noah, out of breath.

Malik sat on the bale and smiled. "A fucking grand? Who am I fighting? Tyson Fury?"

Noah laughed and sat next to Malik. "No, son, you're gonna fight the Albanian. But I've gotta warn ya, he ain't been beat yet."

Looking down at his hands, Malik knew then that they really were going to make him some serious money.

"How does it work? I mean, can I bet on meself?"

The men were amused by the innocence of this remark. "Cor, mush, you ain't fought for money before, 'ave ya?" grinned Vinnie Joe.

Malik shook his head. "Nah, but I ain't lost a fight either, so can I bet on meself?"

Noah nodded. "Right, this is how it's gonna work. I'm gonna bet two grand you win, the Albanian will bet two grand, and whoever wins gets the money. Now, the others are gonna bet with each other, yeah, so like Vinnie Joe may gamble with Callum, it's that simple. But there's money to be had in this fight, boy, 'cos unless anyone sees you fight, of course they're gonna bet on the Albanian. So, the odds will be stacked in his favour, and that's where I can cash in, see?"

Malik nodded. "Right, I best get meself fit, then."

"You won't let me down, boy, will ya?"

Malik sighed. "I'm a man of my word. Besides, I need the money."

As he walked away, Noah crept up behind him. "Between me and you, boy, you're eighteen, right?"

Malik turned to face him with a sardonic grin. "Noah, I'll be fucking a hundred and five, if it means I can earn a grand."

"Good lad," said Noah, as he nodded, man to man.

Malik left the site with a spring in his step. A grand would see his girls all right. He could even save up and learn to drive. Secretly, he was wishing his life away, but in the forefront of his mind was the need to keep his family together. In less than a year he would be eighteen. There would be no way the authorities could get their hands on his sisters, as he would be old enough to take care of them himself. He shuddered; reaching eighteen seemed like a lifetime away.

The icy wind blew through his well-worn coat and he pulled it tighter around him. The lane was narrow, and with no pedestrian path, he had to watch for oncoming traffic. There, in front, swerving all over the road, was a flash-looking Bentley. Malik pushed himself against the bushes and hoped the nutter would straighten up and not hit him. He was in luck: his fate was not sealed on this occasion. The car came to an abrupt stop and skidded into the hedgerow. The man jumped out swearing and waving his hands above his head like a mad man. Malik recognised him and laughed, before running over, grinning from ear-to-ear. "Oi, what's up, Mr Reardon!" he called out.

Cyril had been stung by a dopey wasp. It was totally unexpected, especially as it was in the middle of winter, but it had happened, and he was livid. Cyril stopped dancing about and glanced over at Malakai. "Fucking wasp stung me, the cunting thing."

Malik laughed. "No way, it's too cold. Shouldn't they be all hibernating?"

"Well, fucking clever bollocks, I got one down me back that's on speed, 'cos he sure as 'ell ain't ready for a long kip."

Malik laughed again, amused by the animated man.

"How's ya hand, Malik? I was gonna call by, but I thought maybe …"

Malik looked at his hand and then at Cyril. "It's all right now, but it took fucking weeks to heal, though."

Cyril was mumbling under his breath. "Yeah, sorry about that, boy."

Malik eyed up the Bentley and then he admired Cyril's sheepskin coat and brand-new shoes. He figured that Cyril was a wealthy man and an idea formed in his mind. Cyril owed him a favour, so he was going to call it in.

"Mr Reardon?"

"Call me Cyril, will ya, son. Mr Reardon makes me sound old."

Malik smirked, "Well, you are old, ain't ya?"

"Oi, you cheeky fucker, I ain't old. Anyway, you were saying?"

Whilst Malik started to crack his knuckles, a habit of his when he was concentrating on something, Cyril simply stared at him. It was like watching Eddie Raven when he was a kid. With the recognisable glint in his eyes and the roguish look, this young fucker was his double.

"Ya know ya said I could call in a favour?"

Cyril raised his eyebrow and slowly nodded. "Yes, son, what d'ya want?" His voice was captivating; it was a real East Ender's accent, without a doubt.

"I've got this fight on Saturday against an Albanian and I'm gonna win. Well, I need a few hundred quid to bet on meself, see, and, well, I ain't got much saved, so I was wondering if I can borrow it? You'll get it back on Sunday."

Cyril took a step back and looked Malik over. "Why don't ya get in the car, son? I'm fucking freezing. I hate the bastard cold. I've got to go home and collect something. D'ya wanna come with me, so we can talk?"

Malik agreed, and he climbed into the sumptuous leather interior of the grandest car he'd ever laid eyes on.

As Cyril pulled away, he asked Malik, "So, what's all this about, then?"

Still on a high with the idea of having a grand in his back pocket, Malik went on to tell Cyril in detail about the plan for the fight. Cyril listened intently. The more he heard Malik speaking, the more he was convinced he was Eddie Raven's son all right with a bit of his grandfather, Marcus, thrown in for good measure.

Before Malik knew it, Cyril had pulled up outside his mansion. Malik looked on in amazement at the spectacle in front of him. It was like looking at the huge house in the TV series *Downton Abbey*, which he remembered seeing when he and his family were living in the East End, and there was a semblance of normality in their lives. "Cor, blimey! Is this all yours, Cyril?"

Cyril laughed his way. "Yep, I'm lord of me own fucking manor, would ya believe!"

Malik laughed with him, and it was at this point he realised it was probably the most he had smiled in a long time. The idea of earning some money was lifting his desolate mood, which was something that had lingered for as long as he could remember.

"Right, Malik, my business can wait. I think me and you need a chat, so come inside, and we'll have a drink and a bite to eat. How does that sound?"

Malik was warming to Cyril. His lord-like clothes, the fuck-off mansion, and the magnificent Bentley, it all seemed far removed from his cockney voice and funny ways. But, then, he was yet to learn that Cyril was a one-off geezer, a larger-than-life personality, who made you feel very comfortable in his company.

Mary was in the kitchen and didn't see or even hear Cyril come in. He had forgotten about the dog, and as he pushed open the huge ten-foot oak door, both Frank and Stein came into view. Stein ran at Malik but stopped dead. Malik wasn't afraid. He put his scarred hand out under Stein's nose and said, "Yeah, boy, you have a good sniff, 'cos that's what ya did."

The dog had his ears back and sniffed Malik's hand. Cyril watched in amazement. The boy was fearless, and the dog sensed it. "You ain't afraid of dogs, then?"

Malik shook his head. "Nah, it's people who do more damage. I don't think Stein meant to hurt me. It was just a reaction to you shouting. He was probably protecting his master."

Cyril led him into the drawing room with all its plush finery, where, of course, the oil painting of himself above the fireplace didn't go unnoticed. Malik looked up and struggled to stifle a laugh.

"I'll call Maggie for a brew, or d'ya fancy something stronger?"

Malik shook his head. "I don't drink alcohol, so tea's fine, thanks."

Cyril used the internal phone on the wall to call down to the kitchen. "Maggs, fetch some tea, there's a good girl. I've got a guest here, so knock up some sandwiches, with that chutney stuff you make, and bring it all up into the drawing room, will ya?"

He chuckled, as he replaced the receiver. "Cor, she's going off on one. Maggie is really called Mary, but I wind her up something rotten. She hates it."

"Me grandmother had two names like me little sister. Her real name was Chantilly, but everyone called her Tilly."

"I knew ya grandmother, she was a lovely woman. To be honest, wiv ya, I knew ya grandfather well. Old Marcus was a mate of mine. Well, he kinda worked for me."

Having never known his grandparents, Malik tuned out, as he didn't have much interest. As far as he was concerned, they had left him and his sisters to be brought up by a pot-headed waste of space. "So, Cyril, how about it, then? D'ya fancy lending me the money? You could make a few quid yaself." He gazed around the room. "Not that ya need it, like."

Cyril was surprised that Malik had changed the subject. Cyril knew he may look like a bit of an old fool, but that pretence had on more than one occasion been a huge advantage in deals to be done, not least that tremendously satisfying game of poker he'd had when he'd won this house in a battle of wits with Lord Chambers. Therefore, he got the message loud and clear that Malik had no interest in Marcus, but it was bugging him as to why. "So, did ya see much of Marcus before he passed away?"

Malik shot him a glance; his smile had left his face, and Cyril saw the man in the boy. "Let me lay me cards on the table, Cyril, 'cos I get what you are, right? All this, and you ain't no lord. I know where ya came from. You're a villain and a right clever one an' all, I suspect. So, I can guess me grandfather was one, too. But I never met him, and if he was alive today, I'd fuck him off. Ya see, me muvver is a no-good cunt, and me and me sisters are practically bringing ourselves up, 'cos she ain't fucking capable. So, as I see it, me grandfather, me grandmother, and even me ol' man, can rot in hell, 'cos where the fuck were they all, when we needed them? You tell me that!"

Cyril was taken aback by the force and indignation of the young man's words, and so he took a deep breath before he could reply. What

103

he saw in front of him was intense anger in the boy's eyes, and he knew he shouldn't push it. It was, however, no surprise to him at all. He'd known Jean for a very long time, and yes, she was a fucking slapper, albeit with an innocent face. She would pretend she was all sweet, like butter wouldn't melt, but really, she was a conniving slut of the first order. He never imagined that Malik was parenting the children alone, although he suspected that Jean was probably a heroin or crack cocaine addict, spending most of the time out of her box and leaving Malik to get on with it. He decided it would be better not to get involved in Malik's affairs at home. After all, it wasn't any of his business, and it wasn't as if he knew the boy.

"All right, son, you wanna earn a few bob. I'll front the money. I'll even 'ave a wager meself. D'ya reckon they'll wager ten grand?"

Malik's eyes were like saucers at this point. Excitedly, he replied, "I dunno, but we can find out on Saturday."

Cyril shared Malik's good humour. "I'm coming with ya, boy, 'cos I don't trust pikeys. Tell me, who's put you up to it?"

"Noah. A big lump, he is."

With spiked interest, Cyril gave Malik a controlled nod. "Yep, I know him. Well, I'm gonna bring me gun, 'cos he is, as you rightly say, a fucking big lump and no mistake. I'm sure he won't try no nonsense, but I like a bit of reassurance."

Malik agreed. "Thanks, Cyril, I feel a bit better now, 'cos, ya need to know, I ain't afraid of fighting. Nah, far from it, in fact, but I want what's rightfully mine, if I win, that is."

Mary entered the room with a tray of tea and fully loaded sandwiches. As she glanced over at Malik, she was riveted to the spot, as if she'd seen a ghost. Cyril hadn't been exaggerating. The boy really was Kelly's double. If he had a long wig and tits, it would be her. As Malik smiled, his charming expression lit up his face, and Mary felt unusually flustered; there was something in that grin that touched her. She had no doubt that he was going to grow up to be a charismatic bad boy with a twinkle in his eye. She glanced at Cyril, who could also charm his way into good company, but then there was his other side: on one of his off days, he had as much appeal as a hippo stuck in a mud hole.

Malik scooped two large teaspoons of sugar, a rarity in his home, and stirred his tea noisily. He eyed up the sandwiches and felt his mouth water.

"Help yaself, son. Ol' Maggs makes a fair decent bit o' grub."

Mary left the room with a soft smile on her face, not even bothering to banter with Cyril or tick him off about calling her Maggs.

"Now then, Malik, this Albanian. I've watched a few of 'em in my time, and I reckon this one will be like the others, one hard bastard. Well, they all are over in that neck of the woods. They're as hard as nails, the lot of 'em. Are you sure you're ready, 'cos if he catches ya with a swing, he may knock ya off your feet?"

Malik didn't care; he was all out to win and couldn't even face the possibility of a defeat. That money was his and his sisters' futures.

"Cyril, whether or not I'm ready, it's happening, and I'm gonna win ... I *have* to."

They finished their lunch and spoke about the history of boxing and prizefighting. One of the most famous Irish fighters was Patrick Rooney. He, too, was a small man. There was not much meat on his arms, but what he lacked in bulk, he made up in fortitude and skill and was fast and furious. Much like Malik, he also had a family to support, and his sure way to earn a living was by bare-knuckle fighting, which he did to great effect. That was over a hundred years ago, but despite the huge gap in time, people to this day would still speak of him with undisguised respect.

Malik was fascinated by this lesson in history. He wanted to be like this great man, so he would look up to Patrick Rooney as his role model. One day, he would have a name for himself and a home fit for three princesses.

CHAPTER SIX

Saturday morning, Malik was up and dressed; he wasn't nervous at all, but he was excited, and he could feel his heart rate climbing the charts. He looked in the mirror, which he rarely ever did, and grinned. Tonight, he would be returning home with a wage – a fair, honest, and decent wage – he hoped. As he opened the front door, there on the step was a parcel addressed to him, along with a handwritten note. It was from Cyril, saying he would pick him up at nine o'clock. He chuckled to himself. Cyril was a card, but he had a generous spirit. He liked the old boy. Inside the parcel was a grey tracksuit, a T-shirt, shorts, and a pair of trainers. He hurried back up the stairs and put them on. The inside of the tracksuit was soft and comfortable, and the trainers fitted like a glove. **RIVER** was emblazoned in red thread across the back. For the first time ever, Malik felt proud – he was actually someone now, and it felt good. He thought about his name; for years he'd despised it, as Malakai River sounded like a fairy out of a fantasy book, but just then, looking at the name on the back of that tracksuit, he changed his mind. He would be humble and thankful for the gifts bestowed on him. He knew now who he was and where he was going – and there would be no stopping him. No more looking at the floor in shame, he would hold his head up high and fight his way through life. Yes, if God had given him a talent, he was certainly going to use it.

Dead on the dot, the Bentley arrived outside the cottage, leaving very little room for anyone to get past on what was a narrow road. Cyril might be a man of many attributes but parking his motor was not

107

one of them. Malik skipped down the drive, punching the air. He spun around to show Cyril the back of the top and did a boxer's shuffle, as he laughed. "Nice one, Cyril."

As Malik went to get in the front, he noticed another man sitting beside Cyril, a big guy, roughly sixty years old, possibly a bit younger than Cyril, dressed in a suit and looking very dapper in a thick blue Crombie. Malik opened the back door and got in. The privacy glass had obscured his view, and once inside, he realised there was a third man, probably in his late sixties, who was also not short of a bob or two, if his clothes were anything to go by.

"Malik, these here are friends of mine, Frank and Blakey."

Malik greeted them politely but a touch nervously. After ten minutes or so, following a bit of banter between the older men, Malik realised that they had probably never paid taxes to HM Revenue & Customs: they looked like villains, they spoke like villains, and the manner in which they held themselves, it made Malik convinced they actually were villains. They were big men, especially Frank, who had hands like proverbial shovels and narrow dark eyes. Malik knew he would have been very dangerous in his younger days, just by the sheer heaviness of his frame; little did he know, though, that he was menacing even at this age. Blakey was the better-looking of the three; Malik put him in mind of an older version of Paul Newman, with his piercing blue eyes, whereas Cyril could almost have passed for Bob Hoskins, if he'd only been a couple of feet shorter.

"Blakey's gonna 'ave a wager, and Frank likes a good fight, don't ya, son?"

Blakey appraised the boy critically; there was definitely a resemblance to Eddie Raven.

Cyril noticed in his rear-view mirror how the boy held his head up; maybe it was the rig-out that gave him pride, or the fact he felt confident he was going to smash the Albanian. However, looking at Malik's size, there was a nagging misgiving crossing his own mind. The lad had never boxed before, and without a shadow of a doubt, he was going into the fight of his life, if Cyril's contacts were accurate about the boy's chances. He kept that information to himself. *No good putting a dampener on things at the first hurdle*, he thought.

As soon as they entered the site, Malik was overwhelmed with the number of cars, trucks, and men, and his adrenaline levels shot up even more. This was it now. There would be no turning back, not if he wanted to fulfil his dreams and maintain the level of respect he felt he had earned with his pre-match spar against Noah. There was virtually no feminine presence at all, which surprised him, for when his mother let him watch boxing on TV, it seemed as though it was the women who were doing all the hollering and screaming. Strange that. This wasn't just a roll around between the straw walls, this was big business. Eyes were on them, as the newly polished Bentley stood resplendently nearby. Malik sensed the atmosphere. He was good at reading people and surmised that they were sizing him up. The men and Malik got out and all strode with purpose towards the ring. Noah saw them and headed their way. He was pumped up and excited. "All right, Malakai River?"

Malik nodded. "Yep!" He was, too.

Noah looked at Cyril and smirked. "I didn't know you were into the sport, Mr Reardon." He was trying to suss out what Cyril and the other two men were there for. Noah was well aware of who they were, and he was immediately curious as to why they were escorting Malakai.

Cyril smiled, almost sarcastically. "Well, it seems to me that me boy 'ere is taking up this sport, and, well, I thought we best come along and watch, 'cos ya see, he's new at this, and as I see it, he might need a bit of guidance. Know what I mean?" He cocked his head to the side and raised his eyebrow.

Noah never understood these gangsters' riddles, but the one thing he did understand was reputation, and as old as the three men were, they were more dangerous than any gypsy on his site. They were wealthy old-school villains who would shoot you dead and bury you. And if they didn't do it, then they had plenty of men on their firm who would. There was a mutual respect though. Noah was a hard bastard – and his own name was revered within gypsy circles – and although his world was far removed from Cyril's, he was a man to be respected. Both men nodded at each other and shook hands. Noah had a hunch that their motives were to make sure the boy wasn't hurt or cheated out of his money. He looked at their thick Crombie coats and assumed that somewhere inside were shotguns.

Noah ruffled the youngster's hair to lighten the mood. "Are ya ready, then, boy?"

Malik laughed. "Oh yeah, more than ever."

Noah glanced once more at Cyril. He was still puzzled as to why Cyril and his friends, Frank 'the butcher' and Blakey, were looking out for this kid. As he understood it, the boy was just a nobody. The last time he saw Malakai, he had rags on his back. He pushed the thought aside and began giving him advice about the Albanian. "His weakness is his left ribs. He got them broken in his last fight, so, boy, you need to fire in quick jabs, to wind the fucker."

Malik was listening intently whilst his minders followed, clocking the set-up.

"Cor, Cyril, that's fucking Eddie Raven all right. He's the spit outta his mouth. But, to be honest, I was never keen on Eddie, yet, I kinda like the kid. 'Ave ya told Kelly yet?" asked Blakey.

Cyril shook his head. "Nah, I dunno what to say. I can't be sure. I mean, Eddie never mentioned he had a son. All I know is that Jean River was seeing Eddie in the prison chapel, and ya know what that means, the sly, dirty bastard. Yeah, getting his fucking helmet wet."

Frank, in his deep voice said, "Well, I can bet a million quid that he's a Raven. He is Kelly's double, and that mocking grin, it says it all. He has Eddie's genes. Just look at his colouring and his eyes. I have no doubts. Anyway, if he is Kelly's brother, we best keep an eye on him."

A crowd gathered around the straw walls. In the main, they were local gypsies, but some had heard about a special fight taking place here and had travelled as far as London, Essex, and Ireland, where an even greater gypsy population lived. A non-gypsy onlooker would have had a field day watching this crowd. They were of all heights and sizes; some were wearing Dealer boots and braces, and others were absolutely dripping in gold, and that was before you looked inside their mouths. Malik couldn't really understand their lingo, but he sensed they were eyeing him up. He watched money changing hands and other boys getting ready for their fights. It was clear that this was not just a one-fight competition but a real boxing fest. Some distance behind the straw ring was a fire over which hung a huge pig in the process of being spit-roasted, and in close proximity, there was an informal bar with bottles of beer stacked up as high as they could go. And then there was the banter. It was crazy stuff, with so many languages in play, but even to a blind man, it was perfectly obvious that these men were having the time of their lives. It was a bit like a cattle market, where the serious business was being discussed, and the buying, selling, and wagering were all taking place in a febrile atmosphere. The tension and the excitement were rising by the minute, and as Noah marched Malik into the ring, the crowd respectfully stepped aside. Noah clocked the name embroidered on Malik's back, and he had a secret grin, as he suspected the boy's minders had been hard at work getting him dressed for the part. So, as the two of them stepped inside the arena, Noah proudly raised Malik's arm aloft, and with his loud, deep voice resounding around the site, he duly introduced Malik. "This, 'ere, is River. He's gonna fight Albi, so all wagers are on!"

The crowd good-humouredly cheered, some laughed, and plenty shook their heads at the sight of this young man, who looked ill-equipped as a boxer. Malik closed his ears to the hoots of derision which were coming his way. He didn't care less what they thought; he knew he was there to earn a grand, and that was all he would focus on.

Cyril and the other two were watching closely, until Blakey piped up, "I'm gonna 'ave a bet. D'ya reckon there's anyone 'ere who will wager me thirty grand?"

Cyril then pointed to a group of men just behind the hog roast. They were big men, all wearing leather coats, and they each had a square-shaped head. "I reckon that little Russian crew over there will want a decent bet."

Blakey mumbled under his breath, "I hate the fucking Ruskies. They don't play fair and will need watching."

The Russian crew were, in fact, Albanian, and they were also ready to bet big money because their man had never lost a fight. They had sized the boy up, with his clean hands and girlish good looks and thought the odds were in their favour. Surely, Noah was having a laugh, as the kid looked a runt in comparison to Albi? To any American observer, this was a slam dunk; to those outside America, it was a foregone conclusion. Whichever way you looked at it, Malik was toast.

112

There was a table in front of them with scraps of paper and a pile of money. The tall Albanian, Movec, was the guy in charge. He was taking the bets, which, right now, were not many. The gypsies were reluctant to have a wager on Malik; he looked like he couldn't fight his way through a fag paper. Movec was pissed off: all he had on the table was four grand and he was hoping for at least twenty. He and the other Albanians were off that night back to Eastern Europe; they had already turned over a site up north, and this was to be their last venture. Their method was really pretty simple: to wait until the fight was on, and then, when everyone else was distracted with the fight, they would scarper with the money. Up in Northumberland, they had made two hundred and fifty grand, so they reasoned, there was absolutely no basis for why their plan wouldn't work well this time.

Movec watched the three smartly dressed old men approach. He didn't think much of them until Cyril spoke, and then he realised they weren't farmers up for a gamble, but they were more serious. He'd met their kind in London, when he was drug dealing. They didn't fuck about: crime and corruption were in their blood. So, he knew that if he wasn't careful, they would be quick to pull out a gun. Still, their money was as good as anyone else's.

"D'ya want a serious bet?" asked Cyril, with a cheeky smirk.

Movec studied him carefully. "How serious?" His accent was so strong, it was difficult to understand.

Blakey hated the Eastern Europeans; they always made his blood run cold. "Thirty grand says River wins."

Movec gave a false laugh. "I thought you said you were interested in a serious bet."

Taking offence to the man's tone, Cyril snapped, "Make it a hundred grand, then, cocky bollocks."

Somewhat amused by the way Cyril spoke, Movec nodded. "Yes, but put your cash on the table."

Cyril was only too keen to put his hand inside his coat and pull out a fat envelope. "There's my seventy, and Blakey, 'ere, is gonna wager you another thirty."

Blakey reached deep into his pockets. Retrieving his money, he also slapped his cash down hard on the table. There were a few onlookers having a good chinwag as they eyed up the money. It was then that some of the older gypsies got wise, and so they decided it may well be a good idea to have a stake on Malakai. Movec didn't give a shit if Albi won or not, though, as he was still going to take the money and run.

Malik was with Noah, taking all the advice he could; he was skipping and jumping around, warming up his muscles. The other boys, due to fight later on, watched Malik carefully. He was fast: when he punched the air, his hands were difficult to detect by the naked eye. It was like trying to spot the movement of a bird's wings in flight.

The ring was empty and ready for the main event. Johnnie joined Noah. "I've wagered a grand, meself, so let's hope you're right about this mush."

Noah swallowed hard. "Me too, bruv. I've wagered four grand. That's all me fucking savings." They laughed and waited for the Albanian to appear. There was silence, as Malik sat on a straw bale, in anticipation.

Then, a short but very powerful-looking man, whose body rippled with muscles, stepped out of a caravan. He was roughly twenty years old, and like the other Albanians, he had a mean-looking square head and jaw. His nose was a mess and the bones above his eyes were prominent, which made those eyes look all the more intense and bright. He didn't have a height advantage, but he was certainly more heavily built than Malik, probably by another seventy pounds. Another Albanian, his trainer, hurried over and gave him a swig of beer, and then he placed a hand under Albi's nose, so the boxer could snort a long line of cocaine. Malik was taking it all in. For a split second, he felt his stomach churn. But the touch of nerves only lasted two ticks; he thought about the grand he would receive if he won. *No*, he thought, *make that when I win*. This would be his focus, his motivation. Noah raised River's arm again and shouted his name. "River!" The crowd cheered. Malik gazed around the ring and realised it was packed. Most of the men were cheering for him, making him feel prouder than he'd ever felt in his life.

Albi flared his nostrils and glared into Malik's eyes. The crowd were shocked when Malik faced him off with a smirk. It was that trademark look which convinced Cyril, Blakey, and Frank that he was Eddie Raven's son.

The referee was a young and fit gypsy who went by the name of Red, on account of his ginger hair. He was a fair man, and he knew the game well, having been brought up on prizefighting.

Albi threw the first punch. He assumed that within two blows the skinny kid would be out cold, and so he could then take his earnings and be home by lunchtime. Malik swerved the punch and danced around. Albi launched another and again Malik swerved. After three more missed swings, a man from the crowd shouted, "What's this, a

115

fucking River dance? Michael fucking Flatley? Get in there and fight, boy!"

Malik knew what he was doing though. He was carefully watching how his opponent swung a punch, and when the fifth blow missed, Malik went for him, with a fast thrust into the ribs, again and again. The punches were so fast as to appear almost invisible to the spectators. Then, the Albanian counter-attacked, with a sharp jab which caught his opponent on the side of his head. Malik had never been hit so hard, and for a moment, he saw stars. All the excitement of the fight was short-lived: the buzzing sound of the crowd was silent, as Malik's body reeled from this heavy blow. He became deafened, his eyes blurred, and he felt his knees buckle. He could only stagger back, in an attempt to regroup from such a lethal punch. The Albanian took full advantage of Malik's senses being in lockdown and cracked him again, this time on the other side of his head. It was all Malik could do to stay upright and repeat that mantra in his head, *I want that thousand-pound prize.* He then heard Cyril shouting, "Kill the cunt, Malik, fucking smack him!"

Cyril loved a good boxing match and was no stranger to ringside seats at the big heavyweight matches. He had watched Frank Bruno and Mike Tyson in their younger days, and now he was witnessing what could possibly be a future lightweight champion. Of course, prizefighting the gypsy way had different rules. For a start, there were no defined rounds, and the referee never stopped a fight unless the man was out cold, or on the ground, having been beaten unfairly. If the loser felt he couldn't carry on, he would hold up his hand and say, "my best," meaning he'd given his all, and the fight was justly won by his opponent.

In desperation, Malik found the strength from somewhere. He pushed himself off the bale and launched himself in the air. With an almighty effort, he produced an uppercut which connected with Albi's jaw. This was exactly what the punters in the crowd wanted to see – a real fight, since it had looked very uneven, up to now. Albi wobbled, and the crowd cheered. Malik was now in full swing, letting rip with a succession of jabs. Although these were not lethal in themselves, by the nature of Malik's physique, they were, nevertheless, delivered with pinpoint accuracy, rather like laser-guided missiles. The result was that his Albanian opponent was being smashed all around the ring. Malik couldn't stop: he knew that if he didn't maintain the momentum, his opponent would try to get back into the fight. With a final and an even more precise uppercut, Albi fell to the ground, barely conscious. For a second there was silence, but it was soon followed by wild screaming from the huge crowd who had witnessed in effect a David and Goliath mismatch.

Whilst Noah was almost crying with pride, Cyril climbed inside the ring and grabbed Malik, hugging him like the son he'd never had. "Ya fucking did it, boy, ya fucking did it!"

But the euphoria didn't last long. Frank, in his deep voice, called out, "Oi, the cunts have fucked off with the money!"

Cyril let go of Malik and spun around. "Look, there they are!"

The Albanians were running across the field and heading to their car, their master plan now in full swing.

Frank, Blakey, and Cyril wasted no time in running to the Bentley. The gypsies were all dumbfounded and scattered in every direction, hell-bent on getting their money back as well. No way were these bastards stealing their dosh. Cyril jumped in the car and had it started up before Frank and Blakey were fully inside. Despite a bit of a reputation for being a reckless driver over the years, Cyril had got them away on many a job. It was an old joke that Cyril had been their getaway driver, but back then, bank jobs were easier, as there was no such thing as CCTV. The boys often reminisced about the good old days and how Cyril would have a car remodelled with a faster engine, ready to have it tearing away with their loot only to end up with a car that looked like it had been in a stock car race. He would hit every kerb, post, and fence on the way. He never let on at that time, he didn't possess a valid licence.

He was chasing what looked like a typical mid-sized BMW, carrying the Albanians and their money.

"Dirty no-good cunts!" shouted Blakey.

Cyril was swerving all over the road. "Cor, blimey, I'm too old for this," he said, coughing and spluttering.

Frank laughed, "You're always complaining, ya fucking big girl's blouse. Now, Cyril, look where you're going. They're in front of us!"

"Frank, get ya shooter out and blow their fucking tyres, will ya, while I keep the beast steady," yelled Cyril.

Frank tried to pull his gun from his pocket, but the coat had become caught in the door when they'd rushed off in the car. Cyril was swerving around the bend so fast, Frank hit his head on the window. "Frank, get ya shooter out, for fuck's sake!"

Frank was getting in a right flap. "I can't! It's in me coat, and that's shut in the fucking door, Cyril!"

Cyril reached down, pulled out his gun, and lowered the window. "Take the fucking wheel, Frank!" As Frank grabbed the wheel, Cyril leaned out of the window. At the same time, Blakey had his own window open and was aiming his gun.

But the men were beset by several problems, none of which had been anticipated. First, the road surface was proving to be a real pain in the arse. It was patchy at best, a prime example of council road maintenance cuts. Then, there was the strong and piercing wind which was causing their eyes to water at these high speeds. They were already doing eighty miles per hour on a road which was really only suitable for half this speed. And, finally, the *coup de grâce,* as far as the Albanians were concerned: it was all about the specification of the two cars. On the face of it, the Bentley looked the faster of the two motors. It was what gave Cyril confidence that he would easily catch up these men. But although his car was definitely the more superior beast – sporting a power-to-weight ratio twenty per cent greater than the BMW M5 V10 and a top speed in excess of one hundred and eighty-five miles per hour – being one thousand pounds heavier was proving to be the main problem. The men were not racing down an airport runway but through the glorious Kent countryside on twisty roads. So, although Cyril and Blakey managed to discharge at least one round each, they went nowhere near their intended target.

"Fuck! How the hell am I going to hit those bastards?"

At this point, Cyril was working himself up to a full-blown heart attack, such was the adrenaline running through his system. The men realised that their weapons wouldn't do the trick, and so they settled back into the car, with their only hope of catching the Albanians being the superior speed of the Bentley. However, the BMW was now out of sight. Things were looking bleak, to say the least.

After what seemed like an age to the occupants but was probably only a few minutes later, the men heard a sound like a bomb going off up ahead. Blakey looked at Frank and just shrugged his shoulders. As Cyril drove around the next bend, he was met by an old bloke who was lying sprawled across the road with his bike in the ditch. He frantically waved his hands to the driver to stop his car, which Cyril did.

"What's up with you, mate?" asked Cyril, as he lowered his window to speak to the man.

The old guy looked pretty badly hurt, with cuts across his cheeks, but he rushed his words out urgently.

"You'll struggle to get down the road, squire. There's a film of diesel all the way across it and the surface is real slippery. I've just seen a car take off into a field ahead!"

Cyril thanked the man for the heads-up, and he then decided he would not risk getting his much loved Bentley smashed to pieces. Parking on the verge, the men got out with their shotguns hidden beneath their Crombies and set off up the road. As they walked around the next bend, there was carnage. A car was flipped over, with smoke pouring out of the engine. A man was trying to get out of the vehicle. On reaching him, Cyril saw that it was Movec.

The car was a total wreck and the toerags were in a bad way. The money, luckily, was in a holdall and not in the boot of the car, which had caved in and would probably require an oxyacetylene torch to open it. Frank almost ripped the door off its hinges as he dragged Movec out by his hair. Movec was still clutching the bag. Frank saw the state of the man's face and knew his injuries were life-threatening. As Frank snatched the holdall, he threw Movec on the ground. "Ya dirty foreign cunt." Then he kicked him hard in the head. Walking back to the Bentley, they saw a few of the gypsy vans piling up behind. Frank held the bag up and the body language on the gypsies instantly transformed from anger and gloom to joy and palpable relief.

By the time everyone except the Albanians had returned to the site, it transpired that Albi had no clue as to the plan hatched by those Eastern European crooks. He was angrier than anyone else because he had a reputation to uphold.

Malik was slumped on one of the straw bales, fuming that some men had run off with his grand, but he soon sat up straight when he saw Cyril walking towards him with half the site trailing behind. Noah patted the older man on the back. "Well done, Mr Reardon, I thought they were gone – the no-good rats."

Cyril carried the holdall over to the table and looked at the betting slips before he handed over the money to the rightful owners. Then, he grinned when he gave Blakey his sixty grand and managed an even bigger smile when he took his own money. This had been quite a pay day for them, apart from the Albanians, of course.

Malik was looking over eagerly at all the comings and goings while basking in the congratulations and adulation from many of the gypsy boys. Noah counted out two grand. "'Ere, boy, ya rightfully earned it, fair and square, eh?"

Fixing his gaze on the money, Malik then studied Noah. "Yeah, I did, but that's two grand, and our deal was a grand, and Noah, you know me. I only take what's rightfully mine."

Cyril and Frank were amazed by the boy's morals.

"River, I bet four grand, me life savings, and you earned me two and yourself two, so now I've got six grand, so fair's fair. Boy, ya did me proud."

Malik was bursting with pride. Two grand was so much money. He could live like a king in his castle. No more searching for scraps. He shook Noah's hand and walked away silently.

Cyril drove him home, past the upturned and still smouldering BMW. There was no sign though of the Albanians, who must have crawled away. Malik glanced over and smirked. "Got a puncture, did they?"

Cyril looked in his rear-view mirror and winked. "Looks like it."

As they pulled up outside the cottage, Malik saw the smoke billowing from the chimney. That was a relief; at least the fire was still going. She was a good girl, his Sassy.

He thanked Cyril for the lift and was about to get out of the car, but Blakey abruptly stopped him. "Hold on, son, we've got ya winnings here."

Malik sat back down and frowned. "What d'ya mean?"

Cyril laughed. "Ya don't think Noah was the only one who bet on ya, did ya? You said you wanted me to lend ya a couple of quid to bet on yaself, right?"

Malik shrugged his shoulders. "Well, yeah, but, Cyril, Noah put me up on a wage. The deal was he paid me to fight, and if I won, he paid me half his winnings."

Blakey laughed. "Yeah, well, who the fuck is Noah? We look after ya now, son."

Malik frowned at Cyril; he was unsure of what was going on.

"Blakey's right. See, I was friends with ya grandad, and it's only right and proper we look out for you. Old Marcus wouldn't expect any less. So, take ya fucking winnings, and don't bleedin' question it."

Blakey handed the heavy packet over. "Fifty grand, and don't put it in the bank, as you can't say ya won it."

Malik felt his heart racing. Fifty grand! He wanted to pinch himself. The three pairs of eyes were staring at him. He was numb with shock. "I, er, I mean … I don't know what to say …" He looked at the packet and felt his eyes welling up. "You know, I'll have to owe ya, 'cos, as I see it, you've done good by me. One day, I'll return the favour."

Cyril chuckled. "Malik, don't forget, boy, I still owe *you* a favour."

As they watched the boy strut up the garden path, Cyril nodded. "Well, if that ain't Eddie Raven walking up there, then I'll fucking eat me underpants."

Blakey laughed. "Ya silly ol' bastard, ya would catch the bluebonnet plague."

Cyril laughed with him. "I swear, Blakey, ya wanna read more. Fucking bluebonnet, my arse. The word's bubonic."

CHAPTER SEVEN

After cleaning the whole house from top to bottom, Sassy was now making the beds and waiting anxiously for Malik to return. The younger girls were not in the best of moods, and although they helped Sassy, they were not their usual giggly selves.

As soon as he skipped through the door, Sassy was there to see he was okay. "Cor, fucking 'ell, I've been so worried. I take it ya won ya fight? I can see bruises, but at least you don't look like the elephant man."

Malik wore the biggest grin, which lit up his face. "Yes, I won, and we are rich, Sass. I mean fucking caked."

Sassy assumed he'd won the thousand pounds and flung her arms around him, which took Malik by surprise, since Sassy was not one for affection.

The two little ones stood watching but their faces were still sad. Malik, sensing something was wrong, looked back at Sassy for answers.

"I might as well tell ya now, the school's going on a trip to the zoo, and I said we can't afford it. All Tilly's friends are going, and Star's, too."

"Well, so they can now! How much is it?"

Sassy took a deep breath. "Twenty pounds each. But they also have to wear their own clothes, like a tracksuit, and they ain't got one. So, I said, to tell their teacher they can't go."

Malik kneeled down and put his arms out for the girls to give him a hug. They were confused, not knowing if they could go or not, but still, they ran to him and cuddled him.

"Right, girls, get ya coats on. We're going shopping, 'cos you'll need a nice bit of clobber for the trip, won't ya?"

Tilly and Star squealed with excitement and hugged him even tighter. Sassy felt her eyes well up. She saw the bruises on the side of his face and the joy in her sisters' eyes, and her heart went out to him. She was old enough to know that her brother was having his face punched in to support them. She glared over at the photo of her mother on the mantelpiece and felt the urge to throw it on the fire. Her hate for their mother was increasing at every turn.

He used the home phone to call a taxi, and soon after, they were off to the shopping centre in style. He was going to spoil his girls.

After wandering around all the shops and buying new clothes, shoes, and coats, they stopped at a Burger King, which was a real treat for the kids. Sassy noticed a group of boys over by the tills; they were looking over and whispering. As the family got up to leave, the boys walked over to Malik and shook his hand. Sassy then realised that her brother had earned their respect that morning; the boys were from the gypsy site and recognised Malik from the fight. She listened to their praises and how they held him in high esteem. It was a triumphant moment, but it was then spoiled by one of the gypsies who was having a good gawp at Sassy. He made a remark to Malik, who, in a flash, grabbed the boy by the scruff of his neck. "She's me sister! She's too young for dating, got it!" Malik's eyes were red and angry. The gypsy boy nodded and lowered his gaze. "Sorry, mush, I didn't know."

Sassy wanted to laugh; those boys were shit-scared of her brother, and she knew then that he was one hard bastard.

Seven months later

Jean paced the floor: she was nervous. Adam Carter was out of prison and living in a plush home on the outskirts of Bromley. He had met up with Jean at a party, and they'd taken up where they'd left off, years before. She loved Adam; he was the one man she would give up everything for, but when he got banged up for his part in a big drugs run, she had to cut off all ties and move on. She loved sex too much to stay loyal and wait for him while he served his time.

But now, there he was, back on the scene, flashing the cash and living it up. He was out two days when he met up with Jean, and having been shut away like the proverbial monk, he was happy to screw the life out of her. As he remembered her, she was always a good fuck. The days of screwing turned into weeks and then months. Then, once he'd had enough and wanted to get on with his life, she threw him the ultimate hook. Her youngest daughter, Star, was his baby.

She had felt twinges of guilt for leaving her children, yet after a line of cocaine was shoved under her nose, or a lavish shopping spree was hers for the taking, she soon switched off from thoughts of her offspring. She consoled herself with the notion that she was going to make a better life for them, with Adam's money. In reality, she was making a life for herself. Adam was a good catch, with a muscular frame and attractive blue eyes. He wasn't shy of a few girlfriends either. He was perfect, if you liked cocky thugs with money and a reputation.

127

Adam Carter was a criminal from a well-known family who were running North London. She wasn't a stranger to that world; in fact, she grew up in it. Her father, Marcus, was a prominent Face, and so hooking up with the odd villain showing his worth was par for the course and always had been, until they all got to know her for what she was – a slapper.

Too easily led, Jean had wandered from one man to the next, looking for comfort, which inevitably led to her popping out babies – something she certainly didn't want and could have prevented, had she shown a bit of savvy. Malakai and Saskia were born from sordid relationships. Jean would shudder every time she thought of their fathers, including Eddie Raven and the quick shags in the prison chapel.

Malakai was the most problematic; he was ruling her, and she resented him. He should never have threatened her friends, her extended hippy family, as she saw them. Then, there was her wayward, mouthy daughter, Saskia. She'd never liked her since the day she was born. Her red hair and wild ways were too much like her father's and she hated him. But she couldn't hate Star for the simple reason that she had no idea who her father was. Yet she wanted to hang on to Adam, and so when he said he wanted to live his own life without her, she let him believe Star was his, knowing full well that he would want his child. If he wanted Star, then she came with a mum, and that was her.

She took the beating Adam gave her, when she announced that her youngest daughter was his. She knew he would, too; he was always handy with his fists. In fact, he was not like the older villains, like her father, who would have seen red if they caught him hurting a woman or child. Nevertheless, she was nothing if not a realist, and so she would suffer the odd backhander, if it meant she could live like a woman of leisure. As soon as he knew that Star was his, he demanded she went and collected the child.

"It's not that easy, Adam," she said, with her sorrowful, pathetic expression. He glared with contempt.

"You fucking listen to me! I ain't having no child of mine being dragged up by her brother, and by all accounts, your fucking son is a nutjob. I've done my research and he's a fucker. So, I want my kid here with me."

Jean was nervous now; she hadn't seen her children for months and would be throwing herself to the wolves, if what Adam said about Malakai was true. She'd always known that he had his father's temper, just by the glint in his eyes, and she guessed that by the time he reached manhood, he would show it in more than just a sneer.

That morning, Adam watched her get dressed in her Karen Millen floral blouse and teal fitted trousers. She slipped her feet into a pair of flat sandals and dialled a cab.

"What if Malakai stops me taking her?"

Adam jumped from his chair, a monster of a man. "Then, use your fucking charms, like you fucking do on me, and make sure you bring her home. If you come back without my child, don't expect to stay."

Instantly, he changed his crazed expression to a compassionate smile and gently kissed her on the lips. "Go on, babe, you'll be fine. I'm looking forward to seeing my little girl."

❦*❦

Malik had taken on another ten big fights and bet on himself. His reputation was growing among the big-timers, and they were keen enough to stake large wagers from their loot, which had been accumulated largely through dishonest means. No gypsy worth his salt

129

would put his money in a Nationwide savings account. Cyril became his minder, driver, and genial 'uncle,' as he accompanied him to every fight, making sure everyone knew he wasn't on his own, and that he had the hardcore villains on his side.

The priority was to spend money on updating the house. No way did Malik and his sisters want another winter like the last one. The house was fitted with central heating, the kitchen was replaced with new gadgets and units, and the property benefited by having a damp-proof course, and so now the cottage was a warm and inviting home. One extra benefit was that Sassy gained her own room. The little ones had put on weight and looked a picture of health. Malik was clever; he had kept them all off the radar, when it came to the authorities and anyone else who might have been nosing around. He attended each school's open evenings, and he made it very clear that as his mother was unwell, he was her carer. Sassy learned to copy her mother's signature to perfection, and so no one questioned a thing. The schools had no reason to be suspicious, since all the girls were doing well: their attendance was exemplary, and they always appeared bright-eyed and well-clothed. In fact, they were better turned out than many of their contemporaries and that went for the posh kids too.

Early October, the long summer was coming to an end, the air was cool, and Malik was preparing to put the new garden furniture away in the log cabin he had built. He'd had it modelled on Penelope's classy structure. Sassy was cleaning the barbecue and the two little girls were playing with the new litter of kittens. It was a peaceful day spent in the back garden. They had enjoyed the summer. Malik had employed two landscape gardeners to transform the messy rambling lawn and overgrown bushes into the perfect outdoor space to entertain and for the girls to play safely on their swings. He'd also installed a hot tub and a large decking area.

Sassy had grown another two inches over the holidays. She was looking even more womanly, with her hair as wild as ever and now down almost to her backside.

All at once, Malik dropped the chair he was carrying, and Sassy turned to see what was going on. *Would you believe it?* thought Malik. There, standing as bold as brass in the garden was their mother.

Tilly and Star didn't run over to her as anyone would have expected; instead, they hurried to Malik's side, holding his legs as they had always done. Glaring with utter contempt, Sassy screamed, "You had better fuck right off!" She was holding a barbecue fork in one hand and pointing at her mother with the other. "Go on, I mean it, Jean. You'd best fuck off now, or I'll fucking stab ya."

Malik stayed silent. He decided not to intervene. The last thing he wanted to do was to show up his sister by taking control at this stage. As far as he was concerned, Sassy had every right and needed to get her negative feelings towards her mother off her chest.

Jean looked very different from when she left the home a year ago. Dressed in a modern outfit, not the hippy rags she wore before, she looked a picture of innocence, standing there with her wild hair recently styled. She was actually wearing make-up – that was a first.

"Go on, spin on ya heels and do one. You ain't wanted 'ere!" shouted Sassy, who was now edging towards Jean, brandishing the lethal-looking fork. Her eyes were like saucers and held anger like Malik had never seen before. Sassy easily towered over her mother; her strong and tall frame had grown so much. Tilly could only grip Malik's leg tighter. She was clearly terrified, and he could feel her shaking.

"Please, please, listen …" Jean's words begged forgiveness.

Malik then stepped forward, the little ones close behind, and he reached over and took the fork from the incensed Sassy. "It's all right, Sass, Muvver was just leaving." His voice was placid, yet Sassy knew underneath Malik's cool exterior, there was a volcano ready to erupt.

He turned around to face the girls. "Go to your room. I'll be up later."

Tilly and Star nodded and ran as fast as they could to the back door and up the stairs. Tilly slammed the bedroom door shut and turned the key to lock them both in. She was afraid that their mother would take them away. She'd been only seven at the time, but she remembered life being so bleak when their mother was there, and she knew it was Malik who had kept them safe and warm.

Side by side, like two Rottweilers ready to pounce, Malik and Sassy stood there, immobile, facing their mother.

Jean could feel her eyes filling up. It wasn't sadness for her children, though; it was the fear of not being able to go home to Adam with her baby. She'd been given an ultimatum: in effect, it was to take Star back with her, or don't bother to return.

She'd been nervous and expected an icy reception but not the reaction she was faced with. Offering a better life was going to be the excuse for staying away, and yet looking around, it was apparent that without her, they were doing just fine. The rumours Adam had heard about her son must have been true. He was earning big money from unlicensed fights. In her mind, she imagined the house was still run down and the kids as they were before. With Malakai battered and bruised, she would be their saviour, and they would accept her offerings. Malakai was almost eighteen now. Tall and broad, his face was that of a man — a hardman. Saskia, coming up to seventeen, had grown into a beautiful yet fiery woman. The excuse Jean had rattling around in her brain was pathetic and she knew it.

"Please, please … listen, I don't want to fight, I came to …" She stopped for a second to search their faces for any signs of compassion – there weren't any. "Star's father wants to meet her. He wants to give her a home, a good life, and—"

Before she could continue, Sassy launched forward to attack Jean. Malik anticipated this though and just managed to grab her arm and pull her back. "No, Sass!" he shouted.

Sassy was trying to shake Malik off to get to her mother. Malik was the tough one in the family, but Sassy was not far behind him. Her anger at every hardship that had endured over the last year was saved up and aimed at Jean.

He could feel Sassy's rage, and he held her tightly, knowing if he let go, she would kill Jean with her bare hands.

"I fucking hate you, ya stinking rodent. You left us to rot in hell! I swear to God, if you don't fuck off, you'll be shitting ya own heart out!"

Jean was shaking. She knew Saskia meant every word of it.

Malik empathised with his sister, but he could also see this situation getting out of hand. "Sass, go inside with the girls and leave this to me."

With her eyes wide and red, she took a deep breath and tried to calm herself. She nodded her white spiteful face and stomped towards the back door, still glaring at her mother.

Malik watched until Sassy was out of sight. In a low, menacing tone, he said, "Muvver, Sassy would have tried to murder you and that just wouldn't be fair."

Jean gave him a gentle smile, deluded by his words. "Thank you, Malakai. You have always been such a good son."

He held his hand up to silence her from going on. "No, Muvver, I didn't stop her because I didn't think she had a good reason. She did! But, it wouldn't be fair for her to end up in prison over a low-life rat like you. I don't want to argue, but I do want you to listen and listen very fucking carefully. You left us to die."

"Ah, come on, Malakai. You wouldn't have died. I was just looking for a better life for all of us."

He moved closer, almost stepping on her toes. "You left us to die. You gave up your rights as a mother the day you fucked off and left us to beg and steal for food. Those babies were sick with cold and white from hunger and cried themselves to sleep. Sassy became their mother, a fucking kid herself, doing *your* fucking job. So, as far as we're concerned, you're dead, Jean River. You are fucking dead and buried. Leave us alone, never come back, and I swear to God, if you so much as even look at Tilly or Star, I will come for you. I will hunt you down, and you'll wish you'd never been born."

Jean's shoulders slumped, and her knees felt weak. Never did she dream that her son, Malakai, would put the fear of God in her. As she walked away, her distress turned to annoyance, and she suddenly spun around and made a threat she would one day regret. "Adam Carter is Star's father, and he will come for her, Malakai, and you won't stop him."

Sassy had the front window open and heard Jean's words. In a second, she was down the stairs, out of the front door, and dragging her mother down the path towards the gate. Malik managed, in among the torrent of punches, to grab Sassy's waist and pull her off Jean before pushing his sister back into the house. He then looked down at the bloodied mess of Jean's face. His mother didn't look so sweet now. Her expression, although bashed and severely bruised, was one of pure hatred. Slowly, she managed to get to her feet and limp away.

The two little ones were now comforting Sassy.

"Come on, girls, let's get out of 'ere!" said Malik. "Go and pack some bags."

Concerned that Jean would return with this Adam guy, claiming to be Star's father, Malik took control. He had a feeling they wouldn't be returning to the cottage for quite a while. He and Sassy packed their clothes whilst Tilly and Star went off to hunt for a few of their toys and books. The children, of course, didn't question him at all. He was their big brother, their father figure, and their best friend, all rolled into one. The one thing they had learnt in their short lives was that they must stick together.

❧*❧

Cyril was trying out one of Mary's new recipes, sticky toffee pudding, when the phone rang. It was Malik.

"Cyril, I need your help. That favour you owe me. Well, I want to call it in."

Desperately trying to clear his throat, as the sticky toffee had almost glued his false teeth together, Cyril choked, "Oh, yeah, and what's that then, boy?"

"Can you come and pick us up from me house? I'll explain when you arrive."

He sensed the urgency in Malik's tone. "On me way, boy. Do I need any tools, or is everything okay?"

Malik laughed to himself, despite their predicament. "Nah, just come as soon as you can, please."

Cyril liked the fact that Malik was so polite and respectful.

Within fifteen minutes, Cyril arrived and beeped his horn. Everyone was ready and waiting, by this time. They all hurried down the front path to the big Bentley. As soon as Cyril saw the girls, he sat upright and frowned. Malik opened the back door and ushered his sisters inside and then he hopped in the front. "Cheers, Cyril."

Detecting the panic, Cyril wasted no time in pulling away. "So, what's going on, boy?"

Malik glanced over at his fearful sisters in the back. "Cyril, do you mind if we stay at your house, just until I can figure out what to do?"

Cyril nodded; he wouldn't talk in front of the girls. He'd never suspected that Malik was looking after his sisters alone and it had never been a discussion point between them. Their talks were about the fights and getting him trained up, so, other than that, it was small talk.

Once they reached the mansion, the girls were wide-eyed, never having seen a house so big. Star squeezed Tilly's hand and she let out a chuckle. Sassy looked at her two little sisters and winked; this wasn't going to be so bad after all. Whether they were moving into this mansion for good, or just a few days, it didn't matter. For now, they would be safe. Cyril called for Mary to take the girls with her into the kitchen. Not having children of his own, he had no idea what to do with them. It was easier to pass them off to his housekeeper, so he could get down to the business of the day.

Sassy wanted to stay with Malik, but with one nod from him, she knew she had to do as she was told. Star and Tilly were happy to skip away with the soft-faced woman; her suggestion of baking cakes was enticing and exciting to the little ones. Sassy followed, trying to take it all in. The huge hallway, the grand furnishings, and the fact that her brother was friends with a lord, or a duke, or even a prince, was hard to believe.

"So, son, what's going on?" asked Cyril, as he sat down heavily on the sofa.

Malik sat opposite, nervously rubbing his hands together. "Cyril, I know you've been good to me, 'cos ya knew me grandfather, and I appreciate all you've done. The truth is, and I hate to admit it, you're the only man I know, really. I've got no one." He paused, thinking of the right words to say.

Cyril gave him a look which said he already knew that.

"I ain't been honest with ya, Cyril, but, I ain't lied, either. The thing is, me muvver left us, me and the girls, twelve months ago, and well, I didn't want me sisters to go into care, so I tried to keep us safe but together. The problem now is the ol' cunt 'as just shown up and wants to take me little sister, the baby. She reckons her father wants her."

Cyril sat back and watched Malik's uneasy expression and the way he appeared so vulnerable. Little did Cyril know that behind those damp walls of the cottage, Malik was trying to fend for his family. He was just a kid.

Now, Cyril felt the boy's pain. He remembered the boy trying to chop wood for a fire and facing his first fight with the Albanian. It struck him that his perspective of Malik, not that it had ever been bad at all, had been ill-founded. In a heartbeat, it changed dramatically: he saw this young man as not only brave and courageous but someone he should hold in high esteem.

"Have you been looking after those kiddies on ya fucking own, then?"

Malik lowered his head and nodded in shame. "I couldn't tell anyone, in case the social services took 'em away."

Cyril, as tough as he was, felt a lump lodge in his throat. He was mentally kicking himself for not taking a greater interest when the two of them had last met here in his home when Malik wanted help with his first fight. "Christ, son, why haven't ya told me? I could 'ave ..." He didn't know what he could have done, but he knew he would have helped, in some way or another.

"I was too afraid, ya see. I probably needed them as much as they needed me. Me muvver, well, she never really looked after us. I did most of it, when I could."

Cyril nodded. "All right, son, what do ya want me to do?"

Malik shrugged. "I dunno, Cyril. I dunno what to do. She reckons that this fella of hers is gonna come and fuck me over and take me youngest sister, the fucking baby. I swear, Cyril, I'll kill him, if he touches her."

"Don't you think it's better if the social serv——" He never finished the sentence, when Malik was on his feet.

"See, I wished I'd never fucking told ya." He was about to storm out of the room but was called back.

"Malik, boy, wait, it's all right. I ain't gonna call no one."

Malik stopped in his tracks and unexpectedly fell to his knees with his hands over his face and sobbed. The pain and suffering his sisters and he had endured finally hit him all at once. Cyril rushed up from his chair and pulled Malik to his feet. He wasn't used to consoling people, but somehow putting his arms around the boy came naturally. "Listen, son, you've no need to worry. Uncle Cyril will help ya sort out this mess."

Malik stopped crying and wiped his face. "I'm sorry about that. I just feel tired. I'm sick of worrying about the girls, and when that ol' cunt turned up, it took all me strength not to fucking throttle her. Sassy gave her a good hiding, and I don't blame her. Me sisters have been to hell and back, all because of her."

Guiding Malik back to his seat, Cyril headed over to the drinks cabinet and poured them both large brandies. "'Ere, son, get ya laughing gear round that."

Malik took the brandy, and in one gulp, it was gone. He screwed up his face, swallowed, and gritted his teeth. The warm liquid burned his throat, but as his muscles relaxed, he felt a comfort and held out the glass for another one. Cyril chuckled. "Easy, boy, ya don't drink, do ya?"

Malik smiled. "Well, I think I needed one, 'cos, Cyril, I don't cry either."

"So, son, you mentioned that ya mother wants to take the baby to meet her father. What baby?"

"Oh, sorry, I mean Star. We call her the baby. Actually, we call both the little 'uns babies. I forget they're not." Malik sipped his drink and shook his head. "And as for Star meeting her father, it's a joke, 'cos Jean doesn't really know who our fathers are. She shagged everything, the fucking dirty tramp. Now, she's with some geezer called Adam Carter, and she reckons he's gonna come and take Star from us. Knowing her, she has lied about that, too, but she's probably sucked this bloke in, like she does everyone, with her airy-fairy ways."

"Adam Carter, you say?"

Malik nodded. "D'ya know him, then?"

Cyril took a deep breath and stared into space. Malik waited for an answer.

"It's best, boy, that you and ya sisters stay 'ere until we get this mess sorted."

Malik sensed the concern in Cyril's voice. "You know who this bloke is, don't ya?"

With a spiteful look in his eyes, he nodded. "Yeah, son, I do, and to put it bluntly, he's a right 'orrible piece o' work. A dangerous one at that. So, for now, Malik, you and the girls must stay 'ere."

Malik gradually relaxed in his chair. He trusted this old geezer. He'd come to respect and actually love him like a father, and he knew that if anyone could help his family, it would be good old Cyril.

By the end of the day, it was agreed that the River family would be staying in the mansion indefinitely, so Cyril had taken Malik back to the house and collected all the kids' belongings and had them settled into their rooms at his home. Sassy was in her element, wandering around the house like the lady of the manor. She'd never seen such finery and was lapping it up. She knew she and her sisters would never be bored, what with the heated indoor pool, the games room, and the huge flat-screen TV. And her own bedroom, with a four-poster bed and a long window with the extensive view across the fields, was so peaceful. Her sisters had their bedroom next door, and like Sassy, they considered themselves to be princesses for the time they would be living there. But, most of all, they felt safe being here with the old man, who, it was clear, was very fond of their big brother. No longer did they feel uneasy: it was a great feeling. Mary was at hand and loved fussing over the children – a far cry from the banter with Cyril. She didn't have children of her own and always fantasised about having at least one, but she was way too old now, and so she enjoyed what she had. Cyril was secretly pleased too; he wasn't used to small children, they had no place in his life until now, but in a trice, he felt years younger. Tilly, especially, was his favourite; she was quiet and reserved, and that smile of hers – well, it melted his heart.

They all sat together over a roast dinner and especially enjoyed the cakes made by the girls. Cyril felt proud of Malik, knowing that when he was his age, he could never have coped anything like as well. *The boy had done good*, he thought; he was raising three girls and was not much more than a kid himself. The way in which they behaved was also impressive. Really, he couldn't have asked for nicer children – polite and sweet was an understatement. However, what struck him the most was how the girls looked up to Malik, almost hanging on to his every word.

Once they'd finished the meal, little Tilly passed Cyril a cake. "'Ere, Uncle Cyril, I made this one just for you."

Cyril felt his eyes mist over. Her cute little face and infectious lisp turned him into a softy, and by calling him 'uncle', it gave him a wave

141

of fulfilment like he'd never felt before. He took the over-iced cupcake from her chubby little fingers and pinched her cheeks, which made her giggle contentedly.

Sassy, though, was unusually quiet; the whole fight with her mother had left her with more than enough to think about. If she was honest, she wished she'd been given the chance to finish off Jean once and for all. She had enjoyed roaming around the mansion, yet when her mind wasn't occupied, she filled it with hateful thoughts towards her mother.

The dining room had huge floor-to-ceiling windows which faced the well-lit drive, and in the distance, Cyril could see a Range Rover gliding its way towards the house. As it reached the portico, the lights beamed through the windows. Cyril held his breath. He knew exactly who the car belonged to and now he would have some explaining to do. He looked at Sassy. "'Ere, darling, do us a favour, will ya? Take the kiddies upstairs or in the games room. I gotta bit o' business to sort out."

Sassy smiled and took the girls' hands to leave, but on leaving the dining room with them, she encountered the visitor who had just entered the house through the massive stone porch. As if someone had hit her around the head with a bat, Sassy couldn't have been more shocked. The tall lady, wearing an exquisite Dolce and Gabbana dress, was smiling at her with the most amazing green eyes set against a glowing suntanned complexion she'd ever seen. But there was something about her features and expression which made Sassy do a double take, as she watched the young woman look down at her own two little sisters. "Well, hello," said the visitor.

Sassy was now glaring at her, in utter bewilderment.

Cyril rushed to the front door before Kelly had a chance to meet Malik. He was met with Sassy as white as a sheet and transfixed on the person who was just taking off her soutache jacket.

"Go on, Sassy, take the girls upstairs," he urged.

Sassy snapped out of her gaze and hurried the girls away. The day had been a mix of emotions, and now she questioned if she was seeing things. *What's going on?* she thought.

Kelly kissed Cyril and walked past him down the enormous entrance hall and into the drawing room, throwing her bag on the sofa. "I need to talk, Cyril," she said over her shoulder. "I've got a few issues with the business. Oh yeah, and who are those girls? I never knew you had a family."

She stopped when she saw the uncomfortable expression on Cyril's face. "What's up?"

But before Cyril could get a word out, Malik entered the drawing room. He looked at the visitor and froze. Malik and Kelly simply stared at one another. Kelly finally stepped back and blinked furiously. Her heart began to race and her stomach knotted up. She turned to Cyril and cocked her head to the side, looking for answers. Malik was totally unaware of what was going on. Yet, he was gripped by an unexpected sensation that he couldn't explain.

"I think you two had better take a seat," urged the usually unflappable Cyril.

Kelly was covered in goosebumps – the boy was her father, Eddie's double.

She didn't know whether to run away or hug him. He wasn't Eddie Raven – obviously – because Eddie was dead. Yet this young man was so like him, it was bizarre.

Malik giggled with nerves because the tension was almost like an elastic band ready to snap.

"Kelly, meet Malakai River, Malik, meet, er …"

Kelly took a deep breath, as she gave the young man a curious look. "I'm Kelly Raven."

Malik was amazed to see that they were like peas in a pod – a mirror image, in fact. His mind was an avalanche of strange emotions. How could this be, seeing his double and in such circumstances? What were the chances of this happening to anyone? It was surreal, to say the least.

Interrupting the moment, Sassy burst into the room. She was pumped up with so much anxiety, she had to find out what was going on, and although she would normally do as she was told, the idea that this woman was somehow related to her brother was eating away at her.

"Who are ya?" she asked, with spite on her face.

"Sassy!" Malik raised his voice, annoyed with her rudeness.

"Well, look at her, Malik! She looks like you!" She turned to face Kelly. "Well, missus, you do, don't ya?"

Kelly swallowed hard before she nodded. "Yeah, you're right, we do look alike. Who's your father, Malakai?" she asked, turning her back on Cyril.

Malik's eyes flitted from one person to another and he shrugged his shoulders. "Fucked if I know. Every one of my family seems to have a different father. By the way, I'm Malik."

Cyril put his hands up. "All right, all right, everyone. You, Sassy, sit ya arse down. I s'pose this includes you, too, babe." Kelly went over to her favourite armchair by the enormous fire, whilst Sassy, none too willingly, stomped across to the table to sit down and wait for Cyril to make some kind of pronouncement. Meanwhile, he phoned down to the kitchen to order everyone refreshments.

Cyril didn't sit down himself. He took a deep breath before he delivered what he suspected would be quite a bombshell. "I might be mistaken, Malik, but your mother, Jean, had a thing with a man called Eddie Raven, Kelly's father."

Kelly stared at Malik and frowned. "No, Cyril, he can't be his son. Eddie was in prison. I take it you're about seventeen or eighteen?"

"Eighteen, in a couple of weeks," replied Malik.

Cyril shook his head. He knew this conversation would be a difficult one. "Well, yes, Eddie was inside, but as far as I know, Jean went on a few visits, and, well, he bragged that he'd shagged the life out of her in the prison chapel." He held his hands up and waited for the eruption. Instead, Malik and Kelly merely stared at each other. But the shock of these developments was sending off wild signals to all present. Sassy felt particularly vulnerable and was understandably angry and frightened. He was her brother – there was no room for anyone else.

Malik smiled a half-smile, like Eddie's. "Well, I reckon you must be me sister, then."

Kelly felt overcome; she'd never had a sibling and now she did — lots of them, in fact. However, she was also nervous because Malakai was her father's son all right — they didn't need a DNA test for that.

Sassy was so eaten up with jealousy, her face was saying it all for her. "He ain't your real brother, not like mine. I mean, you don't even know him." Her tone was ugly, and there was now an unpleasant undercurrent felt by everyone in the room.

Kelly turned to face Sassy and sensed her pain and worry. The sadness and fear were written all over the young girl's face. Kelly rose from her armchair and went over to sit down next to her. Enclosing Sassy's hands in hers, she said, "So, Sassy, if he is me half-brother, then I guess you're me half-sister, too, and those little girls, they are also family."

Sassy saw the sympathy in Kelly's eyes and immediately felt foolish. "I'm sorry. I didn't mean to … well, what I mean is …" She stopped, and a huge tear trickled down her face.

Kelly leaned towards her and hugged the girl. "You've nothing to worry about, sweetheart. I'm not about to take your place."

Malik watched as his recently discovered sister embraced his wild Sassy, and unlike her usual self, she allowed Kelly to comfort her. The little ones were called to the room and introduced to Kelly, who was delighted to meet such charming children.

At that moment, Mary came into the drawing room laden with tea, coffee, a selection of soft drinks, and biscuits for everybody. She smiled broadly to them all and left discreetly. She could see that they were preoccupied, and she didn't want her presence to distract them.

146

Kelly was initially annoyed with Cyril for keeping this secret hidden from her. If only she'd been informed about her new family, she would have helped them. They shouldn't have had to suffer like this. As far as she was concerned, he was family. But the more they talked and laughed, the more she realised he wasn't like Eddie: in looks and expression, yes, but in his heart – no.

Malik, however, was just pleased that he had a big sister. The fact that she was obviously loaded and had a serious reputation was mind-boggling. In twelve months, his life had been turned completely upside down, and the ironic thing was that if it hadn't been for that bitch of a mother, none of this would have happened. How weird was that?

She made a fuss of Sassy too. She liked the girl's gumption and sensed she was afraid of losing her brother. As soon as Sassy realised that Kelly was no threat, she relaxed and began to marvel at the woman. Sassy wanted to grow up and hold herself in the same manner and aspired to be just as attractive.

Kelly looked at her watch and sighed. "Well, with all that talking and catching up, it's too late for me to go home now. Besides, Mary makes a lovely breakfast." Tilly and Star squealed with excitement.

Once Malik's sisters went to bed, Kelly turned to him, with a gentle expression. "It's a shame, Malik, because I would have loved to have known I had a brother. My life was pretty shit growing up, and if it weren't for our ol' man, I may have had the chance of a normal family. He was a greedy bully who left me to be dragged up by his wife, a nutcase. Anyway, I'm telling you this because your father is dead, and it's a good job, too. At least, he can't get his paws on you."

"Well, sis," he said, having listened with avid interest to this revelation, "it seems like we were both dealt a shitty hand. Me muvver's not the full ticket, leaving us for someone called Adam

147

Carter. I hate her more than anything. I worry about the little 'uns, but now I worry about our Sassy. She really suffered, ya know. Well, not anymore. I'm gonna make sure she has a normal life, whatever that looks like."

Kelly tossed her head in annoyance. "Adam Carter, eh? So, Jean's got her shoes well and truly under his bed, then!" After a few seconds of contemplation, she said, "The Carters have taken a few liberties lately, ya know. I've been wondering why. But, I think I have a fucking good idea."

Malik's eyes widened. "Do you know Adam Carter?"

Kelly shook her head. "No, but I think I need to tell you the extent of my business."

Malik was looking at his own flesh and blood with respect. She was no idiot. Secretly, he liked the idea of his sister being a gangster.

"Our father had money and muscle. He owned pubs, a club, and a protection racket. He also had a serious cocaine business going on with his brother-in-law, a man called Patrick Mahoney, who, by the way, I killed and served time over." She waited to see Malik's reaction, not wanting to frighten him off. He nodded for her to go on.

"When Eddie died, being that I was the only child, well, so we all thought, I got it all: the houses, the businesses, and the protection racket. I inherited a considerable amount of money and responsibility, and that's why Cyril, here, has my back. You see, Frank, Blakey, and Cyril gave me the option to continue with the businesses or take the money and run. I left school with no qualifications. All my lessons were learnt in prison. So, with their help, I took over. The biggest problem I expected to face was the Carters. Yes, Adam Carter's family. However, once Patrick and Eddie were dead, the drugs dried up

148

because the Colombians wouldn't deal with anyone else, including the Carters. Lucky for me, though, the Colombians saw me as someone they could do business with, and they decided to take a chance on me. And I've never let them down. This didn't matter to the Carters. That family wanted to earn their money by other means, but it meant stepping on my toes."

Cyril frowned. "So why are the Carters taking liberties now?"

Kelly was surprised that he hadn't worked it out for himself. "Adam Carter is a reckless bully. He was inside for the last five years, but he came out some months ago, and he wants a cut of my business. He has already knifed two of me best men, and badly, too. That's why I came over tonight, to have a chat about taking on more muscle. But then, of course, I got sidetracked with more important matters," she winked at Malik.

Malik was listening to this conversation, as if he were watching a scene from a gangster movie. It all seemed illusional. So much was happening to him and Kelly, that his brain was working overtime in trying to process a swiftly moving story of events. But although it was unreal to him, it all made so much sense. And, furthermore, looking around the mansion with all its wealth, and at his rich sister, who was rigged out in designer gear, he wanted to be a part of it. Kelly and he were not only alike in looks but had come from a similar background and without any formal qualifications. What else could he do except fight for money? He knew that this type of work may be short-lived, but this was his life, as he saw it.

Suddenly, he jumped in. "Sis, I can help. Count me in. I can fight."

Kelly noticed his eager expression and felt an overwhelming sense of closeness. It was as if he had always been there; maybe he was her mirror image and had the same traits, but there was a bond, and it was that emotional connection which would be the important thing, which would bind them together, as brother and sister.

"Sis, I need to earn a wage to look after the girls, so will you put me on your payroll?"

Kelly looked at Cyril and laughed. "He really doesn't know me yet, does he?"

Malik felt awkward; he'd pushed her too far, and besides, she didn't know him, so how could she trust him to take him on?

"Malik, listen to me. You are my brother, there is no disputing that. Family is everything to me, and one day, you will understand that. But I'm a very rich woman, thanks to our father, which also means that you are well off, too. Eddie's money is ours to share, that goes without saying. You won't ever need to bruise those knuckles again. No, if you wanna work, then you can run any one of the businesses, but life will be far easier for you from now on. All ya need to do is learn the ropes, and Cyril, here, was my best teacher. Besides, all that, I think you'll look kinda handsome in a suit, so perhaps you shouldn't go down the boxing route sporting a boxer's nose and cauliflower ears!"

Kelly was well aware that his looks alone had her father's stamp and would have the other firms quacking in their boots, if they thought that Malik was half as reckless as Eddie.

"We have a problem right now and that's our Star," she said.

Malik felt goosebumps cover his body. She just said, "our Star." It was as if a thousand bricks had been lifted from his shoulders.

"I've had Beano do some serious homework on this cunt Adam, for my own purposes, and by all accounts, he's a loose cannon, a reckless tosser," she stated, with a look of ice in her eyes.

Malik saw his new-found sister turn from a soft-featured woman to a hard-faced one of substance. There was so much to her, and he was just glad she was on his side.

By the end of the night, they had agreed to take Adam Carter head-on.

Let the fun begin.

CHAPTER EIGHT

Kimi sat in the chair next to her father's bed. He lay there, with pain etched on his face. She was exhausted. The cancer had spread to his bones and he was as weak as a kitten. Yet, he refused to go to the hospice and expected Trisha, his wife, and Kimi, his daughter, to care for him. Kimi didn't mind at all; she loved her father, although Trisha was another story. She was too up her own arse to lower herself to play the nurse. It was as if she was oblivious to the whole situation, carrying on as if he was at work or on the golf course. She went off on her shopping trips as per usual and continued enjoying her afternoon teas with her la-di-da friends. Kimi was left to clean, feed, and see to his medication. She had barely eaten in days, afraid to leave her father's side. Her bed was cold too, not having been slept in. So, her current bed was the chair and a throw, next to her father.

She thought about Malik every day and longed to go back to the store, just to see if he returned. That Christmas was the worst ever. Her father had collapsed and was rushed to hospital, and she was too consumed with grief, when they told her he had cancer and was not going to see out another ten months. She never returned to work; her job was caring for him.

And care for him she did, day and night, as he fought to stay alive. Now, she stared at his once handsome face, which had become thin and gaunt with a yellow tinge. He wasn't her father anymore, he was just the ghost of the man he once was. A tear worked its way down to her lip and she choked back the second one. She thought she couldn't cry any longer, yet that tear was for herself this time. She had no one except her father. Trisha had told her, in so many words, that once he was dead and buried, she would be out on her ear. All his assets were in their joint names, and so she wouldn't even see a penny. She did have her car, a decent enough motor, which would have to be her home until she could secure a job.

Her thoughts returned to Malik, as they always did. It was strange because she barely knew him; however, she was drawn to him, with his smouldering eyes and his cheeky smirk, and even the way he spoke, with that sexy beguiling voice, turned her on. He had intrigued her from the very first day she met him, and when she saw him walking two little girls to school, she knew then that the food and toys were for them. She even followed him to his house and waited in her car to watch. She had no idea what went on behind those walls, but she could imagine, and she really wished she was there with him.

She held her father's hand as the death rattle in his throat became worse. The nurse who came every day said he only had hours to go. She left Kimi in peace to spend the last few moments alone with him. Trisha was out of the house when he finally passed away. Kimi didn't break down in sobs; she had cried all the while she watched him dying. Carefully, she crossed his arms, lowered his eyelids, kissed him on the head, and then she returned to her room.

As she lay there on her bed, with her eyes closed, she drifted off to sleep … but not for long. She was rudely awoken by the front door slamming shut. Trisha was never quiet.

154

In a daze, Kimi got up from her bed and met Trisha at the top of the staircase. "I'm sorry, Trisha, but he has just passed away … peaceful, it was."

Trisha's forehead tightened and her thin malicious lips, which stiffened whenever she was annoyed, were ready to snap, like a taut rubber band. "And you couldn't even call me?" she shrieked.

Kimi stepped back, not ready for her malicious words. "He has only just gone. I didn't know … I, er …" She was stumped for words.

"Oh, you knew all right. You just ignored the fact that I should have been the one he said his last goodbyes to. Me! It should have been me! Not you, you're nothing but, oh, never mind. Have you called the nurse?"

Kimi shook her head. "Like I said, he has only just gone."

Trisha hardly looked the grieving widow. Dressed in a Chanel suit and Tiffany jewels, she looked like she was going to a fashion show with her face heavily made-up and her hair neatly curled and piled high. Kimi, on the other hand, hadn't even showered, and as for curling her hair, she hadn't even had time to brush it. Her naturally red hair had been dyed over the years, but when her father in his sick bed asked her to wash out the colour, so he could see her as she used to be, she rushed to the nearest chemist and bought a box of red dye – anything to please her father. There was no point in wearing make-up; it would only run, along with the endless tears.

"Right, call the nurse and get the body taken away. He'll start stinking."

Kimi was in shock. She knew her stepmother was a trollop, but she assumed that she had some compassion; he was her husband, after all.

She couldn't have been more wrong. Her dad was Trisha's meal ticket, and she had another side to her life, one that they knew nothing about. Kimi was too tired to work all of this out for herself, her mind on the immediate tasks ahead, so she grabbed the phone and made the necessary arrangements. The black van arrived and very gently the undertakers placed her father into a body bag and carried him away on a stretcher.

Once they had gone, the house was silent. Kimi returned to her room and lay down again; it was all too much to take in. She closed her eyes but not for long, since Trisha was standing at her bedroom door. "Right, Kimi, now your father's gone, there's no need for you to stay. There are two suitcases in the spare room. You can use those."

Kimi sat upright and glared at Trisha. "This is my home. I have nowhere to go."

Trisha folded her arms and pursed her lips. "This is my house now. You were only living in it because of your father. I never wanted children. I was just doing you a favour, allowing you to live with us. So now he's gone, it's time for you to do the same."

Kimi was gobsmacked. She'd always known that at some point Trisha would ask her to leave but not the very day her father died. "Trisha, he's not even fucking cold and you're throwing me out?"

A satisfied smile crossed Trisha's lips. "Yes, I am, silly girl. You don't think I could have you and your foul mouth living under the same roof as me, do you? I never wanted you here in the first place. We both know that."

Kimi didn't have the strength to argue, let alone fight. "Did you ever love my dad?" was all she could ask.

156

Trisha chuckled. "Gawd, girl, you have no idea, do ya? I fought fucking hard to get to this position, and I ain't about to have a silly teenager ruin me plans. 'Course I never loved ya ol' man. In fact, sweetheart, he repulsed me. 'Aving to suck his dick for all this, it made me puke. But, oh well, it's all mine now and with no smelly helmet to lick."

Kimi was almost blown over. She'd never heard Trisha speak like that. Then it dawned on her, she was never a hoity high-class woman; she was just council house trash pretending to be something she wasn't. However, Kimi wasn't going to stand by and allow this bitch to tarnish her father's image. She took a deep breath, jumped up from the bed, and punched Trisha right between the eyes, knocking her off balance. Shocked by her own reaction, she didn't hang around to wait for the backlash but grabbed her coat, pulled on an old pair of boots, and left the front door open, as she legged it down the street. She didn't have time to grab her car keys and could have kicked herself. Then she realised she had nowhere to go; she had no family now, no friends, and she was alone.

A sudden urge to see Malik gripped her, and the only place she knew where she would find him was at his house. It had been so long, she thought that perhaps he might have moved on and maybe had a girlfriend. But she had nothing to lose in finding out. As she reached a parked car, she stopped and peered in the side mirror and noticed just how rough she actually looked. Her red hair was wild, and without make-up, her eyes appeared to have sunk. She couldn't do anything about it, not now, with no money, no home, and no car. Malik's house looked different from when she'd last seen it. The front was tidy and the cottage itself now had a fresh lick of paint. Kimi stood at the gate and pondered for a while, not having noticed a car parked opposite or the man who was sitting inside watching her – Adam Carter.

After the awful fight with Sassy, Jean had returned to Adam, hoping the marks on her face would prove to him that she had fought hard to get their daughter, and he would forgive her for not returning with Star. She secretly wanted Adam to be mad — not with her but with Malakai and Saskia. Hoping he would wage war on the pair of them, she sobbed like a baby, insisting she'd done her best.

Adam had no reason to doubt her and was alarmed by the bruising on Jean's face. He figured that Malakai had done it, and in his book, there are rules. The key one was you never hit your mother. Mind you, he wasn't averse to hitting women *per se*, as he had aptly demonstrated throughout his evil life. Now it was his turn to get involved. In his eyes, this nutter, Malakai, had his daughter and that made it his business. Before he left to collect what was his, he grabbed Jean's face and turned it to the light, to see the extent of her injuries.

"It weren't just Malakai, Saskia hit me as well." Of course, this only fuelled his anger. Son or not, Malakai was a grown man who was taking liberties, bashing his mother. However, it never really took a lot to raise his temper. As the shrink put it, he was wired up all wrong. At six-foot four and built like a brick shithouse, he was certainly the biggest of his four brothers. Unfortunately, brawn doesn't equate to brain though.

Leaving prison, he found that their business in North London had been taken over, and they had been left with a small area to run. This had riled him up, and then, when he heard it was a woman behind the firm who was responsible, he was livid. His eldest brother, Johnnie, told him to back off and wait until they had enough money to take on more muscle. He had to agree, but that anger festered like a pressure cooker ready to blow. Now, the slightest thing would irritate him, so this issue with Jean's son was giving him serious cause for concern. If he got his hands on Malakai, he would let him have it big time, with no holds barred.

Adam sat in his car, waiting for Malakai to appear. He'd already knocked at the cottage and knew no one was at home. Determined to bash the fuck out of the young man, he remained and watched. Then, with a stroke of luck, he saw the girl who he assumed was Saskia, from the clear description Jean had given him – her age and that wild red hair. He cast an eye over her neat little body, admiring her auburn locks blowing in the wind, and he felt a sudden stirring in his groin. He couldn't quite work out what she was doing, just hanging around there, but still, she had caught his interest, that was for sure. He wanted his daughter, Star, and would get her by any means he could. After looking up and down the quiet lane, he stepped out of the car. Kimi didn't hear him, as he crept up behind her. She was too consumed by grief and confusion. It happened so quickly: one second, she was debating whether or not to knock at the door, the next she felt a large hand over her mouth and being lifted off the ground and dragged down the side of the cottage into the back garden. In a panic, she wriggled liked a feral cat, but he was too strong, and his voice put the fear of God in her. That deep, raspy voice, which could only belong to a mad man, was whispering in her ear, "Stop moving, or I'll blow ya fucking brains out." He shoved his automatic into her back, at which point, she nearly wet herself. Instantly, she stopped trying to struggle and began to tremble.

"You shout or scream and you're dead, got it?"

Kimi's mouth was dry, her ears were ringing, and her head felt as though a thousand needles were piercing her skin. She had never experienced fear like it. Adam removed his hand from her mouth and spun her around to face him, still holding the weapon.

159

Kimi looked up at the giant; his broad chest and square jaw spoke volumes. She was face-to-face with a lethal man. Her knees went weak, and she wanted to speak, but her tongue felt as though it had doubled in size.

Adam sneered at the girl, enjoying the look of terror on her face. She was a pretty little thing; her breasts were plump and oozing out of her see-through blouse, and as she tried to catch her breath, he watched them heave up and down. Then, he felt that stirring in his pants. He was bulging, and as Kimi lowered her gaze in trepidation, she couldn't help but notice the huge erection sticking through his tracksuit bottoms.

"Ya should never 'ave hit ya own mother like that."

Kimi was bewildered. *How did this man know she had hit Trisha, and how had he managed to track her down in less than an hour?*

"Please, I never meant to hurt her." She was pleading with the man. Afraid for her life now because he wasn't messing around, she knew by the mad expression in his piercing blue eyes that she was in some serious shit, and she would be lucky to come away unscathed. The guy was evil.

"Shut it and open the fucking door." He pointed to the back door.

Kimi frowned. "I, er, I don't have a key."

In a second, he grabbed her hair and pulled her face close to his. "Don't fuck with me, you little bitch."

Kimi's hands were shaking, as she hoped the door would be unlocked. She was too afraid to argue. The handle turned, and when she pushed the door, she discovered it wasn't locked. Holding the gun to her head, he shoved her inside and marched her through the kitchen, down the hall, and into the living room. There was an eerie silence. The cottage was empty and they both knew it.

"Where's Malakai and Star?" His voice, although calm, was scary, which unnerved Kimi.

Tilting her head down, she whispered, "I don't know." She had wanted Malik to be there. More than anything in the world, she wanted someone to be there.

"Fucking liar! Where are they?" he screamed, so close to her ear that she felt nearly deafened.

"I don't know, I swear. Please, mister, I don't know!"

Adam was thoroughly annoyed, as he had wanted to get into the cottage, take his daughter, and leave. But now his original plan had been scuppered. Everyone was out except this nutter Saskia, who'd had the temerity to bash up his girlfriend. He was angry now, studying the girl, who certainly didn't look anything like the hard nut Jean had described. He'd been mugged off. His temper was gaining momentum and it was now ready to erupt. As his breathing intensified, he felt his heart pumping furiously. The girl was either faking her terrified expression, or Jean was lying through her back teeth, begging him to believe her daughter was a vicious sod.

"So, you think you're hard, hitting ya mother? Well, I'll fucking show you, ya little strumpet."

He snatched her by the hair again and threw her onto the sofa. She didn't fight back; he was too powerful. The first slap was like a punch to the side of the head. Kimi screamed in terror.

Adam was excited by her pleas and slapped her again. This time she begged him to stop, but this only aroused him more, as she wailed like a little girl. With her wild hair across her face and her ample breasts tight and pert, he wanted to see more and ripped her top down to view the neatly placed bosoms in her lace bra. Adam hadn't seen young smooth skin for a long time. His urge was off the scales now and his anger overpowering. Kimi's facial expressions were proving to be such an irresistible turn-on. She tried to scramble off the sofa, pulling her top back up, but Adam was too strong, and his massive hands grabbed her throat and threw her back down. He didn't bother with the gun: this little hussy was totally at his mercy, and she knew it.

"Take ya fucking gear off!" he demanded, through clenched teeth. Kimi froze. *What did he say?*

"I said, take ya fucking gear off!" he shouted again, this time with a fierceness that petrified her.

Kimi jumped, her teeth chattered away, and then she shook uncontrollably. The realisation hit her that he was going to rape her, and she knew then he wasn't playing games: if she didn't strip, he would kill her.

Her sudden calm exterior masked the hysterical sobbing she held inside. A warm tear escaped and fell. He was revelling in the power he had over this young woman, as he'd done before with others.

Slowly, Kimi removed virtually every inch of her clothing and stood stark naked, save for her boots. Adam licked his lips and gazed at the perfectly shaped figure. A childish giggle escaped his mouth and Kimi closed her eyes. She couldn't bear to look at the man who was going to abuse her body. She wasn't afraid of sex, or even a stranger to it, yet this was different – this time she was out of her depth.

162

"Bend over!" he demanded.

Kimi didn't hesitate; she wanted it over and done with, so he would leave her alone. The humiliation was nothing compared to the terror. The gun, his evil eyes, and the fear of dying were enough to do as he said to survive this sordid ordeal. Now bent over the sofa arm, she shut her eyes to what she knew would be an experience from hell. He was like a monster inside her. As he banged away, his cock felt like a red-hot spear. But this was just the *hors d'oeuvre*. He then grabbed her so hard by the hair, it felt like he was almost breaking her neck. She screamed with the pain, and when he hit her hard across the head, it should have been enough to knock her out cold. But she was damned if she was going to go down without a fight. She pretended to slump her body. As Adam stopped humping her and extracted himself, she turned, and with all the strength she could muster, she kicked him hard in the balls and followed that up by spitting the biggest gob all over his face. And she hadn't finished. With one final burst of energy, she launched a punch which struck him hard in his left eye. She knew those blows had hurt him. Unfortunately, though, there was only going to be one winner in this contest of beauty and the beast. Adam was one hard bastard and took the punishment as a matter of course. Drawing breath, he merely grinned and smacked her one so hard across her face, she slumped onto the floor. Her capitulation infuriated him, as this fight was the best one he'd had in his life. *No, I want her awake,* he thought. He didn't want to flog a dead horse, and with his anger along with his urge to come, it sent him into a frenzy. As he entered her again, his hands forming a vice-like grip round her creamy-coloured throat, he squeezed, shouting, "Wake up, you little cunt, fucking wake up!" Finally, when he came and removed himself, he looked down at the girl who was lying in an awkward position and not breathing. He hoisted his tracksuit bottoms back up and snatched her arm, shaking her to wake up. She was lifeless and white. Without any warning, she let out a final breath of air which sounded like a sigh. Adam assumed

163

she was just unconscious. He picked up his gun, took one last look at the girl, and left. His anger subsided but his determination had not, as he thought, *that will teach Saskia not to mess with him. That fear in her eyes would surely send a clear message back to Malakai to hand over Star, or he would get worse.*

Satisfied that he'd made a point, Adam headed back to London. He now needed a drink and drove to the Mitcham Mint. After downing a few whiskies and snorting a few lines, he mulled over his actions. If Saskia called "rape", then it would be her word against his. She'd led him on, inviting him into her home. After all, he thought, in his own twisted mind, she wanted it as much as he did. He rushed to the men's toilets, cut another line of cocaine, this time a fat one, and snorted it. His worry turned to euphoria; he was on a high, and so he returned to his seat to enjoy a few more whiskies, his favourite tipple.

As the drugs wore off, Adam went over the event and his brain started to process what he'd actually done at the cottage. He shuddered. It was always the same; his anger and urges seemed to distract him from the serious business at hand. He had left that cottage without smashing the life out of Malakai and most importantly without the boy's baby sister, Star. The one consolation was that he'd given Saskia a good roasting. He couldn't go back to prison, not again. He was enjoying his freedom. His thoughts turned to Jean. He wished he'd never met her; all she did was cause trouble. It was her fault. She had made him go. He wouldn't be worried about what he'd done, if it wasn't for Jean. She was nothing to him but a regular shag. Living with her was a pain in the arse, and her whining and neediness were driving him mad. Yet, she had his kid, and he was lumbered because with Star came the mother – or did it?

Jean was pacing the floor in a right state. For a few days now, she'd been awaiting a call from Adam, anxious to know what had occurred. She daren't phone him because he always told her, "Unless it's a fucking emergency, like your legs are hanging off, then never call me."

When her phone rang, she almost dropped it, with her hands shaking so much. He called only to ask if anyone had been to his home. Jean was by now pulling her hair out. "What happened!" she shrieked.

Adam didn't like her tone. "Nothing fucking happened. Malakai and Star weren't there."

"I've been worried sick! Where are you and where have ya been?" she asked in desperation.

Adam was fuming. He had no need to answer to her. After all, she was the one who had caused the problem in the frigging first place. "Oi, cunt, stop with the nagging. I'm away with a friend." He wasn't exactly lying either. He'd just spent a couple of days off his face on drugs with an old pal in the East End.

"When are ya coming home, Adam?"

Adam stared at the phone and gave this question serious thought. He contemplated whether or not to go back. He was relieved that no one had come to his apartment asking questions, as he assumed that Saskia had kept her mouth shut about the whole incident. However, he wasn't ready for the list of questions that would surely be on the tip of snoopy Jean's tongue. "I'll be home when I'm fucking good and ready. Now, get your gear together and fuck off!"

After slamming the phone down in a temper, Adam was quizzed on the phone call, and Johnnie found out from his brother that according to Jean, the Carters had a child in the family that they never knew they had. Johnnie shrugged his shoulders at the news. Adam's sex life was nothing to do with him.

"So, Johnnie, what's the plan?"

Johnnie smirked, "You, my old son, are too fucking impatient. And who or what gave you a good 'un in your left eye? No, don't tell me, you ran into a door! Anyway, where was I? I'm thinking of promoting young Mason Rye and his brother Fynn in the firm, the fuckers. I swear, there ain't a full brain between 'em, but they can 'ave it all right. Fearless, they are."

"About bleedin' time, Johnnie. I mean, I get locked up, come out, and find our cunting manor is taken over by a fucking woman! It ain't right. I don't give a rat's arse that she's Eddie Cako Raven's kid. She's still a bird and has no right raining down on my fucking parade."

Johnnie agreed wholeheartedly. "I know what ya are saying, Adam, but it ain't the fact that she's a bird. She has the Colombians backing her and that motley crew headed by ol' war horse Cyril behind her."

Adam downed the dregs of his pint, having given up on the whisky, and giggled like a school boy. "Cyril is nothing now, the old cunt. He's gotta be a hundred and five."

Johnnie wished his brother was sensible, instead of a reckless twat. "He might be knocking on, but he still calls the shots. Him, Frank, and Blakey ain't ready to throw in the towel. Ya see, it's a way of life to them. One thing you have to bear in mind is this — Cyril may look a daft old git, but he has connections and respect, and most of all, the men he has in his circle, he can trust with his life."

166

The landlord of the Mitcham Mint pub stayed at the other end of the bar. The Carter brothers were nasty bastards, and this was not their manor. If Cyril or Frank wandered in, then there would be no pub left. He kept a keen eye, hoping Johnnie and Adam would leave once their pints were empty. His heart sank though when Johnnie waved his glass and threw a handful of change on the counter. The pub had a bad reputation, and try as he might, he couldn't get it cleaned up. If it kicked off in here again, then the authorities would close it down. Yet, he wasn't going to argue with the Carters, especially that animal Adam.

Just as he was about to serve Johnnie, in walked Lacey, his daughter. "I'll serve the gentleman, dad," she said, in her sweetest voice. Roy, the landlord, swallowed hard. His daughter was perfect to reel in the punters, but she was barely out of her school uniform. She had taken to spending money on home improvements, as she called them. Having her lips enlarged along with her tits, and her once soft fair hair totally bleached with extensions, he hardly recognised her these days. He watched as Adam's eyes nearly popped out of his head and then he sighed. She was at it again; any man who looked like they had clout and money, she was on to them in a nanosecond, oozing her wares over the counter, just like Rose, her mother.

Adam was almost over the jump with his tongue metaphorically hanging out.

"'Ere, Roy, ya daughter's grown up since the last time I saw her. A right stunner, if ya ask me," said Adam, to which Lacey blushed with excitement.

Roy was hot under the collar: he was too fond of his girl to allow the likes of Adam or any of the Carters touching her. "Yes, she is for a kid, but she's got too much make-up on for my liking, though." He tried to get the message across.

Adam stood upright and twisted his head in an awkward position like a contorted mad man. "What are ya trying to say to me, Roy?"

"Nothing, Mr Carter, only that she's a kid and should really behave like one."

Lacey tutted. "Dad, I'm eighteen now. I'm no kid."

Johnnie knew that look on Adam's face, and so he decided to calm the situation, before all hell broke loose. "Come and sit over here, Adam." He pointed to a table against the wall, well away from the bar. "I've got serious business to discuss."

Adam shot a sideways sneer at Roy. "'Old on a minute. Is this cunt trying to mug me off? Ain't I fucking good enough for his daughter?"

"Oi, oi, slow down, Adam. She's a kid. Let's take a seat over in the corner."

Adam's shoulders relaxed, as he walked to the table with the drinks, leering back at Roy. He was angry for being put in his place. Lacey was right up his street. The sex he'd had with Jean's daughter had been the best for a long time, and it made him even keener to seek out a younger girl. He now had a sudden appetite for teenagers, and in his own completely twisted and narcissistic mind, he thought he could make out with these girls better than the young men could. He had, in fact, always liked them young, but after almost five years in the clink, his urge had grown. Jean was all right for a dirty screw, but after putting up with her for a few months, he was after something else now – he craved for fresh meat.

Roy's mouth was as dry as a granny's fanny and his face was like a beetroot. "Lacey, get ya fucking arse back upstairs before you cause a fucking war," he hissed quietly. Lacey had never heard him speak like that before; even so, she gave him a defiant sneer and stepped back behind the pillar, out of view of the customers.

Adam had one eye on his brother and the other on the bar. He scowled when he saw Lacey disappear. "Fuck Roy," he muttered to himself.

Johnnie was sitting on hot coals and knew his brother was ready for a ruck. "Leave it, Adam. She's Rose's daughter, for fuck's sake. She's barely eighteen."

Adam glared at Johnnie and wanted to punch him in the face, but there was a code they all shared: there was no fighting with each other.

"Adam, listen, we can't go in all guns blazing because this Kelly Raven is no silly slip of a kid, mark my words. She's Eddie Raven's daughter, all right. It's like she's carried on where he left off. She has a lot of backing."

Adam swallowed a slug of his beer and shook his head. "I don't give a fucking monkey's uncle. I ain't shying away from no bird. As I see it, she's taken a liberty."

Johnnie put his hand up. "Wait, Adam, you don't know the facts."

Adam took a deep breath and allowed his brother to fill him in.

"She served time for killing Patrick Mahoney." By the look on Adam's face, Johnnie could see that the intent behind his words had fallen on deaf ears.

"So, if she hadn't killed him, then I probably would have. He was another cunt getting too big for his boots and—"

"You know what?" Johnnie rudely interrupted. "You really are a thick twat at times. Your answer to everything is violence. Well, sunshine, you need to listen very carefully before you and your reckless ways have us all fucking shot."

Very rarely did Johnnie raise his voice, but when his youngest brother had mad notions that could have an adverse effect on the whole family, then he would reel him in. Nutjob or not, Adam was going to listen.

"Kelly Raven was fucking fifteen when she killed Patrick Mahoney. She also took on her father and aunt, by all accounts. And not to put too fine a point on it, Kelly managed almost single-handedly to take over the south and the north manors of the city. Now, you might find it a fucking joke, me ol' son, but when the most ruthless and dangerous woman we know – yes, Adam, you know who I mean – Patrick Mahoney's sister, Sheila, goes missing, along with her two boys, who was the finger pointed at?"

Adam sat up straight. He knew exactly who Patrick's sister was, and yes, he had to admit, along with Eddie Raven, Sheila had been one lethal mare reigning her terror over in Ireland, and when she'd needed to, she'd also caused mayhem in London. "So, I guess, then, the finger was pointed at us?"

Johnnie rolled his eyes in frustration. "No, you fucking crank, at Kelly Raven. So, little brother, before you shoot ya mouth off making threats, ya wanna know what you're walking into, because in my book, that so-called Kelly Cako Raven has more fucking nerve and clout than you realise."

Adam was grinning and it infuriated Johnnie. "It ain't no fucking laughing matter, Adam."

"Perhaps I should meet this Kelly, spin her a yarn, and fuck the life out of her."

Johnnie rolled his eyes again. "You might think you're God's gift, mate, but you're the wrong colour."

"What, she likes a black cock?"

"See, Adam, she ain't only got the Colombians. She also has Cyril's lot and Keffa Jackson, her fella, all backing her. I tell ya this for nothing, you touch her, mate, and take ya pick, 'cos one of them will come for ya, and it won't be pretty, that's for fucking sure. The first time I met her was at a funeral, and I swear to God, before I had a chance to shake her hand, there were three men ready to gun me down. They came out of nowhere. She might look like some kinda model, but her eyes are Eddie's all right. I ain't kidding. My fucking blood ran cold when she glared at me."

Adam rolled his eyes and protruded his jaw in annoyance. "Aw, for fuck's sake, even President Kennedy got shot. She ain't invincible."

"And neither are you, so, for once in your life, stop thinking with ya toe cap boots and use ya brain. Right up until the point you decided to stick ya fucking oar in, I had a decent business going. She plays fair and we earn enough. I'm not sure that taking on an army is a good idea. The Ryes will come in handy for our own safety, but you need to keep your hands to yourself and leave well alone."

By this time in the conversation, Adam had already tuned out Johnnie. His mind was back on Lacey. Unbeknown to Adam, Lacey's thoughts were centred on him.

The pub suddenly went quiet. Johnnie was the first to turn around to see who had just walked in, and he was taken aback to see a few of

171

the punters jump up and leave. There at the entrance and coolly surveying the pub were three of the biggest black guys you were ever likely to see. They were standing behind a smartly dressed individual, whose skin was less dark. His eyes were green, and his hair was neatly cane rolled. There was no doubt he was a looker but dangerous was probably the byword. Confidence seeped from every bone in his body. He stepped forward and allowed the others to enter the pub. Johnnie swallowed hard because in among them were Frank and Blakey. Frank was a sick bastard, and that was on a good day. His tool kit was as infamous as the man himself. He was used to getting exactly what he needed – information.

Adam was grinning like an idiot; he liked a good ruck, and these men weren't here for a tea party.

By the time the light-skinned black man reached the bar, all the other punters had left. Roy was shaking in his boots, and when he glanced across to the other end of the bar to see his daughter leaning over the counter, flashing her assets, his heart rate soared. Keffa Jackson ordered a brandy from Roy and turned to study the Carter brothers.

Johnnie stood up; he was faster on his feet. They all stared at each other for a few seconds, and then Johnnie spoke. "All right, Keffa?" He tried to sound firm, yet inside, he was shitting it.

Keffa walked over to where the Carters were sitting, indicating to Johnnie he should sit down, whilst Lacey, ignoring her father's expression, brazenly poured the drink herself. Eager to attract Keffa's attention, she brought it over and smiled at him suggestively. But her smile froze when she saw the way Keffa deliberately ignored her, as if she were a piece of dirt off his shoe. She cringed with embarrassment and walked forlornly back to the bar. Keffa, meanwhile, carried on as

172

if nothing untoward had happened. His movements were concise and controlled, as he stared into the eyes of both Carter brothers in turn and casually sipped his drink. Johnnie hoped this was going to be a conversation, not a blood bath.

Adam gave Keffa an evil glare, acting like the hardman, as always. Until now, Adam had no idea what Keffa looked like because they'd never met. However, he was aware of his reputation, and he was fully cognisant that Keffa was the brains behind the drug business with the Yardies. Like many others, Adam expected Keffa to be a skunk-smoking, dreadlocked waster. Far from it. Keffa was a businessman and never touched drugs himself. Adam surveyed the room, taking note of the men surrounding him. The tension was tight. His mood changed, and he sneered in Frank's direction. By his reckoning, the old cunt should have retired years ago.

Keffa leaned on his left arm, facing Johnnie, turning his back on Adam. The man was an utter arsehole. "Ya overstepped the mark, Johnnie. Those two men, ya fucking brother stabbed up, were working for Kelly." He shuffled back in his seat, plucked at a bit of stray fluff, which had settled on his cashmere mid-length overcoat, and waited for a reaction.

Adam was tapping his foot; the anger was building up, and he wanted more than anything to let rip and cause bedlam. Johnnie could see that incensed expression on his brother's face and prayed that Adam would remain seated. Yet, in his heart, he also knew that his brother was a hot-headed bastard who never backed away from anyone. Ever since he was five years old, he'd earned a reputation for himself as being the most vicious brother in their family. There were four of them in total, all running the same business. Adam had his uses though: he was the muscle.

173

Adam looked at Keffa with madness in his eyes, and just as he was about to headbutt the man, he felt a gun shoved fiercely into his stomach. "Reel ya neck in, or I can guarantee I will do it for ya. Got me?" growled Keffa.

This was some piss-take. Adam was livid, being forced to contain his temper, because right now the look on Keffa's face said he was a dead man, if he so much as raised his voice.

"You are a cunt, and I hate that word, but that is what you are. So, this is the thing, see. Your brother 'ere and Kelly had an agreement. You Carters can have North London for your line of work, and then you will keep ya nose out of any other business. Ain't that right, Johnnie?"

Johnnie nodded, with resignation in his eyes.

"But, Adam, that little arrangement was fucked up when you came on the scene, carving up her staff. So, as she sees it, those men need a little compensation, at fifty grand a pop."

Johnnie took a deep breath. He was grateful that she was offering a deal and not an eye for an eye, as he would certainly have done. "She wants a hundred grand and no comebacks?" asked Johnnie.

Keffa nodded. "See, Kelly is a fair woman. She ain't no bully, she plays by the rules." He shot a glance Adam's way, shoving the weapon harder into his stomach. "But, Johnnie, any more fucking silliness by loopy drawers here and ..." he tapped Johnnie's face, "let's just say, Frank will be sharpening his toolkit."

That was it. Adam had had enough of this man and his condescending manner. He couldn't contain himself any longer.

Flaring his nostrils, he gave Frank the death glare. "Ha, that old cunt, couldn't sharpen his own prick!"

Frank hated to be called old. Like a deranged combat soldier, he jumped the stool that was in between them, and before Adam could leap from his chair, Frank plunged a long thin spiked instrument into the younger man's shoulder. The hot sharp pain shot down his arm and he yelled aloud and clutched the injury. "Ah, you cunt!" he screamed.

Johnnie was shocked by the speed at which the other men were there with guns aimed at him. Keffa calmly stood up and faced Adam. "You need to curb ya tongue. See, acting like a fool will get ya hurt. Any more nonsense, and Johnnie boy, 'ere, will be planning your fucking funeral. I want a hundred grand by Monday."

Johnnie was like a nodding dog, agreeing to the world. He didn't want any grief from Kelly's firm because his own wasn't strong-handed, and his men would all be dead and buried, if they fucked up again. He clocked the menacing expression on Frank's face, and he thought that maybe there was no point in taking on Cyril Reardon and Kelly Raven's men, even if he brought in more muscle. The extent of her influence was really not known. She could have a whole fucking army, for all he knew. Adam, however, was fuming, and he took note of what each and every one of them looked like. He was on his own mission and would take them out, one by one.

Lacey observed the action. She loved a rebel and wanted in on that lifestyle. For years, she had watched the dolly birds draped over the hardcore villains and that was the career she was going to take.

As soon as Keffa and his mob left, Roy could breathe. He thanked God that they had left his pub intact. He knew for sure that a fight between Frank's lot and the Carters would not be clean. So worked up about the potential fight, Roy didn't notice his daughter scurry her way

175

around the bar with a wet bar towel offering to help Adam. As soon as he spotted her, Roy's heart was in his mouth. *She was really taking the piss now*, he thought. Adam was like a time bomb ready to go off, and there was his kid, in her skimpy dress and fluffy ways, ready to play Florence Nightingale.

Adam had taken off his T-shirt and was looking at the wound. His eyes lit up when he saw two boobs almost loose outside a short tight dress. Lacey's doll-like face beamed, and she gave him a real schoolgirl grin. His pain subsided, as he watched her fussing over him. He also saw her gawping at his toned six-pack. He may not be the best looking, yet girls seemed to love his blue eyes and his big athletic build. He was proud of his own body and worked out three times a week. Johnnie was always amazed at how many birds drooled over his youngest brother. Johnnie was the looker, the prettier of the brothers, so his mother had said. He was darker but had the blue eyes and a thinner face, like two of his other brothers.

"Sorry, love, could ya leave us for a minute?" asked Johnnie.

Lacey smiled sweetly again and hurried away but only to stand at the bar. She was waiting to see if Adam would call her over when they finished their chat. She admired his tough exterior and was sucked in by his seductive eyes. He threw her a sideways glance and winked. Lacey was totally hooked; she wanted him and was going to defy her father to have the life she wanted. She didn't care that this hulk was twice her age: he was a villain, and she was ready to parade around on his arm. Besides, the man she really loved had pushed her aside for his so-called wife, and so Lacey wanted more than anything to get back at him.

"Listen, Adam, that was a warning. Now, do you see what we're up against? You need to keep away. I'll make sure you have your cut, and you'll have your regular poke, but for now, you stay clear. Got it?"

Adam was still eyeing up Lacey and only listening with half an ear. His concentration span had always been short, like a kid's; he would never pay attention to anything unless it suited him, and right now, it didn't. Getting Lacey's knickers off was the only thing on his mind.

"Yeah, yeah, yeah, all right, Johnnie. Keep ya fucking hair on. I've other matters to deal with, like getting me daughter back."

Johnnie shook his head. "For Christ's sake, the kid could be anyone's. That Jean is a dirty whore, fucking any man with a flash car and a fifty-pound note."

Adam wasn't listening again; he was watching Lacey pouting her plump lips and waiting his chance.

Johnnie looked at his oaf of a brother and decided to leave him to it. There was no point in talking when he was obsessed with shagging the barmaid or distracted by the notion that this kid of Jean's was his. Johnnie and half of the crooks in London knew Jean was after any gangster who would keep her sweet with drugs and sex.

Once Johnnie left the pub, Adam stood up at the bar opposite Lacey. Between the two of them, they could have cleared the glasses and shagged on the counter. The sexual tension was sickening to Roy, yet he was too afraid to say a word. Adam left to make a call, before he invited Lacey out for dinner.

When he was out of earshot, he rang Jean again. "Have you gone, like I told you to? I'm coming home, and when I get there, I don't want to see you or any of your stuff there. Got it?"

Jean was gutted; she had fallen in love with Adam all over again, and she wasn't going to give up on him that easily. "Adam, no, please, I love you," she begged.

Adam sighed. He hated her pleading; it was irritating. "I told you to bring my kid to me, but you didn't, and I also told you, if you didn't, then don't bother coming back, but ya did. So, Jean, like I said, when I come home, I want you fucking gone. You can come back when you have my kid in tow."

Jean was snivelling. "I tried, Adam, I swear I tried, but Saskia and Malakai beat me up. I thought you were going to get her."

Adam's mind then went back to the girl and the shag he had. "Jean, I forgot to tell ya earlier. Your daughter, Saskia, was alone when I got there, and she's so much like you. She loves a good hard shag." His tone was harsh and spiteful.

There was a second of silence, as Jean tried to process what Adam had just said.

"What?" Her voice was shrill and on the verge of hysteria.

"Gawd, woman, do I have to spell it out? You're too old. The only thing you can bring to me table is me own fucking daughter. Now, if ya want to stay in me house, then, like I said, do whatever it takes to bring me what's mine."

"Did you say you screwed my Saskia?" She waited and then heard the sickening laugh. She really hoped he was joking, just to wind her up.

"Yeah, Jean, I have to say she threw herself on me. She's a bit like you in that way. But the thing is, she's younger, tighter, and a damn sight better looking."

"You cunt!" she screamed down the phone.

Adam laughed. "Now, now, there's no need for language like that. Keep it in the family, I say. So, Jean, I mean what I say. You'd better be gone when I get back, or, trust me, woman, you'll wish you had."

Jean was beside herself with grief and anger. She was so in love with Adam that the thought of her own daughter taking him away from her, her own mother, sent her over the edge. She didn't bother packing her bags; the only things she took were her handbag, a bag of cocaine, and a grand in fifty-pound notes, there on the kitchen side. Fuelled by rage, she hailed a taxi and headed for Otford. She would show her daughter who was boss, the fucking little sod. If Malakai got in the way, she would give him a piece of her mind as well. She brought them into the world; well, she could find a way to take them out, couldn't she?

With tears rolling down her face, she sat almost slumped in the back of the taxi. How could he be so cold, so cruel? She had been the perfect lover, keeping the house spotless, cooking him his favourite Italian dishes, and always ensuring his apartment was well stocked with food and booze, just to see a smile on his face. She washed his clothes, poured his drinks, and even sucked his dick every day and night. Now he wanted shot of her, and what really incensed her was that he'd had the brass nerve to shag Saskia. This was the daughter she detested the most, the one she'd spent years struggling to pretend she loved. She shuddered when she thought of how she'd conceived the little ginger shit – it had been a living nightmare.

The local villains, including Eddie Raven's firm, had got shot of her. They'd snubbed her after Malakai was born, all at some point having screwed the life out of her, and what did she have to show for it? Fuck all, that's what. The other dolly birds had their five-bedroom detached homes with the pool, all the flash cars, but what did she get? A council house, a bun in the oven, and herpes was the sum total of his affections.

The Hells Angels were in town, and for a few months, they'd completely taken over the local pub. Jean liked the fun, all the drinking, and taking any drug on offer. They were hard, vicious men, not at all rich and suave, but they had money, and it was enough to keep her filled with cocaine or ecstasy. She took it – no questions asked – and for three weeks, she was off her face, flirting and teasing the head honcho, who was a big grizzly bear of a man called Cyrus. She wasn't the only woman flirting; he had many girls fighting for his affections, but she was determined to be the one he wanted. She was prettier back then, with her long hair and sweet features. The gang decided they had stayed long enough, and they planned to leave, come the morning. Cyrus had also taken over an abandoned warehouse, and so with all the bikes lined up outside, they had made a makeshift living room and sleeping quarters inside the building.

That night, they took the party from the pub back to the warehouse. It was summer, and the evening air was still warm. An old oil drum had been cut in half and used to make an outside barbecue. The other half was filled with ice and bottles of beer. They danced, snorted, puffed, and drank. Cyrus was watching Jean. He wanted payback for all the freebies he'd handed over to her. Two other bikers, older men, each having greasy skin and a pot belly, wanted in on the action too, as they always did, and they looked over to Cyrus with an unspoken agreement. Jean was as high as a kite and dancing her arse off in full view of all of them. On impulse, he got up from his seat and snatched her hand; she didn't stop him, she liked a bit of rough. He took her into the warehouse, and at first, she thought the set-up was

180

romantic with red candles lighting the living area. Fur rugs and patterned pillows were scattered on the floor. He was silent as he undid his belt and removed his shirt. Jean remembered giggling, as she removed her clothes, but she soon stopped, when, without any warning, he threw her to the ground. She liked a bit of heavy-handedness, of course, but landing hard on the rug was a little too aggressive. He was strong, and in the half-light, she saw the look in his eyes. It wasn't passion for sex: it was an angry passion for power. Jean was a woman of the world. She realised she was in deep shit, she was in the buff, and she guessed escape was pretty pointless. She now saw him for what he was. He wasn't at all the man she fancied anymore; his appearance and bearing frightened her. As she looked at his white skin and his crooked teeth, and smelled the stench on his breath, it was as if she'd just awoken from a dream, only to be faced with the awful reality that Cyrus was a dirty, smelly old man, and if he hadn't been surrounded by leather and Harley-Davidsons, he could have passed as a street wino, begging for the odd few pence. She tried to get on her feet, but with brute force, he threw her back down. She couldn't scream or cry for help because she was there on the floor with nothing on. Then the door was pulled open and in walked the two other men. She remembered saying, "No, I don't want this", and their chilling reply, as if it were yesterday. They'd said, "Well, you don't think the drugs were free, do you?"

They held her down and all took turns, laughing and teasing, like she was a wild animal. She'd never had sex as violent as this. She tried to go along with it at first, pretending she was enjoying it, but inside, she prayed it would soon be over. It was as if they didn't want her to enjoy it. They wanted her to struggle, to be in pain, and especially to prolong the agony. The more she put on the pleasurable moans, the rougher they got, until eventually, two of them held her down whilst Cyrus did the unthinkable and almost ripped her a new arsehole. She screamed that night, as the pain of his abnormally large penis entered

181

her anus. She was fucked for two hours and eventually they took it in turns to shoot their loads. The sick, sordid bastards were cruel and dirty. She grabbed her summer dress, fled the site, and headed back to her little council house with her baby, Malakai, still asleep in his cot. The internal tears took months to heal, and by the time the doctor told her she was pregnant, it was too late for an abortion, and so she had to endure an unwanted baby growing inside her and the awful labour that would last for three days. So, she hated Saskia from the day she was born. The minute she saw the red hair, she was repulsed, and as Sassy grew older and the wild attitude set in, Jean only saw Cyrus. She was never actually cruel to Saskia, but she just didn't like her, and so she treated the child as if she were someone else's.

CHAPTER NINE

Jean arrived outside the cottage, determined to give Saskia what for and to stop Malakai in his tracks, if he tried to get in her way. She slapped the driver a fifty-pound note in his hand and traipsed down the garden path. Just as she was about to knock at the front door, she paused and took a deep breath. A sudden rush of nervousness left her trembling, and so she reached inside her bag for the cocaine. After scooping a bit, using her long painted fingernail, she snorted hard and gagged on the bitter taste at the back of her throat. The adrenaline rush gripped her instantly, and in anger, she almost smashed the door down with her heavy banging. "Open up, Malakai!"

She stepped back and waited. There was no answer, not even a murmur from inside. The silence annoyed her, and so she marched to the back door to find it ajar. A sudden whoosh of wind blew the door wide open and Jean entered. She'd barely got through the door, when it banged behind her, in the fierce wind. Now, everything suddenly went very quiet. Jean wondered why the house was unlocked, as she looked around, noticing the changes. It was as if she had stepped into someone else's property. This was not the house she had left behind; the kitchen was like a show home, with all the brand-new units and appliances. But it seemed strange somehow. She knew why. The plant in the kitchen window was nearly dead, there was a wasp eating a rotten apple that someone had left in the sink, and when she had a nosy look in the American fridge, there was spilt milk and unwrapped chicken, which had clearly been left for a while, judging by the smell which hit her as she peered inside. Gingerly now, she walked towards the living room, clocking the freshly painted hallway and soft new carpet. Her anger had turned to a high level of awareness and she listened for any creak or whisper. It was so quiet; all she heard was her own heartbeat and her frantic breathing. There was something not right. A premonition, which had almost become second nature to her ways of living dangerously, alerted her and an icy chill shot down her spine.

As soon as she entered the living room, that's when she saw her. Her eyes widened, and an unexpected gasp left her mouth. There, lying naked on the floor, was a girl – a body – with long red hair. She was almost face down and her wild red locks were like a veil hiding her eyes. She looked more closely at the girl, noticed the bruising around her neck and the fact that she was naked, and deduced she had been raped. This hadn't just happened either. There were sure signs of decay, and if she hadn't lined her nose with so much cocaine, she probably would have got a whiff of death.

Jean was paralysed with shock. It was obvious the girl was dead; her skin was an unnatural grey colour. At first, she thought it was Saskia, and her heart felt as though it had been ripped away. She may have disliked Saskia, but, underneath, she probably did love her. The trembling and the sick feeling in her stomach somehow sobered her up enough to get a grip of herself. She bent down and moved the hair away from the dead girl's face. It wasn't Saskia. Another blast of wind slammed the door once more and Jean jumped. She called out, "Malakai!" but again, there was an eerie, peculiar silence.

Jean's instincts quickly moved up the gears, her mind focusing on the here and now, not her emotions. She was alone with a naked dead girl who had probably been raped. How long had she been lying there?

184

How long would it be before someone came to the cottage? Had the police already been alerted? These questions – and others – were whirling around in her head, as her heart rate steadily increased. Her forehead felt clammy, but she still shivered, as she saw the girl's eyes stare up towards her and a fly weaving in and out of her lashes.

She knew she had every right to come to the cottage, but the circumstances were such that she would have to answer all kinds of tricky questions, if she stayed and waited for the emergency services. Her mind was in turmoil and the comedown from the cocaine had left her unable to think straight – she had to get away as fast as she could. Hurrying from the living room back into the hall and then across into the kitchen to leave by the back door, her eyes suddenly fixed on a poster stuck to the fridge by Blu-Tack. It showed a fight scheduled for a Saturday next month, with Malakai holding a trophy from his last bout. There was also a newspaper cutting from the *Sevenoaks Chronicle* which appeared at first glance to be an account of a recent contest that had taken place. Without even thinking, she ripped both the poster and the newspaper cutting from the fridge and shoved them in her bag. After a final furtive glance around, she slipped out of the kitchen via the back door.

Leaving the cottage, she marched quickly with her head down towards the garden gate. Rather than call for a taxi to pick her up here, which would draw unnecessary attention to herself, she decided to head to the superstore, a short walk away. She shied her head away from the traffic in case anyone should recognise her. So much was going through her mind. *Who was that dead girl, for Christ's sake? What had she got to do with her family?*

To those who knew Jean well, and who were aware of the facts as they stood, they would have agreed that Jean was far too stupid to put two and two together. And they would have been right. She hadn't

185

considered the possibility that when Adam told her he'd shagged Saskia, it was actually this young woman with long red hair.

Trying hard to put those disturbing images she'd just seen out of her mind, for a moment, she assessed the present situation. She'd arrived to take Star back to Adam's home. Without her, she knew that her relationship with Adam was history, as far as he was concerned. It was obvious her kids were not living at home now. If she could find Malakai, then she would locate her other children as well.

A sudden cold sensation gripped her as her thoughts somehow moved on to Eddie Raven. She was always doing this to herself. His sick acts were plastered all over the papers, once he'd been found dead in his home. She swallowed hard. *Was what she had seen the work of her son? Was that why there was no one at home?* Her somewhat fanciful mentality could see him following in his father's footsteps. He was his father's son all right, with his looks, his smirk, and his newly acquired muscles. She didn't want a rapist looking after her youngest daughter. She had to get her away from Malik and to Adam.

She pulled her phone from her bag and dialled Adam's number; he would know what to do. His phone was switched off. She dialled again, within sight of the store now. Still no answer. She was building up a sweat, and it wasn't from the fast pace she was walking either. Events were overtaking themselves, and she felt herself beginning to panic. She needed to be clever about this situation, but her track record to date hadn't been good.

Arriving at the store, she searched for a cab, but the only one there was waiting at the pickup point to take a lady home with her shopping. The driver told her he wouldn't be very long, if she cared to wait. It seemed the best thing to do, so they agreed on a time. Going over to the store entrance, she found a bench and sat down. She rummaged through her bag, eager to discover what she'd taken off the door of the fridge. She guessed her son had been the one to find all the money for the home improvements. Hopefully, the newspaper cutting and the poster might tell her more about what he'd been doing.

The cutting told her nothing useful, except Malakai was definitely following in Eddie's footsteps, as far as muscle was concerned. Jean stared at the picture of her son fighting his opponent and felt a sense of sadness. There was the proof: he *was* a man of athletic physique. And then there was that smile: she had never noticed just how handsome he was when he smiled because he'd never done so in her company. He had always been such a serious-looking kid with a menacing glare. Yet that smile told another story. *Did he have a split personality like Eddie?*

Then she studied the poster in more detail and read the name of his manager. Cyril Reardon, his manager? It was too far-fetched. The Cyril she knew was her father's friend, a well-known crook. She recalled him when she was a kid. Her father had shown the man so much respect to the extent that he'd virtually knelt down and kissed his fucking feet. She remembered, when she was around fifteen, being grabbed by Cyril and thrown in the car and taken home. At that age, the whole ordeal had been so humiliating because at the time she'd been sneaking into nightclubs, getting wasted. The night Cyril caught her, he didn't care that her friends were laughing, he was so preoccupied on getting her back to her father. She never argued because she knew that Cyril was, in his own way, looking out for her, yet when she was older and acting out of turn, he sneered at her, shaking his head. She'd lost his respect, and that was also the case with her own father and his colleagues. That was probably why she fell into the open arms of Eddie Raven because he didn't look at her like that. He treated her like a beautiful woman — if only for a short while.

As she reached for her bag to put away what she'd read, she observed the cab coming towards her. Standing up, she stretched her

187

aching muscles, which had become so tight from sitting on a most uncomfortable bench seat. All she needed to do was to go up to Reardon's place and she would find her kids. Bingo. Cyril was a man of reason, especially when it came to matters of murder. She was confident he would side with her and take her to Malakai and order him to hand over her kids. There was no way Cyril would want any Ol' Bill sniffing around.

She climbed into the cab and headed to the mansion. It wasn't a secret as to where Cyril lived; he bragged about being the lord of the manor.

The cab driver pressed the buzzer to be allowed entry into the grounds and waited. After a few moments, there was an answer. "Yeah, who is it?"

It was Cyril's voice.

Jean tapped the driver on the arm and said, "Tell him it's Jean River."

The cab driver did as she asked but was rudely denied access.

Jean got out of the cab and pressed the buzzer. Cyril impolitely told her to fuck off.

"Cyril, unless you want this place swarming with the police, I suggest you let me in, 'cos I've something to tell you, and I ain't gonna do it through a fucking intercom."

Cyril looked at Malik and Sassy and nodded for them to go upstairs.

He clicked the open button and watched as the car drove up the long drive.

Kelly was intrigued. "So, this is Malik's mother, I assume?"

Cyril nodded. "Yep, a right drippy prat."

Peering through the window, she replied, "Well, Cyril, she doesn't look that drippy to me. Maybe a bit cocky, though."

Kelly stood up and smoothed down her figure-hugging black dress. "I want to hear what this minx has to say. After everything those kids have told me about her, I've a good mind to fucking hammer the woman meself."

She turned to face Cyril with an icy stare. "She ain't getting hold of Star. I was raised at the hands of a nutcase. That baby ain't gonna be, not if I can do anything about it."

Cyril smiled. He loved Kelly as if she were his own daughter and was proud of the person she had become. That soft protective nature was just one of her many traits.

The door knocker was heavy and it thudded loudly against the front door. Jean could hear a clip-clop of high-heeled shoes before the door was swung open. She stepped back when she saw a tall, slim stunning-looking woman, who certainly didn't look like any housekeeper. Jean's throat tightened, when she met the cold glare from Kelly. She recognised her as Eddie Raven's daughter, her son's double, for sure. Jean had read about Kelly in the newspapers at the trial. She knew all about her past and that of her family. For a second, she gawped, taking it all in. Kelly Raven was a baby when she first saw her, and when she was only a teenager herself.

Kelly looked Jean up and down. She was so similar in appearance to her own so-called mother, it was uncanny. If looks could kill, Jean would have been struck down faster than lightning.

So many thoughts went through Jean's head, as she just stood there, totally bemused, seeing Kelly Raven larger than life. This world was so far removed from her former hippy existence and when flower power ruled her life, that for a second, she wanted to run and bury her head in the sand. A short time ago, when she was high on cocaine, she imagined she could sort out her son and eldest daughter with ease. But now, she felt totally insecure.

Kelly wasn't about to put her arm around Jean and welcome her inside. Instead, she remained rooted to the spot, as she watched Jean squirm with discomfort.

"I, er … I want to speak to Cyril," she mumbled.

Kelly moved forwards and Jean jumped back, off the stone step.

"It seems to me, Jean River, that you're playing a very fucking dangerous game. Now, correct me if I'm wrong, but did you not threaten my brother with Adam Carter?" She cocked her head to the side and gave Jean a smirk that had Eddie's name written all over it.

Jean swallowed hard; her throat was drying up. Those words and that sneer showed such an uncanny likeness to Eddie, it was incredible. In fact, so much so, it completely put the wind up her.

Malik had crept down the stairs and was hiding behind the door. He could see Kelly but not Jean. His sister's cold disposition and her confidence were new to him. His eyes lit up when he witnessed her shitting the life out of his mother.

"Your brother?" asked Jean.

"Please don't insult my fucking intelligence by denying the fact, 'cos ya see, it's like this. I don't take too kindly to people who try and mug me off. So, a word of warning. Be upfront or fuck off."

Jean knew at that point Kelly was no silly kid. Every word coming from the woman's mouth was spoken with calm assuredness.

Kelly gave Jean a snarling glare.

"Look, I don't want to argue, I just need to speak with Cyril or … well, find out if my son's here …"

Kelly gave a false laugh. "Your *son*? Did I hear you correctly? You've some nerve, I'll give ya that, lady. That kid has brought up those girls, while you fucked off filling ya fanny with an absolute scumbag by the name of Adam Carter. So, don't you call that boy your son, 'cos in my book, you haven't earned the right. And let me tell ya something else for nothing. Anything you have to say to Cyril, you can say to me. Have ya got that in ya thick skull?"

Jean's face was a picture. Being confronted with this glamour puss who easily had the looks of a model on any catwalk you cared to name, and who could, at the drop of a hat, speak like a real East End gangster, Jean had to contend with a quite terrifying but spectacular sight. Those inside the house were having a ball listening to Kelly.

But Jean wouldn't cower to this young woman: she was having none of it. She nodded and decided to go for the jugular. "Well, you can tell Malakai and Cyril that there's a dead body in the cottage, and I'm going to call the police, unless my son hands over Star. I don't want my youngest girl wrapped around a fucking murderer!"

191

Kelly's eyes widened, and in an instant, she grabbed Jean around the throat. Malik was by her side in a flash. "What the fuck are you on about?"

Kelly let go and pushed Jean up the steps. "Get inside, you!" She pointed to Jean who was coughing from the choke hold. Kelly then snatched her arm and marched her through the front door.

"Cyril!" she called.

He appeared in the hallway, as cool as a cucumber.

"Cyril, this no-good skank is pulling a dangerous stroke here."

Jean shook her arm free. "I ain't, there *is* a dead body in the house." Instantly, she felt foolish. How could she really accuse Malakai? The truth was that an hour ago she thought she'd devised a convincing plan, which actually seemed quite logical, yet now, faced with Kelly and Cyril, she was in over her head.

"Who is he?" asked Malik quickly, searching his mother's face for answers.

Jean's shoulders slumped. Her tactics looked to have been blown out of the water by this crazy young woman, and she sure wasn't going to get any help from the others here. And now, it was obvious it wasn't her son's doing. "It's not a he, it's a girl. She's lying there dead in the living room, with hardly a stitch on."

Malik was livid that his mother would firstly accuse him and secondly use this to get her hands on Star. He stepped forward, an inch from her nose. "You are one sly, devious cunt, d'ya know that? Instead of calling the Ol' Bill, you wanna try and set me up to get ya fucking hands on Star. Well, you fucked up, 'cos I'll call the police meself. I ain't killed no one, but if you don't fuck off right now, I just might murder you!"

"Hold on, boy!" cried Cyril. He pulled Malik away. "Let's try and sort this out calmly, shall we? Now you, Jean, you'd better start talking. I wanna hear all the facts, so no fannying around. This is not a silly game no more."

Jean watched Kelly close the front door. Her stomach was in knots. If only she'd just walked away.

Malik was white and pasty, and he felt a sinking feeling in his stomach. He had no idea who the dead girl could be.

Clocking the worried expression on Malik's face, Kelly glared at Jean. "When and where did you find this dead girl?"

"Just now, in the cottage, on the floor, by the sofa, naked, except for her boots," she replied, in a very matter-of-fact voice, as if this was entirely commonplace in her life.

Kelly raised her eyebrow. "And you or your fella had nothing to do with it? Only, Jean, I find all this a bit fucking strange."

Jean searched Cyril's face for some kind of support – she might have known there would be none.

"Look, I turned up to talk to Malakai and there was no answer, so I went in through the back door and found her. I had nothing to do with it, I promise, and neither did Adam."

Kelly smirked. "And you can be sure about that, though, can ya? Only, Malik tells me you threatened that Adam will be coming for what's his. It seems to me, you're knocking on the wrong door, and I think I should do your duty for you and call the police myself."

It hit Jean that Kelly was a clever woman. Perhaps she had a point. Adam had gone to the cottage, so he'd said. A part of her actually believed Kelly. But her initial assessment that he probably hadn't killed the girl proved stronger than this woman's instincts. Jean just could not imagine him killing a kid, end of. Yes, he was a hard bastard, but fist fights with grown men were more up his street. She started to chew her lip and her hands shook. The cocaine was out of her system, yet the after-effects were apparent. Kelly noticed it right away and felt disgust for Jean.

As Malik and Kelly stood side by side, Jean felt her heart sinking. There was clearly a bond between them and the likeness was visually disturbing. She had lost her son to Kelly. She was his family now, and there was no changing it.

As if things couldn't get any worse for Jean, they just did. She heard a noise from the staircase, and as her head turned to see who else was there, she saw, surprise, surprise, her bastard daughter Saskia descending on her like a bat out of hell, with that long wild hair.

"You, fucking whore-bag. I told ya to stay away." She was hurtling towards Jean with a rage in her eyes like a rabid dog. Yet, just as Sassy was about to lunge for Jean, Kelly turned and faced her.

"No, Sassy!"

Sassy stopped dead in front of them all. She looked a picture of contorted rage, as she began to scream and cry at the same time, her arms flailing like a marionette. "Kelly, you don't understand what that piece of shit put us through!"

Kelly remained between Jean and her daughter, preventing Sassy from attacking her. She put her arms out to comfort the shaking child, but Sassy was too incensed to be held or fussed. She screamed and

194

pointed her finger over Kelly's shoulder. "I hate you. I fucking hate you so much, Jean, I wish you would just curl up and die!"

The tears of anger poured down her face, as she kneeled down and sobbed. Kelly knew then that the stories of how the kids had struggled after their mother left them were not woeful tales of exaggeration.

Kelly tried again to hold Sassy and calm her down, and this time she succeeded. Sassy fell into Kelly's arms and sobbed away even more so.

This action somehow pricked a nerve in Jean. Maybe it was jealousy or even hate, but either way, she had heard and seen enough. She spun on her heels and headed for the door so fast that no one had a chance to stop her. But this woman wasn't finished yet, despite being outnumbered four to one. Her mouth ran as fast as she did. "You won't get away with this, Kelly Raven. They are *my* kids and you are no one to them. And you, Saskia, ya dirty slut, putting it on a plate for Adam to help himself, ya make me sick."

She was saying all this, as she headed out and down the steps, too chicken to say it face-to-face. Yet that was Jean all over: she talked a good game, but when push came to shove, she was nothing.

Kelly's character was rather different, though, and she wasn't going to let this woman get away with that crap. Letting go of Sassy, she skirted past Malik, kicked off her shoes, and shot out of the mansion like her arse was on fire. Jean suddenly panicked; she hadn't really expected the sophisticated woman to ditch her stilettos, hoist up her dress, and tear after her. Before Jean had time to build up a sprint to get away, Kelly had her by the hair, spinning her around to face her. With an evil glare, Kelly headbutted Jean. Her nose split, with blood splattered across her features. Then Kelly let go of her and took a deep breath. "Don't you dare tell me they ain't my family. Malik is my

195

brother. He may be your sordid little secret, but he fucking ain't mine. You had best get it in your thick head, that from now on, those kids are my family, not yours. You, ya bitch, lost that right. And for the record, I'm filing an order to the court today to become their legal guardian, and there ain't nothing you can do about it. 'Cos, Jean, if ya fucking try any silly stunt, I will come for you and ya silly boyfriend, and I'll fucking kill you both! And, just to let you know, I'm more than capable of murder!"

Jean was wiping the blood from her face. The broken nose didn't hurt but she knew the damage was bad. She was in so over her head, there was nothing more she could say except mumble "okay". Kelly was strong and violent, just like her father, and so Jean felt too scared to argue back. That headbutt was probably a warning. In the distance, she saw her children all comforting each other. Cyril had a disgusted sneer on his face, but it wasn't aimed at Kelly, it was directed at her. Kelly looked totally unperturbed, with the hateful glare that spoke volumes, leaving Jean to walk away in abject defeat.

On entering the house, Kelly saw that Sassy was still shaking and she put an arm around the younger girl's shoulders. "It's all right, Sassy, she won't be back. You heard what I said."

"Oh my God, what was she talking about, 'putting it on a plate'?" she sobbed uncontrollably.

"Don't worry, Sassy, she's deluded. Too many drugs, I suspect." Yet Kelly knew there was obviously more to this saga, and she was not going to let Jean get away with it.

Malik was taking it all in. There was his sister, Kelly, a classy-looking woman, who, in a flutter of a prostitute's eyelashes, could switch into a violent lunatic and not even flinch. She stood up for them and showed her true worth, without hesitation. She was going to look out for them, and she'd already proved she was more than capable. Sassy softened; her wild, erratic mouth and fiery fists were a front. Inside, she was the gentlest of souls, and now she had Kelly to do all the shouting. She could be the seventeen-year-old she should be. She had no need to fight the world in defence; she had a big sister now.

Later on, once emotions had subsided, they sat together, discussing the way forward. Sassy wasn't excluded, since she was old enough to be in on the decision-making. It suited her down to the ground.

Kelly called her lawyer and had the request for a residential order on the kids backdated by two days. Michael Delmonte only had a handful of clients – all belonging to the criminal fraternity. Kelly knew he was bent; he had to be, if he'd been working for Cyril for twenty years.

She winked at Sassy. "Right, all sorted. By tomorrow night, the courts should approve the court order and you, Saskia River, will be under my supervision. So, no more lip." She gave Sassy a sweet smile and tapped her gently on the nose.

Cyril called Mary and the two youngest girls to the drawing room, and as they entered, he chortled, "Maggie, me ol' girl, I'm gonna up ya wages, 'cos, it seems, you're gonna be rushed off your feet."

Mary tilted her head to the side.

"Our Kelly has just adopted a family, and so they'll be living 'ere for the foreseeable."

Mary clapped her hands together in sheer delight.

"Oh, wonderful! At least, I ain't gotta listen to your whining, and ya best stop wearing them poxy nightshirts that hardly cover ya bare spotty arse."

Kelly burst out laughing. "Gawd, Cyril, you'll give the kiddies nightmares!"

They all sat together, enjoying the banter. Perhaps they knew that at last things could only get better.

Once night fell, the serious business as to what to do about the murdered girl in the cottage was addressed. By this time, the little ones were bathed and ready for bed. Mary took her new role very seriously, and so she decided to read them a bedtime story. Not having children, let alone grandchildren, she savoured the moment.

Kelly paced the floor, thinking. "This is a mad situation and a bit worrying because if we call the Ol' Bill, then for sure, Malik, they'll call you in."

"I can get rid of the body, that's not a problem, but who is it? Malik, do you know any young woman that would be at your house?" Cyril asked.

Malik shook his head. "I don't know any ..." he paused, and then his eyes widened. "Oh, hang on, maybe ... The only girl I know is Kimi. She hasn't been to my house, yet I've got a feeling she followed me because ... oh, it's a long story."

Kelly frowned. "Well, Malik, we have all night, so tell me everything you know. We've a serious decision to make."

Malik noticed the concerned expression on Kelly's face. He told her about his acquaintance with Kimi and how she'd played a part in

198

helping to feed and clothe him and his sisters over the previous winter. He thought it best not to elaborate on his first sexual experience.

"Did you have an argument or a fight with her?" she asked coldly.

Malik was hurt. "Kelly!"

Kelly gave him a sorrowful smile. "Malik, I'm not questioning whether or not you killed her, but if we call the Ol' Bill, then trust me, that will almost certainly be the question they'll ask, because they'll want to pin this on someone."

Malik took a deep breath. "Call them! I didn't kill anyone, so I'm not afraid of the law."

Kelly shot Cyril a glance. He shrugged his shoulders. This wasn't a murder they needed to cover up.

Malik looked visibly wounded. He liked Kimi. She was such a kind-hearted soul. He hoped that his mother was lying. But if she wasn't, he hoped even more that his worst fears weren't about to become a reality.

CHAPTER TEN

Jean called a cab, having walked for miles to get a signal. The same cab driver picked her up and hardly recognised her. She had a misshapen nose, to add to her injured feelings, from the assault on her up at the mansion. Still, it wasn't his place to ask questions. He was a local man and knew full well who lived in the mansion and thought it best not to delve.

Eventually, she arrived outside Adam's apartment and was still shaking when she tried to put the key in the door. Being so upset, she wasn't aware of her surroundings and had assumed that Adam was still out. The apartment was quiet. She flung her bag on the sofa and clicked the kettle on, in dire need of a sweet tea. That's when she saw the long black leather boots strewn over the floor, along with a pair of knickers. Eaten up with jealousy, she charged into the bedroom to find Adam's big naked body sprawled out on the bed and next to him a kid – both were sound asleep. She wanted to put a knife through the pair of them, but all she could do was torture herself by staring at the perfect tight body of an attractive young girl. She was in despair – the pair in bed, her children with hate in their eyes, and herself, an old has-been, with saggy tits and wrinkled skin. The man she loved was a no-good bastard.

She silently retreated from the room, knowing that if he saw her, he would give her a slap. She wasn't supposed to be there; he'd made it very clear. "Make sure you bring her home. If you come back without my child, don't expect to stay," he'd told her.

She returned to the kitchen and quietly sipped her tea, pretending she was alone and what she just saw was a dream. Her nose hurt now, so she took the wet dishcloth and wiped her face.

Lacey had been disturbed, and without any hesitation, she got up from her bed. Still naked, she sauntered into the kitchen to get a drink before she woke up Adam for another good session. The lounge and kitchen were open-plan. It was a big room with a huge window which looked onto a park. It was one of the upper-class dwellings. Lacey liked the pad and could see herself living there one day.

Jean was shocked and genuinely at a loss for words when the girl sauntered into the room with a brazen assurance.

Lacey smiled. "Oops, sorry, love. I didn't know he had a cleaner. I'll just get dressed." With that, she toddled off, wiggling her neat arse.

Jean was mortified and yet she still didn't have the balls to say anything. She hurried to the sofa to snatch her bag, but before she could leave, Adam was there like a raging bull, with Lacey behind him. They were both still in the buff.

"Didn't I fucking tell ya? Well, didn't I?"

"Adam, listen, please!" she cried, but her voice tailed off, as she became distracted by the naked girl. Her eyes were so familiar somehow, but she couldn't place where she had seen her, if at all.

Lacey realised the woman was no cleaner and obviously his bird. She'd already made up her mind that she wanted Adam, and come what may, she was going to have him. But as young as she was, her only way of fighting was to be catty like a child. She pushed past Adam, and with her hands on her bare hips, she laughed, mocking Jean.

"Oh, darling, please don't embarrass yaself. As you can see, he wants you out, and I do too, so that I can get back down to business, unless you wanna watch." Her voice was full of spite and wickedness.

Jean was humiliated and hurt to think that Adam was just laughing at her. Then he smiled. "That's an idea, Lacey. Come in the bedroom, Jean. My little Lacey here will show you how it's really done." He unashamedly pulled Lacey away and grabbed her tits, showing Jean that he didn't give a shit about her or her feelings.

Lacey giggled. "Come on, Adam, let's go back to bed. I've got a clit ready to be tickled."

Jean was mortified at how Adam could seriously want a girl so rude, but then again, she was a very good-looking kid. If the truth be known, she was looking at a mirror image of herself in her younger days. She clutched her bag and was about to leave, before the tears fell like Niagara Falls, when she had a last-minute dig.

"Well, Adam, let's hope that the dead kid I found at my house has nothing to do with you because Kelly Raven is calling the police!"

Astonished by this news, Adam let go of Lacey and glared. "You what?"

Jean knew then she had his attention. "Yeah, you heard it right. Kelly Raven is calling the police."

Lacey sensed this was not her business, so she crept away, back to the bedroom. As much as she hated Kelly Raven, and for no reason other than pure jealousy, she also knew that it was time to leave.

"What the fuck has Kelly Raven got to do with you?"

His ears pricked up. He had no clue as to how Kelly, in any shape or form, was connected with Jean.

"Oh, ya wanna listen now, don't ya, Adam?" She was now very much aware that she had the upper hand and decided to make the most of this opportunity. It was the only way to call the shots. "You'd better tell ya strumpet to fuck off, so we can talk. Best she doesn't know, eh?"

Adam was fuming. He called to Lacey, through gritted teeth, without taking his eyes off Jean. "Lacey, get ya gear on and go."

The tone in his voice was sufficiently clear for Lacey to justify a swift exit. She was dressed within a few seconds and was back in the living room. Popping her knickers in her bag and pulling on her boots, she said, "Call me, babe!" as she headed out the door. Adam's expression was severe, and he stood there motionless, at a loss for words.

At last, Jean had his undivided attention. "Adam, I went to the cottage to get Star, but my family were gone, and there on the floor was a fucking dead kid."

Adam pointed at her. "You wait there!" He left to get dressed; somehow, this conversation felt too serious to be standing with his todger on show.

He returned in a tracksuit. "How the fuck do you know Kelly Raven?"

"She's Malakai's sister." She wanted to smirk; it was all mad and complicated, and yet Adam looked worried. Jean had no idea that Adam was caught up with a Carter versus Raven feud.

"You never fucking told me that he was Eddie Raven's son!"

Jean looked down in shame. She'd never told anyone about her debauched way of life and had certainly kept to herself who the children's fathers were. But now she would use everything to get Adam back in her pocket and carry on like it was before.

Adam grabbed the packet of fags from the side and lit one up. "I suppose he gave ya that fucked-up hooter as well?"

Jean shook her head. "No, that was Kelly Raven, the evil cunt. She reckons, she's adopting Star." Jean knew that would get up his nose.

Adam slowly nodded his head. "Well, that gives me two reasons to fucking smash the life outta the silly cunt. She's taking too many liberties. Who the fuck does she think she—?"

"Like I just said, she's Eddie Raven's daughter, that's who she is," piped up Jean, bravely.

Adam glared at her. "Well, I should have put a bullet in his head years ago, the flash wanker. Cor, when I fucking get my hands on her, I'm gonna …" He stopped and ground his teeth.

"Adam, did you not hear me? She's gonna call the Ol' Bill about the dead body!"

Adam frowned. "So, what's that gotta do with me?"

Jean assumed then that Adam wasn't the killer, or he would have panicked. "Not a lot, I s'pose, if you had nothing to do with that dead girl."

Adam lurched forward and grabbed Jean's neck. "You wanna watch ya fucking mouth, woman, before I fucking throttle ya." He slowly let her go and watched as she eventually stopped coughing.

"You went to the house, Adam. Ya fucked me daughter, so you'll have prints all over the place. That was a right 'orrible move, you bastard. I really thought ya felt something for me. I never did you no harm." Her voice was trailing off into one of her whines again.

Adam stubbed his cigarette out. He appeared a worried man. The consequences of his actions were coming home to roost big style, and once again, he cursed his stupidity for his cock dictating his life choices. His intense expression resembled a man in meltdown.

"What's the matter, Adam?" asked Jean, hoping he was having second thoughts and would hold her tight, pleading to be forgiven.

There was no anger in his eyes, no fiery words, or flaring of the nostrils. She guessed then he was seriously troubled.

"Where was this Kelly bitch, when you spoke to her?"

Jean assumed she was back on board with Adam and together they would join in a fantasy quest to save their daughter. "She was at Cyril Reardon's estate and Malakai was there as well."

"Oh, it just gets fucking better. Cyril poxy Reardon?"

Jean stepped forward and stroked his arm. "It's all right, Adam. We can work this out. Kelly can play happy families. I'll find a way to get Star."

Adam wasn't listening. "Who else was there?"

Jean frowned. "No one, apart from Saskia. I guess they hid the two girls upstairs. Why?"

Adam smiled. "Saskia, you say? What, she was there? You actually saw her?"

Jean was confused yet hurt. "Yeah, why?" Her tone changed out of anger. "What, ya wanna take off with her now, do ya?"

Adam shook his head. "Shut up, ya silly tart. The only girl I saw at that house was your fucking daughter, so I reckon either your boy or ya girl may have done away with the kid. Desperate times call for desperate measures."

The vision of the dead girl, who – initially – she herself had thought was Saskia, along with the uncomfortable look on Adam's face, was a light bulb moment. Adam *had* raped and killed that girl, thinking she was Saskia. It was all falling into place. Jean could see that Adam believed the girl was her daughter, from the description she'd given him. It was some comfort that Saskia hadn't been a victim of his perverted desires. She might hate her daughter, but she was her flesh and blood, when all was said and done. And she recalled earlier Malakai's completely genuine expression when he'd asked, "Who is he?" It gave her all the conviction she needed to believe her son was innocent.

Adam was beginning to think that the idea of claiming back his daughter just wasn't worth the aggravation. It was okay before when he assumed that Malakai was just a nobody, but the boy was wrapped around Kelly, his enemy, and Cyril, a Face. He thought about Cyril and shuddered. There was a time when he took a real hiding from the man. That was

207

over twenty years ago although the scars around his left ear were a constant reminder.

He was only nineteen at the time. His brothers were in their twenties and had a reputation and money. They kept their business over in North London, away from the likes of Cyril and Eddie Raven. He realised Johnnie, Frazer, and Matt were the sleeker-looking brothers; they took after their mother for their looks. Adam was his father's double, and although he always had a bird on his arm, it was his older brothers who had the real pick of a bit of skirt. Johnnie, being the eldest, called the shots. Frazer was the quiet, studious one and worked out the finances. Matt was the charmer, but he had sly tendencies, and on a scale from one to ten, he was verging on the eight mark for a psychopath. Adam, however, was the baby and as such was treated like one. When they discussed business, they regarded his input as unimportant. He hated it when they said, "Just do as you're told." It was something constantly thrown in his face. The day he told his brothers to go and fuck themselves was the day he realised he should have listened.

They were working their way up in a firm run by Patrick Mahoney, an Irishman, who was born into money. He bought his way into the criminal world. His money lured in the most violent muscle, and within a few years, Patrick and Sheila were running the whole of North London. They specialised in protection rackets and a few night clubs. The Carters had the cocaine business pretty much sewn up, and so they fell under Patrick Mahoney's umbrella. At the time, all those years ago, it had worked well. Patrick took a cut from their profits, and he, in return, would watch over their manor. But the day Patrick went to visit Eddie Raven, to give him a word of warning not to fuck with his business, the tables turned, and Patrick, in his arrogance, found that he had underestimated Eddie.

The altercation between them that day changed the whole dynamics. The Carters were not going to wage a war that they couldn't win, so they accepted the deal, and that was that, as far as they were concerned. Although they would be handing over a bigger cut to Patrick to pay off Eddie, they earned enough to waive that extra poke and so decided it was easier to leave things as they were.

Adam, however, was not happy; he took umbrage at this piss-take, which, to be fair to him, it certainly was, and so he decided to take matters into his own hands. Without any planning, or giving his brothers the heads-up, or even consulting them first – that was never going to happen – he rushed into Eddie Raven's pub, the Cedar Arms, in the East End, like a man possessed and started on the fixtures and fittings by swinging a bat. To any sane man he was not only dangerous but a complete nutjob, and so the pub quickly emptied. Sitting in the corner were Frank and Cyril.

The pub was now clear, all except the two old men, as Adam saw them. He was a fool not to have listened to his brothers. Cyril and Frank were notorious, yet Adam thought he was invincible.

Adam ignored the two men and began smashing up the tables, in between shouting for Eddie Raven to come down the stairs and face him. The barmaid was screaming and hid herself behind the bar. The pint glasses, which had been abandoned on the counter, were smashed with one swoop of the bat. That was when Cyril jumped up. He liked the barmaid, Flossie; she was a good girl, and he wasn't going to stand for this man's vile behaviour which would put an innocent kid in danger.

"Oi, cunt, what d'ya think you're doing?"

Adam was raging; he had it in his head to take this as a personal vendetta, completely going against his brothers' words of warning. He stupidly thought he would one day take over and went on the rampage to show his worth. He turned and looked at what he classed as two jokers. They weren't even old then, although, being only nineteen, he saw anyone over the age of thirty as being in their dotage.

"Fuck off you, ya stupid old man!"

Cyril looked at Frank and calmly placed his pint glass on the table and stood up.

"Did you fucking hear that, Frank? This cunt 'as just insulted me twice. He called me stupid and then he called me fucking old."

Frank shook his head, gravely. "Oh, dear me, you hate being called old, Cyril, don't ya?"

Adam gripped his bat tightly, the level of anger now reaching its peak, and there, in front of him, were two geezers taking the piss. He was ready to smash the life out of someone, and if these two wanted to flex their muscles, then he was going to annihilate them.

"You wasters had better fuck off before I pulverise ya with me bat."

Cyril laughed at him. "'Ere, Frank, I reckon it's true what they say about that Carter family."

"Yeah, Cyril, what's that, then?"

Adam was seething, but before he would tear into them, he wanted to hear what they had to say.

Cyril looked Adam over; he knew exactly who Adam was.

"Yeah, they reckon when the youngest was born, he was dropped on his head. That's why he's so stupid, but it don't account for him being a cunt, though."

Frank roared with laughter.

Adam was now so incensed, he ran towards them waving his bat. He was going to knock the old git off his feet. His anger did him no favours: in attempting to whack Cyril, his whole approach wasn't carefully planned out at all. Swinging the bat, without consideration for the consequences, left him wide open, and as he missed, Cyril cracked him hard on the side of the head. The punch was fast and left a deep gash, due to the knuckleduster worn on Cyril's hand. Adam toppled and was then met with a torrential downpour of savage blows. He was out of his depth, and within a few seconds, his unconscious form was splayed out with blood pouring from his skull. Cyril was so out of breath, it made Frank laugh. "Cor, mate, he may have a point. Look at you, ya unfit old bastard."

Cyril was bent over, with his hands on his knees and taking deep breaths. "Fuck off, Frank, I was doing all the work, ya cheeky fucker."

Frank walked over to the bar and gave the barmaid a concerned look. She was on the floor in the brace position. "Are you all right, Flossie, me sweetheart?"

Flossie was too afraid to move. She didn't mind a bit of aggro, but it was the insane look in Adam's eyes that had utterly freaked her out. "Get up, Floss, you're all right. Babe, pour me and Cyril a brandy. The old man needs a livener."

Cyril stepped over the battered body and laughed. "Less of the fucking old."

They downed their drinks and looked back at Adam.

"D'ya know, I was really looking forward to me pie and chips. I can't believe that idiot has ruined me dinner. I guess we'd best take him downstairs and give him a little reminder as to what happens when someone insults us," said Cyril. He faced Flossie and winked. "Do us a favour, babe. Could ya lock the doors and fetch us our grub?"

Flossie, now visibly more relaxed, hurried over to the main entrance and locked up before she left to cook Cyril's and Frank's pie and chips. She was fully aware of who she was working for and was glad both men were in that day. Of course, she knew the rules: see nothing, hear nothing, do nothing.

They dragged Adam down to the basement. The room was large; half of it was for the beer kegs, and the other half for any private discussions, or, as in this case, a little reminder of what happens if ya fuck with Cyril's firm. They heaved the unconscious man onto the chair under the central light fixture and bound him tightly. Frank was annoyed. If he got out his tools from his bag, then he at least wanted his victim to be awake. But the head bashing was so severe that Adam remained out of it.

"I dunno, Cyril. I ain't cut an unconscious man before."

Cyril tutted. "I know, mate, it does go against the grain, but me pie and chips will get cold. Tell ya what. Cut half his ear off. I want that delinquent to go back to his little mob with a warning. If he ain't listening, then he doesn't need two fucking great lug holes."

It was fortunate the floor was covered with lino: it would make it easier for the staff to clean up the mess.

Adam remembered waking up on the pavement outside the back of the pub. He was disorientated, until he felt some soreness, and he realised that his left ear was hanging off. Lucky for him, the slice was neat, and so the surgeon was able to sew it back on again.

∞*∞

That was so long ago, yet he'd learnt a valuable lesson not to underestimate Cyril and his firm. It was different now, though. They really were too old; they must be well over sixty, and although Frank had been quick with his tool, plunging that metal rod in his arm, he was still well past his prime, and there was no way now that he could compete with someone younger and stronger like himself.

Adam ignored Jean as if she wasn't there. He snapped open a can of beer and wandered off into the lounge area sitting heavily on the couch. He had a lot on his mind – Jean's son, Malakai, and Malakai's sister, Kelly Raven, were all under his arch-enemy Cyril Reardon's roof. In among all this shit was a random dead bird in Jean's house. *Had he actually killed her?* It was obvious from what Jean had said that he hadn't raped her daughter. He found it difficult to process the complexities, and so he switched off from it all. Lacey popped into his head and he glanced at Jean. She stood there with her nose purple and crooked, with a pathetic, needy expression slapped across her face and an air of unease. It was Lacey he wanted to look at, not Jean, the pitiful wreck. The sight of her annoyed him.

"What the fuck are you doing still 'ere? Ya bring me nothing but grief. Get outta my apartment!"

Despite knowing that Adam had killed that girl, Jean still wanted him, and in a plea of desperation, she ran to him, throwing her arms around his neck. "Please, Adam, don't do this. I love you. We have a baby. Don't throw me out. I've got nowhere to go." Of course, she

213

did have a few fallbacks if need be, but she wouldn't be telling Adam anything about those.

Adam's head was too full of anxiety and Jean was to blame. He jumped up, grabbed her arms, and almost launched her through the window. With a bang, she bounced off the glass and slid to the floor. He towered over her, spittle forming at the sides of his mouth. She had never seen a man go from calm to rage in less than a second. His malicious look and cruel words totally shook her.

"Get the fuck away from me, ya skanky old whore. I should never have brought you into my life. You're nothing but a waste of oxygen. Look at ya!" He gritted his back teeth and then spat in her face. "Get up, Jean! Get ya fucking gear and fuck off, before I destroy you!"

Jean managed to get to her feet and choked back the tears. There was no point in crying; tears weren't going to work on him now. Slowly, she stepped over to the sofa to retrieve her bag, watched by Adam.

"Stop acting like a fucking div and get out!"

She thought about pleading with him one last time but then decided against it. Instead, she threw the bag over her shoulder and headed to the door.

"Oh, and just so we're clear, you can keep ya daughter. I ain't interested. And another thing. You may have been a dirty fuck for a while, but remember this, Jean. That's all you were. So, don't come back, leave the keys on the side, and never fucking cross my path again. Got it?"

"Oh, yeah, I've got the message all right, Adam, and you take one from me. You'll be sorry, mark my fucking words." Jean had her back to Adam, when the smirk ran across her face. She dropped his front door keys on the side table and left.

She was gutted it was over. Nevertheless, as if she had just woken up from her worst nightmare, she consoled herself with the thought that, other than those bastards Eddie and Cyrus, Adam was no different from all the other men she'd been involved with, and at least she had benefited from those relationships as much as them. In fact, she knew herself perfectly. She'd never been a revengeful person, and when one dalliance petered out, she'd always relied on using her looks to move on to the next conquest.

But, now, this time, it was different. Her looks had changed. No longer was she the pretty chick with the neat body; she was much older — too old to pretend she was a beauty — and all the drugs had taken their toll. She couldn't compete with the likes of Lacey or her own daughter. However, she wasn't going to take any more shit lying down. Revenge would be sweet, and she had a sudden taste for it.

CHAPTER ELEVEN

Kelly asked Malik if he was sure he wanted the police called. When she'd gone on the run, six years ago now, after the Patrick Mahoney incident, she'd been very fortunate to meet Rudy Jameson, who took her into his home. He became one of her closest friends, along with other members of his so-called family, namely, Tulip, Ditto, and Reggie. She had long experience of how the filth could mistreat people and intuitively preferred to keep well away from them, if she could. *But if needs must*, she thought.

"Yeah, of course, I do. I didn't kill anyone, and really, I've no choice."

Kelly looked at Cyril. This was Malik's call to make.

"They're gonna ask why you're here, why your mother came to you asking for Star. It will get messy, I can tell ya that much. They'll wanna pin this on someone."

Malik was seated and looked up at Kelly fearfully, his eyes full of vulnerability. "I don't know, Kelly, I want to call the police, but will they treat me fairly?"

Cyril shrugged his shoulders. "We can remove the body, but that mother of yours may call the Ol' Bill herself."

"I wanna sleep on it. I'm fucking shattered," said Malik, rubbing his eyes.

Kelly agreed. She needed to go home and talk to Keffa; she was also missing him.

It was one o'clock in the morning when Malik woke up. He had tossed and turned all night, and when he finally drifted off to sleep, he dreamed of what he would imagine the horrific scene inside the cottage would look like. The nightmare left him in a cold sweat. He sprang from his bed and slipped into his clothes. He had to go and see for himself or he would never rest. Meanwhile, Star had also woken up. After all the sweet fizzy drinks that Mary had plied her with, she'd been unable to go into a deep sleep. An urge to pee seemed a good enough reason to see what was going on in the house, and so she put on her new thick, fluffy dressing gown and went to the bathroom, with an ear to sounds coming up from downstairs. But the house was silent. Once she finished, she strolled back, but then, she just made out Malik about to creep down the back staircase. Thinking he was about to run away, she panicked. She decided to follow him. Down he went and into the kitchen, and then he hurried out of the back door. She didn't want to call after him, in case she woke up the rest of the house. Frantically, she searched for her wellington boots. They were by the front door, along with her coat. She had to be quick. It was dark outside, and if she didn't catch him up, she could lose him.

Malik was heading for the cottage. It wasn't too long a walk across the field and past the woods. Even so, he would be quicker if he went via the back of Cyril's extensive gardens. He marched with the cool breeze refreshing his face. The air was clear, and the stars were bright. He'd never noticed the sky before, as he usually walked with his head down.

Star had pulled on her wellies and struggled to put her coat on over the dressing gown, but eventually she was ready for the outside. She looked across the field and could just make out a person, a man, perhaps, from his size. So she ran as fast as she could, but then, when she got to where she thought the man was, she realised it wasn't a human being at all, it was a tree. On she went, in search of Malik, despite it being dark and eerie. She had walked so far that when she turned around she could see nothing. There was no mansion, no road, just woods. Assuming her brother was ahead somewhere, she continued to look for him. The wind blew in her face and strange noises unnerved her. She whirled around when a bat flitted past. It caused her to lose her balance. Tripping over a tree root and twisting her ankle in the process, she cried out, "Ouch!" As she yelped in pain, she heard another sound; it was a high-pitched scream and scared her, causing her to stand rigidly in fear and hold her breath. But then, she was able to breathe normally, as she saw that it was only a fox, even though to her it resembled a monster. That was the trouble. For much of her short life she had lived as a townie and had certainly never ventured outside at this time of night. All the scary monster stories that Malik and Sassy would read to her, when she was tucked up in bed, seemed quite fun to listen to, but tonight, she was seeing things for real, and she wished she'd stayed inside. *What was she thinking?* she thought. She called out for Malik but there was no answer. The only sound was from the night animals; an owl hooted, the fox barked and screamed yet again, and the bats darted around. Fear engulfed her, and she sat rocking in a ball, too terrified to move. She hoped Malik would find her; *surely, he would come?* He always looked out for them all.

Meanwhile, Malik had reached the end of his garden and leaped over the fence. It was deathly quiet, and he saw no signs of any police activity or crime tape. He was careful not to make a sound, as he cautiously made his way up the path towards the back door. He hadn't even reached it when the metallic meat-rotting smell hit him. His stomach turned over, and reality smacked him in the face. So, Jean wasn't lying: there *was* a dead body in the house. He had to know who it was. He had a key to the back door but guessed it wasn't locked. It

219

entered his head then that they'd forgotten to lock it when they scarpered up to Cyril's place. Gingerly, he pushed open the back door and tiptoed inside. The wind shot through the hallway and whistled sinisterly. It was creepy and although Malik was a tough cookie, he wasn't so brave around the things that go bump in the night. *But then,* he thought, *who was?* He flicked the lamp on in the living room with one hand and kept the other over his nose and mouth. The smell was so rancid, he suspected he would puke up. As the soft glow lit up the room, he saw her, lying there, just as Jean had said. He had never seen a dead body, let alone a decomposing one. A squeaking sound made him jump. A rat dramatically appeared from within the dead girl's hair. Malik gasped in horror. He had to look away for a second, take a deep breath, and plough on. He slowly squatted down by the head of the corpse and removed the straggly strands of red hair to get a look at the face. *Red hair?* His heart was pounding in his chest and his stomach contents were rising. He could be sick at any moment. *Calm down, Malik, fucking stop it*, he told himself. He took another deep breath, and then, repulsed by the smell, he gagged, but he managed to hold down the vomit. The sight was confirmation of all his worst fears. Despite the girl's hair being red now — *was that its natural colour?* — it *was* poor Kimi. But her face was half-eaten away, her eyes were crawling with maggots, and her lips had been chewed by what he assumed was a rat, making identification very difficult. The unusually warm weather had sped up the sickening putrefaction and attracted the wild life.

Kimi had helped his family so much and had brought light into a life which until then had little purpose. He didn't want to leave her there, all alone in the dark, with no clothes on. He wanted to cover her with a blanket. But there was a risk he might inadvertently tamper with a crime scene, if he touched anything. Even though his mind was partly numb with shock and horror, the other part was telling him to get as far away from this place as possible. He turned off the lamp and whispered, "Good night, my angel. God bless you, my sweetness."

He ran back along the garden path, over the fence, and through the woods. The warm air and sweet smell of the autumn leaves settled his stomach, yet it could not contain the tears. He ran, crying like a baby. How could he ever get that shocking picture out of his head? A cold shiver ran through his body and he knew this night would always haunt him. He couldn't say he loved Kimi, he hadn't known her long enough; and yet he was gutted and felt such sorrow for the girl, who'd not had a chance to fulfil a life of her own. And not only that, but he felt very guilty for involving her in his. If only he'd never met her, then perhaps she would still be alive, giving people her inimitable cheek. He was tired and scared. Yet, at the same time, he was bitterly angry. Who would do such a cruel thing to her? She was a kid, really, just a sweet funny girl, much like his own sister Sassy, and perhaps even more so, now that he'd seen her with long red hair. He stopped running and paused, taking a deep breath. His sorrow was now tainted with a bitterness that he could almost taste. A fierce, twisted, and angry pain clutched him. It was an emotion he had never really felt before – except perhaps when he thought of his mother on the occasions they were near to starvation. Kimi's death must be avenged, that was a given.

As he entered the kitchen, the sound from the large wall-mounted clock and the traces of the smell of cooking from last night's dinner soothed him. He wasn't physically tired, yet emotionally, he was exhausted. Cyril had given him a taste for brandy, and it was a feeling he savoured, but it somehow felt wrong to drink liquor. He flicked the switch on the kettle to make a coffee. He took one of Cyril's funny mugs with 'Old Git' written on the side from a kitchen cabinet and put a heaped spoonful of coffee and two spoonfuls of sugar into the mug. He'd developed a taste for sweet hot drinks. Adding some milk, he was looking forward to removing the vile taste in his mouth which had been left by the smell of death. As soon as the kettle boiled, he poured the water into the mug and gave the contents a good stir. He would have smiled, if he was in the mood, but tonight's turn of events had left a

221

wounded feeling in his heart. Suddenly, he heard a noise by the internal kitchen door, and he assumed it was Frank or Stein, one of the dogs, but there stood Tilly, with her thumb in her mouth, looking wide-eyed and angelic. She leaned against the door frame.

"Hey, what are you doing up? It's far too early."

Tilly tilted her head to the side, when she saw Malik's tears. "Why are ya crying, Malik?"

Malik shook his head. "I'm not. Now, Chantilly River, get yaself back in bed before ya wake ya sister."

Tilly smiled. She liked being called Chantilly, but then she frowned. "Star's not in bed. I thought she was down here with you."

His state of mind still freaked out, he almost dropped the mug of coffee onto the table. In a panic, he ran past Tilly and up the stairs. He pushed open the door to the girls' room and turned on the light. Star's bed was empty. *Oh, shit*! He looked under the bed and then called her name. There was no answer. His vision of Kimi was there in the forefront of his mind and now Star was not where she was supposed to be. He had exaggerated images of his baby sister lying dead somewhere. He called again, but this time he didn't hold back; his panic was rising, and Sassy heard the shrill tone in his voice. She was out of her bed and running down the corridor in a heartbeat.

"What's going on, Malik?"

He turned to face her with a desperate, terrified look. "Star's not here!"

Sassy threw her hands to her mouth and her eyes widened. "Oh, Jesus, she was banging on about going in the pool. Fuck me, she can't swim!"

The commotion had woken Cyril and Mary, who also scrambled from their beds, and they joined Malik to find out what all the fuss was about. Malik was now like a whippet, tearing down the stairs to the swimming pool. His heart was pounding, and his legs were like jelly. *Please God, don't let her be dead!*

The natatorium was stifling hot. Malik ran around the edges in a panic, but his heart rate slowed down, when it was clear that at least she wasn't lying at the bottom of the enormous pool.

Cyril was in his deep burgundy night robe. He looked like Wee Willie Winkie, and in different circumstances, everyone would have had a right laugh at his appearance, but at this hour and with the unexplained disappearance of their baby, this was the last thought on their minds. Quite the opposite, in fact, as what they saw was the expression of a scared old man.

"Right, Sassy, you check all the wardrobes, Tilly you check the games room, Maggie you check the bathrooms, and Malik, you come with me into the kitchen."

Now mentally exhausted and believing he wouldn't be able to think straight, Malik was relieved that Cyril had taken charge.

"What's going on, son? Where have you been?" He cast his eyes down at Malik's trainers.

Malik wasn't about to lie. "I couldn't sleep. I had to see if Jean was telling the truth about a dead body in the cottage. If so, I had to see who it was." A lump in his throat stopped him from talking. He was too close to tears.

Cyril gripped his shoulder, and his immediate reaction was to ask who the person in the cottage was, but he could tell from Malik's face that this would be a question for later on. "All right, son. Listen, we're gonna find Star. She's probably gone sleepwalking."

Malik was swallowing hard against the lump in his throat. Impatiently, he brushed the tears from his eyes.

"He's got her! That cunt Adam has snatched her, ain't he?"

Cyril frowned. "What? No way! He can't get in here. It's like fucking Fort Knox."

Malik shook his head in frustration. "I left the back door open, so I could get in again. I fucked up! Now that bastard's got our Star. I swear to God, I'm gonna kill him!"

Cyril squeezed Malik's shoulder. "Don't jump to conclusions. She's probably in the house somewhere, so let's keep looking."

While they searched the house, Cyril called Kelly, Frank, and Blakey over.

Much later, they finally decided that Star was missing. By this time, Kelly had arrived with Keffa and rushed into the drawing room to find her brother looking like death warmed up and Sassy as white as a ghost.

Keffa had never met Malakai and was taken aback when he noticed the resemblance to Kelly and more to the point Eddie Raven, his old enemy. He hated her father, Eddie. A meeting many years ago with the man, and a long time before he'd first met Kelly, had left Keffa with his throat cut.

224

Although Keffa loved Kelly and had done since the day he met her, when she was only fifteen, it wasn't until she came out of prison at the age of twenty-one, that they finally became an item.

He stepped forward and held out his hand. "Nice to meet you, Malakai, although it's a shame it's in these circumstances. I'm Keffa."

Malik looked up at the confident tall man and gave him a sad smile. He shook his hand and then turned to Kelly. "He's got her, Kel, that bastard Adam, I just know he has."

Kelly put her arms around him and whispered in his ear. "If he has, he's a dead man. We'll get her back, trust me, Malik."

He listened to her words and knew she meant them.

Tilly slid her hand into Cyril's. She understood from the way the adults were talking that her young sister could be in real danger. She was heartbroken. Star was her little sidekick, her shadow, and Tilly was too young and helpless to do anything to help her tiny sister.

Cyril looked down at Tilly's big sad eyes and squeezed her hand. He nodded for Mary to take her into the kitchen. She shouldn't be hearing this conversation.

At that moment, the door flew open and in walked Frank with Blakey. "'ave ya found her?" asked Frank. His voice had always been deep and gruff.

Malik shook his head. "That Adam has her. I fucking left the back door open. I reckon he snuck in and grabbed her from her bed." His mouth was dry, and his voice cracked.

Kelly rubbed his back. "Don't worry, we'll find her."

Kelly raised her eyebrow at Cyril, and he quickly understood her expression and spoke to his buddies. "Frank, Blakey, you two come with me. We're gonna pay this Adam a visit."

Frank smirked. "He's nursing a wound from one of me tools. He obviously ain't learnt his lesson. Does the prick know that Malik is your brother, Kelly?"

Kelly shrugged her shoulders. "Well, Jean, Malik's mother, knows, so I guess he does now. After that little episode when she came here to get Star, she no doubt went running back blabbering her mouth off. Therefore, it stands to reason, Adam turning up and taking her. That man has some front, I'll give him that!"

Cyril took a deep breath. "Who does he think he is? He wants to take over the manor and fuck with me family, does he? I've a good mind to feed him to me brother's pigs. The liberty-taking tosspot."

Frank sneered. "Well, by all accounts, he's a lone ranger, 'cos, I don't think he'll have the Carter brothers backing him. Keffa, 'ere, gave Johnnie a word of warning, and by the look on Johnnie's face, he was shitting hot bricks. Nah, Adam's on his own. But, if they want a fucking war, they'll have one."

Sassy watched and listened. Impressed by the tone in their voices and the way they treated this situation as a personal attack on all of them, she knew whose corner she wanted to be in. It was galling though to be told she had to remain in the mansion with Mary and Tilly, with the doors bolted shut.

Keffa drove Kelly and Malik to Adam's apartment, and he sensed the tension in the car. The brother and sister were hyper, looking straight ahead and keeping their thoughts to themselves. They couldn't be more alike if they tried. Cyril and his men followed in the Bentley.

226

They all parked their cars behind the block and gathered in the car park. It was quiet, with not a soul around at this early hour. Frank was putting his black leather gloves on, while Blakey was pulling his woolly hat down just above his eyebrows, hiding his white hair. Of course, they weren't aware that because Adam had the apartment block to himself, they were able to reach his front door without any nosy neighbour having a good gawp.

"Right, I'm gonna kick the door in. You, Blakey, have ya gun ready, just in case the cunt has a shooter. But don't fire unless you have to 'cos the baby might be there," ordered Frank.

Malik, in a cool manner, said, "Why don't we just knock?"

Frank and Blakey looked at him, as if he were mad. It was Frank who said, "Malik, mate, you've a lot to learn. We ain't fucking around 'ere. I want the door off its hinges and that cunt shaking in his daisy roots. Got it?"

Malik realised they were not messing, and he then cast his mind back to the Albanians.

"If you're gonna be part of the firm, you need to know the rules, and the number one rule is you show people who's calling the shots," added Blakey.

Malik took note and nodded. It was at this point in his life that he realised he was not going to be a lawyer, an accountant, or a doctor. And he was pretty sure he didn't really want to work for anyone else either. Who wants to earn a living working in effect for someone who is earning even more off you? In reality, those bosses weren't so different from pimps.

227

So, yes, he really wanted to join Kelly's firm. He was Eddie's son and Kelly's brother. He didn't want to ignore his family history and more to the point his newly acquired sister. And, he'd shown that he was a fighter, in mind and body. All the new people he had encountered recently he liked and felt comfortable with. They might be criminals but so what? They had kind hearts, when it came down to what family was all about. You look after your own because you know no other fucker will do it for you. He would put his trust in Kelly and her firm. Blood is a lot thicker than water, so they say, and he knew family loyalty (not that he'd had much from his wicked old mother) would probably see him okay in the end.

Frank lifted his right leg, and with a hard kick, the door crashed in off its hinges, landing heavily into the living room. They were in, and like cats, they shot in all directions.

Adam was sound asleep in his bed, the wound to his shoulder now very sore. The pain had actually got worse after shagging the life out of Lacey. He'd taken sleeping tablets, downed most of a bottle of whisky, and got into his bed, in that order. Somewhere in the background, he heard a noise, but it was fuzzy, and it took him a while to realise that he was surrounded by Cyril's men. He blinked furiously and tried to get up to face the enemy. He didn't get a chance to draw breath. A blow from the side hit him hard on the cheek. The adrenaline pumped furiously around his body, and in a second, he was wide awake and ready to fight. He turned to see who had thumped him one – it was a young lad, still in his teens.

"Where's me sister?" demanded the kid, his voice laced with venom.

Adam was livid; he hated being caught unawares and lunged forward to give the boy a slap, but he wasn't fast enough. Malik dodged him and then came back with another crack, this time to the nose.

"I said, where's me sister?"

Adam felt the blood go to the back of his throat. That punch was fierce and had broken his nose.

"What the fuck is going on?" shouted Adam.

Removing the blood with the back of his hand, he looked the kid up and down, amazed that someone half his size could fight like that. As his eyes focused, he saw what looked like Eddie Raven – *surely Eddie was dead, wasn't he?* – as the expression, the eyes, and the bearing were the spitting image of the man. It reminded him of the person he feared the most.

Then Kelly stepped forward; that evil intent in her eyes was just like Malik's. "So, you're the fucker, that's been carving up me men!"

Adam guessed who she was. Johnnie had given him a good description, and he was right: that look in her eyes was cold. She was fearless, but he wasn't going to back down as easily as his brothers had. His eyes turned back to Malik. "I've no idea where your sister is. Are you talking about my daughter, Star?"

Malik's jaw shot forward and he flared his nostrils. "She ain't your daughter, ya fucking prick. Jean was shagging for England. Wake up and smell the coffee! She pulled your name out of a hat. So, where the fuck is she?" he screamed.

Adam put his hands up in defeat. "I swear, I don't know. I ain't left me apartment since that cunt," he nodded at Frank, "fucked me shoulder up."

Malik had it in his head that Adam was lying, and he was onto the man, pounding his fist into Adam's face again. The next punch hit him in the ribs. As he bent over, Malik pulled his fist back, and with an almighty clout, he smashed Adam's eye socket. More by luck than judgement, it was the same one which Kimi had had a decent poke at. Adam fell to the floor, with blood seeping from above his eyes, his nose, and chin. Cyril pulled Malik away before he attempted another blow. Adam was out cold and twitching. The men looked at each other in stunned silence. Adam didn't see the blows coming or stand a chance. Even the fight with the Albanian wasn't as brutal as this.

But Kelly seemed totally indifferent to the punishment meted out, seeing this as some recompense for what Adam had done to her men. She walked around the bed and pulled her brother into the living room. She felt his whole body shaking. "Calm down, Malik. It's all right. We'll find her."

Malik sat on the sofa with his face in his hands. All he could think of was his little sister frightened and alone somewhere. Then he had a thought. "Jean. Where is she? I bet she has her!"

Cyril and Frank watched over Adam, and as soon as he showed signs of coming around, they grabbed his arms and pulled him to his wobbly feet and sat him on the bed. Adam was battered and knew it. For the first time in his life, he had taken a beating that shook him.

Cyril must have been telepathic, for he asked, "Where's Jean?"

Adam tried to focus but one eye was completely closed and the other was blurred. He wasn't going to argue. He'd had enough. "I threw her out yesterday. She left around four o'clock. I ain't seen her since, and I swear, I ain't seen the kid."

"Where did she say she was going?" asked Blakey.

Adam coughed, as the blood started to trickle down the back of his throat. "As if I care? She didn't say. I told her to leave her keys and do one."

Malik could hear what was being said and returned to the bedroom.

Trying to focus, Adam could just make him out standing there. He was angry with himself, letting a kid beat him like that.

"Malakai, I haven't got your sister, nor the fuck do I want her. Ya mother left yesterday. I need you and her like a hole in the head. Now, all of ya can fuck off. I didn't deserve this."

Kelly jumped forwards, an inch from his face. "Oh yeah, ya did! You cut me men and ya threatened me brother, so you fucking deserve to get a fucking bullet through ya thick head. So, thank your lucky stars, you ain't dead. If I find out that you had anything to do with Star going missing, I will personally see to it that you will be choking on ya own bollocks!"

Adam held his breath. Kelly's perfume pervaded the room. But he sensed her anger more, which was surging like molten lava. He couldn't get his head around the fact that this woman was acting and talking like a man. It grated on him that she had so much credence, but right now, he wasn't about to argue. He would keep his mouth shut and bide his time. They would pay for this — one day.

CHAPTER TWELVE

It was seven o'clock by the time they all returned to the mansion. Malik was beside himself with worry and his face showed it. Keffa remained quiet until they pulled up in the drive, when he grabbed Kelly's arm, delaying her from getting out. Malik didn't notice, and he joined Cyril for the next plan.

"What's up, Keffa?"

Keffa looked at Kelly with concern and then cleared his throat. "Are you sure about this Malakai fella?"

Kelly frowned and gave Keffa a look of disgust. "You what?" she spat.

"Well, come on, Kel, you saw him back there, like a fucking raging bull. I'm concerned he's another Eddie Raven. That temper, that rage—"

Whatever Keffa intended to say, the words were drowned out. Kelly could feel the blood surging through her body. As much as she loved Keffa, he was treading on extremely thin ice. "Oh yeah! And what? I ain't got a temper!" she spat at him again. She shrugged his hand away. "I suppose it's all right for me to have a temper like me father did, but I have a cute arse and fucking tits, so that makes it all right, does it?" The emotional temperature was rising, with every syllable which came from Kelly's mouth. She shot him a burning glare. "I am well aware that he has a temper and that he looks like fucking Eddie. So do I! But let me tell you, Keffa, he has a heart of gold!"

Keffa's expression softened and he put his hands up in surrender. "Okay, okay, I get what you're saying. But you don't know anything about him. Ya can't just take him on as family." Those words packed a punch, and she felt as though she'd been given a karate kick to the solar plexus by her former instructor, Terry Lawrence.

"You listen to me and listen well! Malik's the only blood relative I've got in this world. His mother is a cunt, as was mine, and if you think fighting to earn money to bring up three little sisters ain't kind-hearted, then you need to pull ya fucking head out of ya arse. I wear the sins of me father and so does that kid, but here's the thing, see. We ain't Eddie Raven, we are different people. Malik can fight, but, Keffa, is he fighting you or me? Nah, he's fighting for those kids. So, in my book, that makes him special, and I, for one, am proud to be his sister, and no one, and I fucking mean no one, will get in the way of that!"

Keffa was astounded by this outburst. She had never spoken to him like that before and it cut him deeply. He sucked his teeth and allowed her to get out of the car. He remained seated, watching her flick her long hair and march like a madam to the mansion. He loved her with all his heart, but he wasn't happy. She'd said, in so many words, that she would put Malakai before anyone. Well, it was pretty obvious that that included him. He felt very empty. They had been through so much together. He'd rescued her – really prevented serious harm to her on several occasions, only a year or so ago, when she'd had confrontations with her father. This didn't seem right at all. For now, though, he would suck it up and keep his mouth shut.

Mary was in the hallway, talking to the men. She had made a telling discovery that along with Star's coat her wellies were missing.

"If Jean or anyone came in and snatched Star, they wouldn't fuck about with coats and boots," pointed out Blakey.

Cyril nodded in agreement. "'Ere, get me dogs and Star's clothes."

Frank shook his head. "Aw, fuck me, Cyril, ya plonker, those animals are Rotties, not bloodhounds. I think we'd best call the filth."

Malik was racking his brains and then a thought entered his head. "Hold on, Cyril has a point. Those dogs love playing with Star. We should try it. But whatever we do, we need to do it now. I can't stand this. All this waiting around is doing me head in."

Kelly put her arm around his shoulders. "Babe, we *will* find her. Look, it's not cold, so if she went out in the night, she won't have frozen to death."

Malik thought about her words and he took comfort from them. Once he'd fetched Star's favourite jumper and let the dogs sniff it, they were itching to go outside. Everyone took different directions, calling Star's name. Stein was charging full steam ahead and then he stopped and chased a rabbit. Cyril was angry. He had never had a real family of his own, and so the arrival of Malik and the girls brought a new meaning to his life. For some reason, he was particularly attached to the little ones and the thought of Star being harmed or worse made him terrified. Now, Stein was pissing him off. "You fuckwit of a dog, go and find Star!" he hollered. Stein stopped in his tracks, and it was as if he knew what Cyril was saying. He began weaving in and out of the trees. Keffa was close by, so Cyril called to him. "Keffa, get your legs moving and follow Stein. I can't bleedin' keep up!" Out of breath and wheezing, Cyril knew he was out of condition.

235

Keffa was not happy that his new handmade leather shoes and bespoke suit were getting covered in the thick grey mud, but he knew he was fit and could outrun all of them. He chased after the dog, hoping that the animal didn't do a U-turn. He was afraid of dogs, always had been, in fact. Stein was still running until finally he was out of sight. Keffa followed in the direction the dog took. He thought it was all a bit mad; they were not equipped to go on a missing person hunt, so why hadn't they called the police? Then, he spotted Stein sniffing around a tree and beside it there was a bright pink coat. He hurried over, slipping and sliding on the wet leaves, and stopped when he reached the pink object. His heart was in his mouth, when he looked down. He didn't want to touch the child who was curled in a ball. She was motionless, with her face buried between her knees and propped up against a tree. He bent down and whispered her name although he was convinced she was dead. There was no answer. Stein nudged her with his nose, but she still didn't move. He nudged her again and then Keffa saw her slowly lift her head. The sense of relief was overwhelming, and he screamed, "She's here! She's here!"

Star peered up, shivering. All she saw was a big dark-skinned man with green eyes, until she focused on Stein. She knew then she was safe from the bogeyman and the wild animals of the night.

"Come on, darlin', let's take you to your brother, hey?" His voice was soft and gentle, and his big smile was a comforting sign. Star put her arms out for Keffa to pick her up like a baby.

Her huge round eyes were tired and sad. "Fank you," she whispered.

Keffa felt his heart melt; she was so cute and sweet. Now in his arms, she hugged him. He'd never held a child before and the

236

sweetness of her turned him weak at the knees. "Are you okay, Star? Are you hurt?"

Star laid her head on his shoulder. "I can't move me foot. I can't find me bruvver. He ran away in the woods." She choked back a tear.

Holding her tighter, he scrambled his way over the raised slippery roots and towards the open field. "Don't worry, darlin', your brother's here. He's looking for you."

Cyril had heard Keffa and was already on his phone giving the others the news. It was Malik who tore back across the field to meet Keffa. His face was tear-stained, and as soon as he reached them, he took Star and fell to his knees with her in his arms. He cried like a baby, holding and rocking her. "I thought you were … Oh my God, Star, I thought I had lost you!" The tears streamed down his face, as he kissed her head a hundred times.

Keffa stepped back – he wondered how he could have been so wrong about Malakai.

Malik looked up at Keffa, and there was so much warmth in his expression. "Thank you, Keffa, thank you so very much."

Mary made everyone a cup of hot chocolate and encouraged Star to drink hers. Although it had been a warm night for October, by the time they had found Star in the early hours, the temperature had fallen considerably because of the clear skies. Star was frozen and very weak. Her ankle looked slightly swollen, but once she had warmed up and had virtually forgotten about those dark shapes and scary sounds in the dead of night, she managed to stand without any assistance. She was fussed over by all of them, but it was Sassy and Tilly who held each of her hands, as they waited for Mary to take her off to bed.

"So, Malik, what were you doing last night?" asked Cyril.

All eyes were on him, as he relived the whole scene. "I had to go and see who was dead and if Jean was telling the truth. It was Kimi lying there, the girl I met who worked at the store, the one who gave us food and stuff last Christmas. I suspected it." His voice cracked, as he choked, "She was our saviour, ya know. She was just a kid! Why the fuck did someone kill her? I can't leave her there, it's not right. Her cold body being eaten by all the wild life, it's fucking wicked."

"Well, son, we've two choices. We bury her ourselves or we call the Ol' Bill. But, Malik, if we do that, you'll get pulled in for it, that's a dead cert."

"Then, so be it. I didn't kill her, bless her heart." Malik looked at Kelly. "Kel, will you look after the girls until I get out of the nick?"

Kelly nodded. "It goes without saying. Like I said, they're my family now."

Malik nodded. "I mean, if for whatever reason they do me for it, will ya …"

Kelly spoke for him. "Listen, Malik, you didn't do it, and if you do go down for it, then you have my word. The girls will stay with me."

After much deliberation, as to what was to be said, they all agreed to call the police, and at that point, Frank and Blakey left. After all, they'd had no part in it. Cyril had to swallow hard because he hated the filth, as he called them, more than anyone. Kelly stayed upstairs with Keffa and the girls. She was on their radar, but luckily for her, they never had anything on her, although the police knew full well she was running a tight ship.

≪*≫

It was Detective Superintendent Valerie Campbell, a woman in her early forties, who was to head the case, and as soon as the call came in, she was like a rat up a drain pipe. Her eyes nearly popped out of her head when she realised that the person reporting a serious incident was staying at Cyril Reardon's place. A team was called in, the cottage taped off, and forensics instructed to go in there within the hour. Deciding not to wait for a report or even to see if it was true, she flew up the drive of Cyril's mansion, in a confident mood. Her colleagues were all men and it was hard climbing to the top. She had to prove her worth every single day. This case was a special one because Cyril Reardon was somehow involved, and she wanted nothing more than to take down that firm. They had run amok for over thirty years. Since she became a police constable in London, their names would crop up on a fairly regular basis, and now she was a superintendent, she was determined to have them convicted. She'd never compromised her integrity by taking a backhander, unlike some of her colleagues, yet she was capable of far worse. She strongly suspected who the rogue officers were, though, and who, in particular, was in the pocket of Cyril Reardon.

The name Malakai River didn't come up on any database. He wasn't a known villain and had never even been pulled in on any suspected charge. In her mind, Malakai River was probably one of Reardon's men who had escaped any form of capture.

Mary answered the door and politely invited the superintendent in. Campbell gazed around the ornate, spacious entrance hall. This was a slap in the face for her, knowing that Cyril was not only a Face but one who had landed himself a fucking estate to boot.

"Please follow me into the drawing room. Malakai is waiting. I will fetch some refreshments," said Mary.

Campbell was annoyed. She wanted to go in wearing her air of authority, but instead, she was having to be polite in observing the pleasantries. She didn't do nice, especially when she was on a mission to convict Reardon, the devious bastard. And to add insult to injury, she felt insignificant, being asked to follow the maid.

The drawing room was just as grand as the hall and had money seeping from every grain of wood. Malik was sitting by one of the tall windows on a high back chair. He didn't look nervous; in fact, he appeared calm and collected.

Campbell had forgotten about the officers who were supposed to meet her here. She was too intent on getting inside and grilling Malakai River and Cyril Reardon. She was surprised to see the young man stand up and approach her with his hand outstretched to greet her formally. It knocked her off guard.

"Hello, I am Malakai River, but you can call me Malik."

Campbell stared for a second, as she appraised the man. Malakai looked young, and yet his approach was mature. "Yes, Superintendent Campbell." Her handshake was cold and perfunctory, and she deliberately avoided eye contact.

She expected a negative reaction, with her cold and deliberate response, but instead, he replied, "Thank you for coming. Please, do take a seat. I assume Mary will be bringing in refreshments."

Campbell wanted to soften. His expression and that glint in his eyes stirred something inside her, a strange déjà vu feeling. Nevertheless, she was a prig and her emotions were put to the side.

240

The upward climb through her career had made her bitter, and over the years, she'd developed a habit of looking down on people. One of her ex-Met colleagues, Detective Inspector Spencer, had once referred to her as a bolshie vamp, which she'd wryly taken as a compliment.

As she sat opposite, Malakai noticed she was concise with her movements and her cold expression would make a clock stop cold. She wasn't much of a looker, with sharp pointy features and her hair tied back in a ponytail. Yet she didn't appear interested in improving her appearance by paying careful attention to her facial features or by wearing a well-thought-out outfit either. With not even a dusting of make-up and dressed in a rather bland suit and wearing flat shoes, she didn't look the sort of person who was interested in using her femininity to gain advantage in what was still a male-dominated police force.

Campbell pulled from her briefcase a notebook and pen, still avoiding looking at the young man sitting there.

She then went over the notes taken from the call he made to the station. Malik watched her as she methodically scanned the meticulously written pages. At last, she looked up and studied him properly. She noticed how downbeat he was, as if he was reliving the moment when he'd relayed to the officer taking the call that his mother had said there was a dead girl in the cottage.

"Tell me, Malakai, why are you here, and what is your connection with Mr Reardon?"

Malik's expression changed in an instant and he smirked. "He's my manager!"

Campbell sat upright. "Oh, is he?" Her heart did a flutter with this unexpected revelation. This was it; she would squeeze from him all the

241

knowledge Malakai had about the firm. He was young enough to manipulate: this would be a walk in the park.

"What do you mean by 'my manager'?" she asked.

"I am training to be a boxer." Malakai had been given strict advice by Cyril to be careful in what he told the superintendent and to reveal as little information as possible.

"Tell me about this career choice and what is your relationship with Mr Reardon?"

It was an open-ended question to get him talking. It was very cleverly worded too, but even though Malik lacked much formal education, he had acquired an inner cunning which had stood him in good stead. And behind this false *façade* was a steely determination to give this officer a run for her money.

"Mr Reardon likes boxing, I like boxing, and that's it, really."

Campbell paused, waiting for more; she had developed this knack that the longer she managed the pauses the more likely she could intimidate the interviewee. She had learnt that when she'd worked under DI Spencer. Malik waited for the next question.

She'd hardly opened her mouth when her phone rang. Hastily, she took the call with an annoyed tone in her voice. "Yes!" she snapped.

Malik watched her raise her eyebrows, and she stared at him with a smug look on her face. "Thank you." She placed the phone back in her bag. "Well, it looks like your mother was telling the truth. There *is* a body of a young woman in your home. She's been there for four days, according to the forensics team. So, Malakai, where were you four days ago?"

Malik didn't flinch or even blink, which Campbell found strange.

"I was here. I have been for the last five days."

"Why?"

Malik knew this was the point at which he would have to explain himself, and he suspected it would sound odd. He clasped his hands together and took a deep breath. "My muvver left me and my three sisters twelve months ago. I had to bring them up." He paused to gauge the look on Campbell's face. She nodded for him to carry on.

"Well, then, she turned up at the cottage and threatened to take my youngest sister, Star. When I told her to leave, she then told me her boyfriend, a man called Adam Carter, would come, as he was the father, and take Star, whether I liked it or not. I didn't know her boyfriend personally, and in a panic, I called Mr Reardon to help me take the children away for their own safety. Then, yesterday morning, my muvver turns up here telling me there's a dead girl in the cottage, and unless I handed over Star, she would call the police. But, at first, I thought she was joking, and I didn't think much of it. So, this morning, I thought it best that I call you guys."

Campbell surveyed closely his expression and listened intently to his words. His face gave nothing away and his tone was matter-of-fact. It didn't add up. But the name Adam Carter was a name she knew very well; another villain with shit for brains. She would deal with him later, but for now, she wanted to find anything to link Reardon to the dead girl. He would be her biggest catch and it was a long time coming.

Mary came in carrying a tray full of biscuits and cups of tea. "There you go, love, help yourself. There are officers at the door. Shall I show them in?"

This woman is really doing my head in, with all these niceties, thought Campbell. She waved her hands, summarily dismissing Mary, as if she was just an annoying fly. This angered Malik. He may have been brought up by a wacky hippy, but he'd still managed to observe that kindness should be reciprocated. He clenched his fists, trying to control his temper, and then he smiled at Mary.

"Thank you so much, Mary. You're too kind."

Campbell realised she had been overly rude by her dismissive manner and heard in Malakai's voice the first sign of annoyance and a lack of respect for her. After a few further questions, she abruptly sat up straight, glaring fiercely at him.

"I now need to speak with Cyril, while you wait with my officers."

Malik nodded. "I am sure that will be okay with *Mr Reardon*." He emphasised the words Mr Reardon.

There was no question in her mind that he found her rude. Campbell smirked back at Malik; she knew she'd got up his nose, and that was, in effect, her *modus operandi,* when interviewing potential villains. Anger and upset made them react. It usually produced the desired effect in bringing the truth out of people.

She gazed around the room, whilst Malik went to fetch Cyril. Her eyes then focused on the huge portrait of the man in all his finery. *Good God*, she thought, *he looks so absurd, like Heathcliff out of Wuthering Heights.* She had to quickly suppress a giggle, even though she was not in a laughing mood.

When Cyril arrived, she blatantly looked him up and down, as if he were a pile of shit. He, however, smiled genially as if nothing was amiss. In fact, he was totally unperturbed by her act of authority. He was used to jumped-up coppers, all itching to take him down.

"Before I take you all down to the station, you and I will have a nice little chat." Her voice was laced with sarcasm.

Meanwhile, officers were waiting with Malakai outside the drawing room. They had been given strict instructions back at the station and so didn't question her; she was too quick to shout them down.

"So, Cyril, tell me what was Malakai doing here? I mean, a girl is found dead in his cottage. From the forensics, we have learnt that she died about four days ago. Strangely enough, Malakai tells me he has been here for five days. It's all a bit odd, don't you think?"

Malik, from the hallway, heard her strident tones and wanted to jump in, but instead he stayed calm, bit his lip, and observed.

"Correct me if I'm wrong, but I don't remember us being buddies, so cut out the friendly first-name business. It's Mr Reardon to you," growled Cyril.

Campbell felt her hair stand on end. Her expression hardened, but Cyril returned a sarcastic smile.

"No, I don't think it's odd at all, Superintendent. The boy was threatened by his mother and he came here to keep his sisters out of harm's way."

Campbell chortled, "Come on, *Mr Reardon*, this whole picture stinks, and you know it."

Cyril turned to her, his face enraged at the insinuation and by her childish manner. "No, darling, but you wanna make it stink because

245

that's your fucking job. That kid came here five days ago, protecting his family. What happened at the house after that has nothing to do with him. I can vouch for that and so can me housekeeper. So, you can bark up the wrong tree all ya like."

"Well, I expected no less. You all stick together, you and your lot." She stood up and walked towards him.

"I don't like your accusations, madam, and I suggest you watch ya tongue, 'cos saying things like that gets you into trouble."

Superintendent Campbell stiffened her back, expressing outrage. "Are you threatening me, Mr Reardon?"

Cyril laughed. "Threatening you? No, love! But I am suggesting you'll get a right going over from your governor, if you start all this malarkey. So, stop playing silly games, and go and look for the real killer, unless, of course, the girl died of natural causes."

Malik could just make out Cyril's expression and hear him from his vantage point in the hall. He was surprised to see that Cyril's whole attitude to the detective had changed almost in the blink of an eye. The cheeky one-liners and laid-back attitude – which were such an integral part of who Cyril was – were missing. Now, Malik saw something else entirely – a look of animosity, coated with antagonism and steeped in confidence.

Valerie Campbell had stupidly assumed she could handle the likes of Reardon and his crew; even so, she'd been warned by all her predecessors that they were hard nuts to crack. The only breakthrough they'd had was when they found Eddie Raven dead in his house. Eddie had the worst reputation; he was a nasty piece of work and originally worked under the Reardon umbrella. She had met Eddie in the past and was unsettled by his whole conduct. If she was truthful to herself, she would have to admit that she'd been seriously sexually attracted to the man, even though at the time he was unstable and a danger to society.

She attended the funeral of Kelly's mother, but really it had been more for her own nosiness than anything else and not at her superior's behest. Reardon along with his cronies Frank and Blakey were all there. She knew they had checked her out because they could smell the police a mile away. She'd got a kick out of being there too, although, had she but known it, no one was bothered in the least; she was nothing in their eyes, just a wannabe commissioner, shrouded in self-importance.

"I shall want to interview the housekeeper and Malakai's sisters."

Cyril nodded. "Yep, ya can talk to Mary, but not the girls. They ain't old enough." His tongue was sharp; she had definitely hit a nerve.

"Oh dear, I guess I'll have to call social services." She waited for a reaction: there was none.

"If you're thinking that the social services need to be involved to question the kids, and I guess you are assuming that Malakai is their unofficial guardian, then you're mistaken. They *have* a legal guardian."

Campbell shot her jaw forward in frustration. "Oh yeah, and who might that be?"

Cyril paused for a moment. It hadn't been his intention to involve Kelly. The less attention drawn towards her, the better, in his view. You could never tell with this lot. Any pretext, and you could almost guarantee that they would be sniffing around the woman's businesses like flies around shit.

"Some relation of Malakai's has guardianship and a residential order, I believe. And if you need to question his six and eight-year-old sisters, then rest assured, I will be in that interview room with you."

Campbell frowned. "And what about the third sister? Only Malakai said he has three sisters."

Cyril was now irritated by the poker-faced woman. "Ya mean Saskia? Yeah, well, you can question her, as she is seventeen, but only if I am present," he conceded, with a dark frown on his face.

Campbell tilted her head to the side. "You seem to have a keen interest in these girls. Anything you want to tell me?"

Cyril felt his anger rising. *What an absolute piss-take.* She was pushing her luck and pressing his buttons. But years of being questioned by the police made him an expert in dealing with any kind of officialdom. He kept his cool and smiled. "Yeah, of course I do. They are innocent little kiddies with a tough past, and I wanna make sure they have a good future. They deserve that much after what their mother has put them through. But, see, the likes of you wouldn't understand that because you don't live in the real world, do you? I might be who I am, and we both know what that is, but don't tar the family with the same brush."

Campbell rolled her eyes. "Really, Mr Reardon, and you are their knight in shining armour?"

"Well, darlin', I ain't the grim reaper. Look, those kids have had it rough and that boy has done his best to care for them. So, do your job, find the real killer and leave that boy alone. You can have an interview with Mary, Saskia, and me, so you can tick the boxes, but then, do one, eh?"

248

"Oh, trust me, Mr Reardon, I will be crawling all over this place and right under your skin, until I get what I want. Mark my words."

"No doubt you will, and mark *my* words, all the time you spend sniffing in the wrong places, the real killer will be living it up and probably drinking to your incompetence. Are we done?"

Campbell sniffed the air and looked down her thin pointed nose. "Right, enough of this. My officers will take you, your housekeeper, and the older children down to the station for questioning."

"No need. I will drive us there. You see, they will be only too willing to help, so, as I see it, they are doing you a favour, right?"

She knew she had nothing. The interviews would have to be by the book, since Cyril's crew had the best solicitor and wouldn't stand for any nonsense.

As soon as she left, Cyril got to work. He called Michael Delmonte. "All right, Mike, it's Cyril. I need ya down the nick. I'll meet you in fifteen."

Delmonte was semi-retired now and only dealt with a few clients. A hard-faced man in his sixties, tall, broad-shouldered, and with a full head of grey hair and dressed impeccably, he was so meticulous that he could have the station wrapped around his little finger. He was the superintendent's worst nightmare. As the solicitor entered the station, the officers looked at each other, as if to say, "Here we go."

Sassy's emotions were at screaming point, angry and frustrated that they had taken her brother away but more afraid of the possible outcome. Cyril winked at her. "Listen, babe, you just tell the truth, everything you know, and it will all be fine. Oh, but don't mention

Kelly. Just tell them ya mother came here and told us there was a corpse in the cottage."

Sassy almost spluttered – she wanted to laugh at the madness of it all and the way Cyril was so down-to-earth. "Yeah, don't worry about me."

Cyril nodded. "Just think before ya speak, 'cos ol' vinegar tits is one spiteful bitch, and she will want to pin this on someone, as soon as she can. 'Cos, ya see, there are two types of women in the police force: there are those that sleep their way to the top, and, by the looks of her, the ol' prune fucking face, that ain't gonna to 'appen, and then there are those that are so fucking determined to have as many captures under their belt as they can, they will fight their way up, and that, my darlin', is her to a T."

"I'll keep schtum, don't worry."

Cyril pinched her cheek and winked.

At the police station, Michael Delmonte and Cyril shook hands. Cyril gave him the whole story in preparation.

"Cyril, I'll have them out of here within the hour. I would have said half an hour, but that new super, Campbell, is a keen cow. If she gets a whiff that these kids are anything to do with Kelly, then she'll be all over them."

Cyril took a deep breath. "Oh, is that so?"

Delmonte nodded, and his intense eyes narrowed. "DI Spencer from the Met warned me that Campbell is looking for promotion and wants to bag the big fish. She was after Eddie Raven for years, and now he's dead, she has her eye on Kelly. But, Cyril, she has nothing on her, and she knows it."

"Mike, I'd better warn ya. Malakai is Kelly's brother, Eddie Raven's son, although they don't have the same surname. I'll let you see for yaself, mate."

"Oh, I see. That's why she wanted guardianship?"

Cyril slowly nodded. "Those kiddies have had a hard time, and they are good kids an' all."

"Getting soft in ya old age?"

"Fucking looks like it."

Cyril waited with Mary and Sassy in the waiting room, whilst Delmonte signed in.

The interview room hadn't changed in twenty years, although the tape recorder had been replaced with a digital one. As soon as Delmonte entered, Superintendent Campbell stood up. With her flushed face and her teeth bared in an angry grimace, she looked an intimidating sight. He didn't say a word. He removed his expensive suit jacket and placed it over the back of the chair. Then, he reached in his briefcase for a legal pad before sitting down next to his client. His glare across at Campbell made her feel very uneasy. Despite extensive experience in putting away all the criminals she could, she had yet to meet another lawyer who could match Michael Delmonte's reputation and formidable legal skills. He wasn't cheap either: for this hour alone, he was probably paid more than what she would take home in a week.

"We are about to start the interview."

Delmonte shook his head. "No, you're not. You're about to leave, so my client and I may have a few words. He needs to sign some papers first. You know the drill."

Campbell, once again, felt uncomfortable and intimidated. She hated Delmonte with a passion. If it wasn't for him, she would have been made her present grade years ago. She had Frank Marsden banged to rights, until he pulled the entrapment card. It transpired she couldn't produce the requisite paperwork to show she had a warrant of any kind or a court order for surveillance. Campbell slammed the door behind her. Delmonte turned sideways to face his client and was immediately caught off guard. The resemblance to Eddie Raven was surreal.

Staring impassively at the boy for a second, he smiled, which softened his businesslike face, and then he got to work. "Right, Malakai, I'm your brief, Michael Delmonte. Cyril called me."

Malik shook his hand pleasantly and the lawyer noticed it was a firm grip. He thought this was a good start. The lad had made an instant impression on him.

Malik nodded. "Pleased to meet ya."

Delmonte noticed his cool expression and conduct. "I knew ya ol' man."

"I didn't! A right bastard, by all accounts!"

Delmonte's eyes twinkled at this and he gave a wry smile. "Yep, no argument there. He certainly was. Anyway, two things. First, I'm going to give you a crash course in lawyer-client confidentiality. You can tell me anything you like, and it is between us. In lawyer-speak, it is called the lawyer-client privilege. You could have killed the poor lass

252

and even tell me about it. But I am governed by the privilege and so cannot reveal anything you don't want me to. Second, when they ask you a question, you look at me. I will nod, if you should answer, or I will interrupt, if I need you to say nothing. Keep your answers short, don't ramble on."

≈*≈

Valerie Campbell was pacing the floor. She was suffering from a hangover and could have kicked herself. She hadn't been assigned to an interesting case in a while, not one she could get her teeth into, and so last night she'd drunk a bottle of vodka, going through old photos. Her life had been so consumed by reaching the top, she had neglected the fact that her biological clock had ticked away, and with no husband or children, she was a lonely woman, with just a cat to keep her company.

There was something else bugging her. It was Malakai. He reminded her so much of Eddie, it was playing tricks on her mind. Perhaps she was going mad after all. She could never get over Eddie and was only too relieved and pleased he was dead, as she could then pretend that her lust for him all that time ago was a distant memory. But, in reality, her vibrator had his name on it. Seeing Cyril and now Eddie's lawyer, Delmonte, had brought back a fantasy, and she was, in a peculiar way, envisioning this boy, with his green smoky eyes, to be Eddie.

≈*≈

The Superintendent entered the interview room, feeling hot under the collar. Whenever she felt uncomfortable, which was now, her neck and face would start to glow red, as if she were a teenager meeting her first date. It was acutely embarrassing, and in her profession, it did her no favours.

253

Sitting opposite Michael Delmonte and Malakai River, and once she could see they were ready, she turned on the recorder. "Please state your name for the record."

Malik did as he was told, and as the interview went on, he saw no reason to look at Michael. The questions were straightforward, and he answered as required, with short one-word responses, until she asked what his relationship with his mother was like. He looked at his hands and pushed himself back in the chair.

"I dunno, really, but she isn't like other mums, that's for sure." He glanced at his lawyer, who nodded encouragingly for him to continue.

"She isn't a good muvver, that's a fact. She's a bit drippy. When she was at home, she always left me to look after me sisters."

"And how did you do that, Malakai?"

Delmonte spotted the subtext and intervened. "Irrelevant, Superintendent. That has nothing to do with this, so cut the psychological interrogation, please."

Campbell's hackles rose. She didn't like his tone. "Well, it does actually. You see, he lied to the authorities, he lied to the school, so, Malakai, what else are you lying about?"

Malik smirked at the question, but he didn't lose his temper. In fact, he was really enjoying this interview and knew that he had a solid lawyer beside him which gave him confidence. So, instead, he relaxed his shoulders and said, "I never lied, I just didn't inform anyone that we were alone. I did my best. I made sure we were safe, well fed, warm, and *together*." He hoped the emphasis on 'together' would steer her on to other matters.

254

"Where is your mother, Malakai?"

Malik shrugged his shoulders. "Dunno."

For a second, Campbell lost her train of thought. Images of Eddie were appearing all over her mind like a rash. The experience was uncanny to say the least. Looking now at the young man, she was seeing Eddie almost as if he were alive: there before her was his cool expression and that same intensity in his eyes. She tried to swallow, but her mouth was dry, and out of pure impulse, she said, "Did you know who Eddie Raven was?" No sooner were the words out of her mouth, she regretted asking the question.

Malik smiled at her. Shrewdly, he'd already picked up on the vibes coming off the superintendent, and he could hardly not notice how flushed her face and neck were. *Wow*, he thought, *had she really fancied his father?*

She had a hunch she saw Malakai wink. Her heart was beating so fast, her mind went into a spin, and her damned neck, she knew, would be redder than ever. *How embarrassing*, she thought.

"No," he replied.

She knew then he was lying; he was far too composed.

She had nothing to go on; she couldn't hold him any longer and had to let him go, yet her bullshit monitor was telling her there was something not quite right.

The interview with Saskia proved to be just as unsatisfactory. Cyril said little, yet it backed up Malakai's statement. Mary's interview yielded nothing useful.

After the interviews had been concluded, Campbell was on her way to her office, when she saw Cyril Reardon walking towards her. She looked him up and down. "No doubt, Mr Reardon, I will be seeing you again. You can bank on it," spat the superintendent.

"Well, next time, do me a favour. Slap a bit of make-up on, 'cos honestly, woman, you're enough to give me nightmares."

❧*❧

Once they had left the station, she called DI Sampson to join her. They were going to pay Adam Carter a visit.

Sampson gritted his teeth. He was supposed to have landed the job of superintendent and was bitter. His little indiscretion had pushed him to the back of the queue. He knew who had grassed him, and she was standing there in front of him. He did smile, however, because for once she looked worried. Her eyes were glassy, and a thin layer of greasy sweat covered her forehead. Something was bothering her. He didn't care; if she fucked this up, then her days were over, and he would be wearing her shoes.

Adam's apartment was on the top floor of three. A single block, it was set in attractive gardens. The properties below were not occupied; they were bought purely for their investment potential, so he was there alone, and that's just how he liked it. The squad car waited outside and DI Sampson along with Campbell climbed the stairs. As soon as they reached the top, they stopped dead in their tracks. The door to Adam's apartment was off its hinges, and there, in front of them, was blood up the wall. Sampson radioed down to the officers waiting in the car. "Call for backup."

Campbell was inside first, walking towards the claret which had splattered across one wall. Then she saw him behind the sofa, slumped

256

in a sitting position, with a bullet through his head and the back of his skull gone. Two officers shot up the stairs. The youngest PC almost threw up on the spot at the gruesome sight of Adam Carter. They searched through all the rooms and found no other person inside.

"Right, all out! Call forensics!" she commanded, and then, as she whirled around to leave, she spotted a gun thrown on the sofa. "Sampson, I think we have our murder weapon, and I can guarantee that Carter hasn't been dead for more than an hour."

Sampson stared at the corpse and agreed; the blood was still fresh and dripping onto the carpet.

"Well, whoever did this, it was personal. Not a contract killing. Look at the bruises on his face. They certainly worked him over pretty thoroughly," Campbell remarked.

Campbell took one last look and realised she'd made a mistake by stating the obvious. Of course, it was personal. Contract killers don't usually mark their victims, they shoot and leave. The whole Eddie thing was messing with her head. She really needed to get a grip, or she would fuck things up. "Right, I want the area outside swarming with officers, I want neighbours questioned, CCTV footage looked at, and no one entering here until forensics have done their job. I'm going to get to the bottom of this, and I bet that Cyril Reardon is somewhere in the middle of it all."

Sampson knew she was probably right because he'd heard that some of Kelly Raven's firm had been assaulted by Adam Carter and no way would the likes of Cyril and Kelly let that go. He kept that nugget to himself. He wouldn't help Campbell; as far as he was concerned, if she wanted to wear the badge of superintendent, then she should show her worth and not rely on him to do her groundwork. He had a grudge, but she didn't know it.

257

Campbell was keen to find out the time of death; she wanted to pin this on someone and quickly. She and Sampson waited outside the apartment for the head of the forensics team, Alan Cartwright, who arrived five minutes later and made a determination at the scene. By using his thermometer, he could safely say the victim had died within the hour. The superintendent was pissed off that she couldn't directly blame this on Cyril though; he was being interviewed at the police station by her at that time. "Get that gun checked and report back to me ASAP."

Cartwright wasn't used to being spoken to in such an abrupt manner and he raised his eyebrows. "You will have the results when they're ready." He said no more and walked away. Campbell, though, was used to being snubbed by the team. It was par for the course. She put on this callous act, yet inside she had a burning desire to be respected for the right reasons and to see an affectionate smile every once in a while. No one liked her, except her cat.

Back at the station, Campbell called a meeting with the team. She stood by the big whiteboard and began writing notes and underlining names. Then, she turned around to find the sullen-looking faces. They were keen to get working on the two cases but not under her supervision.

"So, we have a Jane Doe, dead five days, awaiting the lab report, and Adam Carter, who was released from prison just a few months previously, found shot dead in his home around two to three hours ago."

"Is there a common denominator, Gov?" asked Victoria Hanson, the niece of the commissioner, who was a detective from the Met police assigned to the case. Campbell knew the one person in the room she needed to suck up to was her. A lower-ranking detective she may

258

be, but Hanson's credentials made her ideally placed to put in a good word.

"Good question, Hanson. At the moment, the answer is no. However, there are certain links between Adam Carter, Cyril Reardon, and Jane Doe."

She turned back to the board and wrote a list of names from left to right. Underneath, she recorded the names of Cyril Reardon, Malakai River, and Kelly Raven. She circled the first two names. "The dead girl was found at the home of Malakai River. Malakai was staying at Cyril Reardon's house at the time." She curled her two fingers, symbolizing it was not a known fact just yet. Then, she glared at Sampson. "And I have reason to believe that Adam Carter has a vendetta against Cyril Reardon and his firm."

Sampson bit his lip. *So, she'd done her homework, had she? Well, it was about time.* By the look she gave him, he could see that she'd marked his card for not handing over his knowledge of the situation. His informant had told him that there had been a fight quite recently at the Mitcham Mint at which Frank Marsden and Freddy Blake, otherwise known as Blakey, were present. DI Sampson was an old-school detective. He knew the villains, and as far as he was concerned, they had turned to the business of protection. Long gone were the days of bank jobs. Campbell wanted them all nicked and off the streets, but she had no idea what that would cause, and in his eyes, it would be one huge fuck-up.

"Gov, any clues as to why?" asked Hanson.

The superintendent would have torn into her, had she not been related to the commissioner, but instead she politely answered, "No, not yet. We'll have a clearer picture when we get the lab results. For now, I want everybody to hit the ground running. Call in all informants. I want surveillance on Reardon's place and their pubs and the club, and I want to know who has guardianship over those two River kids, Star and Chantilly ... fucking stupid names. Oh, and I want Jean River found and brought in for questioning."

CHAPTER THIRTEEN

Kelly had taken the kids to the Glades Shopping Centre. She thought a change of scene might help the youngsters to take their minds off all the drama. Keffa was quiet and almost moody.

"What's up, Keffa?" she asked.

"Look, Kelly, it's all very well playing fucking happy families, but I've got business to attend to, and so have you. Johnnie Carter has a wad waiting for us, and you have a shipment to dispose of. Taking your eye off the ball will leave you wide open."

Kelly smiled down at the two girls holding her hands. Their huge round eyes looked up at her, and she knew she had to hold in her annoyance. They were her family now. She might not know them, or Malik for that matter, but, nevertheless, they were hers. Keffa had been acting distant lately, by either demanding her attention or having serious mood swings. Both were pissing her off.

The toy store was just ahead of them. "Go and have a look around, girls, and stay together. I'll be in soon."

Tilly and Star giggled happily at each other and skipped away, leaving Kelly to it.

"In case you haven't noticed, there's a bigger problem at hand, and I intend to sort out my family first," she snarled at Keffa.

"Ya know what, Kelly? You've changed. I don't know you anymore."

Kelly narrowed her eyes. "Oh, for fuck's sake, I've only just met me brother. I'm trying to help him and his siblings. I guess that means you're on the back burner for a while. Well, I thought you were more man than that!"

Keffa stared down at her. "I'm not just talking about the last few days. I mean, the last year. You used to be so … It doesn't matter. I guess you are who you are meant to be." He kept his deep voice low, not wanting to draw attention.

"And what's that supposed to mean?"

Keffa shook his head. "Come on, Kel, it used to be me and you against the world. Now, it's you and a fucking army. I don't see you, and you never have time for me. You're always too busy jumping onto another scam. Now, it's this new-found family."

The trouble was, Kelly knew in some ways he was right; she really didn't have much time for him. Her business was growing exponentially into one of the biggest crime firms in the country and she was enjoying the challenges. It wasn't as if she had been in the life for very long. Not much time then to assimilate what was needed to learn quickly a fast-growing business and keep all the sharks out there at bay. It was full-on, twenty-four seven, and it took up her time emotionally as well. It was a big deal to her, but she guessed that Keffa would not see things from her perspective.

He was much older than her; in fact, he had just turned forty and had been in the life since he had left London School of Economics and Political Science (LSE). He was bright enough to have gone to Oxford University but had opted for LSE because his dear old mum had been having a few issues with her heart, and he wanted to stay close in Peckham.

And then there was her — who she was. She was a Raven, for good or bad. In fact, if she was true to herself, she had more Eddie Raven in her than not. The only difference was she was fair and not cruel. Aside from this, though, she could at least understand why her boyfriend was jealous of Malik and the girls because they would take up more of her time.

As she peered into his green eyes, she saw a vulnerable sadness and realised that she was hurting him, and yet there was something else. She thought she knew him well, but for the life of her, she couldn't fathom it at all: he seemed on edge, twitchy even.

They decided to call it a day and head back to Cyril's. The girls had enjoyed the shopping trip, and besides, she was anxious to find out how the others had got on down the nick. Malik was on her mind. She prayed they wouldn't try to pin the girl's death on him.

Mary had put on a big roast dinner. She wanted to ease the tension in the home. They were all there, waiting for news on the dead girl. Malik knew he was innocent and hoped Campbell left them alone. As they were sitting around the table finishing their meal, Cyril's phone rang. Rising quickly from his seat, Cyril snatched it from the side cabinet. Everyone looked and watched him scrutinise the number. He lifted his finger to his lips, telling them to be quiet.

"Hello, me ol' son, what can I do ya for?"

Sampson whispered, "The superintendent is out to nick you. She's after promotion. Just a word of warning. Adam Carter is dead, a bullet through his head. Whoever did it, they left a gun behind. If there's a sniff that it was anything to do with you, the squad will be running all over your gaff. That never came from me, all right?"

Cyril took on a concerned expression. "Cheers, mate, I appreciate the heads-up. Keep me up to date." Quickly, Cyril turned to Kelly.

"Kel, call Frank and Blakey. I need me basement emptied. Adam Carter's dead and a gun was left at the scene. Sampson reckons the superintendent is after nicking me. Better be safe than sorry."

Kelly immediately rose from her seat. She knew exactly what Cyril kept down there, and it would lock him up for years. There was a complete arsenal of weapons, his pride and joy.

"Keffa, will ya go down to the garages? There's another Bentley. Bring it around the back."

Malik looked at Cyril. "What can I do?"

Cyril glanced at Kelly for permission. She straightaway switched off from thinking about the ramifications of this phone call to Cyril and nodded at him.

"Come with me, boy. Mary, keep the girls up here, will ya, love?"

Mary tried to look a picture of tranquillity, but butterflies were racing through her stomach. She couldn't recall a time when Cyril's nefarious activities had ever come home to roost, as it were. He was usually meticulous about keeping his affairs well away from his home. She assumed things were serious: he rarely called her Mary.

In contrast to Mary's feeling of doom, Malik was excited. Adrenaline was racing through his veins. He was now in the big boys' world and he was loving it. He followed Cyril down to the basement. As soon as Cyril pulled back the Persian rug, Malik could see a large door made from oak.

"Pull that up. It's a bit heavy for me." Cyril pointed to the inlaid lever to the trap door.

Although it was heavy, Malik managed to pull it open with ease. The staircase led to the lower basement, and as Malik clambered down, he was astounded firstly by the size of the room and secondly by the amount of arsenal. Even a REME officer would be impressed with the scale of things down here and by some of the specialist weaponry.

Cyril was behind him. "Right, boy, see those gloves? Put them on. We need to get this lot shifted pretty fucking quick."

Hastily, Malik put the gloves on and began to remove the guns from the upright boxes and fill the holdalls that Cyril had thrown his way.

"Cyril, what ya gonna do with 'em?"

"Stick 'em in the other Bentley for now. It's still licensed in Lord Chambers' nephew's name, so no one will frisk it."

Within an hour, Malik, Cyril, and Keffa had the basement cleaned out, with everything all neatly packed away in the massive boot of the old Bentley.

As soon as Frank and Blakey arrived, the latter drove the old car and its cargo off to a location that only the firm knew about.

Frank looked tired and yet perplexed. All this running around was taking its toll, and he was seriously thinking of retiring. "So, I reckon we're in for a war, then? Either the Carters are gonna come after us, because I bet ya bottom dollar, they'll think we shot Adam, or the filth will. Whichever way you look at it, some cunt's gonna come knocking."

The youngsters were taken to bed, leaving the others to have a discussion around the table.

In the coldness of it all, Mary was actually enlivened, after the earlier flutter of nerves. Working for the very old Lord Chambers had been rather dull and boring, although she hadn't really minded all the rules, and she had accepted that living and working here came with it responsibilities, and so maintaining etiquette at all times was a priority. When she was taken on, she just assumed that this type of life style was the acceptable way to live. Of course, she'd been an avid viewer of *Downton Abbey*, and so she knew all about how life worked both downstairs and upstairs. In fact, she could be a bit of a snob herself, when she was minded to. She showed off to her friends, when she went for tea, but really, her work life wasn't so exciting.

She came from Bethnal Green, one of the roughest parts of the East End, so living in a country manor was like a dream come true. However, when all was said and done, you can take the girl out of the East End, but you can't take the East End out of the girl. How true that was in Mary's case. And it was one of the reasons why she and Cyril got on so well, despite his piss-taking antics where she was concerned.

So, when Cyril won the estate in a game of poker, and she was offered the opportunity to keep her job as housemaid-cum-cook and general bottle washer, she agreed on the spot. However, she'd nearly had a nervous breakdown, when she learned who Cyril Reardon was, and, more to the point, what he represented. Did she *really* want to

266

work for someone who had earned himself something of a reputation almost on a par with the Kray twins? Therefore, working for Cyril was a far cry from Lord Chambers, and at first, she resented him. He couldn't be more different, what with his foul mouth and lack of decorum, but as the years rolled on, she found herself amused by him and began to enjoy the more laid-back style of running the house.

This present situation, however, was anything but boring. She would wake up and wonder what her day would bring. It was exciting as it was stressful, but now she felt she had a purpose; besides, it was easier for her to live in among the villains than the toffs. She could be herself. She tucked the children up in their beds and hurried back downstairs to make her special doorstep beef sandwiches with another one of her home-made chutneys. Her 'family' needed nourishing.

"Who do ya think shot him?" asked Kelly.

Frank laughed. "Could 'ave been anyone. He was one 'orrible cunt."

"Jean!" exclaimed Malik. All eyes were on him. Up until now in the discussions, he had kept his own counsel, as he wasn't part of their firm just yet. He knew when not to open his mouth, but he did believe Jean may have had something to do with it.

"Why do ya say that?" asked Kelly. Her tone was soft, when she spoke to her brother.

"Well, I reckon she's gone on the missing list 'cos that officer Campbell asked me twice where she was and if I knew where she might go. I can't remember everything she asked in that interview 'cos it went on for ages, but she did ask about Jean, that much I do recall."

A faint smile crossed Kelly's lips. "Malik, no disrespect, but she doesn't seem the type. I mean, she fucking shit herself when I chased her down the drive, so, as I see it, she's a fucking wimp."

Malik's expression dulled, as if he was thinking about her. "I think there's another side to her, ya know. She always comes across as a needy bird, always seeking fucking attention, but …" he stopped and glazed over. Everyone waited for him to continue.

"I think she killed someone once, when I was about fifteen. She was fucking the man that worked in the post office. Not many people knew about it, but I did. She sneaked out in the dead of night and would return in the morning." He paused again and looked at Kelly, who was urging him to go on.

"I followed her once, just out of interest. Well, I don't know why, really. She had a key to the bloke's flat and would let herself in. Then, one night, she came home with a right hump, banging and smashing around. She was pissed and mumbling to herself, saying, 'Thinks I'm a scrubber, eh? Well, I'll fucking show him, the cunt.' I remember the words because I thought the same. She *was* an old scrubber. Anyway, the next night, she crept out again, and I watched her through the bedroom window. She looked suspicious, peering up and down the road, and then she took off. I was gonna follow her again, but it was cold, and Star was wheezy that night. I assumed muvver was gonna go and make it up with him, but she returned an hour later. When I got up in the morning, she was asleep on the sofa, with an empty bottle of whisky next to her. The next day, the post office was shut because they'd found the guy dead in his bed. By all accounts, he'd died of a heroin overdose. It shocked the neighbourhood because no one had a clue he was even an addict."

Frank and Cyril looked at each other and nodded. Malik's suspicions seemed very plausible and fitted with what they knew about his mother. Jean's father, Marcus, used heroin as a form of weapon. She must have learnt that trick from him.

"Well, then, if that's the case, Jean's prints will be all over the gun, unless, of course, she wore gloves. Anyway, we need to be ready, just in case," advised Cyril.

Out of the blue, Keffa made his excuses to leave. He gave Kelly a quick kiss on the cheek and was gone. His silence throughout the dinner hadn't gone unnoticed. Cyril gripped Kelly's hand under the table. "Are you all right, my babe?"

Kelly gave him an awkward smile and nodded.

Frank knew it was time to leave them alone. It was obvious Kelly had something on her mind and it was more about Keffa than business.

"I'm gonna go and warn the lads to keep a keen eye. No doubt, the filth will be sniffing around."

Malik liked Frank, with his deep gruff voice and cool manner. "Anything I can do?" he asked, eager to be part of the action.

"Nah, boy, you sit tight and look after ya sisters. We'll have a better idea, once we get the word what's going on down the nick. Ol' Sampson will keep us informed." He patted Malik's back before he left.

Malik turned to Kelly. "Is everything all right, sis?"

Kelly wanted to cry. She was the tough one, the one in charge. Right now, however, she felt weak with uncertainty, and then, when Malik called her "sis", a name she had never been called before, it melted her heart.

"I dunno. Keffa's acting strange. He's moody and quiet. It's like I don't know him." Her voice was gritty with emotion.

Cyril got up and kissed the top of her head. "Listen, babe, he may have a lot on his mind. All this unrest can make a man preoccupied with his own thoughts. I mean, look at me. I'm like a fucking bear with a sore head, when I've a lot on my plate." He tried to make light of it, but it was apparent that Kelly was seriously hurting.

"No, before all this, he was quiet. Don't get me wrong, he ain't been 'orrible, just distant, I s'pose." She stared out of the window sadly and felt the glistening of tears about to form in her eyes.

"You ain't gotta stay with him ya know, if he's making you unhappy. You can fuck him off," suggested Cyril, who hated to see Kelly sad.

"Well, I've got a feeling that's what he wants."

Malik watched as his sister turned from some hard case to a soft and almost helpless child. He would look out for her, and if he found Keffa was up to no good, then he would give him the hiding of his life. No one hurt his sisters and got away with it.

"It's gonna be all right, sis. You've got us now. We might be a pain in the arse, but we're family." He put his arm around her shoulders and kissed her cheek.

Kelly was taken aback by this display of affection. *Her little brother wasn't so little now, was he?* she thought. Leaving her feelings for Keffa to one side for the moment, she realised she had family blood on her side. That amounted to a lot, in her mind.

❦*❧

Lacey was serving a pint to an old man who sat quietly in the corner of the pub. She had a face like a smacked arse and strutted about in her high stilettos, making more noise than she should.

Roy grabbed her arm. "What's the fucking matter with you, girl? Ya go out all hours, come and go as ya please, and when you're 'ere, you're either looking for the next shag or moping about. I'm still angry you defied my order to stay upstairs, when it all kicked off the day Keffa walked in on the Carters. I've had as much as I can stomach from you. Now, if you don't buck up your ideas, you can fuck off. You're too much like ya mother, the old whore."

Lacey shook her arm free and snarled, "You're just a bitter and twisted old man. Me mother fucked everyone in the pub 'cos you couldn't give her what she wanted. You're a useless excuse for a man. Call yaself a farver, eh? You're a wimp," mocked Lacey.

She would have gladly run off to live with her mother, but the truth of it was she had moved up north somewhere, and Lacey hadn't a clue where she was. She looked her father up and down and rolled her eyes. Why couldn't he be like the Faces who drank in the pub? He was such a feeble embarrassment, and she was totally ashamed of him. The only occasion she could be nice was when he dished out the dosh. Really, she had no respect for him at all. He knew it, of course, and the years of trying to hold on to her were gradually becoming more difficult. As much as she disrespected him, he saw her now for what she was. She was always on the lookout for a flash villain and saw him, her own father, as a waste of space.

It was no wonder, therefore, that the two were constantly at loggerheads with each other, and he certainly was beginning to loathe her. He wanted a quiet life, with all the pleasantries and the odd moment, when, in all honesty, he could look at his daughter and be

271

proud of who she had become. However, that was never going to happen: she was her mother's daughter all right, and for a long time, he had been worn down by the sniggering contempt and sneering comments from the local punters. Roy wanted nothing more than to slap her face. She was out of control and he knew it. From the day his wife had fucked off briefly with Tommy Lartan, a well-known crook, Lacey changed.

She was only thirteen years old, when to her astonishment, and very probably her father's, she suddenly became a woman: a woman with her own mind who was fully aware of her own sexuality and the effect it had on men in her own domain. Learning about the causes of the First World War and how to do tricky algebraic equations seemed not only dull but completely irrelevant to her ambitions of being *someone*. Yes, she wanted fame and fortune, and she knew with her looks and an eye for the main chance, she was perfectly capable of realising her lascivious ambitions. So, she put her mind on making the most of herself, and first up was getting the make-up right and wearing clothes which showed off all the curves on her fantastic body. Men, boys, she didn't care who they were – as long as they were bad and loaded, she wanted them.

As far as Roy was concerned, he knew she was no sweet virgin, and it sickened him to hear her fucking some lad's brains out in the back bar when the pub was shut. He thought about chucking it all in and retiring down at the seaside, but that was easier said than done.

Lacey stormed off. Roy knew that all he could do was watch her. He had no power over the girl; she mocked him and laughed in his face. Although he loved her, he also despised her; she was playing games with some dangerous men.

Keffa Jackson walked in and went up to the bar. Roy felt the goosebumps prick his skin; that's all he needed. Lacey was upstairs, and he hoped she didn't clock Keffa on the camera. He'd warned her not to get involved with him. Of all the men, he was the one she had to stay clear of. He was Kelly Raven's fella, and if Kelly or any of her firm got wind that his kid was making a play, then there would be no doubt whatsoever that the young woman would rain down fire and brimstone on his pub.

Keffa took his drink and lowered himself onto a bar stool at the end of the counter, against the wall. Roy wasn't pally with Keffa. After all, this wasn't his manor, and he was fully aware who the man was. Everyone was. He'd been a Face in South London for well over twenty years and now he was known in other parts of London. South West London was a neutral ground for the south and north divide, and, unfortunately, it was Roy's pub, the Mitcham Mint, where they would meet.

Lacey had, of course, detected him on the camera and was adding another layer of make-up for that final effect. She also paid attention to what she was wearing, and so she pulled her V-neck top lower down and slipped out of her skirt, swapping it for an even shorter one.

As soon as she appeared at the bar, Keffa glanced her way and called her over. She ignored him and pretended to be stocking the shelves. Keffa was trying to keep a lid on his temper but her cocky attitude was pissing him off. He got up from the stool, flipped open the entrance flap to the bar, and stepped forward. Roy would never let any customer come behind the jump, but he knew in this case he wouldn't even think of trying to stop Keffa. He watched as Keffa grabbed Lacey's arm and dragged her to the kitchen, away from earshot, and decided to leave well alone. This was one disagreement he was not prepared to fight for his daughter, and why should he? She was a fucking

273

nymphomaniac, for God's sake. He turned a deafened ear to the proceedings and continued serving. However, he did have one intuitive thought: perhaps a few words from the big black man may straighten her out.

"Aw, interested now are ya, Keffa? Well, fuck you!" she hissed.

Keffa wanted to headbutt her, there and then. "You listen to me. I told ya, it's fucking over. You were just a fuck, that's all. You wanted it, ya came on to me, and I obliged, end of. If you even think about going to Kelly, or if you're stupid enough to spread a rumour, then I will fucking brutalise you. Got it?"

Lacey leaned back against the chest freezer, as she'd done when they'd first got together. "Keffa, you know you wouldn't do that. You like this little body of mine too much." She was rubbing her hands up and down her breasts and licking her lips. Keffa tried to contain the urge to slap her. He was annoyed with himself that Lacey had sucked him in and handed him her fanny on a plate, and he was livid that she took it to mean anything more. Worst of it all, she was threatening to tell Kelly.

He lunged forward and gripped her throat and his steely eyes bored into her. "I am fucking warning you, ya two-bit cunt. One word, and I fucking mean one word, and the Thames will be carrying another dead body out to sea."

Lacey had never witnessed Keffa so angry; even the incident with the Carters hadn't left him with so much fury. She coughed and spluttered, when he let go, and tears streamed down her face. She loved Keffa with a craving, and for weeks, she'd kept their affair secret, even though she wanted the world to know, especially that stuck-up cow Kelly Raven. She wanted Keffa for herself; he had everything in a man she desired. He was handsome, strong, and svelte, and he'd given her the best shag she'd ever had. *What was there not to like?* she thought. She hated Kelly – really hated her; it was down to pure jealousy. By hook or by crook, she would have Keffa, even if it meant deviously removing the loathsome bitch from the picture.

"Oh, come on, Keffa, you wanted me. You couldn't get enough of me. You said I was beautiful. Kelly can't be all that, if you're shoving your cock up my fanny."

Keffa cringed at her turn of phrase and glared with a burning anger, hating every word she said, because, in all honesty, he did find her cute. He especially enjoyed the frantic and rough sex, which he would deny up to the point of taking a lie detector test, if his Kelly ever confronted him about it. But Kelly was his woman; she was special, and he would never – even in his drunkest moments – engage in sex with her in the way he'd done with this wild cat. There was no comparison.

"You're nothing, Lacey, just an easy shag. That's all you'll ever be, and don't even mention Kelly's name again. You could never walk in her shoes."

He stepped back and scrutinised her. "Take a look at yourself. You're a fake little girl, with big ideas. Well, let's get something straight, shall we? You ain't far off an ol' brass, and if ya want payment …" he pulled out a wad of notes and threw them at her, "…'ere take these, and don't mention Kelly's name or mine again."

He turned and walked away. Lacey's emotional temperature was off the scales, hearing this. She was completely apoplectic with wrath. "Oh yeah? Well, don't fucking underestimate me, Keffa. I ain't the dolly you think I am. You'd better think very carefully before you threaten me, you bastard."

He spun around to face her. "Don't fucking push it!"

275

Lacey laughed. "Me push it? You wanna watch ya tongue because I've something of yours that may just fall in the wrong hands." The words came out before she had time to consider what she was saying.

Keffa cocked his head to the side, as he walked back to her. "And what might that be, Lacey?" he said, quietly in her left ear.

Lacey's cocky stance dropped. She tilted her head to the side, realising she had made a major fuck-up. "Oh nuffin, Keffa, just fuck off and leave me alone." She had his bracelet. It had fallen off whilst in the midst of a moment of passion, and if she ever got the chance, she was going to put it on her own wrist and parade it in front of Kelly.

Keffa gave her another once-over and left, his mind working overtime. That was no story she was spinning. He racked his brains thinking what she could have of his. Then it hit him. He rushed back to the kitchen to find Lacey with her head in her hands.

"Where's the jacket I left here?" He towered over her.

Lacey looked up from where she was sitting, with a puzzled yet tear-stained face. "I don't know, Keffa. I didn't know you'd left a jacket." Her words were feeble, her face daubed with fear.

"Liar, where's me fucking jacket?" he screamed at her.

Lacey cowered away from him, knowing she had pushed him too far. "Please, Keffa, I swear I don't have it. I was just saying I had something of yours to get your attention. I love you, Keffa, I don't want it to end. When you ignored me that day you came into the pub, I was hurt. Adam was there, wasn't he? He came on to me when you left, and we had a thing, a one-off. But it was nothing. You hurt me, that's all. I'm sorry it happened. I know I shouldn't have gone with Adam, but well, I dunno, I just wanted you to notice me."

276

She took a deep breath; enveloped in panic, she remained tearful and motionless. Keffa saw the terror on her face and decided to leave it at that. It was obvious he had walked on hot coals and was now paying the price. If she shot her mouth off, then that would be it for Kelly and him.

Sitting in his car outside the pub, Keffa turned his thoughts to himself – to his other problems. A three-year wait for Kelly to come out of prison, and then this last year or so, when they'd tried to make something together, it would be unthinkable not to have her in his life. What a prat he'd been. But then he'd been extremely unhappy.

He knew one thing: he couldn't – no make that wouldn't – live without her. She was the love of his life – she made him laugh at the most ridiculous things. She was a wonderful caring person with a kind heart. But she had not been there for him, really, for most of the past twelve months or so. And since they'd come back from their holiday, she'd not been interested in sex at all. Men had needs and his had not been satisfied.

When he first started going out with her properly, after all the sad events which had played out in her life, he knew they were more than compatible, despite the large age gap. Time spent with each other had been truly fantastic. They were like conjoined twins with a telepathy all their own. But in fairness to Kelly, once she'd decided to become a Face in South London, she had responsibilities: to the Colombians, to her firm (Cyril, Frank, and Blakey), and to the other men and women on her payroll who kept the businesses running smoothly.

The latter had mortgages, car finance, and food to put on the table, for God's sake. She was a boss in more ways than one. And she was a great boss too.

He remembered the occasion she'd walked into her nightclub and seen one of the hostesses hide her face and run into the ladies'. Something made Kelly glance over at her and she too scooted into the rest rooms. When she caught sight of Izzie Kendal's grief-stricken face, she went up to her and asked her gently what all the fuss was. It turned out Izzie's ol' man had kicked her out. But that was *after* he'd kicked her in the stomach, when he'd found out she was pregnant, and not by him.

Kelly was totally overcome by hearing this news. In fact, as if a switch had turned on in her mind, she realised that with leadership came responsibilities for everyone in her empire and that included, and very much so, the people at the bottom of the totem pole, like the Izzies of this world. Quickly, she hunted down Keffa and told him the situation. He took three of his men and went to Izzie's flat, which, by coincidence, happened to be in the same block as the one that Kelly's best friend Ruth had lived in when she was with her partner, Connor. He'd been a vile bastard, and Kelly had made it a priority to see that Ruth was properly looked after, when she eventually came out of prison. Dale, Izzie's boyfriend, never knew what hit him. He didn't just get a good talking to – that wasn't exactly Keffa's style. The guy was nearly kicked to death and warned that he would be fish food, if he so much as went within a mile of Izzie. Meanwhile, Kelly had her housed in a comfortable apartment in Peckham, a *pro tem* arrangement, until the young woman could be found a permanent place. This act of some considerable generosity, if not humanity, travelled on the grapevine faster than lager turns to piss. Like a shot, people all the way through Kelly's organisation came to see their boss in a very different light: her kindness and magnanimity of spirit earned her respect by her staff.

Keffa tore away in his Range Rover Sport, with a lot on his mind: the missing jacket, Lacey's big mouth, and now finding out that the stupid girl had turned to his enemy, Adam, had been too much to absorb at once. "Christ!" he shouted aloud, as he slammed on the brakes. He had to go back and find out if Lacey had given his jacket to anyone. It was clear in his mind what he'd done. Retracing his footsteps, he remembered taking off his overcoat and then his jacket, but when he left to go home, he only grabbed the overcoat — what a fool! That jacket had his gun with his prints all over it. A cold sweat coated his skin. Adam was dead. But his own gun was missing. Living in two homes, his apartment and the one at Kelly's, had caused this major fuck-up. After leaving Kelly's house, he now realised he hadn't had his jacket on when he paid the Carters a visit here, and he'd taken his spare gun instead. After that, he went to his apartment. He also knew the jacket wasn't at his apartment because he had a habit of leaving it over the sofa and if his memory served him correctly it wasn't there. So he was sure that the jacket must be in the pub. Now he knew: the jacket must be here ... and with it the fucking gun! *Christ, could things get any worse?* he thought.

Lacey was still in the kitchen, sobbing like a baby. She loved Keffa, and she hoped that one day, he would make it official. She wanted everything Kelly had: the clothes, the cars, the money, and the status. Naïvely, she thought that it was Keffa who was the man in charge of the firm and that Kelly was just his bird. In her eyes, Kelly was boring with her long straight hair, black skintight dresses, and hardly any make-up. She looked cold and serious, whereas Lacey perceived her own self as fun and sexy, with her new tits and bleached curly hair. To be fair to her, she knew how to make a man laugh and she oozed sex. Blinded by the idea that Keffa was working his magic on her, she assumed Kelly was a wet fish. She hadn't a clue that Keffa wasn't getting his oats at home and therefore only after her for a quick shag. She thought offering to give him the blow job of the century was classy, and being a hot-blooded man, he wouldn't say no.

That was the only thing she had got right about him though.

However, Keffa had also been naïve. He assumed that Lacey knew she was a slag. Not for one moment did he think that she'd ever compare herself to someone like Kelly. If Lacey had even a modicum of intelligence, she would have known from the off that Kelly had what other women could only dream of – charisma, style, and a confidence which could never be matched by some silly tart.

He sat outside the pub, bashing his hands on the steering wheel in a right temper. Lacey was stupid and playing with fire. He tried to calm his mood before he throttled her. After a few deep breaths, he walked around to the rear of the pub and entered the back door which led straight into the kitchen. Lacey gasped when she saw him standing there with his threatening stance and fierce expression.

"You'd better tell me where that jacket is, 'cos I ain't fucking being mugged off by the likes of you. I took me jacket off in this kitchen, if I remember rightly."

Lacey was shaking, trying to recall if he'd left a jacket. She racked her brains thinking back to a few days ago, going over the events in her mind.

❧*❧

He had waited until the pub closed and she whispered to him to meet her around the back. Then, she'd pulled him into the kitchen and began snogging his face. She recollected it because he'd told her a few times not to kiss him – he didn't like it. He got rough, when she kept trying to put her lips on his. Thinking it was a game, the more she tried it, the more forceful he became, until, eventually, he ripped off his overcoat, jacket, and shirt and then pinned her to the wall. She undressed herself and was all over him. He took her that night, there, over the freezer.

It was a little rougher than she liked, but it was, as she saw it, fun and very passionate.

Keffa, though, saw it differently; he wanted to release a tension that had been building up for a long time, and so he wasn't overly bothered whether he hurt Lacey or not. After they'd finished, Keffa continued taking deep breaths, while she skipped to the bar, still naked, and poured him a brandy. He downed two or three and they talked. It was nothing too deep, mainly frivolous stuff about sex and what she could do with him. Afterwards, he left.

◦*◦

Keffa grabbed her by the hair and pulled her face close to his. "Where's that jacket?" he growled.

Lacey was weak at the knees, and she recognised the major shit she was in. "Please, Keffa, let me go. I'm sorry, really, I don't know. Please believe me, babe. I love you," she cried.

He pushed her to the wall, holding her shoulders against the cold plaster. Like a sick, twisted creature, he tilted his head, and then he kissed her. She shuddered. He looked deranged.

"Please, Keffa, I'm sorry. I really don't know where it is."

Then he stroked her hair and wiped her tears. "It's all right, my angel, don't cry. Just tell me, though, what you did with it."

She searched his eyes for some form of compassion and forgiveness, but they were eerily black and cold. He gripped her throat again and she had a premonition he would go too far this time. The muscles in Keffa's neck tightened, and he had a compelling urge to smash her face in.

281

Her heart was beating furiously, her breathing fast. She began to snivel again.

"Where. Is. The. Jacket?" His words were slow and deep. "You didn't do anything stupid with it, like give it to Adam Carter, did ya? Ya do know that Adam's dead, don't ya?"

Lacey wore a look of total horror, in part because she could barely breathe, but on hearing the shocking news about her latest conquest, it nearly finished her off.

Keffa could see that he'd gone too far, and he let her go. Lacey collapsed, falling to her knees coughing and gasping for breath.

"Please, Keffa, don't hurt me. Please, Keffa, I didn't give it to Adam or anyone. I swear on my life, I haven't seen it!" she begged.

"You'd better not have been anywhere near his place with my jacket, because now Adam Carter has been found dead, I don't want to be called in for questioning over a silly fucking mistake caused by your stupidity!"

Glaring in disbelief, Lacey watched as Keffa left, slamming the door behind him. With her hands still shaking, she searched the kitchen for the missing jacket and felt sick when it was nowhere to be found.

Christ, she thought, *what the fuck have I got myself into?*

CHAPTER FOURTEEN

Valerie Campbell was standing against the whiteboard with a cringey smirk across her face. She had called the team in to deliver the news about the prints on the gun in Adam's apartment. Then, she took great delight in glaring at Sampson.

"So, forensics are back. Well, well, well. Reardon's little firm have messed up big time, a right sloppy mess. We have our suspect banged to rights. The bullet that blew Adam Carter's brains out belongs to the gun owned by none other than Keffa Jackson. This was the gun we found in the apartment. He's Kelly Raven's partner, a serious member of Cyril Reardon's crew."

Hanson was the first to ask a question. "How do we know the gun belongs to Jackson, Ma'am?"

The soft young voice of the woman grated on Campbell. She had to remain pleasant though. "His prints were all over it," she smiled.

"Any news on the Jane Doe, Gov?" asked Stevens, an up-and-coming detective who was also assigned to the case.

Campbell nodded. "Yes, very interesting and also alarming. The semen sample taken from the girl matched the DNA of Adam Carter. Therefore, whether he murdered her or not, he certainly had sex with her. The coroner also said she had tears associated with a rape victim, but the marks around her neck are, at present, inconclusive as to who strangled her."

"But surely, Gov, if he raped her, he probably murdered her?" commented Stevens.

Campbell took a deep, controlled breath. *Give me strength*, she thought. *This lot couldn't find their own arse, if she paid them.* "Stevens, forensics cannot find evidence that confirms he killed her." Quickly, she changed the subject. "We can't jump to conclusions, but the most important matter at hand is Keffa Jackson. So, I want him brought in for questioning."

She glared again at Sampson. "You come with me. I have a search warrant and we're going to turn Raven's place upside down. Caulstone is going over to Jackson's apartment with a warrant, in case he's there. I have wanted this for a long time, and now we have evidence, so mark my words, by the end of the day, we'll have enough shit on the pair of them to lock 'em up and the rest of the firm, too."

Sampson knew he had to get a message to Cyril, and quickly, but the immediate problem was Campbell. She had her sharp eyes on him. Before she had a chance to whisk him away, the phone rang. As she answered it, he left the room and headed for the men's toilets. He pulled out his phone and dialled Cyril's number.

"Mate, they're after Keffa for Adam Carter's murder. His prints are on the murder weapon. We're heading to Kelly's house now and Keffa's place will be raided as well." Instantly, he heard the door open to the men's rest room, and instinct made him put the phone away. Flushing the toilet, he opened the cubicle door, and there, before him, was Campbell, her hands on her hips, giving him the evil eye. She was ready to explode.

"The ladies' are next door, unless you need a fucking urinal!" He was fuming that she had the audacity to walk into the men's, like she owned the place.

"What the fuck are you up to, Sampson?"

He curled his lip. "'Aving a fucking shit. Is that not allowed in this nick?"

"Yeah, very convenient," she snapped back.

"Look, what's this all about? I mean the filthy looks and following me into the bog?"

Campbell grinned. "I know you, Sampson. Reardon has someone from this station in his back pocket, and I'm betting my poxy pension that it's you, isn't it?"

"Get a grip, Ma'am. I'm a fucking detective and 'ave been since you were in nappies, so don't start that one, because that's a very serious accusation, and I don't take too kindly to it!" His voice took on a raised tone and he hoped that it had hit a nerve. At any rate, he could see he'd ruffled her feathers. She shrugged her shoulders and turned to walk away. Sampson was fuming, though. He despised the woman and would have her for this one day.

Kelly was finishing her breakfast, still in her pyjamas. Her slightly messy hair didn't detract from her soft blushed cheeks, which underlined her prepossessing exterior. When Cyril walked into the room, his usual bubbly countenance had taken on a serious expression. He flicked his head for her to follow him. She laid her knife and fork down beside her plate and gracefully stood up. They went to his man cave, which at one time had been the study belonging to Lord Chambers. It was a beautiful room with oak panelling to three sides, and it commanded magnificent twin views of huge cedar trees standing majestically on the expansive lawns and of oak trees positioned on both sides of the long tarmacadamed drive to the entrance of the property. Once they were away from the others, Cyril felt able to relax. He placed her hands in his and looked at her with such concern on his face that Kelly held her breath, in anticipation of the news to come.

"They're gonna pull Keffa in for Adam's murder."

"What!" she screeched.

"They're gonna turn ya house over, Kelly, and Keffa's an' all. Is there anything there, anything at all, you wouldn't want the Ol' Bill to find?" He kept his voice down, so as not to alarm Malik or the girls.

She took a deep breath and shook her head. "No, Cyril, my home is my home and business is kept away. You know me. I ain't that silly. And Keffa's a bit old in the tooth to slip up like that, ain't he?"

He tapped her hand. "Good girl."

"So why Keffa? What do they have on him? 'Cos no way would he be that fucking reckless, surely to God!"

"The gun used on Adam had Keffa's prints on it. That's all I know, babe."

Kelly quickly retrieved her clean phone from her bag and dialled Keffa's unmarked mobile. It rang three times before he answered it. "Where the fuck are ya?"

"Oh, come on, Kelly, what do you care? For months, now, I've been the last one on your speed dial," he replied, in a flat tone.

Kelly was ready to explode with frustration and rage. "I care 'cos, right now, the murder squad will be on their way to turn over me gaff and arrest you for murdering Adam Carter!"

Keffa was in his old apartment in Peckham, drowning his sorrows. He hadn't slept a wink, going over his life and his future, or not, with Kelly. His heart skipped a beat, as he immediately came out of his introspection and sat up straight. "You what?"

"Yeah, you heard all right! Your prints are on the fucking shooter that killed Adam, so where are ya?" she bellowed down the phone.

Keffa tried to gather his wits about him. "Listen, Kel, I never killed him. I swear to ya, I never shot him."

"If you didn't kill him, then how come they have a gun with your prints on it?" she demanded.

It was a very good question to which he could not give an honest answer. He couldn't tell her the real reason – that he'd left his jacket after shagging some dumb barmaid – yet he was quick to spin Kelly a porky. "I don't know, Kel. All I can think of is one of me old shooters has ended up in the wrong hands."

She knew he was lying. They'd lived in each other's pockets long enough for her to know him virtually inside out. His expressions, the variations in the tone of his voice, his mannerisms, they were all logged in her computer-like brain, so in trying to pull the wool over her eyes, it was a complete and utter joke. "Keffa, don't fucking mug me off. I know you! All your guns are wiped clean before they leave your lock-up, so do me a favour and be upfront, or, well, I can't help ya."

Keffa swallowed hard. She was right. How could she help to get him out of this shit, if he wasn't honest with her? But, if he told her the truth, she would hate him, wouldn't she? He was between a rock and a hard place, and it was deeply worrying for him personally and for their relationship, whatever that was now. He had to get away and give himself enough time to think. A hard knock at the door interrupted his thoughts.

"They're 'ere, Kel, delete the number." With that, he cut her off and deleted her number before removing the chip and rushing to the toilet to flush it away. He searched the living room and racked his brains to think of anything he may have left lying around. He didn't have any further time though as they were through the door, wearing flak jackets and wielding guns.

"Place your hands where I can see them! Now put your face down on the floor!" shouted one of the armed officers. Keffa didn't fight, struggle, or argue. He knew he would get a bullet in the head, if he as much as scratched his arse.

Cyril was staring at Kelly's blank expression. "Well, what's going on?"

"They've nicked him, but something just doesn't add up."

Whilst DI Caulstone and his team were on their way to Keffa Jackson's apartment, Campbell's mind was focused firmly on what she hoped she would find at Kelly Raven's gaff, which explained her silence on the journey to Farnborough Park in Orpington. They stopped at the gates and flashed their badges. Campbell took a good look at the development. It was so far removed from her poky flat. The properties were large statements. Outside every house was a flash car or two. This was a villain's paradise. It was a gated community where each home was set in their own immaculate gardens. In the main, it was occupied by stockbrokers, doctors, and wealthy crooks, and there, at the end of the long drive, she could see Kelly Raven's house. Two squad cars pulled up behind DS Campbell's motor. Two more were parked further down the road; the officers had left them to surround the perimeter of the property on foot – in case Keffa did a runner, if he was even there. Her phone rang: she was informed that they had him in custody.

"Sampson, call off the armed squad. They have him at his own place."

"Are we still going to search the house?"

Campbell gave him another one of her irritating smirks. "Fucking too right we are. I want the wash baskets emptied, the beds stripped, and in fact, Sampson, I want this fucking house turned upside down. I'm going to find more than a T-shirt with gun residue on it."

Sampson eased himself out of the car seat and straightened his new fresh-smelling raincoat, courtesy of his missus. She hated the smell of fags and always sprayed him down with some potion or other, until finally, one day, she'd had enough. She threw his old coat in the bin and bought the new one. He didn't really take his appearance too seriously, and he was constantly nagged at for leaving his hair to grow to unacceptable lengths.

In some ways, as Campbell glanced across at him, he reminded her of a younger Peter Falk from the very popular American TV series *Columbo*. Like Falk, Sampson was the archetype of the maverick cop. His inelegant appearance was, as she well knew, a complete cover for who the man really was. Underneath that laid-back manner was a very shrewd cookie indeed. Well, he had to be, she surmised, because she was damn sure he was pocketing two incomes, and she knew which one was paying him a decent wage.

He smoothed down his coat again and gazed up at the house. A spear of envy pricked him, yet really, he couldn't complain. His house wasn't as grand as Kelly's, and certainly nothing beat Cyril's, but for sitting in two camps, he was well off. His monthly payslip and weekly poke from Cyril, kept him sweet enough. He guessed Campbell would be pig-sick, parading around the mass of wealth sitting there. She often bemoaned the injustice of how the villains were taking the piss with other people's well-earned cash.

No sooner was she through the door, when his boss took up a position in the large hallway and pointed to him to head for the kitchen.

"I'm going to screw these scheming shysters to the fucking floor! So, Sampson, I want every drawer tipped out. I want every piece of evidence there is! Have you got that?" Her sideways glance was enough to let him know she was also on his case.

Gritting her back teeth, she paraded around the house, sneering at every piece of artwork and each carefully chosen ornament, one of which – a beautiful blue ceramic cat – she recognised from a visit to Liberty a few months earlier. The out-of-this-world kitchen had her flummoxed. She wanted to go through the washing machine and the tumble dryer, but try as she might, she couldn't find one among the modern folding highly polished doors. Then she tugged hard on a high stainless steel door, expecting to find a broom cupboard, but only to find instead a walk-in fridge. She slammed the door shut in annoyance, mumbling under her breath, "Ridiculous."

Sampson followed her around and watched the exasperation written on her face. They wandered from room to room opening drawers. Campbell didn't bother closing any; her obvious irritation and envious streak were all too much, and her temper finally snapped. Out came the drawers, straight off their runners, leaving their contents strewn across the Italian marble tiled floor. *Yes*, thought Sampson, *that was a real cunt stunt.*

Once they were in the bedroom, Campbell stared at the bed. With two fingers, she peeled back the bedding only to discover it had not been slept in. The Egyptian cotton sheets were completely wrinkle-free and folded by a pro. They had a cleaner, that was for sure. Everywhere she looked was immaculate. Then, she turned around and frowned. "Where are the wardrobes?" Her movements were quick and jittery, like a clucking chicken.

Sampson smiled. "Gov, a house like this has a dressing room." His sarcastic tone pissed her off and she snarled at him, "Well, then, get a move on. Find it! I want all his clothes bagged up and sent off to forensics."

Sampson made an obvious frown. "Er, Gov, I think we'd better let forensics remove the clothes. I mean, we don't want any fuck-ups, cross-contamination, and all that."

Campbell was biting her tongue. What an idiot she was. She needed to get a grip on herself. She was making errors which could be costly for her job. He was right, and so far, there was nothing in this house. It was like a hotel. It was spotless, and there were no homely trophies, no photos, and no paperwork. Then, a moment of inspiration. "Hey, hold up a minute, this isn't their regular home."

Sampson looked at her as though she were mad. "Yeah, it is. This is in her name, and it's a known fact. Anyway, there's an easy way to check. Look in the bathroom. All women like their favourite perfume and stuff."

Campbell marched on ahead and pushed open the bathroom door. He was right. On a glass stand were toiletries, perfumes, and waxing strips. She stared for a while; it didn't make sense. There were Raven's personal items, but this huge house just did not seem lived in. Somehow, it seemed sterile, almost soulless.

By this time, Sampson had found the walk-in dressing room and he called Campbell over to take a look. It was filled on both sides with clothes in every colour, and opposite to Kelly's, there were racks containing Keffa's clothes. The shirts were all hanging up, having been dry-cleaned and placed in separate covers. Sampson was not surprised at all – after all, he had a toe in the door, so to speak. But the look on his boss's face was absolutely priceless.

Her words were short and succinct. "Well, there's no point in bringing forensics into the house. Everything has all been dry-cleaned, the clever fuckers."

"Well, it looks like Kelly Raven and Keffa Jackson have a case of OCD," said Sampson, with a smug grin.

"My arse, Sampson, they've had this purposefully scrubbed down."

"Actually, I don't agree. My missus is similar. You know, every nook and cranny in our house is the same. I'm lucky if I get to wear my work clothes inside the house. They're in the washing machine before I've sat down!"

Campbell flared her nostrils. "Yeah, but this isn't normal." She thought about her own home and many others she had busted; they were never this tidy and clean.

"Fuck it!" She pulled the mobile from her jacket pocket and dialled DI Caulstone. He was the detective who had just arrested Keffa. "Hi,

292

Caulstone. Tell me, when you nicked Keffa Jackson, did you call forensics to make a swoop of the home, and did you find anything that would incriminate him?"

She paced the floor, clenching her fists.

Caulstone was a younger version of Sampson. He, too, didn't do everything by the book, and, on the whole, he was more eager to find paedophiles and serial killers than get involved in the underworld. After all, they only killed their own kind. "Nothing 'ere, Gov. Bins are clean, there's no dirty washing. In fact, the place is spotless."

She didn't say goodbye. With her trademark disdain for those lower down the pecking order, she cut him off in a temper. Sampson was smiling inside. She was not getting anywhere, and he didn't fancy her chances of finding any incriminating evidence. "No luck, Gov?"

"What d'ya mean, no luck? We have Jackson banged to rights. Trust me, Sampson, I'll have them all, you'll see!"

He followed her out of the house, and as he passed two officers, he said, "Sorry, guys, but can you do us a favour, clean up in there? The guv'nor's had a paddy and ransacked the place."

Campbell was too keen to get back to the station to hear him or she would have flipped. This temper of hers was going to fuck things up, and Sampson wanted to see her pulled down a peg or two. He could have told her that Kelly wouldn't have any matters of business lying around in the house. She was an old hand on young shoulders – very young, in her case. Yes, she was astute and that was a fact. He also knew that she not only had other properties, such as two pubs and a nightclub, but she also owned many smaller businesses and could keep all her paperwork at any one of them. His boss would have to work that out for herself because he was more intent on seeing her fail than help with this inquiry.

Keffa was stripped and had his clothes taken to forensics. He sat in the interview room in a white police suit, after he'd made his entitled phone call to Michael Delmonte.

The measured click-clack sounds of Superintendent Campbell's shoes could be heard along the corridor, as she trudged her way towards the interview room. Then the door swung open and in she stepped. After sizing up the two detectives sitting there, she then studied Keffa. He was calm and collected and sat upright like a gentleman. He certainly didn't give her the impression he was in any way a thug, as she'd imagined.

"Keffa Jackson?"

He nodded. "Yes, and you are?" he asked confidently.

She had briefly seen him in the flesh at Kelly's mother's funeral, although she had never spoken to him, and she was surprised at his London accent. He came across as smart and alert with a professional quality that didn't match his hair style and the cocky sharpness in his green eyes. He was good-looking, in a manly way. She thought he was probably a bit of a babe magnet.

"I'm Superintendent Campbell. I take it you've been read your rights?" she asked brusquely, as she sat heavily on the chair opposite, acknowledging the officers for the first time.

"Yes, I have, and before I answer any questions, my brief is on his way, so I suggest we wait."

294

Campbell was not used to being dictated to and gave him her famous brash smirk.

As soon as he arrived, Michael Delmonte was led to the interview room. He entered in his usual brisk and efficient manner, as ever giving absolutely no clue as to what he was thinking. He looked Campbell over and nodded for her to leave, which she did, with the two detectives in tow.

Once they'd left the room, Delmonte said, "Firstly, Keffa, did you kill him?"

The question was not a surprise, but oddly, it helped Keffa to relax. He settled more comfortably on his chair and looked Delmonte squarely in the eyes. "No! I never did."

Delmonte gave him a hard stare, as he pulled out his legal pad and Montblanc fountain pen. "So how do they have your prints on the gun that killed Adam Carter? You'd better tell me everything, or you, my dear chap, are going down for this."

Keffa stared at his fingernails that were now bitten down and sore. As a rule, he never bit his nails, but the pressure he was now under was giving him a lot to be anxious about. Considering the fragile state of his relationship with Kelly, he believed this could be the final straw, as far as he was concerned. He took a deep breath and told Delmonte the truth about how he'd left his jacket at the pub. He knew he had to be brutally honest with his solicitor, so he left nothing out. He owned up to the fact that he'd been shagging some slip of a kid, which had led to the stupid mistake of leaving his jacket containing his gun at the pub.

By the time he'd confessed to all of this, he felt awful. It was indefensible, back-stabbing, and dishonourable.

"Well, I'm afraid you've no choice but to tell Kelly the facts. Right, where were you the day before yesterday?"

Keffa was so full of worry that he had to really think about it. "I, er … I was with Kelly and two little girls, Malakai's sisters, shopping."

Delmonte nodded and scribbled down notes. "Good, we can pull the CCTV footage, and that will put you far enough away from the scene."

Keffa slumped in his seat and sighed. "Not really. Adam Carter lived in an apartment in Bromley. We were in the Glades Shopping Centre, just up the road."

Delmonte looked up. "Okay, we can match the time of death to the times on the cameras, and let's face it, you can't be in two places at once. I just hope they were all working."

Keffa lowered his head in frustration. Realisation hit him that unless they had clear footage with the times attached, he was going away for a long time.

Meantime, while Keffa was being grilled like a trout, Kelly had troubles of her own: so much just didn't add up. Keffa acting strange, and now his gun at the scene, it was disturbing to put it mildly. She called Frank and Blakey over, to figure out exactly what went on at the Mitcham Mint where Keffa held his meeting with the Carters. She needed to be in possession of the facts, and at present, she was flailing. Did Keffa have some other grudge against them?

Both men were equally flummoxed. After some conferring between them, it was left to Frank to put Kelly in the picture. Blakey would normally never say a word to anyone unless he really wanted to.

"Kel, to be honest, he had his back to me, when he was talking to Johnnie. I couldn't hear much at all. All I heard was Adam call me an old something or other, and I gave him a dig with me metal rod. We left after that. I wish I could help more, but that's all I remember, babe."

"Right, I'm gonna pay the landlord a visit. I want the disks because he must have that pub full of cameras."

Frank smiled. "He does have cameras everywhere, I know that much, but he wipes them clean every night. The man knows not to hand anything over to the filth."

Kelly sneered. "Yeah, well, he might tell the police that, if they came visiting, but I reckon he would keep them, just in case he ever needed to use them. I would, wouldn't you?"

"Yeah, I think you're right. I guess I would."

Just then, Malik entered the study, and hearing the tail end of the discussion, he suddenly piped up, "I'll go with you Kel. I dunno, I've come into your life, and now all this trouble has occurred, I feel responsible."

Kelly ran her hands over his shoulders. "This ain't your fault, but if it makes ya feel better, then, yeah, you can come with us. I might need some muscle." She gently punched him on the arm.

Sassy appeared, dressed in a ruffled smock blouse, skintight jeans, a leather jacket, and high boots, identical to Kelly's. With make-up highlighting her face, she no longer looked the seventeen-year-old she had become but instead more like the twenty-year-old she aspired to. "I'll come, too," she offered. Everyone stood with their mouths open, completely gobsmacked at Sassy's appearance.

Admiring the girl, Kelly realised that underneath the wild hair was a very attractive woman. Once those white eyelashes were coated in black mascara, she was indeed beautiful.

"Sassy, go and take that fucking shit off your face, you're only …" Malik stopped for a second and noticed Sassy look at Kelly for backup.

Kelly looked over at her brother with warmth. He was trying so hard to be Sassy's big brother, her protector, and she got that.

"Malik, she is seventeen, and I bought her the make-up and clothes. You have to remember that Sassy is a woman now. Fuck me, when I was younger than her, I was—" She stopped. She didn't like to recall those years of being on the run for murder, nor the years spent inside. "Never mind, Malik. If she's old enough to play mum to the kids, then she's old enough to look like a woman, and it's time she felt good about herself." She turned to Sassy and grinned. "Ain't that right, sis?"

Sassy was stumped for words, but she was so proud. Kelly saying "sis", it made her feel ten feet tall.

That day the dynamics changed. Sassy loved her brother and would do anything he asked, but now she had Kelly, who, in an inoffensive way, backed her corner.

Malik sighed, sensing that he was being outmanoeuvred. "All right, I suppose so, but no fucking fella, yeah? You're still my little sister, and I don't want to be fighting boys off at the door."

With her hands on her hips and a cocky grin, Sassy mocked her brother. "Malik, I could be a fucking fanny muncher, for all you know."

It was the first time they'd all laughed that day. Sassy's mouth was still foul, but she was comical.

❧*☙

It was midday and Roy was cleaning the pint glasses. Lacey never refilled the top shelf; she couldn't reach. Just as he stretched to place the last glass on the rack, he saw Kelly and Cyril. He swallowed hard and stared. Frank and Blakey were standing behind her, and then he noticed the young man, and for a second, he felt palpitations. Malik's assured swagger and slightly inclined head, along with his half-smile, gave him an edge that suggested he was one dangerous fucker. Roy knew that stance only too well and was instantly on his guard. He blinked hard; no way could it be Eddie Raven, and as the lad approached the bar, he realised he was right. It seemed eerie but what a relief. Roy had had enough dealings with Eddie Raven to last him a lifetime, and if he was honest, he was glad that Eddie was six feet under.

His ex-wife had once had a thing with Eddie; not that he was surprised because she'd had a thing with most men, including the Carters. Roy had heard that his wife was putting it about with one of their regular customers. After hearing noises below one night, he went downstairs to see what was going on. As Rose was just coming out from the kitchen, he saw her face all flushed, her hair in disarray, and the sound of the back door closing quietly. He guessed what she'd been up to, although he didn't know who the bastard was. But he was sickened by her apparent disloyalty. So he installed a CCTV system in the pub, to see if he could get the hard evidence he needed. And it wasn't too long afterwards when he saw more than he bargained for. Roy never forgot to this day the image of his wife on that freezer laughing, whilst

Johnnie Carter was banging her one; it would live with him until the day he died in the pub. But when he showed Rose what they'd done, she stormed off, sticking two fingers up at her husband to live with Johnnie. But that fling only lasted a week or so before she caught him quite by chance one night with a young fella in the back of Johnnie's car outside his home and that was that. It didn't stop her though from shagging her way through the rest of the brothers, or so he was told.

The Carters were evil in his opinion. He was still sickened by the fact that his little girl had been fucking Adam, and it was only eight years earlier, when Lacey was ten years old, that the bastard had been screwing his wife, after Johnnie Carter had finished with her.

⁊*⁊

Sassy felt grown-up in among their crafted walks and serious faces. She'd been watching *Peaky Blinders* on Cyril's TV and was amazed by those characters. She'd once cheekily asked Cyril if he was like them, but he'd laughed her off. She was learning in that short time how to carry herself, and she soon realised that outside the home she was to be silent and to listen; her wild ways and cocky lip were only for private audiences. They sat around the biggest table opposite the bar, carefully checking out who was about.

Frank approached the counter and nodded to Roy. "Five brandies and a Coke with ice and lemon, mate. Bring 'em over."

Roy looked at the man, gave a brief nod, and walked quickly away from the assembled group. He knew then that they wanted a word with him. His heart was beating fast, so much so that he decided to have a sneaky large whisky when he turned his back to pour the drinks. As he arrived at the table, he could sense the tension and realised that whatever they wanted it must be serious. Then he thought about Lacey. Maybe Kelly had got wind about his daughter and Keffa's indiscretion.

300

He placed the tray on the table and sat on the only available chair. He swallowed nervously, waiting for it all to kick off.

Kelly looked him up and down. "So, here's the thing. My ol' man's down the station, accused of shooting Adam Carter. Now, I wanna know how much real grief there was between Keffa and Carter, 'cos some things just don't add up."

Roy was confused. He had nothing to do with their wars. He just ran the pub.

"So, what d'ya want from me?"

Kelly smiled at first, taking her time sipping her brandy, before she looked at him coldly and replied, "I want to see your CCTV footage over the last few weeks."

Roy swallowed hard again and felt his face redden. His adrenaline began to pump furiously because he knew what was on those disks and it wasn't pretty.

"Ah, well, that's a problem, 'cos I wipe 'em clean, ya know, in case the Ol' Bill——"

He'd no sooner got the words out of his mouth when Malik grabbed the man's wrist and slammed it on the table. The movement was so fast, even the others at the table jumped.

"Now, see, mate, correct me if I'm fucking wrong, but do we look like the filth? 'Cos, ya see, I ain't stupid, and if I ran a pub like this, I would keep all the footage, 'cos it's like insurance, ain't it? So, engage your brain and think very carefully before you say another fucking word."

Roy was startled by the boy's actions and even more so by the tone and words he used. He decided there and then not to mug him off.

Kelly smiled at her brother. He wasn't playing. He was the real deal.

Roy's eyes flitted between Kelly and Malik. "Look, I don't want no trouble, okay? All right, you can have the footage, but don't come back to me, if you don't like what you see."

Malik gripped the man's wrist even more tightly and moved to within an inch from his face. "Listen to me, cunt, if I don't like what I fucking see, and it has anything to do with you, then I'll be fucking back, and you might not have a boozer left!"

Roy moved his head back and looked at the men for some kind of reassurance, but he was to be disappointed. Frank leaned on his chair with a nodding approval, proud of Malik's input. The three men had known Eddie Raven since he'd been fifteen years old, and right now, they were watching his son, as if history were repeating itself. Cyril observed how the confident arrogance fitted Malik like a soft leather glove.

Roy took a deep breath and looked at Kelly. "Keffa and Adam were in here together just the once, and you, Frank and Blakey, were here, weren't ya?"

Kelly's antenna was working overtime now. She had a strong feeling there was more to this. "So, Roy, tell me why I won't like what I see on the disks?"

Roy knew then he'd put his foot in it and tried to backtrack. "Well, you know, Frank, don't ya? When ya stabbed Adam, it weren't a pretty sight." He shut up, knowing he was looking like an idiot.

"Yeah, but I already know that, and I'm guessing you know I'm aware of what Frank did to Adam Carter, so I'll say it again, why won't I like what I see, Roy?" The words were cold, her glare deadly.

He said no more and went towards his private quarters, with Frank on his heels. Roy knew that it wouldn't be long before the shit hit the fan, and he didn't fancy Lacey's chances when Kelly Raven saw her beau having that very naughty shag with his daughter. He would need to warn her to get her bags packed and leave pronto. With his mind on this, he headed for his upstairs office. As he turned left at the top of the stairs and entered the long landing, he didn't see Lacey appear from her bedroom in the other direction to go downstairs to the bar. As soon as they were in the office, Frank pushed Roy aside and looked at the monitors, admiringly. "Nice set-up, Roy."

With his hands trembling, Roy's eyes flicked to the shelf in the messy office and focused on the disks clearly marked in order of date. This was it now, the point of no return.

Frank wasn't slow; he spotted them right away and chuckled. In contrast to all the chaos in the room, with various papers, box files, and dirty coffee mugs scattered around, one shelf was meticulously organised. It held numerous disks all neatly lined up in order of month and year. Kelly had asked him to seek out the recordings for the month of October, which would show the occasion when he'd accompanied Keffa to meet the Carters. Carefully, he selected it from the shelf, but on impulse, he ejected the current disk from the machine that was in the process of recording, clearly labelled November, and took both downstairs.

Roy's eyes widened, but there was nothing he could do except stand back and allow this hulk of a man to take what he wanted.

303

Lacey was not in the best of moods. She was still reeling over Keffa's dismissal of her. Then, like a bolt in the head, she saw Kelly and her anger grew. Kelly was impeccably dressed, and her hair was dead straight and pulled to the side with not even a kink in it. Lacey tried to find fault. She was eaten up with jealousy, when she had to admit to herself that Kelly was a looker. And to add insult to injury, the woman had some kind of clout, by the way all the men in her party surrounded her. Lacey's lips curled with anger as she saw this madam sit back looking like the queen. Then, her eyes diverted to the young man by her side. Now, he was a real looker too. In fact, he and Kelly, were so alike, there was no question they were related. And even more interesting, he had bad boy written all over him. Then her attention switched to the tall slim girl with long red hair, who was glaring her way. She was identically dressed to little miss high and mighty. Lacey looked away. The redhead wore an evil expression and it appeared to be aimed at her. She polished a glass and placed it on the shelf before she turned for a surreptitious glance at the young man again. He was definitely her type and probably her age. There was something intriguing about him and yet familiar too.

Blakey got up to order another round. Signalling to Lacey, he remembered her from the other day. He asked for the drinks to be brought over. Lacey smiled; she wanted nothing more than to get a closer look at her next catch.

Before Lacey took the drinks to the table, she pulled her halter top down and pushed up her DD cup size bra.

Sassy was eyeballing her carefully. It was then that she knew who she would model herself on and it wasn't the barmaid. A few months ago, Sassy would have wanted fake boobs, lip fillers, and bleached hair, but not now. Now, she wanted to emulate Kelly and not the silly tart approaching them.

She watched as Lacey lifted the counter flap and wiggled her way through, holding the tray. Her short skintight skirt looked cheap and nasty and the pink high-heeled shoes were so tacky she favoured a reject Barbie doll. Sassy was jarred that the silly tart was eyeing up her brother. As Lacey placed the tray in front of them, she deliberately leaned across Malik, flaunting her big tits across his face. She giggled and apologised. Malik was taken aback. All he could see were two wobbling boobs under his nose. "Easy, tiger, I don't wanna suffocate."

Lacey looked straight into his green dewy eyes and instantly felt an attraction. Thoughts of Keffa went out of the window, and her eyes were now fixed on Malik.

She giggled again. "Sorry about that. These little puppies have a mind of their own."

Malik, in the moment, forgot where he was and laughed along with her. "I ain't complaining." As she walked away, she winked, knowing she had him hooked and with thoughts of reeling him in.

Sassy tutted. "Oh, for fuck's sake, 'ave a bit o' class. That's one ol' skanky slapper."

Cyril laughed at that comment. Sassy's turn of phrase was spot on.

Malik, however, was annoyed. He turned to face Sassy. "Jeez, Sass, you pulled on a pair of fucking high-heeled boots, slapped on war paint, and now ya think ya royalty."

Those words hurt. She knew she came from fuck all, but for the first time in so many years, she felt she could hold her head up.

Kelly threw Malik a harsh glare and decided to give the young girl a bit of slack. "At least Sassy looks like a lady. She runs rings around that barmaid, and you'd best remember that. And, Malik, I really don't think you'd like ya sister to go flashing her wares for all to see, now, would you?" Her tone was serious and held a hint of a warning.

Malik, caught up in all the bravado, realised that he had spoken without thinking. He'd never been cruel before to Sassy.

He turned to face her and noticed the hurt in her eyes. Suddenly, he had the urge to hug her. Sassy was the last person he wanted to upset; she was his rock and always had been. "Aw, fucking 'ell, sis, I was joking. Besides, how can you be royalty? It's ya gob that gives you away." He winked.

Sassy smiled. "Fuck off, cunt." It was her way of joining in the joke.

Roy emerged with Frank and almost knocked Lacey out of the way. He wanted shot of them. They would cause a stink, if any of the Carters turned up. With Adam dead, there would be a bloody war, that was for sure.

"They're 'ere," confirmed Frank, gripping the two disks in his huge hand.

Blakey watched with satisfaction the panic on Roy's face and noticed the layer of sweat across his brow. "All right, Roy?"

Roy gave him a nervous smile. "Yeah, yeah. I just don't want no trouble."

He walked away and gave Lacey a look of disgust. "I wanna a word, when they've gone."

Recognising that grave expression, Lacey knew she was in shit up to her neck. However, that didn't stop her from scribbling her number on a bar mat and handing it to Malik before he slipped away out through the door.

She returned with her conceited grin and it took all of Roy's strength not to slap her face. "So, what's up now?" she spat, with her hands on her hips and defiance in her eyes.

"Look at ya! You really couldn't give a flying shit. Well, Lacey, you have well and truly fucked up this time. Those disks that 'the butcher' had in his hands had the last few weeks' footage of the pub, which, if I'm not mistaken, have you and Keffa on them." He took a harsh breath and ran his fingers through his hair.

Lacey shrugged her shoulders and smirked. "Oh, perving over them was ya, farver?"

The vile thought tipped him over the edge and he pushed her towards the stairs. She lost her balance and fell, landing on her arse on the bottom step.

"You stupid, stupid, girl! That recording will have Kelly Raven wanting your blood. I won't be surprised if she takes this fucking pub down with you in it!"

Lacey wasn't bothered because she really didn't have a clue, too wrapped up in her own selfish world to care. "Oh gawd, as if she can do anything! It's about time someone showed her she ain't all that special. Keffa wanted me, not her, and the sooner she sees the disks, the better."

She went to get up, but Roy pushed her back down. "That woman can have you dead and buried at the click of her fingers, and unless I'm going completely off my rocker, that lad you gave your number to, is Eddie Raven's son. So, Lacey, it's better that you pack your bags and fuck off because I've just about had enough. I warned you, but ya just never listened. Well, now, you're on ya own."

Lacey rolled her eyes. "So, what if he is Eddie Raven's son? That old man is dead, so he ain't no threat."

Roy sighed aloud. "Oh dear, Lacey, if that boy is half the nutter Eddie was, then you, my girl, will have a nasty fucking death. I saw the same look in that kid's eyes. He is his father's son all right."

Lacey was shocked but again she shrugged it off. "They won't touch me. I'm only fucking eighteen. I ain't no grown woman."

At once, Roy felt a deep sorrow for his daughter. "Lacey, Kelly Raven was only fifteen when she bashed Patrick Mahoney's head in with a doorstop. Eighteen in their world is an adult, so, my girl, if you want to live by the sword, you'd better be ready to die by it. You were warned and now I can't help ya."

The two faced each other, at daggers drawn, with Lacey full of contempt for her father, but it then dawned on her how precarious her position was. Her expression transformed from arrogance to despair.

"Listen, you need to pack your stuff and stay away for a while. I can't have you here. They will be back, and your head will roll, and I'm too fucking old in the tooth for bloodshed, or, worse, picking up the remains of a burned down pub!"

"But, Dad, I've nowhere to go," she whimpered.

He raised a sarcastic eyebrow. "Really? You've collected more fucking phone numbers than I collect pint glasses. Just go, Lacey."

She realised that pouting her lips and giving him her childlike expression had worn too thin, and so all she could do was pack her bags and leave.

CHAPTER FIFTEEN

Kelly received the news that Keffa was being charged for Adam Carter's murder. The police had checked the CCTV footage in the shopping centre, but not all of his whereabouts could be accounted for, due to the lack of working cameras, and it was too close to Adam's apartment. The fact that they had his gun as the murder weapon was enough to hold him.

That evening, after the house fell silent, Kelly decided to look at the disks. She wanted to be alone because although Keffa had been acting strangely and nothing added up, she still loved him and would be distraught if he was found guilty. He was her alter ego and her protector. Since she was a kid, almost from their first meeting, she had grown to love him. Once this mess was sorted out, she planned to go away on another holiday, away from the business, and rekindle their relationship. She never wanted it to end; even the thought of it made her feel sick to her stomach.

There was a TV and DVD player at the end of her bed at Cyril's. She inserted the first disk for October and realised that to watch it would take hours, so she sat in front of the TV and had the remote on fast forward. There were four split screens: two of the bar, one of the kitchen, and one of the pub garden. "Fuck," she swore out loud. It would take ages to get to the part she needed to see. Then she noticed the date and time at the bottom left hand corner of the screen. She pressed the superfast forward on the remote, but in doing so, she went to the end of the month, just beyond the all-important 30th October date, the date the meeting took place between Keffa and his men and the Carters. She rewound but went too far back. But then, when she stopped the disk to fast forward to the correct date, she suddenly froze. There, paused on the screen, as clear as day, was Keffa in the kitchen. It was dated 27th October.

Her heart was pounding, and she felt the hairs on the back of her neck stand on end. She pressed play and watched. He was with the barmaid. At first, she thought they were arguing, but then she realised the girl was trying to kiss him. Kelly threw her hands to her mouth to stop the scream that wanted to leave her lips. The pain was like nothing she had felt before. Watching her boyfriend, someone she trusted with her life, take off his overcoat and jacket and run his hands over the girl's body, savagely groping her breasts, almost caused her heart to stop beating. She wanted to stop the recording, but she needed to watch – she needed to be sure. Keffa watched the girl strip down to nothing, and then he threw her around like a rag doll, fiercely fucking the life out of her. That wasn't her Keffa. He was never like that with her: he was gentle, loving, and slow. This was something else. He had her bent over the freezer hammering away with such force that Kelly sensed for a second that the girl was being raped. That was until she saw the girl's face turn towards the camera and smile as if she was in ecstasy. He then spun her over and pulled her legs over his shoulders and carried on. This was no rape, but was it an act of passion? Kelly paused the recording at the point where the barmaid once again smiled at the camera. Staring incredulously at the TV, Kelly started to feel the tears prickle behind her eyelids before they cascaded down her cheeks. It was just bizarre. All those years of having an ideal picture in her head of Keffa and her together – their future, a family of their own – and now to see him like a wild animal with another woman was just beyond belief. She felt her throat constrict, as if an invisible pair of hands was

312

strangling the life out of her. How could he do this, how could she have been so blind? He was the only man she ever wanted, and now, to think it was all based on a lie, it was upsetting beyond description. Cupping her head in her hands, she shook, as the soundless sobbing began, and yet inside, she was screaming. So many contradictory emotions engulfed her. She hated him and loved him in equal measure, and then she thought of herself and panicked. This feeling of grief was going to be her shadow. The picture of him and the barmaid would haunt her dreams and be there when she awoke in the morning. How would she ever get over it? She could blot out the pain from her past, but this was different: this was a love she would never get over. Then, there was the embarrassment, the complete humiliation. How could she live with that too? At once, she took a deep breath and stopped the sobbing. A new emotion – fucking anger – now took hold of her: it was a rage inside that almost tore her head off.

Turning the device to the play position, she continued watching. She wasn't going to be a lovesick teenager; no, she needed to feel angry, as this feeling of contempt was easier to handle. She glared at the footage, and then, out of her haze of anger, she saw simultaneously his jacket slide down the back of the freezer and him leave the pub. She sat upright and wiped away her tears and rewound the device. There! Yes, he'd left the pub in just his shirt, jeans, and overcoat. He always carried his gun inside his jacket pocket and yet he had left without it. She watched more, fast forwarding the images to the point at which Keffa, Frank, and Blakey had their meeting with the Carters. That was when Keffa left the pub, with the barmaid fussing over Adam. Too exhausted to watch anymore, she lay there for a while, mired in grief.

By morning, Kelly had tossed and turned, as she knew she would, with Keffa's image invading her dreams, and so by the time she got up for breakfast, she looked as though she had done several rounds with Olympic taekwondo champion, Jade Jones.

313

Mary had the girls up and dressed, ready for a day at the zoo. She was in her element, playing the nanny. The little ones loved the new adventures, the new family, and, of course, their big room with the enormous beds. Kelly was just coming down the stairs as they left the house.

Malik and Sassy were already at the table with Cyril, talking over yesterday's events. Sassy wore a sympathetic expression when Kelly appeared. She'd heard her crying, and yet she knew Kelly wasn't the type to be fussed over. She would tell them what was wrong in her own time.

"Come and 'ave a nice hot cup o' coffee, babe. We'll get this mess sorted," said Cyril, patting the chair next to him.

Kelly sat down and poured herself a cup, eager to consume some caffeine inside her to get herself moving. She looked out at the grey skies and sighed. "I'm thinking about selling up – the pubs, the club, everything." An unexpected tear left her eye.

Everyone remained silent, not knowing what to say. But they saw the pain on her face, all the same.

"I can't do this alone. I'm not sure I want to do it at all." Her words were robotic.

"You ain't alone, Kel. You've got a big firm, and, of course, us," Cyril reassured her.

She snapped out of her gaze and turned to face him. "Yeah, I know, but I think I got so bogged down with my business, I neglected what I had with Keffa."

"You've both worked hard, babe. Listen, Michael will have him outta there in no time."

Kelly smiled, and her tear-stained cheeks shone as though they had been polished. "It doesn't matter anymore, Cyril. It looks as though it's over between me and him."

"What! Why?" squawked Cyril.

"'Cos, he was fucking that barmaid. Anyway, enough about him. I need to move on and put him and the business behind me. I've just lost my appetite for it all."

Cyril sat with his mouth open. He knew men in this business flashing their cash always had eyes for a bit of dirty skirt and often took what was on offer – it went with the territory. Keffa was different, though. He may be a villain and always had been a good-looking lad with money, but Kelly was no gangster's dolly bird. She ran the firm. She had class and respect.

Malik was confused. "What barmaid?"

Kelly rolled her eyes in frustration. "That skanky slapper, to use Sassy's description of her, the one in the pub who was all over you!"

Sassy abruptly jumped up from the table. "I ain't standing for that. I'm gonna deck her one."

Malik stood up too. "Cyril, can you take us over there? I think that little scum bag deserves a right good beating."

Kelly waved her hand for them both to sit down again. "Oh, don't worry. I will deal with her later. I wouldn't normally lower myself, but under the circumstances, I don't give a shit, and she will get it, that's for sure. Right now, though, it's too risky for any of us to act

315

like loose cannons. I mean, this business with the dead girl in the house, and now Adam shot dead, we can't afford to have the filth looking in our direction. Something stinks, and until I find out what's going on, ol' miss fake tits can wait."

Cyril's phone rang. It was Frank. He sounded out of breath and distraught.

"'Ere, slow down, mate, I can't hear ya."

The look of shock and horror clouded Cyril's face. "You're fucking joking! Jesus, is anyone hurt?"

He put down the phone and shook his head. "You ain't gonna believe this, but those bastards 'ave only gone and burned down Naomi's." He looked at Kelly. "Oh, love, I'm so sorry."

Kelly sighed and nodded resignedly. "I guess they think Keffa killed Adam, then?"

"Yeah, it looks that way. It's your call, kiddo. If ya wanna jack it all in, then just walk away, but ya know what this means, if ya don't?"

Malik searched Kelly's face for an answer. He was ready for the war ahead, no matter what she decided. The news that her club had been destroyed hit Kelly very hard. It had not long been renovated and renamed after her dead mother. The thought of the Carters taking a liberty with her shrine transferred her rage from Keffa to the Carter brothers in an instant. This was a total piss-take and she wouldn't swallow it.

"That club was a sanctuary in her name. I wanted to keep her memory alive, ya know, and well, as I see it, the Carters have just desecrated her grave. I want their fucking heads on a stick. That club wasn't anything to do with Keffa, it was mine."

She turned to Malik. "Actually, Malik, it was ours because we inherited it from Eddie. I didn't know back then that I had a brother." Her thoughts drifted off.

Malik felt sick for her. "If I'd known back then, I'd have called it Naomi's, too. I think that was a nice touch, and I'm damned sure the fucking likes of the Carters ain't getting away with a right bastard stunt like that."

He turned to Cyril. "If the lads can find those weasels, then I'll finish 'em off!"

Cyril saw the keenness in Malik's eyes and knew then he was deadly serious.

"They have a tidy firm of their own now, by all accounts, but I think we can pin 'em down and 'ave a word in their shell-like."

The phone rang again and this time it was Johnnie Carter. "I wanna meet Kelly face-to-face today at the Mitcham Mint, neutral ground, twelve o'clock."

Cyril didn't have time to reply: the phone went dead.

"Well, fuck me, ol' Johnnie Carter wants a meet at midday at the Mint. I think we can accommodate that, can't we?" His voice was deep and sarcastic.

Malik rubbed his hands together and a cruel grin swept across his face. "Too right. Let's do it. It's showtime!"

317

Jean River watched the grey sky from the bedroom window. She lay there listening to the gentle snoring coming from the dead weight next to her. Slowly, she got up from the bed, careful not to wake him. She was still sore from the shag the night before and regretted giving Paddy the bag of cocaine. It made him high and horny, and for hours, he was banging away, before he eventually gave up. She stood at the end of the bed, staring at the great lump. He certainly wasn't a looker, not like Adam, but he was a means to an end.

Paddy Rye was in his late fifties and not the fittest-looking man for his age. When he was in his early twenties, he did turn a head or two and was an up-and-coming Face. Being a descendant from a big Irish family, he had six brothers to box with, so he had plenty of practice. He was dangerous, no question, although the real menacing men, the likes of Frank and the rest of Eddie Raven's crew, regarded his outfit as small fry. That burning desire to take back some of their business ate away at him, and so he hoped that when his own sons were old enough, he could muscle in on the manor. Now he had a family of his own: young Paddy, Fynn, and Mason. They took on their father's looks, big stocky men with square heads and sharp features. Young Paddy, known as Pickle, was the eldest and had a good head on his shoulders. He wasted no time in getting his own business set up; it was a trendy bar in Essex, serving the money spenders in their early twenties. Fynn and Mason had the muscle. They were all doing reasonably well for themselves and each had a reputation of which their father could be proud.

The younger brothers worked in London collecting money for the Carters. They had their eye on a bigger prize, the Carters' business, and were working their way towards taking over. Johnnie had just raised their position in the firm, but like their father, they had no sense of honour, and as far as scruples were concerned, they had none.

Jean's visit was for a whole different reason; she had information that she knew the Ryes would be only too happy to hear. With a little mix from the shit-stirring spoon, she could devise a plan and yet let them believe it was all their idea. She wasted no time in divulging the fact that Adam was dead and Keffa was nicked for it. She just hoped they didn't dig too deeply into how she knew.

Jean had been having a thing with Paddy for years, on and off. He was her first fallback, when no one else was around, and when she wanted her fanny tickled, he was there. He was never nasty to her and took what he could when he could because he knew she would fuck off again when she was done. That's how it was now and how it had been for many years.

Jean slipped into her shirt and jeggings and crept down the stairs to the kitchen to make a coffee. Her mouth was dry and tasted vile. Too much cocaine and champagne had left her with a dying thirst. The kitchen was large and had a long table at the heart of it. Paddy wasn't short of a few quid; with a nice pad, a flash motor, and a real swagger, he gave everyone within his circle the impression he was loaded.

She smiled to herself. In a suit, he looked quite attractive, but upstairs, sprawled out on those white sheets, he was actually pretty gross. His fat beer belly, moles, skin tags, and especially the sweaty armpits, turned her stomach. But to be fair, she wasn't getting any younger herself, although she could still wrap Paddy around her finger. She stirred the coffee, thinking over her life. Her father, Marcus River, was a man of substance and she looked up to him – she always had. Perhaps her life of running from man to man was her way of looking for the love she felt she had lost from her father – well, that's what she had learnt when watching a programme which discussed this issue. Instead of seeking out men, she should have loved her children, but if she was honest (that could be tricky), she didn't love them, and

319

popping out one after the other was a mistake. Why couldn't she have what her mother had – a good man, handsome, and loving, offering to give her the world, and living up to it? Paddy was probably the only guy who would have given her that life; however, he wasn't the Brad Pitt or George Clooney type of man she craved. Adam was everything, except now he was dead.

Just as she was about to put some bread in the toaster, the patio doors opened and in traipsed Mason and Fynn, looking extremely pleased with themselves.

"All right, boys?"

Mason smiled. "Yep! Jean, it went like a dream. Where's me Dad?"

"Upstairs, out for the count."

She poured another two coffees and placed them in front of the boys, and then fetched hers. "Well, it's my guess that Kelly fucking Raven will no doubt assume it was the Carters' way of retribution."

Mason burst out laughing. Excitedly, he said, "That's the plan. Let the Carters and her little crew have their own beef and we …" he punched his brother on the arm, "… we, bruv, can pick up where they left off. Keffa Jackson's in the nick, so the Yardies will be chomping at the bit. Raven's little set-up with the Colombians will crack, as those fuckers won't want to do business with her, if she can't keep her own club safe. Reardon's protection racket will be a laughing stock."

Jean smiled from ear-to-ear, like the cat that had got the cream. She had been used and abused for too long, but now she had the ultimate weapon: the Ryes. Her own son and Kelly Raven would wish they'd never crossed her. As she saw it, Eddie Raven owed her, and now she would have her revenge.

All the time going from one lover to the next, and even the years of living like a hippy, still never changed what she knew. She was, after all, her father's daughter. She had watched and listened to him, from being a child. She wasn't really that stupid, it was just easier to pretend she was.

Mason told her, "Right, Johnnie wants us there at this meeting with Kelly Raven. We're gonna have to go, or else he may suspect we had something to do with the fire."

Jean agreed. "Just act ignorant, go along, be the backup, but listen to 'em. I wanna know all the details."

Mason and Fynn liked Jean. She may not be their mother, but when she was around, their father was happy, and so, in some ways, they respected her. Their own mother died when they were kids and their aunt dragged them up, away from their father. However, she died when they reached their teens, and so they moved back with him. Jean wasn't a permanent fixture, but she had always turned up every so often, and so she just seemed to fit in. They liked the fact that she was no whingy, silly tart just after their father's money; she was more of a free spirit, and she was also an attentive listener and had a few good ideas up her sleeve. Her in-depth knowledge of all the London villains stemmed from her father, old Marcus, and therefore the brothers felt more relaxed in her company when thoughts turned to taking over from the Carters, and even more so, when she contributed her own ideas.

"Jean, how did ya know Adam was shot?" asked Mason, just before he took a large slurp of his coffee.

"Oh, you know me, babe. I always have me ear to the ground."

Fynn laughed. "Nice one, Jean. So, you reckon it was that Jackson geezer, then?"

Jean gave him a satisfied smirk. "Gotta be. It stands to reason."

Her hands trembled as she held the coffee cup. She quickly placed it on the table, before the boys realised she was a nervous wreck. The sight of Adam with the back of his head missing was a picture she would always live with.

"Well, I dunno, Jean. Why him?"

"Oh, I heard that there was some incident in the pub between Adam and him. I know that the Ravens and the Carters have a business agreement but rumbling under that charade is a war waiting to happen. So, it's my guess, Jackson shot Adam. The police have him for it, so they must be holding some proof." She stretched her neck and felt a bead of sweat above her brow, hoping that the Rye brothers wouldn't ask too many questions.

"This is our chance to get in there and stir up enough shit to have them fucking ruined, then. I mean, what better time, eh?" chuckled Fynn.

No one would have guessed from her neutral expression, but inwardly, Jean was having a great time. She knew their father had that burning desire to take out the Carters, the Ravens, and Reardon, so she was ready to fuel the fire and give them the nudge they needed to cause a war. She could then stand back and laugh at all of them. She even had a notion of taking over some of that business for herself, but perhaps that concept was too much like a dream. Nevertheless, she could tolerate being on old Paddy's arm, if it meant she could have the respect, the overseas holidays, and the status. But for now, she would watch from a distance and hope that Fynn and Mason had enough balls

322

to see the job through. She gave them a last endearing smile and headed back upstairs to pamper the old man and keep him sweet. One whiff that she was playing a game and Paddy would have her out on her ear, very likely with a black eye or two.

At twelve o'clock on the dot, Kelly stepped out of her Range Rover, wearing a black trouser suit with her long hair tied neatly back in a ponytail. Feeling emotionally raw, she knew she had to get herself together for this meeting and restrain herself from any distraction in the barmaid's direction, even though she wanted to throttle the little hussy. Kelly figured the fire in her belly would come out sooner or later and now was probably not the right time. Malik jumped out of the car all fired-up; he was ready for a fight and was primed to throw his weight around. Sassy came along because if the barmaid was there, she was going to get it.

Frank, Cyril, and Blakey had arrived a few minutes before, awaiting two of their hardest men, Nicholas and Calvin Lawson.

Nick and Cal, for short, arrived behind Kelly in their Audi TT, which looked like a Noddy car when they stepped out. Even Malik, who was growing quickly and was now well over six feet tall, had to look up at them. Still only in their twenties, Cal and Nick were giants. They were the two doormen at the club. Kelly kept them on when she took over and they were only too pleased to work for her. She was a good boss, unlike Eddie, who could be temperamental at best. When he was in one of his vile moods, he would kick off as soon as look at them.

"All right, Kelly?" asked Nick, the better-looking brother. He noticed the deep sorrow in her eyes. He assumed it was over the fire and Keffa being banged up.

She acknowledged him with a smile. "Yep, let's do this."

Nick stepped forward and stopped Kelly from going inside. "Hold on, Kelly. Me and Cal will go in first."

Kelly approved and allowed the two men to proceed.

Malik was learning. His sister had some clout. Not only had she these two big beasts as her protection, but she also had her three trustworthy 'uncles' who could still have men quaking in their boots.

The pub was empty, except for Johnnie, Frazer, and Matt Carter, sitting at the long table in front of the bar. Over to the side were their own henchmen, Mason and Fynn Rye.

Cyril whispered in Kelly's ear. "Wait here, babe." He gestured to Cal and Dan, who, in turn, approached Johnnie.

"A pat-down, gentlemen, or there's no fucking meeting."

Johnnie stood up, holding his hands in front of him. "No tools, I swear." He looked pale and it was obvious he was a trembling wreck. Frazer rolled his eyes and followed suit, along with his brother, Matt, as they rose from their seats and allowed the Lawsons to frisk them over.

Frank turned to Mason and Fynn. "Hop it, you two, the bar's closed." His voice almost echoed.

Fynn turned towards him. "I don't think so, mate. I'm with them."

It was all too much for Malik. The tension in the room was so tangible now that it stabbed his nerves. He ran forward and ripped the table away from the Rye brothers. It happened so quickly, that everyone was immediately on guard. Fynn was pulled up by his jacket and onto his feet; as he tried to hit back with his fist to punch the kid, Malik headbutted him clean across the bridge of his nose.

"Now, you were fucking asked to leave!"

Frank yanked Mason up by his collar and shoved him into his brother. "Do one, or you'll get the fucking same!"

The Ryes were not expecting some teenager to have so much strength. It caught them completely off guard, and yet they weren't in a position to argue. Mason glanced over at Johnnie, who just nodded.

Fynn was humiliated by the total lack of respect given to him by Malik. He turned to the younger man. "I'll 'ave you!" His voice wasn't as aggressive as usual because he knew now that Malik was harder than a coffin nail and as reckless as a tornado.

Malik appraised him calmly. His recent experience as a boxer was ideally suited to dealing with this kind of situation, and so he wasn't the least concerned by the older man's attempt at bravado.

"Come on then, mate, try it, and I'll bust your jaw to match the nose!" Malik's conceited attitude and crafty smirk made Fynn think twice, but he couldn't resist a parting sneer.

Frank pushed both the Rye brothers outside and told them to make sure they fucked off good and proper.

Kelly was totally unperturbed by her brother's outburst. Johnnie, however, wasn't; he felt a real unease.

As they all took their seats around the table, Johnnie poured the drinks. Kelly glared at the Carters in turn.

"So, this is fucking cosy, and it seems to me, that you either have an apology to make or something else is going on. Which is it?" she asked, in a cool tone.

Frazer gritted his back teeth. He didn't like the idea that he was answering to a woman. "We've heard ya club got burned down. I can tell you, it wasn't us."

"Oh, no? Then, who was it that took a right fucking liberty?" asked Malik, with venom in his voice. He confidently took his seat next to Kelly.

Johnnie glared at the boy and then at Cyril and Frank. This was not the way it should be. He should be discussing important business with these men, and, of course, Kelly. There was no way he should have to answer to some slip of a kid.

"Look, what is this? Who the fuck are you?" spat Johnnie.

Malik leaned forward and replied confidently. "Malakai River ... Raven! Nice to meet you an' all."

Malik's youthful looks belied an almost indefinable personality. Johnnie's suspicions were confirmed. He couldn't help but stare for a second. The room was eerily silent as both parties studied each other's body language.

It was Kelly, in her unruffled manner, who continued. "So, Johnnie, I'm sorry to hear about your brother. I know he was trouble, and he shouldn't have cut my men, but I'm a woman of my word, and you did agree to pay up for his little cock-up, shall we say. This is the thing. Keffa is down the nick, charged with his murder, and I believe different. Keffa had no motive to kill ya brother. I also know that you three wouldn't be here, if you'd burned down my club."

326

Johnnie nodded, relieved she believed him. "Kelly, something is going on, and I swear to you, this ain't our doing. Yeah, I'm gutted about me brother, but I don't want to lose another one. We had an agreement. You have the south and we have the north. You get your weekly poke and we … well, we earn enough. I ain't a greedy man."

Cyril watched for any signs of treachery, and he had to admit to himself, he believed the Carters were kosher.

"The problem we have now is this whole situation, as I see it, has made us look weak and that concerns me, Johnnie," Kelly seethed.

Matt, the youngest surviving brother, tilted his head to the side. "I don't like the sound of what's coming next."

Kelly shrugged her shoulders. "No, you won't like what's coming next, but if you don't go along with it, then, believe me, your firm and mine will be fucked over by anyone wanting to muscle in, and by the looks of things, whoever they are, they have already started, and so until we know who it is, then, I'm sorry, but—"

Johnnie put his hands up. "Oh, come on, Kelly, I don't want bloodshed."

Kelly laughed. "Johnnie, you're in the wrong game for that. I'm not talking about bloodshed."

Matt smiled then. He guessed what her plan was. The others, though, were bewildered and stayed quiet.

"Sorry, Johnnie, but the Queen's Head has to go. If we don't make this look like we're having our own turf war, then the real culprit will bring us down. I want to fucking ease them out of the woodwork, and the only way is to make it look like we're fighting each other."

Johnnie glanced at Frazer and Matt for their agreement.

Cyril felt a warm feeling inside, knowing Kelly was smart and could play the game better than most.

"Shame, that's my best earner," chuckled Johnnie.

Kelly remained unconcerned, as she sarcastically replied, "You have insurance!"

Malik was grinning like a Cheshire cat, and it irritated Frazer because he'd never liked Eddie Raven, and Malik was him all over again.

"Oh, and another thing. I have a strong feeling that the culprit is one of your men. I suggest you think long and hard about your workforce and who might gain from setting us up against each other."

Frazer shook his head. "Nah, love. There's no one, not from our side."

Malik surged forwards, an inch from Frazer's nose. "Listen, mate, if me sister says it's one of your men, then it's fucking one of your men. Got it?"

Kelly pulled him back in his chair. "Malik, I think they've got the message."

Johnnie watched the siblings' dynamic forces at work. She held his leash, and for now, he was tamed, but in a few years, that would change, and he knew all hell would break loose. Still, by the time the kid was in charge, he would be long gone, either lying on a sunbed somewhere in Spain, or, worst case scenario, on a cold mortuary slab. For now, he knew that he would have to go along with it. Kelly was the only person the Colombians would deal with. She also had the protection racket sewn up, and if that all collapsed, then that would probably have a knock-on effect, and their own business would suffer. She had them by the short and curlies, although, on the other hand, the arrangement worked fine for both parties. Adam may have tried to upset the apple cart, but Johnnie had respect for the woman and therefore he was willing to pay up for his brother's reckless behaviour.

"This has to be a first, eh, the Ravens and the Carters on the same side!" mocked Frazer, with a conceited tone to his voice evident to all.

Kelly raised her eyebrow. "Frazer, I didn't think there were sides. As I see it, and correct me if I'm wrong, we've an agreement, and that's called business, not feuding between ourselves."

Frazer was caught off guard by her controlled manner. The atmosphere was bordering on hostile and the tension was rising to uncomfortable levels.

Kelly didn't move a muscle and neither did Malik. The Carters, however, shifted in their seats.

It was left to Johnnie to pour oil on troubled waters. "You're right, Kelly. There is no battle between us, and it does appear that there's a third party among us, trying to damage our reputations. I agree, we do need to work together. The Queen's Head will be burned to the ground by the end of the week. If you get wind of any underhanded shit, keep us informed, and we'll look at our own men. I can promise you this, though. With my hand on my heart, we ain't out to cause trouble, but I'll kill the louse that shot Adam."

Kelly was pleased with that intervention. "Johnnie, I will give you the fucking gun, if it helps."

Malik listened intently and his gift for reading people paid off. Their innocence was confirmed. He held out his hand, and Johnnie, without hesitation, shook it.

"I suggest you inform those two meatheads that we're at war. I'd have the cunts followed, 'cos, I've a bad feeling about them," prompted Malik.

Johnnie smiled. It was a genuine smile for the first time. "Well, Malakai River, Raven, I reckon they've a bad feeling about you, since you wrote off Fynn's nose."

The tension had gone at this point, and they all laughed, mainly from relief but also from seeing Malik take on a man who was twice his size. It was quite a shock and one that would embed deeply in their minds.

Cyril glanced across at his men. They understood that look and nodded back in silent agreement that the young ones, Kelly and Malik, had handled the situation like pros, as they would have done a good few years ago.

Sassy was silent and kept one eye on the bar, waiting for any sign of the barmaid. The only person there was Roy, who looked remarkably nervous for a man pouring drinks. Her fixed gaze caught his attention, and like a mouse, he scurried away. Sassy then turned to the men around the table to find Matt giving her the once over.

"So, who's this little cracker?" he remarked, as he flicked his head in Sassy's direction.

Before Malik could leap down his throat, Sassy answered, "I'm Sassy, and I'm well outta your league, mate."

"Hey, 'old ya horses, it was just a compliment. I ain't into kiddies." He held his hands up exaggerating. "Gutsy one, you, ain't ya?"

Kelly laughed. "No wimps in this family."

After finishing their drinks, the Carters left the pub first, to find Mason and Fynn outside waiting, both puffing on a joint. Johnnie cast a belittling grin in Mason's direction. "Some security you bunch of pussies are!"

Mason approached Johnnie, offering him a puff of his joint. "So, what did they say, then?"

Johnnie waved the joint away and studied him closely. "A bit curious, to say the least, ain't ya?"

Fynn, who was standing a few feet away, came over to join them, wiping the last of the blood from his nose. "So, what's the crack, then?"

Frazer and Matt walked away. They weren't going to discuss business with two money collectors and were surprised that Johnnie was even engaging with them.

"I just wanna get something straight with you two. Firstly, your name ain't Carter, so my business meetings are no concern of yours, and secondly, you're lucky me and me brothers weren't hurt because you were paid as me heavies. Instead, you rolled over at the first fucking headbutt. Now, I think it's probably best if you just stick to collecting me money, because after today's meeting, I need real men I can rely on – got it?"

Fynn and Mason walked away, deep in thought. As the three brothers climbed into a top-of-the-range Mercedes and sped away, the Ryes were left literally out in the cold.

331

Mason took a cab to meet up with some mates in the West End, whilst Fynn decided to drive over to Otford. He wanted nothing more than to see his girlfriend, now fiancée. His escape from the world of ducking and diving was to indulge in the finer things in life: good food, holidays abroad, and going to the theatre. His father always said he was born to silk and wondered if he'd done the right thing allowing Fynn to enter the world of villainy instead of taking a professional job or going to university. But how could his father have encouraged a white-collar job or academia, when he didn't know the first thing about either of them? Fynn did all right with what he had and could blag his way around the rich London toffs. He had a thing about posh birds, though, and had secured himself a right tasty little sort. Taking his girlfriend to meet his father, however, would have been a total no-no. She would have sussed him out right away – he was no London city slicker. As if.

She was oblivious to his day job, believing he was in finance and working in the city, and the fact that he didn't speak with a plum in his mouth was endearing. But she also had her secrets. Little did he know that she came from a council estate and could handle herself when needed.

As he pulled up outside her house, he sighed. He wanted to move on to bigger things and take over from the Carters, but that little notion was looking a harder feat than he initially believed. For now, he would bide his time and enjoy a lobster dinner with his sophisticated bird in her classy home, which, one day soon, he would be moving into.

Penelope was wearing her red jersey dress with her hair piled high. She was just about to apply another layer of hairspray, when she heard the front door bell ring. "Damn," she said aloud. Running late for a very important appointment in her line of work wasn't acceptable. Leaving her shoes on the soft luxurious carpet, she hurried down the stairs to find Fynn standing at the front door with a huge grin across his face.

"Well, are you gonna stand there looking gorgeous, or are you going to invite me in?"

What's he doing here? She had to think quickly. The obvious going to work excuse would not cut it.

"Oh, I, er … wasn't expecting you, and I've a meeting with some investors."

She wasn't lying either. She did have a meeting, but if he knew the truth, he would have gone spare. The fact was she had been coaxed into launching a sexy underwear line with a rich friend. The lingerie was aimed at the more mature market, and she was going to a photo shoot to model the designs herself. She liked Fynn because he had money and had an edge to him. She could see him in the ducking and diving world, possibly even within the criminal fraternity. But he told her he was a professional businessman and she believed him, at least until quite recently. She could pull off the successful chick herself with her friends, and she had to admit, she found the new life a thrill, ditching the cockney accent and playing the classy wealthy woman.

Fynn's smile turned to a growl. "Call and say you can't make it. You've better things to do, like making your husband-to-be happy."

Penelope cast a look of annoyance which didn't go unnoticed.

"I can't, Fynn. I'm really sorry, but I have to go. I'm already late for the meeting as it is. Look, you can stay here, if you would like to. I'll be back tomorrow, but I really must dash."

She left him at the door and hurried back upstairs. Her mini suitcase was open on the bed, revealing all her sexy outfits. She sensed his presence behind her and tried to fasten the case before he saw it. Unfortunately, she was seconds too late.

"Oh yeah, and what fucking investors would these be, then? Do fucking tell me?" he demanded, as his eyes opened wide at the sight of the underwear. It certainly wasn't lingerie he had seen her wear and that pissed him off even more.

Penelope froze to the spot, her mind in a frantic panic. "No, Fynn, this isn't for tonight. It's stuff I'm packing up to send back to a sales rep who asked me to try them on. But you know me. It's not really my scene." She continued to zip up the suitcase with her back to him, hoping he'd bought that little piece of fiction.

"So, if you're away overnight, where's the bag?"

Penelope felt her tongue stick to the roof of her mouth, and a flaming hot flush swamped her. "Well, like I said, I'm in a rush. I haven't packed it yet." Nervously, she turned to attack mode. "Look, Fynn, what's all this about? I'm in a hurry, and we didn't make any arrangements to spend the evening together, so perhaps it's better that you come back tomorrow, and you can have my full attention."

Fynn was suspicious and didn't like the idea of being mugged off twice in one day. "You're my fiancée and you ain't fobbing me off, love. You need to get your priorities right. Call these people and tell them you ain't coming because we've a meeting of our own."

She looked at the bruise across his nose, the anger in his eyes, and felt cornered. He was her future, with the money and means to keep her in the standard to which she was accustomed. But Penelope was streetwise, cunning, and a good bullshitter herself when she needed to be, and if she was being honest, she still had her doubts about him. It was little things, like the day he came back from what he said was his "professional job" with cuts to his left eye and his knuckles bruised and bloodied. He'd laughed it off – said he'd been cornered, travelling on the London Underground, one night at a Spurs v Arsenal game. But she hadn't been convinced. Curious, she had checked on her iPad the next morning for matches played that Tuesday evening and found only three games which were all in the Championship. Although the wedding was a year off, she was beginning to wonder whether or not he was the right one. In the last month or so, his soft nature had subsided. She'd witnessed his quick temper and thought he was not as smooth as he'd first come across. That fictitious Tuesday night Premier Division match, therefore, had been revealing, to say the least.

She stepped back away from him and took a deep breath. "No, Fynn, I cannot and will not cancel. This is my work and I won't be dictated to by you. So, leave me to it, and I'll see you tomorrow or at the weekend. Fynn, I'm in a hurry. Please, move!"

He knew she was uncomfortable. You can't kid a kidder, and had she but known it, he could have gained a first-class degree in bullshitting, if it had been on the university curriculum. Grabbing her arm, he coarsely spun her around to face him. "We're getting married next year, and you need to learn to put me first 'cos that's what it's all about," he scowled.

Penelope then showed him she wasn't the delicate woman she portrayed, and instantly shook him off. With both hands on his chest, she thrust him away from her. "Don't you ever put your hands on me again!" She screamed so loudly that Fynn took another step back. Having never seen her act like this, he realised she was not as prim and proper as he thought she was. The look in her eyes certainly told him a whole other story. In fact, he was right: she could fight off an attacker.

The last man who had tried it had come off worse, but the terrifying incident had left her with nightmares.

Still tense from the humiliation in the pub, he vented his anger by slapping her so hard across the face, she fell onto the bed. The minute his hand touched her, he regretted it. As he went to help her up and apologise, she lifted her foot and kicked him hard between the legs. He fell to his knees, holding his balls. His face drained of blood, while he tried to take deep breaths. Penelope didn't waste time. She jumped to her feet and scooted out of the room and into the bathroom, where she locked herself in. She scanned the room, looking for a tool she could use for protection, if needed, but she was out of luck. Her perfect bathroom was always kept spotless; white tiles covered the floors and the walls, with just the usual toiletries. Taking a deep breath, she tried to calm her nerves and think straight. Hopefully, he would have got the message and just leave quietly or offer an apology through the door. Listening intently, she heard nothing. It suddenly dawned on her, the phone was on the bed, and if he saw the messages, then her life as she knew it – and the forthcoming marriage – would be over, PDQ. "Shit!" she said quietly. There were hundreds of images of herself posing in that same underwear. And to make matters worse, all the photos had been texted to Damian Right, the buyer interested in the collection. How the hell would that look? She had no choice but to face Fynn and hope he hadn't seen the messages. She flew out of the bathroom and back into her bedroom, but sure enough, there he was, scrolling through her phone. Her adrenaline was pumping out of fear and anger. She leaped towards him, trying to snatch it from his hand, but he backhanded her away. Again, she ran at him, and this time he didn't bother with a shove. He punched her in the mouth and then delivered an even harder blow to her right eye, knocking her to the ground. Clutching her bleeding face, she tried to crawl away. Fynn was now at the peak of his temper and the red mist descended, sending him into an uncontrollable blind fury. He threw the phone at her head, just missing her, as it crashed into the Sony wall-mounted TV. He then followed that up by kicking her so hard in the chest that she let out a blood-curdling scream. Whilst she was really suffering now, he decided to continue the punishment. His hand reached down and tore at her neatly piled hair, ripping chunks from her roots, and as he lifted her off the ground, he shook her like a piece of wet lettuce. Spittle left his mouth, as he screamed obscenities. "You whore! You no-good dirty whore!"

Terrified of what he would do next, she didn't fight back – she had no strength left – as he dragged her to the stairs and threw her down. The forward tumble was like seeing death before her eyes. To this day, she couldn't describe the following few seconds. However, she tried to grab the bannister, only to fail miserably. Eventually, she landed in a heap on the hall floor, barely able to breathe. The fall had taken the wind out of her and she began to lose consciousness. But she was still able to hear him run down the stairs and tower over her, screaming more disgusting words. She remained motionless, praying he would just leave. Relief came when she heard the front door open, but horror took over, when she realised he was standing outside shouting his mouth off for her neighbours to hear. The outside sensor lights were on and the whole front drive was floodlit for all to see. It was an embarrassment of Herculean proportions, but that was the least of Penelope's problems. *Sod the neighbours*, she thought, as she lay there in excruciating agony with ripped finger nails, broken ribs, her face feeling as though she'd been punched out of the ring, and to cap it all, a badly torn leg muscle. *What else could possibly go wrong?* she thought wryly. She wondered if she would ever come out of this alive.

Malik and Kelly were sitting in her car. He wanted some time alone to talk, away from everyone. After all, they'd only had a short time to get to know each other, and their coming together for the first time had taken place in such awful circumstances, with so much going on, they really hadn't found an opportunity to talk about themselves.

"Are you okay, Kelly? I mean about Keffa?" asked Malik.

She was numb from it all and still in shock. "I dunno, I s'pose I'll have to be. I don't have a lot of choice, and with all that's going on, I need to concentrate on more serious matters. I want to know who's behind all this mess. Someone has shot that Adam Carter, and I really don't believe it was Keffa, and now my club, I mean our club, has been burned to the ground. There's also the business of the girl, God rest her soul."

Malik swallowed hard. He was still struggling himself with trying to get that picture of Kimi's face being eaten away. He shuddered. "Sis, do ya think this is the right life for you? After all, you being a woman and this being a man's world, it must be very hard."

Kelly would have taken offence at that remark, if it had come from anyone else. "Oh, Malik, I do sometimes wonder, but then I think, what else do I know? I hardly finished school. My younger years were spent in prison, and with a manslaughter conviction over my head, who is going to employ me? I did think about selling it all and just buying a sweet shop."

Malik burst out laughing and was soon joined by Kelly. "Oh yeah, sis, you could call it a gobstopper short of a sweetshop, get it, like a sandwich short of a picnic," he chuckled.

"Malik, that's very funny, ha bloody ha."

He noticed the trace of a smile that lifted her cheek bones and admired her for being so strong, when this, to him, was a tough time.

338

They drove along the A21 in Kent and turned off towards Otford. Kelly only knew the route which passed Malik's cottage to get to Cyril's. "Do you mind us passing your place, or shall I go another way?"

"No, it's fine. I'll have to go back soon, anyway. The police called yesterday and said it was okay for me to return. But I've been thinking. That house has such bad memories for me and the girls. I've a few fights lined up, and I'll be able to earn a quid or two, so I thought we should move away. Perhaps this is the right time to have a clean break."

"Malik, I've a house in London, a nice place. I'll put it in your name. It was out of Eddie's estate, and besides, I owe you half of everything—"

Before she could carry on, Malik said, "Slow down, sis, what's going on over there? Look, the Ol' Bill. What are they doing?"

Kelly could see two police cars parked up with their lights flashing, one at the end of someone's drive opposite Malik's cottage.

"Yeah, looks like they've arrested someone. He's slumped over the bonnet."

"Kelly, stop the car a minute! I know the woman that lives there."

Kelly pulled over and turned the ignition off. "Malik, listen, we don't want to be on their radar. How do you know her?"

Malik was leaning forward to get a closer look at the man being handcuffed.

"Fucking hell! What's going on? Ain't that one of the men me and Frank threw out of the pub?"

Kelly's interest now became keener, as she stared across to what was happening. "Oh yeah. What the hell is he doing in this neck of the woods, I wonder? I don't like it, Malik. How would he know where you live?"

Malik shook his head. "No idea, but look, there's an ambulance and a copper at the door. I don't think he was here for me. Something's going on. I don't know. All these coincidences, they're putting me on edge."

"I think we should go, before they notice us."

Malik was almost across Kelly's seat trying to get a better view. "Sis, look! The paramedic is with her. I bet that cunt's bashed her up. I swear to God, if he's hurt her, I'll finish him off, good and proper."

Kelly started the engine and slowly drove away. "Malik, look, she's safe. The police and the ambulance are there. We need to go. I just asked you how you know her?"

He sat back and put his seat belt on, not wanting to argue. She was right. He couldn't step in and cause a scene. "A while ago, when I was trying to earn a few bob, I washed her car, and she gave me a lot of money. It was Christmas time and she did me a right favour. She's a real nice bird, classy she is, and well, it's hard to explain. I liked her. She was special, ya know."

"So, what happened? Did you have a fling or what?"

Malik was silent for a few seconds. "No, she's older than me, and to be honest, I had nuffin to offer her at the time. I couldn't even afford a poxy haircut, let alone any decent clobber. She was way outta my league."

Kelly's own sadness over Keffa was replaced with pain for her brother, knowing that he struggled to look after his sisters, leaving him no room for a life of his own. The rest of the journey was undertaken in silence, each contemplating their own future.

CHAPTER SIXTEEN

Malik awoke the next morning, having had only a few hours of sleep.

A meeting had taken place in the early hours at Cyril's, with men from the pubs and club who were part of the firm invited to attend. Kelly still had her doubts about the Carters' ability to pin down who from their lot was causing a war, so she assigned her own men to do the digging and keep a keen eye. Beano arrived shortly after one o'clock, to give his findings. He was a Native American tracker, or so Kelly called him. He was good at playing the detective and only worked for a handful of people. He wasn't on anyone's firm, as such, but he was paid for his information, which was always spot on. Training at a few gyms and playing poker, he was privy to gossip from many of the club's bouncers. Like a hairdresser, where women poured out their life stories, Beano had a knack for teasing out information. As far as anyone was concerned, he was just a harmless man who was friends with everyone.

Kelly looked white and pasty. She was tired from the grief and stress, and she needed her bed, but as soon as Beano revealed his discoveries, she sat upright with a burst of energy. Malik gulped his fresh orange juice to remove a bitter taste in his mouth.

"Beano, are you one hundred per cent sure that Jean is in cahoots with Paddy Rye?" asked Kelly.

He nodded. "I went to Paddy Rye's son's bar, and I got talking to him. Apparently, his old man was in a good mood and it was all down to Jean River. Paddy has been seeing Jean on and off over the years. They have this mad relationship, and it's a family joke because if ol' Paddy has a smile on his face, then that means Jean's around. Otherwise, he's a miserable bastard."

Malik could see why Beano was able to get what he wanted. His cool, laid-back presence and a face that was so innocent-looking along with a deceptive laconic style of talking suggested he was not an intrusive person. This worked very much to his advantage, as he was seen as the guy people could go up to, to pour out their gossip or tales of woe.

Sassy was trying to control her rage. "The fucking dirty whore. I swear to God, if I get me hands on her scrawny neck, I'll ring it like a chicken."

Cyril ruffled her hair. "Easy, darlin', you won't get ya hands dirty. I'll not 'ave ya getting in trouble an' all, and that's enough of the bad language. Ya need to be a lady."

Sassy softened. Cyril was becoming more like the dad she'd never had, and now, she wished he'd been hers.

"Sorry, but she makes me sick. I hate her, the filthy cu ... woman!" she tried to stop herself from swearing.

"I ain't shocked, really. Let's face it, Sass. Our muvver has waltzed her way through life, going from one dickhead to another, place to place, and all for her own needs. I mean, did we really even know her? I'm sure as hell, I never did. She never spoke to me about herself. The only conversation was about babysitting. What did she ever talk to you about?"

Sassy lowered her gaze from Malik, in self-pity. "Nothing. She never spoke to me, did she? I was the one she detested the most."

It reminded Kelly of her so-called mother. All she ever did was preach the Bible or scream at her. And, of course, there were the beatings. It was strange how they'd almost had the same upbringing.

"Do you know any of her boyfriends?" she asked.

Sassy laughed aloud. "Apart from the hippies and a drip called Dennis, no we don't. She used to fuck off for days at a time. She was a bit like a chameleon she was, dressing up in different outfits. It's all hard to explain." She looked across at Malik for answers.

He smiled compassionately. "Yeah, I know what you're saying, Sass. Muvver was a secretive person. I thought it was just her personality, but it was more than that. Apart from her year of being a hippy, where she was around a lot, along with her beansprout crunching mates, we never really saw much of her. She would go off for days, sometimes dressed to impress, and every time she was different. I hardly recognised her at times. I used to get annoyed with her because we had nothing, and there she would stand, checking herself in the mirror, always rigged out in something nice, all made-up, and off she would go, ready for another trip away. She would leave us either with a teenage babysitter from the estate, or we'd be all alone."

Beano's eyes darted from Malik to Sassy. "There's something else you should know. I asked this Pickle bloke if Jean had any children, and he told me that she hadn't any. So, she may have kept her fellas a secret, but she also kept you all a secret from Paddy."

"It doesn't surprise me!" spat Sassy, with hate clearly in the tone of her voice. "That's what we were – her dirty little secrets. Well, apart

345

from Star, when our muvver was trying to pass her off as Adam Carter's. I hate that woman so much!"

"I think we should pay our muvver a little visit. I wanna know what's going on, and I bet my last tenner she's behind it," declared Malik.

Kelly shook her head. "Nah, surely she ain't that cute? I mean, if she was in control of a plan that big to take us out, she wouldn't have been churning out fatherless kids and living on a rough estate. No disrespect, Malik, but seriously, I don't think she has the brains or the bottle."

It was Cyril who surprised them all with his comment. "I knew Jean as a kid. She ain't stupid, and she has a lotta bottle. A right wayward bastard, she was then. If she's her father's daughter, then she's more than capable. Poor Marcus was pulling his hair out with her. She was on a downward spiral from the age of five. I never liked her. There was something dark about the kid. So, I, for one, wouldn't rule her out of the equation."

Beano agreed. "I also need to tell you that Paddy Rye holds a grudge against Eddie Raven and Johnnie Carter. I'm not sure of the details, but he's said for years that he would bring them down one day and get his muddy paws on their business."

Beano departed at two o'clock in the morning.

It was nine o'clock and Valerie was awake with a splitting headache, the remains of a bottle of Grey Goose vodka standing on the bedside table. She poured a strong cup of coffee and pulled open the drawer to find she had no paracetamol left. Her hangover was a daily occurrence, and now she would have to face the hard beads of water bouncing off her head from the shower. She stared at her clothes lying strewn across the floor and decided just to get dressed and head to work, stopping at the chemist on the way. No one gave a shit what she looked like anyway. Adding her appearance to the long list of jibes wouldn't make any difference. After putting her hair back into a ponytail, she made just one concession: she paid particular attention to cleaning her teeth, just in case the commissioner came too close and smelled any alcohol on her breath.

Just as she stepped onto the pavement, the heavens opened, and for a second, she contemplated climbing back up the stairs to her flat to grab her raincoat. However, her head was throbbing so much that she abandoned that thought and instead hurried to her car to drive to the nearest Boots store for painkillers.

The shop assistant looked her up and down. "Sorry, miss, but we can only sell two packets to any one customer."

Valerie was not in the best of moods. "Ridiculous, what do you think I'm going to do, kill myself?"

The attractive young assistant raised her eyebrow and replied, "Rules are rules, love, so do you want these two or not?"

Valerie slammed the money on the counter, snatched the tablets, and left. Once she was back in her car, she crammed two at the back of her throat and almost gagged trying to swallow them without any liquid to ease them down. The day was not off to a good start and she was feeling the pressure. The commissioner wanted to know what was going on with the case, as he was not entirely convinced that Keffa was the right man behind bars. She needed to buck up her ideas and be one step ahead or her career would go down the pan. It wasn't looking good. Adam Carter was dead, the young girl had still not been identified, Kelly Raven's club had just been burned to the ground, and last night Fynn Rye was arrested opposite Malakai River's cottage, although she had to concede he had been charged about an incident involving a woman who happened to live nearby. But still, either it was all a huge coincidence, or there was more to it. Of greater importance, she was in the firing line, if she didn't get some answers quickly.

No sooner had she arrived at the station, when she was greeted by a smug grin from Sampson. "Morning, Ma'am." His exaggerated smile grated on her like fingernails running down a blackboard.

"Any news on the fire or the dead girl?" she fumed.

"No, Ma'am."

"Well, don't just stand there looking like a fucking wet weekend. Have you organised an interview with Kelly Raven? I want answers, and I want them today."

Sampson was revelling in her frustrations. It was very clear she was losing the plot and it showed. He had smelled the vodka on her breath every day for the past week, despite her unsubtle ways of trying to disguise it, and her dishevelled appearance had been remarked on by a number of her colleagues.

"She's not at any of her addresses. We've left messages to contact us."

She gave him a sneering response. "Not good enough. I want her in here and today. Got it?"

Sampson nodded, knowing he couldn't push his boss too far. She would take her frustration out on him and she was more than capable of being nasty. He hurried away back to the men's toilets and dialled

Cyril's number, with one ear to the phone and the other listening for Campbell to enter the restroom.

"The super is on the fucking war path. She wants to speak to Kelly Raven, and one way or another, she'll have her dragged in. Would she come in of her own accord? Oh, and tell her to bring her brief. Campbell wants blood, and she's at breaking point, so I'm not too sure what road she's going down."

Cyril had felt an inkling this was coming. "All right, I'll have a word."

Kelly was still looking a little pasty and Cyril noticed her sluggish moves and drained expression. He approached her with a cup of tea and sat down slowly alongside her.

"Kelly, that was the DI. They want to talk to ya. I can tell them you ain't feeling chipper. It's up to you."

Kelly sat upright and took the cup, gently lifting it to her lips and sipping graciously. "Yeah, Cyril, I'll go. They'll think it's fishy, if I'm not available to answer questions about the fire."

"Kel, are you all right, love?"

Kelly displayed the despair on her face and blinked back her tears before they plummeted down her cheeks. "I will be. I just feel gutted. I mean, Keffa of all men doing that to me. I thought he loved me. I mean really loved me. I guess I was so wrong. It hurts, Cyril, like you wouldn't believe, and now I have this new family, and I need to be strong for them."

Cyril slid his huge arm around her shoulders. "Oh, Kel, you forget you ain't long outta nappies yaself. You may be the big sister, but this

349

is all new to you. Malik is used to looking out for the girls. You ain't supposed to take over. Ya need time to get over Keffa, and the latest fiasco is all too much to deal with on ya own. Give yaself a break, eh?"

Kelly gave Cyril a wan smile. "Yeah, well, after this is sorted, I'll go off to Spain for a few weeks. Maybe, I'll take the girls with me. Malik can start to learn the ropes with the club when it's rebuilt and also look after the pubs. He'll need to get used to how the businesses work. Where is Malik, by the way?"

Cyril shifted his gaze away from Kelly. He detested lying to her. "He has to sort out plans for his next fight."

Kelly was too tired to notice the awkwardness in Cyril's body language. That was lucky for Cyril because he hated keeping secrets, but he'd just promised Malik he would keep silent over the fact that the boy was going on a prison visit to see Keffa. The VO had arrived with a note not to tell Kelly. That had not gone down well at all. Malik being Malik, he decided he would give Keffa a piece of his mind.

∽*∾

Blakey offered to drive Malik to Brixton Prison. He had his own business to attend to in London, so he wasn't exactly going out of his way. As they pulled up outside the gate, Blakey turned to the young man. "Now, don't you go throwing ya weight around in there, son, or they'll have you behind bars as well. Also, it ain't my business, but Keffa does love Kelly. I don't know why he was fucking around with that silly tart, but I do know he worships the ground Kelly walks on. So, go easy, eh?"

Malik listened intently to the sober words which left Blakey's mouth and decided to go along with his advice. He knew the man was not the most talkative of souls, but he respected his common-sense

350

approach to life. So Malik decided not to prejudge Keffa before the man had given his version of events. He stepped out of the car and joined the queue. Two young women in front turned and smiled, nudging each other and giggling away. It didn't take a brain surgeon to work out why. Malik had noticed lately the admiring glances he was constantly receiving and guessed it was the new clothes and haircut. He held his shoulders back now and his head high. The mirror was not such a stranger either. He took great pride in his appearance, and despite the rush to get ready for the visit, he'd still found the time to check himself over before he left the house.

The prison's main doors opened and slowly they began to enter. Malik had never been to a prison and so had no idea of the process. Little did he know that his father had spent a long time inside, a chunk of it in Brixton. As soon as it was his turn to hand over the VO, he became uneasy. The prison officer, an older man, stared for more than was necessary and examined the paperwork closely. "River, is that your name?"

"Yes. Why, is something wrong, mate?" He tilted his head to the side and smiled.

The officer's eyes were like saucers, as he glared at Malik. "Er, no, everything is fine. Sorry, you look like someone else, that's all."

Malik took back the VO and followed the queue inside the main waiting room. He gazed around at the visitors. They were all kinds — men, women, and babies, but there was a difference. Some were wealthy, dripping in designer gear, and there were those who looked like they had dragged themselves off the street, with their thin colourless faces and eyes that gave a strong clue they were hooked on heroin. Malik's name was called, and he followed the officer into the search areas. Here, he had to pass a detector and was required to

351

remove his belt and shoes and then have a pat-down. He hated the whole set-up: the smell of the prison, the banging of the metal doors, and especially the attitude of the officers. It all felt like he was a prisoner himself. He assumed that they never switched off and treated everyone the same. He shuddered, as he was led into another short corridor where the doors were shut behind him. The sight of the barred gates and the cold colours of the walls were probably a deterrent for any young teenager to get into serious trouble. Eventually, he was escorted into the visiting room, where again the doors were locked behind him. A row of tables stretched across the room and most of the inmates were already seated. Malik couldn't miss Keffa, by the sheer size of the man. A guard stood by his side with his arms crossed. Keffa looked over and nodded at Malik to join him.

Once seated, Malik, forgetting what he'd just promised Blakey, wasted no time in getting his point across. "You fucked up big time with me sister." He didn't shout but his voice was deep and intimidating, taking Keffa by surprise.

"Malik, never mind all that. This is serious, right? I need to sort shit out." He leaned forward. "I need your help." Then he stared up at the screw, still by his side. "'Ere, mate, do you fucking mind? You're earwigging."

The officer was a big lump but the look on his face said it all. He was on edge, and Malik assumed that Keffa had clout, even in the nick.

Once the prison officer moved back out of hearing, Keffa continued. "Malik, firstly I love ya sister, and trust me on that score. I've loved her since she was fifteen, and I fucked up, screwing that little tart, Lacey. I hold my hands up, and I don't blame Kelly for not wanting to know me. But I need to know she's being taken care of."

Malik sat back on his chair and gave Keffa a sinister sneer. "Well, she ain't your fucking problem now, is she!"

Keffa shook his head. "Malik, you don't understand. She's vulnerable out there alone——"

Before he could finish, Malik moved forward and spat through gritted teeth. "What planet are you on? She ain't alone. She's with Cyril and she's got me now. So, don't go worrying your little head on that score."

Keffa rolled his eyes. "We ain't got long, and I need you to listen and listen hard. Kelly out there without me is in danger. She doesn't really run the fucking cocaine business, I do. She's the front woman that's all. She deals with the Colombians, but my men do all the running around. When the Rastas get wind that I'm in 'ere for a long stretch, they will run amok. She'll be left wide fucking open. The Carters will take over the manor and God knows who will seize South London."

Malik realised this was no game; Keffa was serious. He nodded for him to continue.

"Malik, I know you're still young, and you don't know the business, but who can I trust? Cyril and Frank, along with their crew, aren't getting any younger, and the new wannabes play a whole different game. There are no fucking rules! Do you love ya sister? I mean, you've only known her for a short while, haven't ya?"

"Keffa, I don't know your business, but I will learn fucking quick, if it means I can help Kelly. Yes, I love her. But you're right, I don't know her that well. Even so, it's this feeling I have. It's like she's always been there, and like all me sisters, I would die for 'em."

Keffa smiled. "Ya know, mate, I believe you. I watched how you are with those little ones, and I have to give it to ya, you're a good man."

"Why, Keffa, why did ya do it? Kelly is devastated, ya know."

"Malik, I was an idiot and I fucked up. Me and Kel, we, er, sort of got wrapped up in work, and she seemed to push me aside, and that Lacey bird offered it on a plate, and I was a fucking prick to take it. Now, I look back, I think Kelly took on too much too quickly. But she's a determined woman. If she does anything, she does it well, and I guess I was put on the back burner for a while. I think I was probably jealous about that, but still, I would rather chop me own hand off than hurt her."

Malik was listening and thinking at the same time. "I think she will be far safer with you outta here than me learning the ropes. I have to tell ya, she doesn't believe you shot Adam, and neither do I."

Keffa shook his head. "I didn't kill him. The problem was, though, I left my jacket at the pub." He looked to the floor in shame. "When I was with Lacey, the gun was in the pocket. To be honest, Lacey wouldn't have the guts to shoot Adam or anyone. She may have shagged him, but she was probably shagging the whole pub, the dirty slut. Anyway, I need you to help me. Go and see a guy called Ditto. He's one of my men and like a brother to Kelly. Let him know what's going on. You can trust him with your life, I promise you. He'll know what to do. Organise men to be on the doors at the pubs, and also the club, when it's up and running again, and choose the biggest fuckers on the payroll. Tell Kelly to change her car. I don't want her driving the Range Rover. If she goes out on business with the Colombians, go with her, and talk to the boys on the firm. I wanna know who's burned down Naomi's."

Malik was taking it all in. "It weren't the Carters. They are working with Kelly to find out who is behind it all. I have my suspicions it has something to do with the Ryes, but I can't be sure yet."

Keffa showed a look of surprise at the mention of the Ryes. "What, as in Paddy Rye?"

Malik nodded. "Yeah, and his sons." He smirked. "I gave one of them a right bashing. They're supposed to be the Carters' protection, the fucking wimps."

"I'm glad you came, Malik. I feel like I can do my bird now, knowing you'll have your sister's back. I appreciate you're young, but I know you're one dangerous fucker. You're your father's son. I know because he was the only man who ever scared the shit out of me." He moved his collar to reveal a scar across his neck.

Malik peered closer. "Fuck me! Did he do that?"

"He was a ruthless man and not many people fucked with him and got away with it. Ask Cyril. See, this is the thing. Kelly is respected because she's his daughter, and his name still has people shitting their pants. It might be an idea to change your name to Raven. Mad I know, but you, my friend, are his fucking double. Ya look like him, ya walk like him, and odd as it seems, ya talk like him. With his reputation, I don't think many would mess with you, especially if they thought you had a mere smidgen of his reckless temper."

"I ain't him though, Keffa. From what I've heard about him, I could never hurt my family like he did. He was one evil psycho."

"No, I know, and Kelly feels the same, but like her, you still have his traits. Your sister is one of the toughest women around. She served time as a kid, like it was water off a duck's back, and as young as she was, she fronted me out with no fear in her eyes. You're the same, I can see it, so use it, mate. Use everything you have, to look after your family. I'll do whatever I can to help, but it's down to you, Malik."

Malik left the prison with a very different outlook and a whole new perspective on Keffa as a person and on his own instincts about the threats to Kelly. Keffa was right. Malik would use his father's reputation in any way he could to run the manor and take care of business until Keffa was released.

CHAPTER SEVENTEEN

Blakey was there waiting for Malik. As he watched the visitors spill out from the main gates, his thoughts turned to events over thirty-five years ago.

❧*❧

Frank, Cyril, a new guy called Basil, and himself had robbed a bank. Back then, it was easier, with no CCTV footage. Basil had been a security guard and gave it all up to join Cyril's firm. Although he thought he was cut out to be a villain, all the perceived bravado in the world couldn't hide the fact that Basil was really a chicken. Stupidly, they trusted the rat because he knew the inside of the bank like the back of his hand. The heist went without a hitch, and all four of them got away with enough money to retire on. That was until the police pulled in Basil. It was just routine questioning, but Basil shit a brick and held his hands up. On the promise of a light sentence for the names of the accomplices, Basil turned Queen's evidence, and thinking he was clever, he bragged that he was doing Frank and Cyril a favour, by keeping their identities out of it and only stringing up Blakey. He wrongly assumed that he would have the protection of Cyril and Frank and be seen as one of their closest men, leaving Blakey to rot in prison for ten years. The trouble was, he really didn't know either man well enough. More than that, he didn't know the rules.

After nine measly months, he was released and naïvely assumed that his waiting car, organised by Cyril, was the resumption of his career in Cyril's firm. So, eagerly he jumped in, giving Cyril a big grin. In his head, they were off to a grand meal, a few drinks, and the keys to a flash pad from the money they'd earned.

"Nice one, mate," said the skinny wimp, whilst simultaneously grinning and showing his fag-stained teeth.

Cyril nodded with a serious dark undertone. He was younger then and had a coldness about him that made him unpredictable, but not this day. This day was carefully planned; it was nothing foolhardy, just urgent business that needed taking care of.

Basil chatted away and hadn't even noticed that Cyril was overly quiet. Basil droned on about the shit food inside and how starving he was. It wasn't until later in the day, as the skies darkened, that he realised they were driving through Epping Forest. Turning quickly to face Cyril, his eyes widened to find an oversized grin spread across the man's face and a gun pointing his way.

"What's going on?" His mouth was dry, but his eyes were wet.

Cyril just continued to smile silently, like a deranged nutcase.

"Aw, come on, mate. I kept you outta the nick, I'm on your side, I had your back." His voice was high-pitched and terrified. "Please, Cyril, please, mate, come on. Look, I can get you in any bank. Blakey was nothing, we don't need him." But then, Basil saw Cyril's brow and lips quiver. That was a telling moment for Basil. He realised, too late, that Cyril was a very angry man.

Once they were deep enough into the woods, the driver stopped the car and stepped out to open the passenger door. Basil got out and looked around, and there, almost making him jump, was Frank, standing by a huge oak tree. A cold chill passed through Basil's stomach, his legs wobbled, and instantly his stomach expelled its contents at the sight before him. A chair was positioned with a flash light so bright that it lit up the whole tree.

Cyril poked the gun into Basil's back. "Strip!"

Basil turned slowly, still retching, to face Cyril. "What?"

"You heard! Take all your fucking clothes off." He said each word like he was talking to a naughty child.

"Wait, er … what are you gonna do?"

Cyril laughed out loud. "Feed you, ya cunt! Ya said you were hungry, didn't ya!" He sniggered and poked him again with the gun. "I won't tell you again. Strip!"

Basil had always wondered how he might leave this world, but he never believed that his final demise would ever be this cruel. But then, he hadn't known Cyril at all well, and not belonging to this gangster's underworld, he'd never understood the depths of Cyril's murderous past.

After he had nervously taken all his clothes off, the driver held out a plastic bag and Basil assumed it was just for his clothes, but he was more shocked to find Cyril and Frank stripping off and placing their clothes in the bags as well. *Jesus, they're gonna rape me*, he stupidly assumed, and then, in a flash, he tried to take off, hoping he could outrun them and dodge a bullet. Frank, predicting this, grabbed him in a twinkling. Basil was thrown onto the chair and tied to the tree.

"Why?" he cried.

Cyril looked at Frank and then down at his own naked body. "Oh, this? Well, it's gonna get pretty messy. I hate getting me new clobber dirty, eh, Frank? You're the same, mate."

"No! Why are you doing this to *me?*"

Cyril and Frank looked at him cruelly and sniggered to each other. It was Cyril who spoke.

"You are one thick bastard, if ever there was one. Did you honestly expect us to swallow what you did to one of our closest mates? Well, did ya?"

Basil looked into Cyril's hooded eyes and tried to speak, but he just couldn't get his mouth to form the words. Instead, his bowels loosened, and a huge stench came off him that was indescribable. He looked what he was, a forlorn and sad man who was seconds away from death.

Frank's deep throaty chuckle unnerved Basil, and the pitiful creature now knew all the begging in the world would never stop them. Cyril, out of pent-up anger, smashed Basil's face in five heavy blows, leaving it a fucked up mess, but Basil was still conscious enough to feel what came next. Frank opened his tool kit, and in a quick movement, he removed Basil's genitalia and shoved them into his mouth. The shock and the fact that he couldn't breathe because his nose was crushed was enough to leave him unconscious, and he bled out an hour later.

Blakey sat in his cell and read his copy of his morning newspaper. It was headline news in *The Mirror*: **Mafia Style Execution in Epping Forest**. He devoured the article faster than his boiled eggs and toast, as he eagerly read the report. A satisfied smile spread across his face. Putting down the newspaper, he laughed to himself. He knew damn well who'd been responsible for the headline: it could only have been Cyril. He paraded around like a Mafia don; he was one cheeky and seriously dangerous fucker, when he had a mind to be. But Blakey realised this was no flash stunt on Cyril's part. A statement had to be made, as rules are rules, and the number one rule was thou shalt not grass. In Cyril's case, he could probably put it more eloquently: if you fuck with my firm, then be prepared to die a wicked death.

෬*෭

Blakey gave a long and satisfied sigh and smiled. He'd never regretted for one moment accepting the offer to be a part of Cyril's outfit. It had its risks but the rewards — well, they were something else entirely. Looking over at Malik, as he appeared from this shithole of a prison, he could see him becoming a successful villain. He had a walk that exuded confidence and a persona that told the world he was not someone to mess with. Blakey grinned to himself and wished he was twenty years younger.

Malik's face lit up when he saw Blakey, and he hurried over, hopping into the front seat. "Nice one, Blakey. Thanks for picking me up."

Blakey pulled away fast. He didn't want to hang around the gloomy old building that held many of his harshest memories. Malik rubbed his hands together to warm them up. "Fucking nippy."

"Yeah, she's a right shifter, this little machine."

Malik laughed. "No, Blakey, I meant the weather!"

Blakey knew then that Malik was probably only up for small talk and perhaps not ready to discuss the visit. They drove through the southern outskirts of south London towards Kent.

Malik's thoughts turned to that incident he'd seen outside Penelope's the other day, and he asked Blakey if he would kindly drop him off at the corner of her road. Blakey assumed he just wanted to go back to the cottage. "So, the Ol' Bill reckon you can go back, then?"

Malik nodded. "Yeah, they used a special cleaning team to sanitise the mess. Christ, it makes me feel ill to think about it all. Anyway, it's all over now. That poor girl." He suddenly felt very flat and disheartened, as he switched his thoughts from Penelope to Kimi. Her body was still in the mortuary because no one had reported her missing. It was breaking Malik's heart. He must think of a way to let the authorities know who she was.

Blakey pulled up outside the cottage. "Shall I wait?"

Malik smiled. "Nah, I'll walk back later. Cheers, Blakey."

It was five o'clock, the sky was black, and the road wasn't very well lit. As Malik approached Penelope's house, he noticed a single light coming from upstairs. It was quiet, and her car was parked in the drive. He hoped she was at home. After he rang the doorbell, he stepped back and waited. A few moments later, a light came on in the hallway, and the outline of a woman, blurred by the frosted glass window, approached the front door. She didn't open it.

"Who is it?" a voice called out, in a despondent voice.

Malik shifted from foot to foot. "Er, it's me, Malakai, although I'm known as Malik. I cleaned ya car some while ago." He stared at the door, now feeling very awkward. What on earth was he really doing here? He hadn't put together any kind of plan when he left the prison, but something told him to come over here to Penelope's place.

There was silence for a few seconds, and then the door opened very slowly. The gap was quite small, so he couldn't see much in the light, but when Penelope opened the door wider, the sight of her battered face made him gasp.

"Jesus, Penelope!"

She lowered her head and beckoned him in. Malik stepped inside, wiping his feet. Penelope didn't say a word; instead, she walked into the living room and sat down in the armchair. Malik followed, closing the front door behind him. When he kneeled in front of her, all he could see was a once beautiful, classy woman, looking up at him in a dazed state. But it was her eyes which caused Malik to swallow heavily. They were partially closed and bereft of any spark of life, and the right eye was badly bruised. She wore a track suit and had her hair in a messy bun. There was not an ounce of make-up on her former exquisite face, which now looked so haggard and dejected. It was clearly apparent that the attack had left her vulnerable and on a downward spiral of depression.

Malik stood up and chose to sit down in an armchair opposite her, leaning forward with his elbows resting on his knees and his hands clenched together. "You remember me, don't ya?"

Penelope tried to smile. "Of course, I do. I could never forget you."

Her sad, pitiful expression was all too much for Malik. He got up from his seat and crouched down again beside her, holding her arms. "Oh, babe, look at ya. Did that bastard do that to ya?"

Penelope frowned. "How do you know?"

Malik averted his eyes from hers, feeling awful that he hadn't made Kelly stop by and be with Penelope at the time of the incident.

"I saw the police arresting a man and the ambulance was here. I'm sorry, really, I am. I should have stopped."

She just nodded, and a tear trickled down her face, following the contour of her nose. Gently, he wiped it away with a tissue from a box which was on the chair arm. She then really looked at Malakai. She liked that name, but, somehow, Malik suited him better. Appraising him carefully – it must be twelve months since she had last seen him – she could see a very different person from that young man with the scruffy clothes. He now looked smart in a sleek leather jacket. He wasn't scrawny either: he was a man, with broad shoulders and eyes which suggested strength and purpose. She tried to tell herself he was still a kid, that he had no place in her future life. Of course, she had felt some attraction for him, when he turned up at her door and worked so hard and expected so little in return, but she hadn't expected this: a guy who appeared so mature and who had the most amazing green eyes. She felt like a princess again, just like the day he told her to go inside to keep warm. Another tear fell, and she tried to fight back the sob that was waiting to be released. He sensed her emotion and leaned forward, wrapping his arms around her. His breath on her neck stirred something inside her. She stopped crying, pulled away to look at his face, and saw the concern in those eyes of his, as he looked at her with so much love. Very gently, not awkwardly but cautiously, he kissed her. She didn't pull away; she needed his embrace and to feel his lips on hers.

"It's gonna be all right, Penelope, I promise." He gently tilted her head up and peered into her eyes. "You have survived what you thought would kill you, now straighten your crown and move forward like the queen you are."

They kissed again, before he carefully pulled her to her feet and held her tight. She ran her hands over his chest, feeling the tight, firm muscles underneath his shirt. "Come upstairs," she whispered.

He held her away and looked into her eyes. "Oh, Penelope, I didn't come here for that."

Penelope looked down in utter shame. What a fool she was. As if this handsome, assured man would want her anyway.

"I'm sorry."

Malik laughed then. "Hey, no! I mean, I didn't come to take advantage of you. I wanted to make sure you were okay. I would love to go upstairs, I want nothing more, but you need time to heal. Look at you! You're bruised and need looking after." He brushed a loose clump of hair from her face and gently kissed her on the lips.

From that moment, the understanding between them changed. He was a strong man with clout and manlier than any man she'd ever met. From the moment she'd set eyes on him, she'd been drawn to his looks and personality. She knew what she wanted now in a relationship. Malik was the one. She longed to be treated as his girl, not a confident woman, but a child. Just the way he looked at her made her feel special, wanted, and loved. It was madness. He had walked into her life a while back and left an unforgettable impression, and here he was again kissing her, as if they had known each other for years. They didn't speak about their connection, it was just a given. She felt so blessed. Her dear old mum, Debra, always used to tell her, "There's nothing sweeter than young love." *Bless her*, she thought, *she was right*.

"Did he hurt you badly?"

Penelope took a deep breath. "My pride and my trust mainly. These bruises, though, will heal."

"Why would you want to be with a degenerate like Fynn Rye?"

Like a thunderbolt screaming overhead, Penelope stood rigidly and stared in disbelief. "How do you know him?" Her tone and appearance turned cold. She had snapped out of the mesmerising clutches of Malik, as if she had awoken from a dream. "Malik, how the fuck do you know his name?"

Malik was stunned by her sudden reaction. He held her arms and sat her back down. "Because he is trying to do over my family, but, more to the point, why are you with a man like him?"

Penelope was trying to get her thoughts in order. "I, er, I met him in a club. We've been dating for …. Actually, Malik, we were getting married."

It was Malik's turn to look at her in outright amazement, hearing this unwelcome news. He paced the floor, running his fingers through his hair. "But you, well you're so elegant and a top-class bird. He's just a fucking thug, a bouncer."

Penelope shook her head. "No, Malik, he owns businesses. He's loaded. He took me on a cruise, and he's paid thousands for my engagement ring."

To his astonishment, it dawned on him that Penelope was talking with a different accent. She wasn't so posh as before, and her East End twang, which had just returned, gave her upbringing away.

"Malik, it was good of you to come and see me, but I'm all right. It's best that you're not here when he gets back."

Malik frowned. "What the fuck do you mean? They ain't gonna let him out! Jesus, he's bashed the fuck outta ya."

Penelope lowered her head and sighed. "Oh, babe, it's complicated and a long story."

Malik threw his hands in the air. "Well, I'm in no rush, so tell me."

Penelope had nothing to lose and being honest would be a breath of fresh air. "I didn't press charges against Fynn, so they are letting him go. I can't face it all. The truth is, I have a past, and it's not pretty. I don't want it dragged up again by the police."

"Penelope, don't mug yaself off. So, what gives him the right to do that?" He pointed at her face.

She huffed. "Who was I trying to kid, eh? Look, the truth is, I wasn't always a rich bird with my business. I was homeless for some time and had to do things I'm not proud of and the police had my card marked."

"Penelope, I don't give a shit where ya came from or who you are. We all have a past and mine ain't too clever, but you ain't no punching bag. I swear, if I get hold of him, I will mangle his face and break his legs."

Penelope liked Malik's sweet nature and his idea of sticking up for her. In contrast, Fynn was no kid, and the bashing she took from him spoke volumes.

"Would you like a cup of tea?" She wanted to change the subject before she told him too much about herself.

He nodded. "Yeah, why not."

Penelope left the room to make a drink whilst Malik stared out of the window. He was livid and would love to smash Fynn's face in. Sometimes, very, very rarely, though, wishes are granted. For there, outside on the drive by Penelope's car, he noticed a man dressed in black, creeping around the perimeter of the garden. Malik moved away from the window and peered from behind the heavy curtains. As the man approached, he realised it was Fynn, and his heart pounded. In one swift movement, he hurried to the kitchen.

"Penelope, listen, Fynn is outside. You go upstairs, yeah, and leave the scumbag to me."

The news Fynn was coming back for round two sent Penelope into a minor panic. She began to shake and dropped the teapot on the kitchen counter. "No, Malik, please, he's a nutter!"

Malik smiled confidently. "And you think I'm scared? That prick doesn't worry me, and I'll make sure he never bothers you again. Oh, and I wanna word with him about some other business."

Penelope was trembling, but she did as she was told. There was something very reassuring in Malik's eyes that convinced her he knew what he was doing. She nodded and ran up the stairs, but this time she had her kitchen knife shoved under the bed and a hammer behind the toilet. No way would she get caught like she did before, even if it meant getting her hands bloodied. After closing her bedroom door, she sat heavily on her bed and shook all over, knowing only too well what Fynn was capable of, if he had a mind to.

Malik turned all the lights off downstairs and crept back to the kitchen and switched the kettle on. He casually removed a mug from the draining board and began spooning in heaped teaspoons of sugar — he liked his tea sweet. The handle on the French doors began to turn. Unperturbed, Malik poured the boiling water into the cup and stirred the sugar. The wall which housed the kitchen units and sink was a few feet back from the French doors, and so Malik could see who was entering without the intruder being able to see him.

As soon as the door opened, Malik stepped into the shadows. He watched to ensure it was definitely Fynn and not a neighbour or the police. The side view confirmed he was right. Malik chuckled aloud, and as soon as Fynn turned to face him, the scalding sugary water was thrown at the intruder. The intense pain was not slow in coming, and instantly, the huge man clutched his face and screamed. Still holding the mug, Malik whacked him hard around the head and then kneed him in the stomach. It was so fast that Fynn didn't stand a chance. He hit the floor, trying to fend off his attacker. Malik stepped away, grabbed one of the kitchen knives held onto the wall by a magnet gizmo, and turned on the light to get a good look.

Malik screamed, "Get up, you stupid bastard!"

Fynn was still in unbearable pain, and all the adrenaline pumping around his body should have left him numb, but it didn't: the burning was insufferable.

"I said, get the fuck up!" repeated Malik, giving the intruder a swift kick to the ribs.

Fynn struggled but eventually managed to pull himself to his feet. His eyes were blurred from the sugary water and were stinging like crazy, but even through the haze, he knew who it was who jumped him.

"What the fuck are you doing 'ere?" he cried, staggering around the kitchen.

"More to the point, what the hell 'ave you come here for, ya dirty no-good fucking wanker?"

Fynn blinked furiously and could make out the door, still open. He wanted to get out and away from this kid; two beatings were enough. He saw the knife and wanted out.

"Listen, I'll go, and I swear, she's all yours. I don't want no trouble. Please, I need the hospital, my fucking face is …" He looked down at his hands to find strips of skin glued to his palm. "Jesus, it's hanging off!"

"You, ya bastard, ain't going nowhere, until I've some fucking answers, so I suggest ya stop moaning like a girl, get ya shit together, and start fucking talking."

Fynn was gripped by pain, but as his eyes began to clear, he glared at his attacker with a hate that he'd never experienced before. It wasn't just that the kid was a cocky little sod: it was the fact that he knew he was now a prisoner, who stood no chance. One false move and the speed of the younger man would have him doubled over again with a knife plunged in his stomach. The hate turned to a cold fear and he didn't rate his chances of surviving this evening. He watched the lad go towards the kettle, convinced he would receive another attack on his face, but instead, the kid grabbed a tea towel, placing it under the running water. Malik was taking no chances, though. With one hand holding the knife, his eyes were glued to Fynn.

"Here, clean yaself up because me and you are gonna have a little chat."

The tone in Malik's voice put the wind up Fynn and left him helpless to do anything but listen. He caught the towel and felt an instant relief as he placed it over his burning face.

"Right, firstly, I wanna know something. What the hell is going on with Jean River and your family?"

Slowly, Fynn removed the wet towel and frowned. Malik's stomach turned over when he saw the man's face blistering and some of the skin hanging loose. He knew he'd done some serious damage.

"Jean River?"

"Oh, come on, mate, don't pretend you don't know her. By all accounts, she's shacked up with ya ol' man."

Fynn couldn't comprehend the connection. "Yeah, I know who she is, but what's she got to do with you?"

Malik leaned forward, still wielding the knife. "I ask the questions, so you just fucking answer them."

Fynn gave a resigned nod. He was overcome with fatigue, and if he didn't sit down soon, he would faint. Carefully, he lowered himself onto the floor and placed the cold towel on his head.

Malik grabbed another mug from the draining board and held it under the tap, still eyeing Fynn.

"'Ere, drink this, ya fucking fanny."

Fynn took the cold drink and gulped it back, pouring the rest over his face.

"Yeah, I do know Jean, and yeah, she's me ol' man's fancy piece."

"And ya ol' man knows she was shacked up with Adam Carter, yeah?" spat Malik.

He wanted to provoke a reaction: the expression on Fynn's face said it all.

"Ha, I guess he didn't know, then?" laughed Malik, sadistically.

The furrowed brow deepened across Fynn's face, and with the immense pain and fear, he struggled to think straight. Jean had never mentioned she was seeing Adam. Fynn now had an eerie feeling and one that would send his mind spinning. He tried to recall the last few conversations with her. She was overly excited with the plan they'd devised to take out the Carters' firm and the one belonging to Cyril Reardon and Kelly Raven. Then, as if someone had turned a light on, he recalled just how much Jean knew about the Carters and the Reardon-Raven firm. He had to think smartly, although he knew he probably wasn't the sharpest member of his family.

"Look, I know you're the one holding the knife, but who are ya, and what's Jean got to do with you?"

Malik, desperate for answers, guessed he wouldn't get them, unless he threw in another shocker. "Jean River is my muvver."

Fynn couldn't have looked more dumbstruck if he tried. Jean had never mentioned children. In fact, she never really talked about where she lived or who with. She was just his father's long-term friend with benefits, and over the years, they'd learned to accept her as part of his life. She was the one who put a smile on his face and theirs, when she was around. Perhaps it was their father's adoration of her that rubbed off on them growing up. Or, maybe, he was happy to put his hand in his pocket and dish out the cash, just to get them out of the house, so he could have his fun. Jean brought out the best in old Paddy, and so there was no reason to dislike the woman, but now it was like a smack in the mouth, and he wondered if the kid was telling the truth.

"But you were with Kelly Raven."

Malik gave a sneering look and then he grinned. "Yeah, Kelly Raven is my sister. I'm Eddie Raven's son." He stopped, noticing the sheer confusion on Fynn's face as he absorbed the shocking news. That should get him thinking.

The thought ticked over in Fynn's brain and then it hit him. The kid was a dead ringer for Eddie and Kelly for that matter, but if their research had been correct, Kelly was an only child. It was like putting together a puzzle where the last piece just wouldn't fit.

"So, Fynn, now you know the family tree, you'd better tell me what Jean's up to, because it's my guess she has killed Adam Carter herself and gone running to your ol' man. For what, I dunno, but I bet she's up to no good."

Fynn couldn't hide his look of horror. Jean had turned up out of the blue, and she'd wasted no time in getting her feet back under the table and flirting with Paddy. She'd quickly got onto the subject of how Paddy could take over with the nugget of information that Adam was dead, which had given them a sense of instability in the Carter-Raven business set-up.

"But Keffa Jackson has been nicked for killing Adam."

Malik raised his eyebrow. "Well, well. She told you that, did she? For the record, he didn't do it because he was with Kelly at the time. But I bet me bottom dollar you heard it from Jean, eh?"

Fynn tried to box clever. "Er, no, actually. I didn't. I heard it mentioned elsewhere."

Malik knew he was lying and wanted to give him another kicking, but looking at the destruction of Fynn's face, he couldn't hurt him anymore.

"So, tell me, Fynn, was it her idea to burn down me sister's club?"

It was over. Fynn and his brother had thought that they were on a home run. No one had suspected them for the arson, and they were convinced at the time that their plan would have worked. The fact that this lad was Jean's son and Kelly's brother, however, made the whole plot messy. They'd fucked up, and he knew that there was no way they would ever get away with it, not from the likes of Reardon's firm or from this nutter. It was a case of grass or die. It was as if Malik had read his mind.

"I'm a fair man, really, so it's like this. I'll let you go on ya way, in exchange for the fucking truth, and if you ain't happy with that, then I've enough boiling water and sugar to turn you into a fucking toffee apple." He flicked the switch on the kettle and grinned.

With several broken ribs and his head throbbing, Fynn knew he'd little choice; that sugar-coating threat wasn't a joke. He was no match for the lad and he knew it.

"Do I 'ave your word that you'll let me go, if I lay it all on the table?"

"You have my word, you can walk out of here with just the marks you have now, if I believe you. Deal?"

Fynn nodded warily and Malik turned off the kettle. Inhaling a lungful of air, as if he was about to go to the gallows, Fynn let his mouth run away with him. "Jean came to us the other night. She told us that Adam was dead and …" he paused and rolled his eyes. "Look, me ol' man was done over by Eddie Raven, years ago. That man bullied me farver into letting him have his business. It was wrong on every level, and it made me dad mad, 'cos he had built up his contacts and played fair. But, overnight, Eddie took everything, and then when he died, me ol' man thought that he could take back what was rightfully his."

Those words resonated with Malik because he lived by the same rules. He only ever wanted what was justly his. "Yeah, so what did ya fucking do, Fynn? I wanna hear everything." He flicked the kettle back on to reheat the water.

Fynn's eyes couldn't widen any further, and he raised his hand. "Look, please, er …"

"Malik, me name's Malik."

"Listen, Malik, I'm being totally upfront. Jean gave us the idea to go in and take back what belonged to us. So, we, er—"

"Ya fucking burned the club down, didn't ya, and you hoped it would cause a war between the Carters and us?"

Fynn looked like a lost child, as he slowly nodded. "Yeah, Malik, we did, and you're right, we wanted you and the Carters to … well, you know that, really, don't ya?"

Fynn lowered his head, waiting for the backlash, but there was only silence for what seemed like ages. As he looked up, he saw Malik reach down and grab him by the arm. "I think you'd better head off to the hospital and get ya face seen to." His calm demeanour rattled Fynn, who, without another word, walked towards the back door.

"Oh, and don't come back here, because if ya do, it won't just be ya face that I wreck. Next time, I won't be so fucking soft. Got it?"

Fynn looked back in defeat. What his fate would be, who knew, but one thing was a dead cert: he and his brother, Mason, were, in all likelihood, dead men walking from this point.

Penelope was sitting on the landing, listening to every word. She was still there when Malik appeared at the foot of the stairs.

"It's all right, Penelope, he's gone, and I don't think he'll be back any time soon."

She hesitantly descended the stairs, unsure who she was more afraid of. "Eddie Raven's son, eh?"

Slowly, Malik nodded. "Did you know my dad, then?"

Penelope's eyes widened. "Wrong question. The real question is, are you like him?"

CHAPTER EIGHTEEN

Delmonte was sitting next to Kelly in the interview room. "You know how it works, Kelly. Just don't lose your temper because I've a hunch that Campbell will want more than just information regarding the fire."

Kelly was washed out, her face pale and sickly once again. She would rather be anywhere than here right now, but with the DS sniffing around, she just had to go through the motions and get the superintendent off her back. It was late, and she should really have left it until the morning, but she thought it best to get this interview over with.

Campbell's face had annoyance written all over it. She'd had the call that Kelly was coming in and so had hung around all afternoon waiting. When the fucking madam had still not graced everyone with her presence by tea time, Campbell was almost climbing the walls in frustration and anger. Then, finally, when Kelly arrived at ten o'clock in the evening, with her brief in tow, Campbell's emotions were almost at screaming point. On entering the interview room, if looks could kill ...

The screech grated on Kelly's nerves, as Campbell pulled the chair away to get herself seated. She stared at Kelly, who did likewise. It was like two female boxers facing each other off at the pre-fight weigh-in. This was the first time Campbell was able to take a close look at Eddie Raven's daughter, and it would be her best chance to gather information. Cyril's firm had kept Kelly off the police radar. It was some accomplishment, considering Campbell understood that Kelly was ranked high in the underworld. The officer had to find a way to crack the nut.

"I am Detective Superintendent Campbell," she coughed. "Thank you for coming to the station. We need to get the matter of the arson attack cleared up."

Kelly studied the officer's face with a quizzical stare. "Well, Superintendent, there's nothing I can shed light on. All I know is my club was burned to the ground."

The superintendent gave her a don't-bullshit-me look.

"So, firstly, where were you the night it happened?"

Poker-faced, Kelly replied, "I was tucked up in bed."

She added no more and glared in defiance.

Campbell chuckled. "But you weren't with Keffa Jackson, though, were you? He's on remand for murder." She was ready with a loaded gun to fire antagonising bullets.

"DS Campbell, I think you're forgetting yourself. We're here on the understanding that my client is to give a statement regarding the

378

arson attack, and I think you've forgotten to turn on the recording device."

Delmonte looked at the device on the wall and levelled his gaze directly at Campbell.

"I was just having a conversation, before we begin."

Kelly felt that it was time to get down to business, to be on the front foot. "Well, I'm not here for a social chat, because you, love, ain't one of me buddies, so I suggest you turn on the recorder and ask what you need to, regarding me fucking club being raised to the ground."

Shocked, Campbell jolted. She hadn't anticipated Kelly to be so sharp with her tongue or to use such profanity. "There's no need to be hostile, Miss Raven. I'm just trying to find out who did it."

"Oh, cut the fucking crap, *Superintendent*." She emphasised the last word sarcastically.

The detective glared at Kelly, and her previously polite tone was replaced with a more vitriolic one. "I know what you're all about, Kelly Raven, living in your father's footsteps. I know more about you than you realise."

Kelly slammed her hands on the table. "Ha, fucking ha. You've no idea, because, lady, if you had half a fucking clue, then you would know that Keffa Jackson didn't murder Adam Carter, because I was with him myself. So, Miss Know-It-All, get this stupid interview over with, and then, I can go home, and you can return to ya game of Cluedo."

Campbell shot Delmonte a glance, only to find a ghost of a smile across his face.

"Push it too far, Miss Raven, and I can guarantee I will have you inside too, on accessory to murder."

Delmonte raised his hands. "Stop right there, *DS Campbell*." He likewise dragged out her rank. "You carry on making threats like that, and I'll go straight to the commissioner and have it noted that you're acting beyond your powers." He raised an eyebrow, asserting his authority.

"I may have grounds for an accessory charge." It was a poorly constructed bluff and she knew it.

But it was Kelly who piped up. "If you had grounds, Detective Superintendent Poirot, then you would have me nicked in a fucking heartbeat. You know, and I fucking know, you've nothing on me, and why? Well, because there's nothing to have, and likewise with my Keffa, but you just can't stand the fact that I'm Eddie Raven's daughter. No doubt, you were another one of his sexual worshippers?"

The notion that she could get under Kelly's skin was short-lived, and now the tables had turned, Campbell felt every nerve in her body being pricked.

"Are we fucking done here?" snapped Kelly.

White-faced and her eyes flashing with fury, Campbell barked back, "For now, Miss Raven, but I'm watching you."

"Pervert! Sorry, I didn't realise ya liked women, but I guess with a boat like yours, you'll take anything. But, sorry, love, you just ain't my type." With those cutting words, Kelly stood up to leave, flicking her long hair over her shoulders and smoothing down her tight black skirt.

Delmonte was still smirking. Leaving his vintage brandy at his gentlemen's club to accompany Kelly to the police station had made him cross at the time, but now, seeing the look on Superintendent Campbell's face, it had been well worth the effort. But Kelly wasn't finished yet.

"You need to get ya head out of ya arse and do some real detective work, because trust me, Superintendent Campbell, when the truth comes out, and Keffa is found innocent, you'll look the incompetent prat that you truly are, and I'll be the one laughing at your face, with egg all over it."

Kelly followed the lawyer out of the room and slammed the door loudly behind her. Campbell was left hot under the collar and with an uneasy feeling. Maybe she'd assumed too much and the young woman did have a point. Building up an image in her head of some bit of a kid with a cocky attitude, who more than likely was too big for her boots, was all wrong. Kelly Raven was more in control than Campbell had given her credit for.

As Kelly marched along the corridor, with Delmonte trailing behind, she nodded at DI Sampson, who had just turned the corner, and winked at him.

Campbell was there in the doorway of the interview room watching Raven walk with elegance and self-assurance, but she also espied Sampson's acknowledgement of the woman. It grated on her that the detective was giving Raven – a villain and a female one at that – respect, whereas it should have been herself that he held in high esteem. Sampson had a look of concern on his face, and with long strides, he headed towards Campbell, holding a note.

She peeled herself away from the door frame and frowned. "What is it, Sampson?" she demanded, as she snatched the paper from his hand.

"Well, well, well. Johnnie Carter, eh? You naughty boy. Now that has put a smile on my face. Pull him in and get forensics over there. I want every computer, phone, and gadget he fucking owns fast tracked to IT."

Sampson nodded and walked away, leaving Campbell on an adrenaline rush. He felt disgust that she could get gratification from arresting someone for that sort of crime, without knowing the full facts or the person involved. Sampson had felt a wave of emotion grip him, when he'd heard the details of the allegations, and found it hard to imagine that Johnnie Carter would be a paedophile. It was ridiculous. As far as he was aware, apart from a brief bisexual encounter, which amounted to nothing, he was too much of a lady's man and wasn't shy about it either. He'd had more flings than Sampson had had hot dinners and there was never a whiff of any noncing by Carter. In fact, all of the brothers, with the possible exception of the late Adam Carter, were as straight as they come. Still, the call that came in was conclusive, and so he couldn't ignore it.

He'd never felt guilty about being in the pocket of Cyril Reardon or any of the other villains because he knew that although their skulduggery was what it was, it was largely unconnected with the general public. He was well paid for tipping his 'clients' the wink. But he would draw the line at violence towards society at large, especially the vulnerable, such as the elderly and children. And his conscience was further insulated from his links with criminals and their crimes by the fact that he'd managed to receive useful tip-offs to the sorts of behaviour which would be anathema to any civil society such as acid attacks, noncing, and sex trafficking.

Therefore, although he would follow up on the information he'd been supplied and see where this investigation led him, he still sensed there was something fishy going on.

The air was cool as Delmonte walked Kelly back to her car and whispered, "You did well, Kelly, but watch her. She's after a promotion. Get yourself off home. No offence, but you do look a tad peaky."

Kelly opened her car door and eased herself onto the seat. "It's late, I guess." She looked up at the stars and noticed how dark the sky was. "I'm just tired. Thank you, Michael, I will do. I think all this business is making me ill. I'm certain Keffa didn't kill Adam, and I've other issues too, so thank you for being there."

Delmonte looked at her tired eyes and smiled. "It was my pleasure, Kelly."

No sooner had she pulled away, when the phone rang. It was Malik.

"Kel, I know who burned the club down. It was Fynn and Mason Rye." He waited for a reaction.

"I thought they seemed shifty, and I suppose you know who is behind it," she replied.

"It was me muvver. Jesus, of all the fucking people, eh? After the fight I've just had with Fynn, I think he'll put old man Paddy right, and I reckon Jean will be turned out on her ear or buried in their back garden. Anyway, are ya on your way to your home or coming back to Cyril's?"

"I'll see you at Cyril's."

Malik sensed the faintness in her tone and concluded his big sister was being dragged down by it all. He would have to step up to the plate and somehow take the pressure off. "Sis, I think I'd better call Johnnie Carter and give him the heads-up."

Kelly felt drained and sick. "Yeah, Malik, if ya don't mind."

This wasn't like his sister at all. She was almost always fierce and lively. Something else was sucking the life out of her, and he wouldn't rest until he got to the bottom of it all. Perhaps he'd underestimated how much she really loved Keffa and the shagging incident had knocked her sideways.

Malik reached the house before Kelly and was met by Cyril, eager for news. "All right, son, how did it go?" Malik had totally forgotten about the prison visit, after the incident with Fynn.

"I've a lot to tell ya, but first we'd better call Johnnie and tell him not to burn down his pride and joy. I know exactly who has been playing with the big shit-stirring spoon. It's the Ryes, no less. Fucking Fynn and his brother Mason burned down Naomi's, and me muvver, the sneaky skank, was behind it."

Cyril nodded. "I had a suspicion and me next move was to pay old Paddy a visit. Looks like you've saved me the job."

Malik, now feeling comfortable in Cyril's mansion, helped himself to a brandy, offering Cyril one. The youngster was so much like Eddie. With his back turned and the black leather jacket defining his now broad shoulders, Malik couldn't see Cyril grinning to himself.

"So, son, I take it you somehow bumped into one of the Rye brothers, then?"

Malik walked over to Cyril with their drinks and chuckled. "Yep, but his own muvver wouldn't recognise him now, the nasty bastard. It was a coincidence, to tell ya the truth. He just 'appened to turn up at the house of an old friend of mine. The cheeky prick had only just bashed the shit out of her, and then he had the nerve to come back! Well, he gotta fucking shock to find me there."

Cyril narrowed his brow. "What friend?"

"Penelope. I don't know her surname. She lives opposite to the cottage. Lovely woman, she is. She helped me out some time ago. Gave me a few quid for cleaning her car and clothes for Sassy, when, to be honest, I didn't know where I was going to get the next quid from. We were literally without food, the electric bill had to be paid. It was a nightmare. The money she gave me saw us all right over Christmas, bless her heart. Anyway, after that meeting at the Mint with Johnnie, remember I bashed that heavy? Well, he's only fucking Fynn Rye. So, to cut a long story short, he was seeing Penelope. He had a bit of a rude awakening to find me in her house, I can tell ya." He chuckled once more.

"So, you reckon Jean is behind it all, then? Is that the situation, son?"

Malik gulped back the brandy and nodded. "Fynn was gobsmacked when I told him that me muvver was shagging Adam Carter, and anyway he squealed like a pig, when I threatened to boil him alive."

With visions of torture, Cyril swallowed his drink and gave Malik a concerned expression. "You be careful, son. Don't go getting yaself a reputation. Sometimes it does no good to be seen as ..." He paused and patted Malik's shoulder. "Well, ya ol' man wasn't liked, he had a lot of enemies, and it's all well and good having men fear ya 'cos ya look like him, but he was always watching his back, forever in a ruck, and you ain't him, Malik. I don't want to see you go down the same

385

road, 'cos it only brings grief to ya door, and you've those kiddies to look out for."

Malik thought for a moment and then tilted his head to the side, and for a second, he looked young again, the hard-faced, manly expression having melted away. "Cyril, I ain't a kid. I mean, I can look after meself, and with Keffa inside and Kelly in a state, I need to do my bit. God gave me these." He looked down at his hands. "And I can use them, ya know that. What else can I offer?"

Shaking his head, Cyril gave Malik a look of sincere compassion. "Christ, it's different with you. See, Kelly is the front woman, but ya know it started as a game really. Me, Blakey, and Frank, called her the guv'nor, and somehow along the way, the likes of the Carters and others took it seriously, and bless her heart, she did too. Of course, we had her back, we still do, and we make sure we have the biggest, ugliest men on the firm all behind her. Then, out of the blue, she secured this mega fucking deal with the Colombians, and the rest is history. So, Malik, you've no need to fight any battles. We've got men to do that. You're still very young, and ya need to live ya life having fun, not being a crook."

"All I know is fighting, one way or another. It's always been that way since I can remember, fighting for the girls, fighting me muvver, fighting for food. I don't know any other life."

Cyril took the glass from Malik's hand and refilled it, pouring himself a double measure. "Take a seat, Malik."

His heart feeling like a brick, Cyril watched him walk over to the chair by a roaring fire. "Son, let me explain something to ya. Guilt is a fucking bastard to carry around with ya, and believe me, I am weighed down by it."

Malik wanted to laugh because Cyril was such a confident and headstrong man.

"The reason I look after Kelly is because of my conscience. That poor kid was a product of Eddie's evilness, and I had a part in it all, you know." He stopped and took a deep breath. "Eddie was younger than you, when he joined my firm, and I liked him back then. He was eager to learn and was fearless, but he had respect for me, and so I laughed at his antics. I even encouraged him to be a fucker, to be honest. I patted him on the back when he took no prisoners, I stood by his side when he took on other manors, and I stepped back when he took over the protection rackets. What I didn't realise was he had a vile streak in him and he took things to a whole other level, and so now I feel guilt like you wouldn't believe."

He swallowed the brandy in one gulp and noticed that Malik was listening intently. "I don't want you to go down the same road, Malik. If people treat you like you're Eddie Raven, then what's to stop ya from becoming him?"

Malik thought about that and what Kelly had told him. And Penelope had intimated as much only an hour or so ago. But the notion disappeared when he looked over Cyril's shoulder. He stood up, pushed his shoulders back, and a large smile emerged. Cyril felt an icy chill because he imagined he was seeing Eddie and he didn't like it. But then he noticed Malik was actually beaming at Tilly and Star.

They ran past Cyril and into Malik's arms, giggling. He picked them up and hugged them tightly. "What are you two monkeys doing still up? It's way past your bedtime."

Cyril realised then that he'd got it wrong about the boy. There was no way Malik could ever be Eddie because the one trait he didn't have was selfishness.

"I'd better give Carter the heads-up before his pub is burned to the ground for no reason."

Malik nodded and continued fussing over the girls.

Cyril left the room and used his virtually untraceable phone. He was surprised that Johnnie didn't answer. He waited a few minutes and tried again but there was nothing. He scratched his head and returned to the study. After a moment's thought, he flicked his head in Malik's direction to follow him. Malik got up from the floor, where he was pretending to wrestle with his sisters, and accompanied Cyril into the hallway. "Listen, Malik, something ain't right. Johnnie ain't answering his phone."

Malik shrugged his shoulders. "So? He might be in the shower or asleep in bed."

Cyril shook his head and stared at the phone. "Nah, he has the phone by his hip and never ignores my calls, ever."

Whilst they racked their brains, Kelly arrived, looking washed out. Both Cyril and Malik were shocked to see her so white, so much so, they instantaneously went to her side, as if she were an old lady. "Kel, are you okay?" asked Malik, as he gripped her arm.

With effort, she nodded, and in a faint whisper, she replied, "I just need me bed. I've got a migraine and I feel absolutely drained."

Cyril placed the phone on the hallway table and clutched her other arm. "Gawd, blimey, girl, you look like you've been through the fucking ringer. Let's get you upstairs."

Kelly didn't resist. Instead, she allowed the two men to help her climb the stairs and guide her into her room. She did feel very weak and wanted nothing more than to feel the soft mattress under her back and the pillow for her sore head. She wondered why she was feeling so tired these days. Was she anaemic? She didn't think so. She made a mental note to make an appointment to visit her doctor's surgery.

"There you go, kid," said Cyril, as he peeled off her shoes and helped to swing her legs around on the bed. Malik felt her forehead to see if she had a fever. He was good at playing nurse because he'd had to be mum and dad so many times with his little sisters. "You feel a bit hot, Kel. I'll make you some camomile tea."

Kelly wanted to cry because Keffa always made her camomile tea. The very first time they'd met, it was under hostile circumstances, but he'd offered her a cup of tea and it was probably at that moment they'd bonded. She thought about Keffa and instantly felt a gut-wrenching feeling in her stomach. How could he have cheated on her like that? He wasn't the man she knew, that was for sure. Seeing him on that recording was like watching a stranger.

Cyril's phone was ringing, and it was a short while before he realised that the stupid birdy song was his ringtone. He looked at Malik and they both headed downstairs. To their horror, they found Tilly with the phone to her ear. It was too late; they only managed to catch her last few words before Cyril managed to snatch the phone away. She had spoken to the caller, confirming the phone was Cyril's, and she would pass on a message. But when Cyril put the phone to his own ear there was silence. Tilly was visibly upset. Her big round eyes brimmed with tears. She searched the floor, convinced she was in serious trouble. Cyril realised he'd been rather sharp when he'd grabbed hold of the damned thing from her. Instantly, he lifted her off the floor and hugged her.

"Aw, baby, I'm so very sorry. I never meant to take it from you like that. Are you okay, darling?"

Tilly looked at him, teary eyed. "I'm sorry, Uncle Cyril. I thought I was helping. Only the lady asked whose phone it was, and she asked if I was okay."

He checked the last call received and it was from Johnnie's number. Cyril looked at Malik in bewilderment and then he gave Tilly a gentle smile and put her down. "You did good, my little angel. Now then, you get yaself off to bed and Uncle Cyril will take ya out tomorrow. We can go and feed the ducks, eh? How about that?" He patted her shoulder and winked, which lightened Tilly's worried face. As soon as she was out of earshot, he sighed. "I don't know what the fuck is going on, but I don't like it at all. That phone never leaves his side. What a strange thing for someone to ask Tilly, and who the fuck was she?" He ran his hands through his thinning hair and shook his head.

Malik's eyes narrowed, as he wondered about the call. "Strange. I agree, that's weird. Why would someone ask if she was all right? I know my Tilly. She never gets anything wrong." He discerned Cyril's apprehension and tried to put him at ease. "It's probably someone dialling the wrong number."

"No, it was definitely Johnnie's number."

Knowing they could do nothing about the situation, they returned to the study and poured themselves another drink. It wasn't long before Sassy joined them. Totally oblivious to the tension in the air, she swanned in with a full face of make-up and with her usually wild hair straightened so it hung past her backside. Malik's eyes widened. "And where do you think you're going, madam?"

Sassy screwed her nose up. "Nowhere, unless pyjamas have suddenly come into fashion." She pointed to her pink satin nightwear.

"So, what's with the war paint, and ya hair, all … er, well, like that," he pointed rudely.

"For fuck's sake, Malik, I ain't a kid."

Cyril laughed and winked at Sassy. "Leave her, son, she's just experimenting, ain't ya, babe, and I for one think you look like a real lady."

Sassy was about to thank him, but Malik jumped in. "Yeah, well, she can be, if she just keeps her mouth shut. Jeez, Sass, ya wanna stop swearing. Anyway, do us a favour and check the little 'uns are tucked up in bed, will ya? I'm bushed and I'm gonna hit the sack." He looked over at Cyril. "I'll see you in the morning, Cyril."

Cyril was staring out of the window in deep thought, still concerned about the phone call.

CHAPTER NINETEEN

Valerie Campbell was like a swan walking in front of the huge board, with her neck stretched long and her hands behind her back. It was six o'clock in the morning and she'd called a meeting. Sampson was shattered: he'd only had three hours' sleep. So, he was bemused to see the superintendent looking remarkably euphoric, for a woman who must only have had a similar amount of time in bed, considering they'd left the station at the same ungodly hour. He noted that her hair had been washed and her dowdy suit was ironed. He, on the other hand, had just climbed into his clothes, where he'd dropped them on the bedroom floor, and he hadn't even bothered to brush his hair. His early fix of coffee was probably still on the kitchen table. He'd only had a sip. However, the super wanted a meeting, and he couldn't be bothered with the backlash, if he wasn't present.

"Right, listen up!" She quietened the buzz in the room. "It seems we've just uncovered some evidence that may well be part of a very serious paedophile racket." She gave the team a knowing grin which irritated Sampson because he knew Johnnie was innocent. They'd dragged him down to the station and sent a team in to confiscate all the computers and phones. Forensics had spent all evening turning over his home, while his two brothers were kept in the holding cells. But it was the look on Johnnie's face when they'd asked where he kept his computer, that Sampson noticed. Innocently, Johnnie pointed to the small office just off the kitchen and asked, "What's all this about?"

Sampson had known Johnnie since he was a lad, virtually knew his every expression, and it certainly wasn't the look of a guilty man.

"IT have just confirmed that Johnnie Carter's computer contains all the makings of a paedophile racket. They are at present running further diagnostics, and we should have the results by this afternoon. Now, I want four of you to go to Cyril Reardon's place. I'll have the squad cars go with you, and I've organised social services to meet you there."

Sampson couldn't believe he was hearing this, and in his tired state, he wasn't too careful in choosing his words. "Are you sure, Ma'am? I mean, what proof do you have that Cyril Reardon is in on this racket—" He was stopped dead by her screeching voice.

"Sampson, shut it, and let's get the facts straight. We have a dead kid found in the River family's cottage, the victim of a rape with Adam Carter's semen all over her, and then we have Kelly Raven's pub burned to the ground. And to top it all, there is Malakai River, who, it turns out, is Kelly's brother, with two little children thrown into the mix, and they are all conveniently under Reardon's roof."

Hanson spoke up. "So, where does Cyril Reardon fit into all of this?"

Trying not to upset the girl, Campbell had to keep calm, if she wanted promotion. If it had been anyone else, she would have torn into them. "The phone we found on Johnnie Carter rang twice, and when we called the number back, it was none other than Reardon's phone."

Hanson tilted her head. "And from that you deduce that Cyril Reardon is a paedophile?" Sampson smirked because even Hanson, as inexperienced as she was, cottoned on to the fact that the evidence was not clear enough to go charging in and have the children taken away by social services.

Campbell counted to three, not wanting to rip Hanson's head off her shoulders. "Hanson, think about it. Look at the board." She pointed to the names and from each one there was an arrow pointing to Cyril Reardon.

However, Hanson wasn't as stupid as she may have sounded, and she certainly wasn't afraid of Campbell's wrath. "Yes, Gov, I can see that, but you could have any one of their names at the bottom because they just happen to be connected, and the circumstances of the two deaths may just be a coincidence. We know the likes of Cyril Reardon, Kelly Raven, and the Carters are, shall we say, in the same line of business, but child porn? Really, I'm not so sure."

Sampson and the team were silent, waiting for the backlash. Campbell would rip into anyone, if they dared question her abilities, and right now, in a polite but assertive manner, that was exactly what Hanson was doing. Campbell took a deep intake of air through her nostrils and gave a compassionate smile. "Hanson, I know you mean well, and it's good that you're beginning to question everything, but in my twenty-five years' experience, I've developed a sixth sense, shall we say, so trust me when I say Cyril Reardon is in shit up to his neck."

With a smile on Hanson's face, Campbell assumed that would be the end of the questions, but that proved somewhat optimistic. The junior colleague wasn't going to be fobbed off so easily. "So, I take it, we have further evidence than just a phone call from Cyril Reardon's phone to the one belonging to Johnnie Carter?"

With a look of frustration, Campbell tried to keep her tone on an even keel. "For the safety of those two youngest children under his roof, I cannot take any chances." She looked beyond Hanson and

395

surveyed the team. She'd had quite enough of this time-waster. "Right, as I said, I want four of you to head off to Reardon's place." Campbell motioned to the four detectives in the room she wanted over at Otford. Then, she continued, "The squad are waiting, the social services will meet you there, and you, Sampson, will come with me."

Hanson raised her eyebrow and got up to leave, before the others had even pushed their chairs away from the tables. Campbell felt uneasy. *Where was the bloody woman going?*

The superintendent's thoughts turned to Sampson. She wanted to go in with all guns blazing and cause a real stink, so she needed to keep her DI with her on as short a leash as possible. Taking the children, his new family, from Reardon would rub them all up the wrong way, and she would have the last laugh. For years, she'd wanted to take Reardon and his firm down and now was her chance. She had her warrant at last and Reardon's mansion would be a mess by the time she'd finished. Even if they couldn't find evidence of any child sex trade taking place, she would find something for which she could nick him. All she needed was a gun, a stash of cocaine, anything, and she would have achieved her ultimate objective.

Sampson was uneasy; this was a dangerous game. No way was Cyril into child porn. It wasn't his thing, and knowing Cyril, if Campbell took those kiddies away, then she might as well kiss her arse goodbye. Campbell had never been able to nick Cyril or his firm and that was because she underestimated him. Behind the old man was a firm so tight that no one would dare go against him, not if they wanted to live. Sampson had known Cyril to kill a well-known paedophile who had gone off the police radar. The detective had mentioned it to Cyril, and with a wink and a nod, the man had turned up dead, left on the bank of the Thames. So, there was no way the firm were into this crap.

"Right, come with me," spat Campbell, as she pulled on her raincoat, which looked distinctly the worse for wear. He had to find a way to get hold of Cyril and going to the men's toilets wouldn't do it. This woman was like a bloodhound, when it suited her to be one. He had no choice but to follow her. With a smug grin etched across her face, she opened the car door and watched Sampson climb in. She knew the bastard was itching to make a call, but she had the measure of the man.

They were ten minutes away from Reardon's place when Sampson's phone rang. With his heart beating fast, he answered the call and prayed that Campbell couldn't hear who was on the line.

"'Ave your lot arrested Johnnie, by any chance?" It was Cyril.

Sampson looked at Campbell who snapped, "Who's that?"

"Er, sorry, Ma'am. It's me mum."

Cyril knew then that Sampson was giving him a tip-off. Accordingly, he lowered his voice.

"Well, mate?"

"Yes, mum. Oh, I forgot to tell you, the vet will come to pick up the kittens this morning." He hoped Cyril was on form and understood coded language.

"What, the kiddies?" asked Cyril.

"Yes, Mum."

"Has that cunt got a warrant?" Cyril was clearly on the ball, so he was able to use closed questions to get the information he wanted.

"Yes, Mum."

"Is the warrant just for me or is it a search?" He hoped Sampson would find a way to answer that one.

"Um, Mum, *you* need to search *everywhere*. You're always losing your keys."

The message was clear enough. Campbell had an arrest warrant and a search warrant.

"Thanks, ol' buddy."

The phone went dead.

It was seven o'clock in the morning, and the only one who was up was Cyril, having plenty on his mind. In panic mode, he stormed up the stairs and screamed at everyone from the landing. "Malik, Kelly, get up quick, the filth are on their way. Get the girls out of here."

Kelly was up already, dressed in a tracksuit top and jeans. She had slept well and was feeling much better. Her migraine had gone, and after a quick shower, she felt alive again.

Malik, like his sister, was up and cleaning his teeth. He rarely slept beyond six o'clock these days and liked his early morning fifty sets: fifty sit-ups, fifty press-ups, and fifty lengths of front crawl. Cyril's words hit him like a bolt of lightning. He dropped the toothbrush and ran to the youngsters' room where both children were sound asleep. He tried to wake them, but they stirred and rolled over, tugging at the bedclothes as he tried to get them up. "Come on, Star, Tilly, you have to get dressed. We're going on an outing."

Kelly ran down the stairs to find Cyril as white as a ghost. "What's going on?" she demanded.

Cyril shook his head. "I've no fucking idea, but Johnnie's been nicked and they're coming for me. They've a warrant to search the place, and for some reason, they're gonna take the kids. Jesus, what the fuck's just happened?"

Kelly, for the first time, took control. "Right, firstly, they can't take the kids, unless there's a serious reason for them to do so. I'm their legal guardian now. Secondly, it will take them a few minutes to get in here. Do you have anything that they can nick ya for?"

Cyril shook his head. "Nah, we cleaned out me arsenal, if you remember."

Kelly had forgotten, what with so much happening at once. She pulled out her iPhone from her back pocket and wasted no time in getting Delmonte to meet them at the house. At least he could stop any wrongdoing.

Sassy awoke from a deep sleep and wasn't in the best of moods. She could hear her brother trying to wake her little sisters and was getting annoyed. After dragging herself from her bed, she marched into the kids' room, and with a face like thunder, she demanded to know what all the fuss was about.

"Sass, quick, help me, will ya? The Ol' Bill are on their way, and we have to get the girls outta here!" he shouted, trying to pull a jumper over Star's sleepy head.

"You fucking what? They ain't gonna take 'em, are they?"

Malik was flustered. "I dunno, Sass, but Cyril said to get them out, so just help, will ya!"

With an immediate sense of panic, she got to work in getting the girls dressed before she got herself ready.

It was too late. The intercom was buzzing, indicating they had visitors. Cyril looked at the monitor and slumped his shoulders. His camera at the main gate showed half the Kent police force gathered outside.

"Fuck me, Kel, they have an army! Jesus, what do they think I've done?"

Kelly was shaking with fear and anger, and she was also very concerned for Cyril, her 'uncle' and mentor. His normally ruddy face had turned a deathly colour, and he looked visibly shocked by this sudden turn in events. She placed an arm around his waist. "I dunno, but you'll be all right. You ain't done nothing and Delmonte will be here any minute now." But she was horrified when she looked at the monitor and saw so many officers. "There he is, already! Look!" Cyril peered at the screen; he felt some relief, in seeing his lawyer talking to Superintendent Campbell.

"I might as well let the fuckers in, then."

Kelly rubbed his arm, reassuringly. "We ain't much choice, have we?"

Cyril pressed the release button and the main gates opened. Then they waited for the inevitable loud thump on the door. Malik decided to stay upstairs with the girls. There was no need for them to see all the comings and goings, if it could possibly be avoided. The only person who would not be subjected to police crawling all over the house was Mary, as it was her weekend off.

"Kelly, go upstairs. There's no need for you to get interrogated as well."

"Not a chance, Cyril. I want to 'ear what that bitch has to say. You ain't doing this alone, mate."

It was as if the tables had turned. She was in charge and Cyril felt relieved. And it wasn't a bad thing. He'd taught her to be strong, and now she was looking out for him.

With a sickly smile, Superintendent Campbell stepped inside the cavernous entrance hall, followed by her assistant, DI Sampson, who looked as if he would rather be anywhere but here.

"So, DS Campbell, to what do I owe this displeasure?"

She glared at Cyril and then at Kelly, before she chuckled. This was what she'd been waiting for: to witness them both squirming. She was in her element and it showed. Her deliberate moves and cocky stance gave her an edge that signalled she was calling the shots now.

"I have a warrant to turn over your premises, and *Mr Reardon*, I'm taking you in," she drawled, with sarcasm. Her expression was weird, as if she was on a high. Her smile was spread across her face and her eyes were alive.

Michael Delmonte pushed past Superintendent Campbell and stood by Cyril's side.

"You can question Mr Reardon down at the station, but I want a word with my client first."

Campbell knew then that she had to go along with it, before the lawyer kicked off and found some legal issue that would put a stop to her ransacking the mansion and taking the kids away. She nodded and allowed Delmonte to take Cyril into his study. They were followed by Kelly. In the meantime, Campbell called in the two social workers.

"Right, the children are here somewhere in this monster of a mansion. Take two officers with you, in case you face any resistance."

Malik and Sassy were descending the stairs with both children behind them when Campbell detected them. "Malakai River, step aside, please! We are here to take Chantilly and Star—"

She got no further. In a fit of uncontrollable rage, Sassy flew past Malik and hurtled down the stairs, where she literally launched herself at the detective. The whole incident was totally unexpected. Like a wild animal, Sassy grabbed the superintendent's hair and almost swung from it, pulling her to the ground. Even with Campbell's defence training, Sassy was too fast for the officer to engage her in any kind of defensive hold. With the superintendent now on the ground, Sassy threw herself on top of the woman, clawing and punching and trying to gouge her eyes out. Quickly, one of the social workers tried to pull Sassy away, but she was backhanded and sent reeling across the floor. Sampson wanted to leave the kid to it – she was doing just fine – but he knew he would get into serious trouble, if he let this assault carry on. The commotion sent Kelly, Cyril, and Delmonte back into the hallway, only to find Sampson restraining Sassy, now completely out of breath, and Campbell, lying on the floor in a dishevelled state. With chunks of her hair strewn on the marble floor and deep claw marks down her face, the officer was quite badly wounded. She put her hand to her face. Sticky blood was oozing from her cheeks, and then she felt her eyes closing up. This was the first time in her career that she'd been hurt, and right now, she was numb with shock. Meanwhile, Sassy was trying to break free to have another go.

"No one fucking touches my sisters, ya 'orrible nasty cunt. I swear to God, if you fucking go anywhere near them, I'll hunt you down and rip out ya fucking heart and burn it in front of ya!"

Everyone was shocked, not so much by the expletives — although these did raise more than a few eyebrows — but by the ferocity of the youngster's tone and with the almost deranged expression across her face. For a second, Sassy did indeed look like the person she portrayed: a mad woman from hell.

More police edged their way in, clearly somewhat confused. Normally, an assault like this on one of their own would have the attacker trussed up in handcuffs and thrown into the back of a meat wagon. But the circumstances were unusual, to say the least. The young woman was fighting to protect her little sisters, and it wasn't completely clear to most of the police officers and social workers that this was a *bona fide* case where the authorities had not only moral standing but also a legal one. Then, there was their senior officer to be considered. Superintendent Campbell was in severe shock and looked as if she was going to pass out at any moment. All eyes were on her struggling to get to her feet. The social worker who had managed to keep out of the way of the skirmish leaned forward and offered a hand, but Campbell pushed it aside in annoyance. As soon as she had two feet on the floor, it was Tilly, normally the shyest in the family, the child who hardly said two words and was often in deep contemplation, who spoke first.

"I'm not going anywhere—"

Before she could utter another syllable, Superintendent Campbell, with spite in her tone, snapped back, "Oh, yes, you are!"

That rejoinder set the tone for what was to follow. The atmosphere suddenly became distinctly tense and even chilly. The officer had

403

shown herself for what she was: a bully. Even the supporting officers were taken aback by her harsh and very unsympathetic words towards the little girl, but it was Tilly's response and the manner in which she made it which made them all take notice. Standing as tall as her little frame would allow, and with her tiny hands clasped in front of her, as if she was about to be presented to the Queen, she gave them pause for thought.

"No, actually, I won't go. I'm not a dog. You can't tell me what to do. I'm a person, you know, and my sister and I have been brought up by my brother Malik and my older sister Sassy, when our mother left us." Her sweet voice had the room silent and engaged as everyone hung on to her words. She took another deep breath. "And I've watched him fight for money so that we could eat. I've seen Sassy go without food so that me and Star wouldn't be hungry. So, if you think you know better than me because you're a grown-up, then you're wrong. The grown-up in our lives left us with nothing, and it was Malik and Sassy that made sure we were safe, protected, warm, and cared for. So, no, missus, I'm not going anywhere, and neither is Star. We're happy here. Uncle Cyril is like a dad to me, and now you're going to take him away, and it ain't right. Why don't you catch the really bad people like me mum, 'cos she *is* a bad person?" With that, she edged over to Cyril and slipped her hand into his.

Everyone was shocked into reticence, including Sassy and Malik. They had never heard their little sister so vocal and articulate and command the attention of others in such a mature fashion, giving nearly everyone present a lot to think about.

All except Superintendent Campbell, though: she was livid. She could almost taste the hate in the air. All eyes were now on her, and she knew she had to redeem the situation and get the children out fast. She wanted Reardon's head on a block, and what better way than a child sex trafficking offence. No villain in the land would side with him. He would be inside on the wing where the nonces were, stripped of his reputation and living a life of hell. She wanted the last laugh if it killed her, but right now, things weren't looking too clever.

Rachael, the social worker, who had been struck by Sassy, leaned against the wall. She didn't hold a grudge. Far from it — she could see the dynamics, and if she had known the history, then she would never have tried to help. Kids that bring themselves up are more protective over their siblings than the average kids in a family, where there is at least one parent present in the home. She had seen it in the children's homes. God help anyone who picked on a younger member of the family; they would face their older sibling's wrath, just like Sassy had shown. She could see it in their eyes that there was a sad story to tell, and the bond they shared was like glue sticking them together. She observed the deep heartbreaking expression on Malik's face; it was enhanced by the way his broad shoulders slumped and his hand gripped the hand of the youngest sister, Star.

Sampson let Sassy go, once he felt her calm down, and she ran to Malik, hiding behind him. Rachael knew he was their rock who held them together.

A social worker, in her late forties, Rachael had enough experience to understand children, and what she had just witnessed made her seriously question the fact that the two girls were in harm's way. Sassy was like a caged animal. She would never let any ill-treatment come to her sisters, so Rachael questioned the notion that these children were in some way being used for child pornography. However, she reasoned, nothing these days was ever that simple. The world had gone mad. Her job had become unbelievably more complicated, and with it came more stress, what with new legislation coming out almost every month, so she could never be one hundred per cent sure. As the lead social worker, she felt she should take control of the situation and be the one who made the decisions.

"Kelly Raven, I understand you have legal guardianship. Is that correct?"

Kelly nodded. "Yes, I do." She turned to face Sassy and winked, giving her reassurance.

"Okay, would you mind if we speak with the girls? We would be happy to do it with you present."

Superintendent Campbell was exasperated. There was a fine line between the social services and the police force, and she wanted the girls removed and the pressure put on Reardon to enable her to make him crack. Her own face was a mess, and that was all she needed to demand an arrest.

"Saskia River, you're under arrest. Take her down to the station!" demanded Campbell.

Delmonte felt the situation was getting out of hand, so he stepped forward. "Hold on a minute. You need to step back from this situation because I can clearly see that your emotions are clouding your judgement."

Campbell glared at him with a face like thunder. "You what!" she exclaimed. "She's under arrest. In case you haven't noticed, she's just fucking physically assaulted me."

Rachael stepped forward. "I think it may be best if you calm yourself down. Language like that in front of the children is quite disgusting."

With a harsh look, Campbell shot a glance at Sassy, and then back at Rachael. "Hello! Did you not hear her screaming obscenities at *me?*"

Rachael, who now had a strong aversion to this police officer, shook her head. "It shouldn't really be necessary for me to remind you who the adult is here."

Campbell couldn't comprehend that she was being taken to task by a social worker and none of her team had made the slightest effort to slap the handcuffs on Saskia.

"Sampson, take her to the station, and I want uniformed officers in here, if there is any more nonsense. These two ladies need to take the children away." She rudely gestured at the social workers.

Rachael took umbrage at this. "You called us in to do a job, and I think it's in the children's best interests if we conduct our own investigations in the comfort of their own home. My job is to ensure the well-being of the children and that's exactly what I intend to do."

With one eye almost closed, Superintendent Campbell tore into the social worker. "If I say these kids need to be removed, they will be. I know what your job is, and I also have a bloody good idea what mine is. Right now, it's to get them out of here and to a safe pace. I don't think you have grasped the seriousness of this situation, or do I need to spell it out?"

Again, there was silence, as they waited for Rachael to react. But she didn't. She didn't need all this hassle.

Campbell tutted loudly and nodded to one of the PCs to arrest Saskia. The young PC called Falon was eager to get in Campbell's good books but even this situation was awkward. He nodded back and walked towards Malik. "Er, step aside, son."

407

Malik let go of Star's hand and whispered to her. "Stand with Uncle Cyril."

Star did as she was told, and Malik stood with his chest puffed out and his legs apart. "Touch her and I'll fucking floor ya." Their eyes met, and for a second, Falon felt his bowels move.

It was left to Delmonte to jump in and bring the standoff to a halt.

"Right, there's no need for the cuffs. As her solicitor, I'll bring her into the station myself. She's still a minor," he said, with a deep intimidating voice. Slowly, Sassy stepped aside with her head down and headed towards Delmonte.

The atmosphere continued to be tense, unpleasant, and unpredictable. It was also gaining a momentum of its own making.

Campbell wanted to remove the kids from the house before there was another eruption. However, as Rachael moved forwards to take the little girls' hands, Sassy was off again, jumping in front and blocking the way. She had gone from a deflated balloon to a wild animal, protecting her young.

"Fuck off, lady. You ain't taking them away to be abused by some shitty foster perverts. They need to be here with us."

Rachael put her hands up, showing she was not in any way trying to be confrontational. "They are not going into foster care, Saskia."

"Huh, don't bank on it," uttered Campbell, in her best sarcastic tone.

Rachael and Sassy both glared at Campbell but for different reasons. In the social services official's case, Rachael felt that the ranking police officer was being deliberatively provocative and unhelpful. Sassy, on the other hand, saw the police officer for who she was — a bully first and foremost. Just as Sassy was about to launch another attack, Falon grabbed her. But in trying to spin the wriggling young woman round to put the handcuffs on her, he was thwarted by Malik who stopped him in his tracks. No one saw him move so fast, as he leaped forward and shoved the PC to the ground.

"Don't you fucking touch her, I said!"

"No, Malik!" screamed Kelly, knowing full well that he would be carted off too.

Within seconds, the other officers charged in and had Sassy face down and handcuffed and Malik with his arm up his back.

"Get them down to the station and outta my sight!" demanded Superintendent Campbell.

Cyril reluctantly handed the two girls over to Rachael.

"Please, Uncle Cyril, don't let them take us away, please," begged Tilly, as she tried to struggle to get away.

Cyril was left helpless and silent, but inside, his heart was beating at an astronomical level. With a lump in his throat, he felt pain like never before. Little Tilly, with her huge round dewy eyes, implored him, but all he could do was look at the floor. He could still hear her crying and pleading, as they dragged the girls away.

Then Delmonte patted his shoulder. "Come on, Cyril, let's get this fiasco over with."

The sounds of vehicles moving away from the house could be heard as Kelly thought about her young family being separated from each other. The only people remaining were Kelly, Sampson, and four other officers. Campbell had gone back to the station to give Sassy, Malik, and Cyril a good grilling.

Kelly, totally gutted, had neither the strength nor the energy to deal with the police. She simply turned on her heels and headed to her bedroom, slamming the door behind her. As she sat on the edge of the bed, she placed her hands over her face and sobbed. How could this all get so out of hand? Nothing made sense anymore. There was Cyril being accused of taking part in a paedophile ring, Keffa in prison for something he didn't do, and now her new family all ripped away from her. It just didn't add up.

Quite some time later, a soft tap at her door interrupted her crying, and as she wiped her face, a voice from outside said, "May I come in, Kelly? I would like a word, but only if you're up to it."

Kelly took a deep breath and wiped her eyes one more time. "Yes, come in," she replied in a compliant tone.

Slowly, the door opened, and Geoff Sampson stepped inside, carefully closing the door behind him. He gave Kelly a weary smile. "May I sit with you?"

She looked up and nodded.

He loosened his tie and sat on an upholstered chair by the window. "Kelly, the officers have just gone. They didn't find anything."

"I'm not surprised. They wouldn't because there's nothing to find. The whole thing stinks. This is all a set-up. That officer bitch wants us one way or another, and she's made sure she hits us where it hurts."

Sampson nodded in agreement. "I know, Kelly, I know. Just for the record, I don't believe any of it. I've known Cyril for years, and he isn't a kiddie fiddler, and neither is Johnnie Carter, for that matter. There's something odd going on, though, and Campbell is so determined to nick you lot, she isn't looking elsewhere. Never mind, I intend to get to the bottom of it. So, Kelly, can you help me?"

Kelly lifted her head to see a concerned inspector watching her anxiously. She blinked furiously to stop the tears from plummeting down her face. Although she wanted to help, she had to ask herself if she could really trust him. After all, he was still a copper, and although he had tipped them off on many occasions in the past, was he truly on their side? But then, what did she have to lose? Keffa was facing a murder charge, and right now, she had no way of proving otherwise, unless she shared something which might just unlock the mystery to her family's troubles. Were the CCTV recordings the key to it all?

But leaving Keffa's predicament and probable innocence aside, what she'd seen had certainly disturbed her. Even if he was released, their relationship was more than likely over.

"Look, Kelly, I'm going to make us both a cup of tea to give you some time to think. Christ, this place is a mansion and a half! Ol' Cyril had a right touch winning that poker game."

He eased himself off the chair and looked around, smiling. "He's a funny sod, eh, but ya know what? He's a good man, one of the best." Just as he opened the bedroom door, in waddled the two Rottweilers, wagging their tails and nudging Sampson's hand for him to stroke them.

"Hello, Frank and Stein, my big fur buddies."

Kelly observed how the two dogs fussed over him. Somehow, it felt all the more reassuring. She was in a bad place right now, emotionally that was. She still remembered her good friend Legend; she became acquainted with him when she ended up with Rudy and his

411

family. Legend's strength and size, which had saved her on more than one occasion in the past, paled into insignificance, though, when compared to his genuine love for his mistress. So, in a way, she felt that if Cyril's beasts were trusting of Sampson, who was she to argue with that?

"They clearly like you," smiled Kelly.

Sampson ruffled each one's head. "Yeah, they should do. I have their sister, my Queenie. I bring her over sometimes, and me and Cyril walk them through the woods. They still remember they are siblings, though. Their mother had thirteen pups."

Kelly felt a lump in her throat. It was only a year ago when Legend succumbed to cancer, and at the time, it had rendered her heartbroken. Even now, there were days when she struggled to come to terms with her loss.

"Thirteen?"

"Yep. I think every villain in the south bought one, and Cyril being Cyril, he bought two." He stopped and tilted his head, as if he'd just mused over something.

"What is it?"

He shook his head. "Oh nothing, really, except I guess I shouldn't be discussing this. Johnnie Carter was nicked yesterday for running a child sex racket. When forensics got to his house, they found the computer in his office with all the evidence on it. He swore blind he never uses the computer. In fact, I know Johnnie hates the things and doesn't trust them. So, there's no way he could put such disgusting things on it. I'm sure he has been set up."

412

Kelly urged him to go on.

"But, if he's right, I'm not so sure how it was put on his computer. You see, they had to get a dog handler there because Johnnie has one of the Rotties, Agro. Now, she is a nutter. I mean, she's all right with me. I guess she can smell my dog on me. But if someone went into his house to set him up, his Agro would rip their arms off."

Deep in thought, Kelly slowly edged herself off the bed. "So, what you're saying is Johnnie is either seriously into child porn, or whoever did set him up, they knew the dog?"

Sampson nodded, and she noticed just how soft his grey eyes were. His dishevelled hair gave his mature face a younger look. For the first time in what seemed like ages, she started to relax and feel more confident.

"Let's get some tea and think this over. I can't have Cyril in there, and I must get the girls home. My Malik has been to hell and back to keep those kids together, and I can't have them taken away over something that has nothing to do with him."

"I agree. My boss is an evil cow. She wants shooting."

They left the bedroom. Taking the smaller staircase, which led directly into the kitchen, they were followed by the two dogs. Sampson marvelled at the sheer size of the room. Although there were modern appliances, it was still set out as it would have been a hundred years ago, with the long oak table and wooden chairs to seat the butler and servants. A huge redundant range was the centre piece, and even the original racks, which would once have held the pots and pans, were still there. For a moment, Sampson thought about a visit he'd made to Highclere Castle only last summer.

He took a seat as Kelly put the kettle on. There was a comfortable silence while the detective absorbed the beautiful traditional character and reflected on that visit to Hampshire.

"Have you never been in the kitchen?" she asked curiously, since he'd given her the impression that he and Cyril were good friends, despite their diametrically opposed professions.

Sampson laughed. "No, and I don't suppose Cyril has either, not all the while he has dear ol' Maggie, er, I mean Mary."

Kelly knew then that they were close, and he was right. Cyril relied on Mary for everything. Kelly watched as Stein slumped on the floor over Sampson's feet.

"He's one great lump, that one, eh?"

Sampson wriggled his feet free from the hefty weight.

"You want to see Johnnie's bitch, Agro. Now, she's twice the size of these two and my little Queenie. Rose, the woman that bred them, was going to keep Agro for herself, but after she shacked up with Johnnie for all of a week, she let him keep the dog."

With two steaming cups in her hand, she sat at the table and placed one in front of Sampson.

"So, what about this Rose? Could she have set him up? The dog wouldn't bite her."

Sampson gave a hearty laugh. "Old Rose would be setting up every villain this side of the river, if that were the case. No, she was the type who liked a good time. She went from one man to the next, and I think she went to live with some bloke from up north, in the end. She did catch Johnnie with a fella, which got up her nose, but she was just as

414

bad, always had two men on the go herself. So, Rose just probably buggered off, leaving the dog behind. I did feel sorry for her old man, though. Poor old Roy. He was a big strapping lad, many moons ago, but her philandering turned him into a sad waif of a fella. I don't know why he hasn't packed up the pub business and retired somewhere. I mean, the flack he gets from the punters in the Mint. I would have cleared off years ago—" Sampson stopped as he observed the shocked expression on Kelly's face.

"Are you okay, Kelly?"

Her mind was an avalanche of thoughts and conspiracies, all of them tripping over themselves. Then she thought back to the disks handed over to her by Roy from the pub and the incident she had witnessed when she watched the recording play out. The shockwave of seeing Keffa with the girl had consumed her and put everything else she'd seen to the back of her mind. It was so painful to even let her mind wander back there, but as if she'd woken up from a dream and stepped into the world of reality, she wondered if Sampson could help her. She did, however, need to play her cards close to her chest and find a way to trust Sampson or go it alone.

"Geoff, if you had the evidence that would prove Keffa's innocence, what would you do with it?"

Sampson placed his cup back on the table and clasped his hands together. "Hmm, that's certainly a leading question, but I'll level with you. I definitely wouldn't hand it over to Campbell, that's for sure, because I don't trust her. That woman is determined to have you lot behind bars. It's almost become an obsession of hers, but it may also prove to be her downfall, and I, for one, cannot wait to see her crumble."

With a flick of her head, she indicated for Sampson to follow her. They returned to the bedroom. Sampson was only too eager to see what Kelly had to show him. He sensed this was going to be important and his heart was beating fast in anticipation. Kelly was no idiot. As far as he was concerned, she had more brains than half the men on his team. He said nothing though and watched as she pulled from the cabinet two disks. He noticed her hands shaking, as she slid one of them into the DVD player.

"I really can't watch it again, it's all too upsetting for me. You'll see what I mean. Here's the remote. You need to fast forward it to the 27ᵗʰ October until you see Keffa. I'll leave you alone, and when you've finished, I'll be in the study. I think you'll see something interesting, but please excuse the porn." Her eyes were moist, as she quickly left the room.

Geoff Sampson settled on the edge of the bed and watched her move gracefully out of the bedroom before he eagerly pressed the play button. At first, he didn't quite get where this recording was taken from, until the picture switched to the bar of the Mitcham Mint, a pub he knew well, and then his eyes widened in disbelief. He did as she instructed and fast forwarded it to 27ᵗʰ October. Then, he watched with disgust the proceedings. Kelly must have been absolutely poleaxed, when she saw those two carrying on. He couldn't digest why Keffa would be having it away with Lacey. The kid was definitely following in her mother's footsteps, gaining a reputation, just as Rose had done. But how could Keffa go from Kelly, a sophisticated woman, who would turn every man's head, to a fake trollop like Roy's daughter? It defied belief.

He then pondered for a while, as the recording showed just an empty room, the kitchen at the side of the pub. He was a little confused because all he had watched was Keffa fucking the life out of Roy's

416

daughter. But he continued to watch the recording, keeping an eye on the date as he did so. Reaching 30th October, he saw the meeting with Keffa, Frank, Blakey, and the Carters. He allowed the recording to carry on until the end but nothing of any relevance seemed to be happening. The disk finished playing and he wiped his brow. He felt distraught for the poor woman, watching her fella doing that. He was still confused but was sure Kelly had more to say.

Leaving the bedroom, he went this time down the magnificent oak staircase and into the study, where he found Kelly sipping from a cut-glass brandy bowl. She looked up at him and gave him a tired smile.

"Would you like one?" She held the glass up and walked over to the bar.

It still puzzled Sampson how Keffa could want anyone other than her.

"Yeah, go on, then. I, er, Kelly, I'm really sorry, love."

She choked back the tears and remained with her back to him, pouring from a decanter. With a deep breath, she turned around. "I hate him for what he's done, for what he's done to me, but, Geoff, I wouldn't want him to serve a life sentence, not when I really don't believe he killed Adam Carter."

He took the drink from her and was saddened by the redness surrounding her eyes. Clearly, she must have been crying.

"I agree, it isn't his style. Kelly, what did you want me to see on the CCTV?"

"Keffa's gun would have been in the pocket of his jacket that slid down behind the freezer. He left the pub with only his overcoat, not his jacket, after screwing that fucking slag, Roy's daughter. The stupid bastard was so intent on getting his fucking oats, he slipped up and may have left the weapon for anyone to use and in his name." She rolled her eyes. "Jesus, what a fucking idiot! Anyone could have gone and shot Adam and with Keffa's prints on the poxy thing. The access to that kitchen is easy. The bloody men's toilets are right next door. He's now the one up for the murder. I just don't know how to feel about it all. I'm so angry with him, and yet I feel bad because in my heart, I know he didn't kill Adam. He had no reason to, and, well, you saw for yourself, he left his jacket behind."

Sampson smiled in agreement. "I also don't believe the Carters torched your club. They're too worried about repercussions from your firm."

Kelly laughed at that observation. "Oh, we know that. Johnnie agreed, and even he didn't think Keffa shot his brother. That little incident was just some small-time wannabes trying to cause a rift between the Carters and us."

Sampson raised his eyebrow. "Who?"

"The Ryes. They're some minor outfit from Essex. They had a grudge against me father years ago, and by all accounts, Jean River was in on it. She probably got the hump because Adam Carter threw her out on her ear. So, she came here to take the youngest girl, Star, pretending she was Carter's daughter, to keep her relationship with Adam alive, but she got a shock, I can tell ya. I smashed her nose for her. The fucking whore of a woman."

Shaking his head, Sampson tried to unravel all the connections, but it was like a knotted ball of wool. "Christ, Kelly, this is such a mess. Do you know where Jean is now?"

418

Kelly shook her head. "No, but Malik told me he sent Fynn Rye packing with the knowledge that Jean was seeing Adam Carter before she took up again with the ol' man Rye. Apparently, he's been seeing her on and off for years. The bitch didn't even tell him she had kids. She would leave them to fend for themselves while she'd go off and get her back doors smashed in by Paddy. I hate her, Geoff, for what she's put those kids through. I mean, who fucking does that – leaves the kids alone with fuck all and all because, like my father, she's a sex addict? Well, she may be anywhere, but I can bet me last penny she isn't with the Ryes now. Their little scam to cause a war was done without prior knowledge that Jean had been living with Adam. So, like you say, it's all a bit messy."

Sampson was sinking deeper into the confusion. "So, the possibilities of who killed Adam are endless! Look, Kelly, I'm going to head back to the station. I'll see what's going on with Cyril. You look washed out. If I get an opportunity, I'll call and give you an update. I say, opportunity, because old crafty knickers, she watches me like a hawk."

Kelly stood up to see him to the door.

"Oh, Kelly, I noticed a second disk. Have you looked at that by any chance?"

With a saddened look, Kelly shook her head. "I just couldn't really bring myself to watch much more. Only the meeting with Keffa and Johnnie, but that never gave any more clues. Maybe I was afraid I would see Keffa return for a second helping."

He patted her arm. "I know, love, it must hurt. Do you think you could watch the second disk? It may or may not shed more light. I mean the jacket may well be still behind the freezer and he might have had his gun in his coat pocket instead. Christ, who knows?" he sighed. "But, anyway, I'll keep what we've discussed to myself for now."

As the afternoon sun shone on Sampson's face, Kelly noticed just how bright his eyes were, and his face was so open and kind. Not the typical hard-faced DI, not by a long stretch, and that gave her reason for hope.

"I will, Geoff. Please, if you get the chance, make sure Malik and Sassy are okay, will you?"

He winked in confirmation. Just as he opened his car door, he glanced back to see Kelly staring towards him, looking especially vulnerable. The way the men described her, she was a chip off the old block and tough as old boots. Was she really that or was it just a front, only for the business? Had Sampson known Kelly much better, he would have realised that she was a master of disguise, both in her facial expression, and in how she talked, which was something she had acquired in her teenage years. She could talk like the Queen or a Millwall supporter, if desired.

Sampson set off for the station, trying to process the events of the past two hours. He was used to Cyril being an old fart at times, but then he knew that behind the violence and cockiness was a comical man with a big heart. In some ways, Kelly shared Cyril's personality traits, having a somewhat Jekyll and Hyde personality. Like many before him, Geoff Sampson was fascinated by how personable she was and by how serene she could be at times, and yet when she had a mind to, she could lose her temper like any man. He had heard as much too. But, as he drove down the drive to the main road, he somehow felt privileged to have seen the more vulnerable side of Kelly Raven.

He suspected he was one of a select few who could claim they had.

CHAPTER TWENTY

Sampson eventually arrived at the station, expecting some grief from Campbell, assuming she would be fuming for many reasons, including the embarrassing marks on her face from a kid, no less. Yet, as soon as he ran up the stairs to reach the first floor where the incident room and the offices were, he noticed people giving him anxious looks. Hanson appeared with a pile of papers under her arm and concern evident on her face. When she realised he was standing there looking somewhat surprised, she approached him. "Geoff, didn't you get my text? The commissioner wants to see you. Campbell's been taken to the hospital."

Sampson automatically assumed it was due to the injuries she sustained during the fight with Saskia. "I didn't think the girl hurt her that badly. Weren't they just superficial wounds?" He placed his hands on his waist and gave an exaggerated frown.

Hanson stared at him incredulously, totally baffled. "Oh, you did hear, then? Only I thought no one could get hold of you. Your phone was switched off."

Sampson was puzzled himself by now. "I was there when we went to arrest Cyril Reardon. Saskia River attacked her. Is there something else, then?"

Her expression changed instantly, and a smarmy grin crept across her face. "Jesus, Geoff, you really haven't heard, then?"

"Heard what?"

But there was no time for Hanson to fill him in on a bit of office gossip doing the rounds at present, as the stentorian tones of their most senior officer could be heard from the other end of the building. In voice and conduct, he would have been at home on the parade ground. Sampson, though, had respect for the man. Although he talked to his officers harshly, he was fair most of the time.

"Sampson! My office, pronto!" shouted Edgar Myers, the commissioner.

Sampson hurried along the corridor and into Myers's office. The tall, commanding figure with a chisel-like jaw, who reminded Sampson of General George S Patton, was standing up reading a police file. On closer inspection, Myers looked uneasy.

"Take a seat, Sampson. We have a very serious bloody problem. It's one that, quite frankly, I could jolly well do without."

Sampson watched as Myers took a seat opposite. After taking an age to settle in his executive chair, the commissioner took a deep breath and came to the point.

"DS Campbell has lost the bloody plot. Christ, she has just messed up on a huge scale. I am not in any position to smooth this one over, either."

"I'm sorry, I've no idea what's going on."

With a heavy sigh, Myers rose from his chair and gave Sampson a hard nod to follow him. "I think it's better you see for yourself. Oh, that stupid, stupid, woman."

Sampson had to almost skip to keep up with the commissioner. When he was on one, he was like the Carly Simon song "Nobody Does It Better".

"Whilst you two were off to arrest Cyril Reardon, we had the camera team in. Oh, it's some new bloody rule. One of the holding cells needs to have cameras fitted for the vulnerable suspect. All this nonsense about high risk and suicides. Well, there they were, in the throes of showing me how the damn thing works – it's high-tech stuff by the way, with crystal clear vision and sound – when, from one of the monitors, we see the superintendent arriving with a girl, Saskia River, in cuffs and – wait for it – she manhandles her, pushing her inside the cell. I couldn't believe my bloody eyes, man!" He took another deep breath, before pushing the door open to the custody suite which also contained a monitoring room for one of the cells. Sampson was still on his tail, with all kinds of thoughts going on in his mind.

"The two men who installed the cameras were both there with me watching the monitor. It was something about the sound not working, and then the bloody thing comes alive. There she was, in full view, and she could be clearly heard on that monitor." He pointed to the new system on the wall, shaking his head.

"Sorry, Gov, but I'm not sure what you're getting at."

Myers flared his nostrils. "Sampson, I think you need to see this because there's no way we'll be able to cover this up, even if we wanted to. Strike that last comment! The two men who fitted the system are civvies, and they made it quite clear they wanted to make a statement there and then. Look. See for yourself."

The commissioner fiddled with some of the buttons and replayed what had happened. He was right: the pictures and sound were as good as any home TV system. Then, he observed the action.

Saskia's hands were cuffed behind her back and she was being pushed fiercely inside the cell. She landed on the solid plastic moulded bed, where she instantly managed to get herself into a seated position upright against the wall. The officer towered over her, and if the cameras hadn't picked up the sound, then no one would have known what was said, and more to the point, would never have been able to prove it. But with the new monitoring system, it was as clear as day. Campbell's sick, twisted words were deliberately being said to put the fear of God into the child.

"Right, you fucking little animal, this is how it works," intoned the superintendent, with steely, intimidating eyes and a threatening stance. Saskia sat stony-faced, then suddenly, she glared up with a curled lip and a fierce fire in her eyes. Campbell felt that she was staring down the barrel of a loaded gun, but she wasn't going to let a kid intimidate her.

"You are going to write a statement saying that Cyril Reardon was going to use your little sisters for his sick video."

Sampson watched the look of horror on Saskia's face, and then he heard her answer back. "No, I fucking ain't, you weird bitch. Cyril would never do anything like that, so you can fuck off!"

"Oh, yes, you will, because if you don't, I'll make sure those girls are taken away to a children's home, where, who fucking knows, they may well be subjected to real abuse, and your brother will go away for a long time for assaulting an officer, and you, you little cunt, will follow suit. I'll see to it that you serve ten years."

With that, she impulsively gave Saskia a hard punch to the ribs. Sampson gasped and then he couldn't believe his eyes. Saskia doubled up, the blow obviously having winded her, but then, tossing her head, she sat up straight, and in a split second, she headbutted the

424

superintendent so hard that she fell down onto the floor. Saskia jumped off the bed, and with her hands still tied behind her back, she began systematically stamping all over Campbell's head. The next shots on the monitor were of police rushing to the scene to sort out the *mêlée* by restraining Saskia and rescuing the beleaguered police officer.

To say Sampson was in shock was a master of the understatement. He had never seen anything like it. He hoped he wouldn't see it again. For a second, he was speechless.

"So, now, can you see my predicament? I've got Delmonte up in bloody arms, and you know what he is like. I have had to promise that I will get this matter cleared up in the next hour, or so, or he will be casting hellfire on me and this force, I can tell you. To be honest, I cannot really blame him on this occasion! But, I know that man. He will cause us no end of damage."

"Where is Saskia at the moment?"

"She is still in the cell. Jesus, they are all still in the cells."

"Gov, may I suggest that the child also goes to the hospital because she may have a broken rib, looking at the hiding she got, and if she has, well, we'll be in real trouble, if we ignore it."

"Good point, Sampson. I will organise it immediately."

"So, the super never had a clue she was on camera?" asked Sampson.

Myers huffed. "No, not even I knew the installation was rescheduled for today. It was originally planned for next month."

Sampson shook his head in a resigned fashion. He was still trying to get his head around these latest developments.

425

"I want your honest opinion. This child sex racket, do you think there is any merit in it? I have known Cyril Reardon and the Carters for many years now, and well, it just doesn't have their stamp on it."

Sampson gave his boss a reassuring smile. "Gov, a phone call to Johnnie Carter from Cyril Reardon doesn't mean he is part of a sex racket. The superintendent is so determined to have Reardon behind bars, but she's pissing in the wind, if she thinks her little hypothesis is a workable one. Please excuse my colourful language, Gov. I, for one, think she's gone a bit too far this time." But he held his hands up, as if to say it's just my view.

"No need to apologise on this occasion, Sampson. You are quite right. She has definitely exceeded her authority, and I will have to pick up the bloody pieces, or it will be *my* job on the line." He looked at the monitor.

Sampson knew he was safe to speak frankly. "Gov, I think maybe I should paint a clearer picture."

With a concerned look across at his detective inspector, Myers nodded for him to continue.

"It's been like a crusade to bring down Cyril Reardon and his gang, an obsession that started a long time ago. She was after Eddie Raven for years before he got sent down, and then, when his daughter Kelly Raven appeared, she has been on her case, too. I mean, she has spent hours looking into her businesses, and when Keffa Jackson was arrested, I felt that she had some kind of vendetta against her. We went to search her house, but she didn't want to stop there. She said she would make sure she would leave it ransacked. It was as if she hated her."

The commissioner's look of concern was replaced by intense anger as he said to Sampson, "Well, I have to agree. Victoria has said as much."

"The thing is, Gov, DS Campbell has a problem, a drink problem. She always reeks of booze. I think this mad obsession is truly making her irrational, and I'm afraid she'll take us all down with her, if we don't do something."

There, he'd said it, and he'd probably set the cat among the pigeons in the process, but he honestly couldn't give a shit right now. Working with her had made his life a misery and recently he had seriously considered jacking it all in. Fuck the pension. There was always Cyril's nice little earner.

"Right, thank you, Sampson. I am going to have a very direct and honest talk to Cyril Reardon myself because, right now, I am facing possible headline news, if I cannot rectify the damage DS Campbell has caused us. By Christ, she is going down for this."

As soon as Myers left, Sampson smiled and pumped the air with his fist. What a result! He'd actually imagined several scenarios where Valerie Campbell would shoot herself in the foot, but this was the mother of all fuck-ups. Perhaps he was looking at promotion. There was always hope.

Sampson went off to check Malakai and Cyril were all right, before entering Saskia's cell. She was still shaking when the officer opened the cell door. Her eyes widened, and she backed further against the wall. Sampson looked over at her and she reminded him of a feral cat forced into the corner of an alleyway. *Poor kid*, he thought. The whole experience must have traumatised the life out of the child and left her so afraid of the people she was supposed to feel safe with. His heart sank.

427

He sat on the bed next to her and gave her a genuine smile. "Saskia, I'm so sorry, love. Are you okay? I mean, do you hurt anywhere?"

His soft eyes and unpretentious nature made her feel protected. "Please can you tell me if me bruvver's all right? I mean, they ain't bashed him up an' all, 'ave they? 'Cos, I swear to God, Cyril ain't like that. He's a good man, and Malik is like me. The police will have to beat the fucking arsehole out of him before he will say anything other than the truth."

Sampson acknowledged what she was saying with a smile. "Yes, Saskia, he's fine, and so is Cyril. Let me take those cuffs off, and we'll go to a room where you can have a cup of tea, and I'll see to it that Malakai can come and join you, eh?"

Sassy nodded and suddenly an unexpected tear trickled down her cheek. Sampson wanted to reach over and hug her, but the cameras were still switched on, and it wouldn't go down too well. Instead, he helped her off the bed and released the cuffs. With his hand on Saskia's shoulder, he gave her a gentle squeeze of affection and guided her outside the cell.

"I bet I'm going down now, eh?" She paused. "I didn't kill her, did I? I just lost me temper. She said, er——"

He interrupted her before she panicked herself into a state. "Saskia, listen to me, will you? Superintendent Campbell is badly hurt and has been taken to hospital. But let me assure you that you acted purely in self-defence. She was totally in the wrong for what she did back there in the cell, and I'm going to make sure I put things right." He looked around, making sure no one could hear him. "I will make it my mission in life to ensure that evil bitch gets locked up for what she did. Now, when we go into the interview room, I want you to write down everything she said, okay?"

428

Sassy nodded. "What, even in the police car?"

"What! Did she travel with you back to here?"

"Yeah, she sat in the back of the car with me, with her fucking scrawny hand pushing my chest against the back seat. As if I could go anywhere, anyway. I had me poxy hands tied behind me back."

"Who else was in the car?" probed Sampson.

Sassy looked over his shoulder and froze, causing Sampson to turn around, only to find Falon, the PC who arrested her, hovering around.

Caught off guard, Falon went to turn on his heels but was swiftly stopped in his tracks. "PC Falon!" called Sampson.

As the PC slowly turned to face him, Sampson grinned maliciously. "So, you were in the car with Saskia River and the superintendent, were you?"

Falon's eyes were like saucers, as he stared at the detective. He had been present and had heard everything that was said in the car, and although he was sucking up to DS Campbell, with his eye on promotion, he also knew that she was in so much trouble, and he didn't want any part of it. "Er, yes, why?"

Sampson's expression told Falon all he needed to know. "I want you in my office, Falon. I want a full statement of everything you can remember because right now this situation needs clarifying, and within the hour or so, this station will be front-line news. Before you start wondering what you should say, I must warn you, it wouldn't be a very good idea to side with the superintendent, unless you want to be tarred with the same brush and face the same consequences as her. Do you understand what I'm saying?"

Falon felt sick. The muscles in his legs were like jelly. *Would he get fired for not stopping Campbell who was grilling the kid, or for not intervening when Campbell almost ripped the hair out of the young girl's head?* With a heavy heart, he walked away.

Sassy was taken to the interview room. She sat down, waiting for Sampson to fetch some tea and a chocolate bar from one of the machines. Delmonte saw him out of the corner of his eye and wasted no time in getting in the detective's face.

"I need your account of all this, and I just hope, for your fucking sake, that you're going to do the right thing and not brush this catastrophe under the carpet," he growled.

Sampson rolled his eyes. "You know me better than that, mate. Saskia is in the interview room." He held up the cup of tea and chocolate. "I'm about to get her to write a statement, which, of course, must be in her own words, except we'd better leave out any bad language," he winked.

Delmonte immediately relaxed his shoulders. "Good lad. Campbell needs putting in a mental asylum."

"Oh, I need to see Malakai. I want him in with Saskia, just to put her mind at rest. The poor kid thinks we are all a load of torturous swines."

Delmonte raised an eyebrow. "No, not all of you. Oh, are you going to charge Malakai with assault?"

Sampson retorted, "What assault? I never saw one."

With a pat on the back from Delmonte, Sampson left to give Saskia her drink and a snack.

Within the hour, Sassy, Malik, and Cyril were released and on their way home. Saskia, it turned out, wasn't badly hurt after all and therefore didn't need to go to the hospital. The commissioner had signed the release papers, with no further action, and a deal was struck whereby as long as the superintendent was at least demoted and totally removed from the case forthwith, then Sassy would not press charges.

Myers called Sampson into his office, where he pulled out a bottle of Scotch. "Close the door, Geoff, will you?"

Sampson had just had a long and stressful day, but he realised that there were still a number of outstanding issues to be dealt with.

"Everything okay, Gov?"

"Not really, Geoff. There is still this web of confusion, and although we have let Reardon's lot go, we need to wrap this case up, and to be honest, with Campbell so bloody hell-bent on arresting Cyril's firm, she has taken her eye off the ball and probably cost us valuable time and money in chasing after a bloody red herring. Look, let me lay it on the line. I know you, Geoff. I know what you are all about, and, well, if the truth be known, I turn a blind eye because you are always after the real scumbags and the likes of the old firms and their dealings don't normally come on my radar or to the attention of the newspapers. So, Geoff, you know these people well. I have Johnnie and his brothers still in the cells. Do you think they were involved in this child sex racket, or what?"

Sampson felt slightly hot under the collar and wondered whether he could trust Myers. Tiredness aside, he was being placed in a problematic place, and whatever he said next in answer to Myers's question could well determine his future career in the police force, and his hopes of promotion. Testing times indeed.

Sampson decided to give himself a moment by taking a slow and satisfying slug of his excellent whisky, while he thought about what he wanted to say. First, there was the commissioner's position on all of this. How much did the man know about Geoff's other life? He suspected that it was not much, and that in any case, Cyril and his men were not really the kind of criminals in whom the commissioner had much interest. Second, if he was careful, he wondered if he could still use these 'contacts' as a means to curry favour with the commissioner? After all, it was public knowledge that the police used criminals for their own purposes, if it suited them.

Finishing his drink, he arrived at a decision. "People like the Carters and Cyril Reardon are clever, crafty bastards. Bank jobs, protection rackets, you name it, they probably have an interest. But here's the thing. One little forewarning that they are into kiddies and that's them screwed to the post. Yeah, it's true, I've known them for over thirty years, and we have an understanding." He looked at the steadfast expression on Myers's face, to see if trouble awaited.

But there was nothing for Sampson to be concerned about. With a gentle smile that totally changed Myers's expression, Sampson felt safe to carry on.

"Well, when the likes of Dennis Solace and Peter Manning were caught and locked away for thirty years each, and, by the way, I would have loved to have been able to take the credit for capturing those perverted, sick bastards, it was actually successful and well-known villains who did the digging and gave me all I needed to have them banged up. They were on our side in that situation. In fact, they would rather chop their own hands off than get mixed up with any of that."

Myers refilled Sampson's glass, eager to continue this conversation. Sometimes, he thought, he didn't spend sufficient time in getting to know his colleagues properly, what with all the paperwork which consumed his every hour. It was not really what he'd entered the police force to do. "I know you are right. I just needed confirmation, that's all."

As the whisky hit the back of his throat, the bitter taste made Sampson tighten his lips. "Gov, there's something going on. I'm not sure what yet, but I do plan on getting to the bottom of it."

The commissioner tilted his head to the side. "Go on, enlighten me."

Sampson noticed for the first time just how immaculate the room was. Every file was neatly lined up, every picture dead straight, and then he glanced at Myers's hands and noticed they were perfectly manicured. He surmised that either his boss was punctilious to a fault, or he was another one with a bad case of OCD.

"If I begin with Keffa Jackson, I don't think he killed Adam Carter, for starters. I know the physical evidence points that way, but it's just not his style. And then there's the pornography found on Johnnie Carter's computer. That doesn't add up, either. It's as if someone wanted to cause a serious feud between Reardon's firm and the Carters, and I intend to find out who is behind it."

Rubbing his chin in contemplation, Myers was in deep thought, and Sampson could see his boss was tired.

"Okay, Geoff, I want you to take over this investigation. Do what you feel is necessary and keep me informed."

CHAPTER TWENTY-ONE

Jean River was nursing her wounds. It wasn't so much the hard backhander she received from Paddy but the humiliation all over again. And it was all because her bastard son had stuck his great oar in. She gazed around the dull, lifeless room which looked almost as if time had stood still: the dark brown corduroy sofa, the square box TV, and the overfilled heavy glass ashtrays on the tile top coffee table. *Jesus,* she thought. *Here I am again, for what seems like the thousandth time. Is this what I always come back to — the fucking dregs of society?* Rubbing her bruised face, she curled her legs around her and sank deeper into the well-worn sofa and sighed. It was back to the same old story, running from one man to the next. Paddy was always her go-to place, when nothing else was on offer, all except this very last resort.

And this was it: this poxy flee-ridden flat. It wasn't so awful years ago, when the corduroy sofa was in fashion and the carpet was brand new and not frayed to pieces. And, of course, when the man on offer wasn't so bad looking. She looked at him now, almost bent over with age and stick thin. He was a far cry from the man he once was. He was a lot older than her, but back in the day, he could hold his own against any man. She watched him nervously puffing on his fifth fag in as many minutes. His once thick dark swept-back hair now consisted of a few long greasy strands behind his ears. Those one-time bright eyes were now dull and held years of pain. Jean wiped her nose with the back of her hand and noticed the blood, a stark reminder of yesterday's shocking events.

435

She had been so busy pampering herself in the bathroom back at Paddy's place, that she hadn't seen it coming. But it wasn't long before she did.

By the time she'd wiped off all the moisturising cream and slipped into her new classy nightgown, she discovered Fynn had given Paddy the rundown on some events that had taken place at Penelope's, whoever the fuck she was. But when Paddy himself screamed up the stairs, she hurried down, only to face three angry scowling faces. Fynn's heavily bandaged head and those scary wailing sounds coming from somewhere behind a mummy-like seal around his face were not only doing her head in, but they were also causing serious concern to her lover as well. That's when everything kicked off, big style.

Paddy was so angry, he made Jean jump out of her skin. But he wasn't content with giving her a telling off. He hit her so hard, it obviously cracked her nose as well as her cheek bone. Never one for losing his cool, he was now yelling so loudly, her ears felt like they would bleed. "You sly ol' trollop. How fucking dare you come into my home and pretend you just came for a visit? You've had all this set-up planned before you even walked through the front door! You've let us believe you were just going along with our plot, when really it was your fucking idea!" He moved so close he almost stood on her toes. "Look at him, Jean. Take a fucking good gawp." He grabbed her hair and thrust her forwards to look at Fynn's face. "Your fucking boy did that! It was your son you failed to tell us about. Jesus Christ!" He let go of her hair and threw his hands above his head. "I thought I knew you, Jean. Years, you've been coming in, getting your fucking end away, taking a bit of poke and fucking off again. I never knew you at all, though, did I? Kids, eh? You have fucking kids! What other secrets do you have, Jean, eh? Any of the kids mine, by any fucking chance?

Oh, yeah. Another little fact you've probably failed to tell me about!" His voice was at its height of anger, when he clenched his fist and cracked her right across the side of her face. She toppled and landed on the sofa. "Adam fucking Carter. You underhanded, nasty cow. You sucked us into your plan to set the Carters against Cyril Reardon and Kelly Raven's mob, but it wasn't for us though, Jean, was it? It was for you to get your revenge, and you, ya dirty fucking tramp, almost got me boy killed. You're a loose cannon and there was me thinking you liked to live alone. I just thought ya didn't want a committed relationship, just a regular bit of fun with me. But all the bloody time you've been bed-hopping from camp to camp and keeping those kiddies a secret. What kinda mother are you?"

She recalled the look of pure hatred on Paddy's face. She knew then that she couldn't deny it, but when she thought it was over, Fynn piped up, "No, Dad, that ain't all. Her boy who fucked me face up is also Kelly Raven's brother!"

Paddy's face then turned from anger to hurt. His head inclined with a gentle frown, as he tried to absorb the information. "What?" he said, in a softer tone. But Jean just stared at them all, as if in a trance. Her brain couldn't work quickly enough to get herself out of this one.

"Yeah, dad. That bitch has taken you for a right royal fucking mug. She was having it away with your arch fucking enemy, Eddie Raven!" screamed Fynn.

Paddy's mind was in turmoil, as he tried to think back to the past, to all those wrongdoings by Eddie Raven, and to work out if she'd played any part in it. He didn't realise that Jean had only been seeing Eddie while he was in the nick, that she'd gained nothing apart from a good shag, and that in no way had she been complicit in the war between them.

However, like a eureka moment, Paddy was now putting two and two together and coming up with ten. That horrific night twenty years ago, when, out of the blue, Eddie appeared in the car park of Paddy's nightclub and bashed the living shit out of him, he'd always sensed that there was an informant in his little firm. He fixed a stony glare at Jean, assuming it was her. She was obviously the one who'd nearly cost him his life. That bashing still made him shudder when he thought back to it. The cracking of his shins, as Eddie beat him relentlessly with his metal bat, was fixed in his mind, and it was remembered in every detail to this day. He still walked with a limp and was intent on getting even.

"How stupid was I? Of all the people, Jean, I never thought you would be the one to take me down. Well, you did, didn't ya, eh? Eddie took my fucking business because no doubt our pillow talk landed on his ears." His words were cold and calculated which shit the life out of her. At no time had she ever seen him like this, and yet he was so very wrong. She'd never been involved like that with Eddie.

But how could she convince him now, after everything he'd just heard? He would never believe her. Her mouth was dry, as she stared at Paddy and his two sons, like lions ready to eat their kill.

"Please," she whispered, knowing her begging would land on deaf ears.

"You played me for a fiddle and you returned out of the blue to use me yet again, slyly sucking me in with your own fucking mission, a vendetta setting the Ravens against the Carters. I don't know, and I don't care, but one thing I'm sure of, you can get your ugly arse outta here, before I fucking mutilate you."

Shaking with fear, Jean got up to leave, but Fynn was fuming. "You ain't gonna let her off that lightly, are ya?"

Paddy pulled Fynn back before he launched into Jean. "Yes, son, I am, because if I don't, I will kill her, and I mean fucking annihilate her. So, Fynn, step aside. Let the piece of dog shit go."

Then and there, she knew that Paddy had genuinely loved her, because even after all she was being accused of, he still hadn't really hurt her; it had been a few hard punches, but that was all. He could have ripped her head off, if he'd wanted to. At least she was grateful she still had a face left.

❧*❧

Jean sighed again and wiped the bloody snot with the back of her hand. Finally, the truth registered: she had now hit rock bottom. Paddy's home was beautiful, with all the mod cons and updated furniture, and she should have hooked up with him, but she was always on the lookout for the main chance – she never did find it. Now, however, here she was, in this stinking flat, where it always reminded her she was on the bones of her arse. It was the place she came to when she needed drugs and had no money to pay for them. Paddy wouldn't touch drugs, and he sure as hell wouldn't buy them for her, although that changed recently, when he needed a snort of cocaine to keep up his stamina.

She thought back to the main men in her life. They just wanted her for sex. Well, the business with Paddy Rye may have been hashed up, but there was always one man she could totally rely on. She knew he would do anything for her because he'd always wanted her, long before he married his wife and long after he was wed. Jean knew his wife could have whoever she wanted. And she did. She shagged the Carters and went from one villain to the next and not because they had her on their terms: it was because she could have the pick. Jean, on the other hand, had to make do with the fucking leftovers. At first, she thought she was being clever all those years ago, believing she had one over on Rose by

439

sleeping with Roy, but that was before she realised that it never bothered Rose because she operated on a different level of morality: she was fucking as if there were no tomorrow and made no secret of the fact.

Jean's deep thoughts were brought back to reality, when Roy started to cough like an old man. He was really coughing his guts up and farting at the same time. She shivered when she thought about what he would want in return for putting her up. Her life unquestionably was swirling down the plughole. To go from a young and butch Adam to chubby Paddy, and now this withered old man sitting before her, it was a travesty, but one of her own making.

"Roy, it's kind of you to offer to put me up and pay for me cab, but do you mind if I shoot off? I've things to sort out." She couldn't say she had somewhere to go because he already knew she was out on her arse.

He looked her way and eyed her up and down. She was another one out to make a mockery of him. They all had: Rose, then the Carters, Keffa – shagging his daughter – and now Jean. His wicked grin, showing his heavily stained teeth, made her feel distinctly uncomfortable.

"What are you smirking for, Roy?" She didn't like his sick, twisted smile; in fact, he'd behaved very oddly since she'd arrived. To begin with, she thought it was because he'd had a few drinks. The flat was untidier than she'd ever seen it before, with plates piled up in the sink and the carpet coated in dog hairs. Ordinarily, she would have been welcomed with open arms, with offers of drink, food, and drugs – in fact, whatever she wanted. He would have been all over her, like a lovesick teenager. There was something strange about him today, though, and she couldn't quite put her finger on it.

440

Slowly, he shook his head and chuckled nastily. "Ya know what, Jean, me little lovey? I have spent my life having people taking the piss out of me. A right laughing stock, I've been."

This was an eerie situation and one which was disturbing to Jean. It was the way he was drawing out his words that put her on edge.

"But I thought at least my little Jeannie would one day put a permanent smile on my face, and I have to admit, years ago, our small indiscretions did grace my face with a smile, but in reality, you are just like them, aren't ya?"

His frightening expression and malevolent eyes were making her tremble, and yet she was unable to move. It was as if he had a weird hold over her, or perhaps it was a compulsion to hear what he was saying, which held her there. The problem was she'd always confided in Roy; he knew more about her than she even knew herself.

"I could have probably forgiven Rose for shagging Johnnie Carter. As for you, it didn't really matter who you were having it away with because I had no claim on you, did I? I could have held a grudge over Eddie Raven, but he's dead now, so he doesn't matter." Roy took a long pause, gazing off into space, but it was a quick jerk of his head that made her jump. "But Adam Carter I couldn't forgive, nor Keffa. My little girl, my sweet little Lacey, she turned into a replica of her mother, and those fucking no-good low-life cunts helped themselves. I never had you, Jean, or me own poxy wife, but I did have me little girl, until they got their filthy hands on her."

Jean frowned. None of what he was saying made sense, until she thought about Adam Carter and the girl in the flat. *It couldn't be.* "Your Lacey? But she's a little girl." The penny dropped: *the tart in the flat was Roy's daughter.* The last time she'd seen the kid was seven years ago, dressed in a school uniform. She was not much of a looker then, just a

441

plain, slight schoolgirl. Jean had never got involved with his daughter. Her time with Roy was always out of view of prying eyes, even those of his daughter. The sickness waves engulfed her; it was a nightmare, there were so many coincidences. She assumed Roy never knew she was seeing Adam Carter. The contempt between Roy and the Carters was apparent to her because she knew the history, and she also knew that Roy would never let her grace his back door, if he found out she'd been seeing Adam, but she had no idea that his hate towards that family ran even deeper than it did for his wife shagging Johnnie Carter. *How did he know about me, though? Had Lacey told him?* She bit her nail nervously.

Then her minded drifted back to the afternoon she'd returned to Adam's flat with a heroin-filled syringe, a good swap for a heap of cocaine. Revenge would be sweet. But she was beaten to it, by less than two minutes, she guessed. She'd seen the culprit walking out of the building, with a balaclava over his head, but she recognised those eyes. He was looking at her now, no doubt congratulating himself on being one step ahead of her for most of her relatively short journey in life.

She had to say something because guilt was written all over her face. But she couldn't and wouldn't own up to the fact that she had been another one of Adam Carter's throwaways. "Er, Adam was a bit old for her."

Roy leaned forward and poured a large measure of whisky in his glass and gulped it back in a single swallow. He banged the glass down and poured another. "Oh, yeah, way too fucking old. But not for you, though, Jean, eh? You were just the right age and the right type of dirty fuck, except he liked kids. Men of his type, they all like fucking kids. Did ya know that Johnnie Carter was fucking my little sister a few years back? Yeah, my little Audrey was twenty fucking years younger than him, and he dipped his wick in her, too."

The tension was rapidly climbing a ladder, and Jean was ready to make a swift exit. The problem was she was glued to the sofa, as if by moving, he would dive on her. The expression on his face was alarming: this wasn't the Roy she knew at all. The soft sensitive man with the ever eager-to-please smile was replaced by a deranged psychotic stranger.

"I know what I am, Jean. I'm everyone's punch bag. For years, I've run this poxy dive and for what, eh? Well, let me tell you. My life is over. It's over, and before I finally kick the bucket, I'm gonna make sure those who did wrong by me fucking pay!"

Just as Jean was about to try to ease the situation, in strolled Lulu. She must have heard Roy raise his voice, and like most dogs, she came to see if her master was okay. Slowly, she mooched over to his side and wearily sat down, allowing him to stroke her head. "There, girl," he said, as he gently patted her back. "Now this bitch here is the only fucking female that has stood by my side. She had thirteen pups, didn't ya, girl, and she still puts me first. Yeah, the only fucking bitch that ever loved me, and it's a bleedin' animal!"

The distraction allowed Jean to get herself together and stand up to leave. "I'll be off, then, Roy," she said apprehensively, now itching to get out. This conversation was totally weird, and she'd had enough of weird for one day. However, the way he cocked a questioning eyebrow aroused a feeling of dread. *Had everything during the last few days caught up with her without warning? Was she becoming paranoid, or was Roy really acting like a leopard holding on to his next meal?*

He let out a chuckle, watching her drinking in the fear. "Nah, Jean, I don't think so, darlin'. You don't have any business, do you, because

I'm thinking that quite frankly you've nothing. You've no family, no friends, and no other man to run to except me." He paused and glared with empty eyes. There was a long silence until finally his mind was able to fast forward from the dark place he kept going back to. "It's funny, Jean, because for years you were my little light in this miserable fucking world. Yeah, ya used to pop in when no one was around, like a little night angel. You made me feel like a real man." He poured another drink and slowly drank it. "I knew you were only fucking me because you needed money, and me, like an idiot, I was too fucking soft to wait for you to ask. I always slipped ya a few quid, gave ya drugs. Madness, 'cos I never in my life took drugs, but I bought them, just in case you came visiting. I looked forward to our little midnight get-togethers."

Jean's eyes skimmed between him and the door. *Could she make a run for it, or should she just let him get whatever it was off his chest?* She decided on the latter course and sat back down.

"Do you think, Jean, we're the saddest people we know?" His tone was edged with sarcasm. It wasn't really a question that required any form of reply, and Jean found herself unable to even form words in response.

"There's me. I've done some shit stuff in my time, but it was all because of what people like yourself have done to me. Then, Jean, there's you. I know what you did. There, I bet you've been wondering just now if I knew all about your little affairs, haven't ya?"

His voice retained that strange eerie tone. "You, Jean, have been the motherfucker of all untold lies – wicked lies. You're a conniving bitch, ain't ya? Maybe you've got away all these years without the men in your life and your kiddies catching on to what you've actually been doing, but your life is a lie, ain't it, Jean? Everything about you is about

444

you! You've manipulated the truth to please yaself. You've denied the children their right to know where they came from, who their fathers were. I suppose, when you left them kiddies to fend for themselves, you deceived them, pretending you just popped out for bread. See, managing this run-down flee pit, I get to hear everything. What about Adam Carter, eh? Oh, yes, love, I knew! What was it? Oh, yeah, Adam Carter is your baby's father! Now that wasn't just deception to allow you to go about your life the way you wanted to live it. That was a downright atrocious lie, weren't it? Yes, Jean, you just kept getting away with it, didn't you? But what fucked me up was the day I saw your little girl with the black curls and deep dimples. You've never told me the truth about her, have you? But I ain't thick, Jean. I *know* who she is!"

Jean felt her stomach turn. "No, you've got that——"

"You never even let me get to know her. You're an evil, scheming monster, Jean. She was *mine* and you knew it. That dear little child was denied even knowing me. But let me tell you this for nothing. We reap what we sow in life, and soon you will find out that your wicked lies will have consequences."

Gripped by an incredible urge to run, Jean leaped from the sofa. With her heart hammering, she went to flee, but in one swift movement and without leaving his seat, Roy grabbed her leg, and she fell awkwardly on top of Lulu. The dog reacted to the shock by sinking her teeth into Jean's arm. The attack was instant, and yet as soon as the dog realised what she'd done, she released her grip and fled from the room. The scream was not long coming, once Jean absorbed the fact that she had gaping holes in her scrawny arm and the blood was oozing, thick and dark. Then the throbbing pain hit her. Sitting bolt upright, she gripped her wounded arm with her other hand and looked up at Roy to do something to help her. There was nothing: nothing at all but

445

a blank look greeting her. It was at that point, realisation hit home. There was no escape, no sympathy, and, even more worrying, no help.

"Please, Roy, I need an ambulance. Look!"

She stared down at the blood seeping through her fingers and dripping everywhere. Whether it was the blood or the pain, it didn't matter. She was about to faint. Through hazy eyes and dizziness, she tried to drag herself away, but in a split second, Roy jumped from his chair, and in one quick movement, he had his arms underneath her and dragged her back to the sofa. "Stay there!" he demanded.

As if she could go anywhere! But Jean sighed with relief as he left the room, hoping that he'd gone to call the paramedics. Seconds later, those hopes were dashed, when he returned with a first aid box.

"Please, Roy, this needs more than a fucking plaster! That poxy animal has bitten me right down to the bone!"

"Yeah, that's Rottweilers for ya. She's given ya a nasty bite, I'm afraid."

Was he so mental he couldn't see that without help she might bleed to death? "What are you doing? I need to go to the hospital. What the fuck's wrong with you!" she cried.

He ignored her and searched through the 1960s first aid box which was covered in a thick layer of dust. Jean could feel the vomit rising to the back of her throat and waves of dizziness engulfing her, but she had to get away, or this man she thought she knew but clearly didn't would leave her to die in this godforsaken shithole.

Armed with a roll of bandage, Roy sat next to her on the sofa, his expression still blank and his eyes lifeless. Jean was weak with pain and blood loss. She watched him try to wrap the dressing around her arm, but every time he added another layer, the blood just soaked it up. Finally, he pulled the bandage tight and stuck a nappy pin in to hold it secure. Jean's eyes were searching the room, trying to see where she had left her bag containing her phone. *Surely, she had brought it?* Then her thoughts drifted back to when Paddy had thrown her out. She hadn't had time to grab any of her belongings, only her purse. The shock hit her, and she began to shake uncontrollably which made her teeth start to chatter. She pleaded with Roy to call an ambulance. The dog had punctured an artery, and there was no way she could pull herself off the sofa and get out of there. She knew it and so did he. The room began to close in around her, and her slight body tilted to the side, until gradually, her face slipped down onto the smelly old cushion.

Roy sat back down and poured another drink. "That's it, Jean. You have a little nap while I make you a special drink."

She was semi-conscious, and although she could just about hear him in the background, she was too hazy and weak to sit back up. Instead, she turned her head and remained still. Roy opened the drawer and pulled from it a packet of brown powder. He then decided to make a cocktail. In went the whisky to disguise the taste of the heroin, and then he stirred the mixture. He thought it was rather clever: what was it he'd said to his daughter recently? Oh, yes — you live by the sword, you die by the sword.

"'Ere, my little Jeannie, drink this. You'll feel better, lovey."

His words sounded genuine, as if he'd switched back to his usual genial self. As he gently lifted her head, she opened her mouth, and he eased the fluid down her throat. She choked, but he didn't stop, and coughing and spluttering, she gulped back the contents to prevent herself from gagging. Then, he laid her head back down, but that strange pitch to his voice returned.

"There you go. You love a bit of the brown stuff, eh? And I've never let you down, my little Jeannie, have I? Daddy will make everything all right. You just go to sleep, my little girl."

Her final thought, as she drifted away, was to ask herself if she would end up in Hell with Eddie Raven. Maybe then she could either have him all to herself or find a way to screw him to the fiery inferno wall.

CHAPTER TWENTY-TWO

Delmonte drove them home in his Lexus. Whilst Cyril and Michael made conversation in the front, Sassy was quiet, contracting her body to take up as little space as possible in the corner of the spacious rear seat, a habit of hers, whenever she was nervous or angry – or both. Malik was sitting next to her, drumming the fingers of his left hand on his left knee repetitively and somewhat annoyingly. There was no conversation between them, their thoughts elsewhere.

The whole incident had left Malik and Sassy with much on their minds, and the whereabouts of their little sisters plagued them the most. For Cyril, the last few hours seemed to have aged him by ten years. Normally, he would have given the police what for, by taking the piss out of them, but this situation had him shocked into silence. The cries from poor Tilly, as they dragged her away, made him sick to his stomach, and until the youngsters were back in his house, he wouldn't rest.

Delmonte, sensing the anxiety, knew he needed to take charge. "Right, when we get back to the house, I'm going to call the social worker and find out where the children are. Edgar Myers has made the call to have the girls released, and now it's up to the social services to hand them over. I'm sure it won't be a problem."

Malik took a deep breath to stop himself from crying. "What if—" he didn't want to say too much in front of Sassy.

Delmonte waved his hand. "There's nothing to worry about, Malik. They will be home in no time."

But Sassy, coming out of her trance-like state, heard this and wasn't so sure. "They'd fucking better be, or else I'll give that long streak of piss a permanent smile with a fucking razor blade. I hate the Ol' Bill. How that woman ain't been shot, I don't know." No one corrected Sassy's bad language – this time she was right.

Just as they approached the mansion, Delmonte's car phone rang. The call was from the social services. There was silence in the car as he spoke to a woman there. Malik was on the edge of his seat with nerves.

"I've just had a call from the commissioner, and he suggested we return Chantilly and Star River. However, I've recommended that they get checked over by a doctor."

Before she could continue, Delmonte stopped her in her tracks. "I'm afraid, Madam, you must have misinterpreted the message, as I've just left the commissioner and all charges against Mr Reardon have been dropped. There's certainly no reason for concern, and under the very sensitive circumstances, we do not want the children subjected to any further stress. I therefore expect the children to be returned immediately."

"But—"

"There are no buts, and I want to make myself perfectly clear. If those children are not returned at once, I will be taking serious action because they've already been wrongly removed from their home, and further delay will be classed as another fallacious decision both by your department and by the local police. I strongly urge you to act quickly before further compliance issues complicate what is already a wrongful arrest."

There was silence, as the official tried to assess the situation and to understand what he'd just said. *Did he just say fallacious?* "Er, I'll have to make some enquiries and get back to you."

"Yes, perhaps you need to contact the commissioner because obviously you've misunderstood his words, and I quote, 'I expect the children to be released immediately'. Do I make myself clear?"

"Yes, perfectly," was the reply, before the phone went dead.

Sassy gripped her brother's arm and sighed with relief.

It was the first time that Cyril had spoken since they'd left the station, and the resigned tone in his voice was noted by all. "Poor little Tilly and Star and it's all my bleedin' fault. I can't have this, it's not fair. Tonight, when the little ones come home, I want you to pack your bags and move in to a place I have in Sussex. It's a lovely house, just right for you all, and it's my gift. I can't have you subjected to this life. Fucking hell, you're only kids."

Sassy felt the sadness in his voice, and it angered her to think that he was a good man, and the police had rendered him guilty by association, when it shouldn't have been that way. "No!" she snapped. "Er, sorry. I don't mean to be rude, but all my life I've wanted a family. I know I've got Malik and the girls, but I've always wanted to have a dad, ya know ..." She trailed off, feeling embarrassed. "Anyway, it's nice having you and Kelly. I've never had older relatives, like uncles and people around me who care, and now we have you. Please don't take that away from us as well."

Malik pulled her close and felt her shaking, ready for the tears to fall.

"Look, let's get inside Cyril's house and we can then sort things out," suggested Delmonte.

Arriving at his home, Cyril heaved himself off the seat, and looking deflated, he leaned against the car door. Sassy, in turn, went to his side and put her arm around his waist. "I mean it, ya silly old fucker."

Cyril kissed her forehead and whispered. "If me and you are gonna remain friends, then I ain't old, got it?"

She giggled. "Nothing wrong with being old, is there? At least you ain't a ginger like me."

Cyril stopped in his tracks and shook with laughter. "And how the fuck would *you* know, smart arse? Me hair's grey. I may well have been ginger, years ago."

As Delmonte drove away and they all walked towards the front door, Kelly appeared. The worn-out look was replaced with a wide smile to show her pleasure at their return.

Kelly pulled Cyril aside. "I need you to come upstairs and cast your eyes on the recording. I didn't watch the last one until just a few minutes ago. I thought I'd seen all I needed to see, but no, there's a lot more. Watching the second CCTV disk, I now know who killed Adam Carter, but what worries me, Cyril, is why Roy would hand those disks over to us? He must know what's on them, surely? Also, Geoff Sampson wants me to call him, if I discover anything that could help with the case, so I'm not sure what to do."

With a heavy sigh, Cyril said, "Go on, then, I'll follow you up. Let me just get the others settled. It's been a right fucking nightmare of a day. Sassy has beaten the granny out of Superintendent Campbell. She's been suspended. All charges against us were dropped, but I somehow feel this ain't the last of it. And as for Roy, well, he didn't exactly hand the disks over. Frank took 'em."

Kelly gave him a weary smile. "See, this is what bothers me. You need to look at the recording. I tell ya, it's made me fucking ill."

Very concerned, Cyril's face instantly paled at the thought of the consequences of what Kelly was telling him. He pushed his shoulders back and held his head up. Gesturing to her he would be with her shortly, he called out to Malik. "Son, I've just got to sort something out. Call me when the girls return."

Malik appeared in the hallway. "Is everything all right, Cyril?"

"Yes, boy, nothing to worry about." He gave an encouraging smile for Malik to go back to the drawing room.

Kelly had already paused the DVD player at the crucial moment, having rewound a few minutes' worth and then hit the play button. With Cyril perched on the end of the bed next to her, they both watched with anticipation. Although Kelly had seen it before, it was still hard to comprehend.

It was 3 a.m. on 1st November. No one was in the kitchen for some time, until Roy appeared. He leaned over the freezer and retrieved Keffa's jacket. Both Cyril and Kelly were drawn to the fact that Roy was wearing gloves. He put his hands into the pocket and pulled out Keffa's gun, placing it on the freezer. He then removed the jacket, but they couldn't see where he took it. It was out of view. An hour later, he returned and unbolted the back door. What then shocked them was who entered the kitchen. Cyril edged forward, peering in disbelief at the screen. "Jesus fucking Christ, it's Superintendent Campbell, would you believe! Now, what are you doing, I wonder?"

They watched as the superintendent handed Roy a flash drive. It was evident the two of them were in deep conversation, and then, as Roy held up the gun, a malicious sneer spread across Campbell's face. She nodded, and in a jiffy, she was gone. Then, from one of the kitchen cupboards, Roy took out a plastic bag into which he quickly placed the gun and the flash drive. He then left through the kitchen door.

"Christ, Kel, you have so much evidence on one disk."

Kelly agreed. "Well, that's it, then. That's all we need for the police to have them nicked and banged up for a long time."

"They will need more evidence than that, but let's not worry about that for the moment. What concerns me is the fact that Roy must know that he was on the disk, surely? And if he did, then he also wanted us to know because otherwise he would have had them well and truly hidden, not for Frank to just take them that easily. The question is therefore why?" He paused in thought.

"Should we call Geoff Sampson?"

Cyril turned away from the blank screen and faced Kelly. "Yes, we will, but for now, I think I may need to pay Roy a visit. You see, Geoff can't get fucking blood out of a stone, but I know a man who can."

Kelly raised her eyebrow and grinned. "Frank, I bet!"

Their conversation was interrupted by Malik hollering up the stairs. "They're 'ere, Cyril, Kelly. I've just buzzed them in."

Kelly could hear the excitement in Malik's voice and decided to join him to welcome the girls. She wished all this nasty business could be over and done with. It had been deeply disturbing to them all, watching Tilly and Star crying and pleading as they were dragged off earlier in the day.

Observing from the drawing room window, Kelly could see the social worker getting out of her car with the girls. Tilly was gripping Star's hand whilst trying to shake off the woman who was holding her other hand. Cyril opened the front door and the official released the girls. They ran up the steps towards Malik and Cyril, as if they were being chased by a zombie. Then again, perhaps that's how they saw the people from the social services right now. Kelly wondered whether Tilly and Star would easily recover from their ordeal.

It was a tearful reunion of mega proportions. Tilly flew into Cyril's arms, as if she hadn't seen him for a year, and Star ran into Malik's. Sassy was also crying, as she rushed out to greet her sisters and give them a hug.

The social worker, a snotty-nosed woman called Iris Mandle, tutted in annoyance. She had been the one taken to task by Delmonte and had found the whole experience frustrating.

"I have some papers here for Kelly Raven to sign to say that the children are now back in her care."

Again, it was Tilly who spoke up and shocked them all. "Don't let the old bag in." She pointed to the woman. "You can wait on the doorstep! We should never have been taken from here in the first place." She turned to Cyril. "Don't let her in, Uncle Cyril. She's nasty."

Sassy couldn't stop herself from giggling. Her little sister had so much gumption.

"Honestly, the child needs to learn some manners. It's very apparent that she was raised by children. As the report states, they should have been in foster care years ago, and I can see why, now." She turned to Malik. "And I suppose you're the silly young man who thought it a good idea to bring up these girls yourself instead of calling us, eh?" spat Iris, with a cruel vibe to her posh voice.

Before Malik or Sassy could respond, Cyril stepped forward and snatched the papers out of her hand. "'Ere, Malik, take these to Kelly and bring them straight back so I can officially fuck the condescending bitch off."

Iris stepped back in astonishment. She had never expected a grown man to speak so rudely to her.

"Well!" was all she could say.

As soon as Malik returned with the signed papers, they cheered as the woman returned to her car with her tail between her legs.

It took a while before the youngsters were able to settle in bed. What with all the stressful events earlier and then the excitement of returning to what they regarded as their new home, their adrenaline levels had soared. And, even now, with the knowledge they were safe at the mansion, they needed the constant reassurance from Malik that it would never happen again. They were safe for now, though. Tilly had said more that evening than she had ever done before. When Malik questioned her about it, she replied, "'Cos, Malik, I let you and Sassy stand up for me and Star, and now, I am old enough to have my say to keep our family together. I watch how brave you are, and I want to be the same."

Kelly and Cyril left the mansion on business. Malik agreed to stay behind with his sisters because Mary hadn't returned yet. He would have done, anyway. They needed time with him to get over their experience.

456

The last of the punters left the Mitcham Mint. Cyril, Blakey, Frank, and Kelly watched from their cars as Roy bolted the front door. It was midnight and now the street was empty. Only a stray cat and the occasional motor vehicle could be heard.

It was time. The party assembled at the back door. Everyone's eyes were focused on Frank. With his tool kit in one hand and crow bar in the other, he was ready to rip open the back door.

But as he turned the handle, the door opened, and Kelly whispered. "Frank, there's a camera over on the opposite wall facing the freezer and this back door. Roy will see us coming. Let me go in and call him downstairs. That way, he'll have to take his eye off the CCTV, that's if he's watching it."

Frank nodded. "Yeah, go on in. Yell, if you need me." He pulled a gun from inside his pocket. "I'll have him shot down in a second."

Kelly entered the kitchen, and in her peripheral vision, she saw the freezer and felt sick. That was where Keffa had thrown away their hopes and dreams of ever being one happy family, when he'd shagged the life out of the barmaid. She dismissed the feeling and headed for the stairs. She was about to call up when she heard a glass clink; she thought it was coming from the bar. Careful not to make a sound, she walked backwards and opened the back door, mouthing the words, "There's someone in the bar."

Like three cat burglars, Frank, Cyril, and Blakey eased their way in and followed Kelly to the bar. The curtains were drawn, and the pub was almost in darkness, but she could just discern Roy, slumped in a chair. He was smoking a fag, with a bottle of Scotch whisky on the table

457

beside him. He didn't even look up but just carried on puffing away and sipping his drink.

Cyril tugged Kelly back. He was going to take charge, but instead of barging in and making horrific threats, Cyril pulled out a chair opposite Roy. Whilst Frank and Blakey stood back, behind Cyril, Kelly went over to the bar and watched.

"Mind if I join you, Roy?" asked Cyril in a calm, composed tone.

Roy looked up, as if he'd just noticed Cyril there. He gestured to him to take a seat.

Cyril waved his hand at Frank to fetch over some glasses. Frank pulled three from the top shelf and handed them to Cyril who filled them almost to the brim. He knew this would be a long night.

"So, Roy, mate, tell me what's going on?" There was no point in going in with all guns blazing because Roy's body language cried out that here was a broken man. Slouched in the chair, with his head tilted down, he looked an old, weary, and dejected character of his former self.

"Hello, Cyril," smiled Roy. His words were soft and resigned. "Nothing, really. I was just having a drink before I turn in for the night."

Frank and Blakey looked at each other and shrugged. It was almost the stuff of fiction and it felt a bit spooky.

Cyril passed the drinks to the others and they joined him at the table. Roy didn't even bother looking to see who else was there. He raised his glass and said, "Cheers."

"What are we drinking to, Roy?"

"I dunno, maybe a few ticks off me bucket list. Ya know how it is, Cyril. Ya make a list of all the things you wanna put right before ya die and——"

"Are ya ill, then, Roy?" Cyril was talking with compassion.

"Yep, six months tops, so the doctors say."

Cyril leaned forward. "Sorry to hear it, mate. So, this bucket list, then. What's all that about?"

Roy grinned then. "Yeah, it's kinda silly, really, but I just thought, now I'm dying, what does anything really matter? Who cares if I get banged up, who cares if I get shot? Not me anymore and that's a fact." He gulped the remains of his drink and followed Cyril's lead by filling his own glass to the brim.

Cyril observed the man's withered hands, with dirt under the nails, and then he took a closer look at Roy's tired, gaunt face. It was true: he really was sick.

"Roy, I saw the CCTV recordings. Ya know the ones I mean, don't ya? But I want to talk about the one with you and the superintendent."

Roy chuckled. "Oh, dear me, I must have forgotten about that one. It's all the drugs for the pain that can make me a bit daft." He turned his head and suddenly noticed Frank sitting there clutching his tool bag. Roy rolled his eyes. "Frank, I'll tell ya this for nothing. If ya try to torture answers out of me, I don't think it will make much difference. Ya see, I've so many poxy tablets for the pain, I'm practically immune."

Frank put the bag down on the floor. "Nah, mate, I ain't gonna hurt ya. So, I think, me old son, you've a lot to get off ya chest, haven't ya? And me, Cyril, and Blakey are all ears, when ya ready, that is."

"Where do I start?"

"At the beginning is a good idea, since ol' Cyril wants an easy life. He doesn't like to get too confused. It's his age, ya see."

Cyril kicked him under the table.

"Right. Well, then, let's start with Rose. Now she was a right whore, ya know. She led me a dog's life, she did, and ya know what? I just can't get it outta my head, my Rose with Johnnie Carter, after she knew he'd fucked me little sister. A virgin she was until he got his filthy fucking hands on her. Then, there's my Lacey, my sweet little girl." He stared into his whisky and tears tumbled effortlessly down his face. "She was just like her mother. I begged her, pleaded with her to stop it, but like Rose, she was another one that wouldn't listen. Still, I never hurt her. As much as I wanted to kill her, I told her to fuck off before I changed me mind."

Cyril looked up at Kelly who was still standing at the bar. "Call Sampson," he mouthed to her.

Quickly, she darted outside. The phone only rang twice. "Geoff, it's Kelly. I'm at the Mitcham Mint with Cyril and his men. Roy's inside, making some mad fucking confession. I think you'd better take over, while he's on a roll, because that last disk had him and the superintendent on it. He was holding Keffa's gun. It's him, Geoff. He shot Adam Carter, but I think there's more, so will you come quickly?"

"Right, I'll be there in ten minutes. I'll have to bring backup, but don't worry. You just keep him there."

"Sneak in the back door, all right?"

She crept back into the pub and took up her position at the bar. She had a sense that tonight's drama would be etched in her memory for many years to come.

Roy was in a trance, staring into his glass. Cyril looked over at Kelly; she put her finger over her lips, signalling to stop talking to him. He needed to make a confession in front of the DI.

"Here, Roy." Cyril offered him a cigarette and Roy took it with a nod of thanks as he told them bitterly, "It makes no difference now. These bastards are what gave me a death sentence. Mind you, Rose, Johnnie and Adam Carter, Keffa, and fucking Jean didn't help, either. They all drove me to drink and fags."

"Yeah, Roy, that lot did give ya a hard time, eh, me ol' son. No one can blame ya for what ya did."

"Mr Reardon, I was never one for violence. I was a bit of a coward, really. I know they laughed at me and took the piss, but why I managed to carry on serving pints and running this joint was, well, it was because I had a secret, ya see. Not that it did me much good, mind. I couldn't reveal the fact that I'd been proper violent once upon a time. But there was no pat on the back, no fear in anyone's eyes." He took a deep drag on his fag. "I thought at least my wife would have been petrified, but she thought I didn't have it in me. Standing there, she was, laughing at me, telling me I was a useless prick with a cock the size of a hamster's and the brains the size of a pea. 'Why don't you grow some fucking balls and be a real man,' she said. So, I did, and I showed her that I had balls. Poor cow never expected me to thump her one, but the trouble was, once she was on the floor, I lost it. Cor, Jesus Christ, I was mad that day. I admit I did go a bit far, but I knew, even when I cut her to ribbons, she was still mocking me. She had this grin, ya see. It was fixed across her face, no matter how many times I ran that blade over her,

461

or how many fucking times I stuck that knife in her chest. She still had that mocking grin. Even when I buried her, she was still laughing at me."

Cyril was mortified and yet morbidly fascinated. He reached across and put his hand over Roy's. "I understand, mate, you did what ya had to do. I would have done the same thing, but afterwards, I would have fed her to the pigs. So where did ya bury her, Roy?"

With a flick of his head, he replied nonchalantly, as if this was commonplace, "Under the patio, of course."

From where he was sitting, Cyril noticed Sampson ease his way in and two coppers appear at the entrance to the bar.

"So, Roy, ya buried Rose under the patio? Only, I thought she had fucked off up north with some fella?"

Roy really laughed at that question. "Nah, I started that little rumour."

"So, me ol' son, what's this all about? Ya know, you and Superintendent Campbell?"

Roy began to cough again and instantly Blakey pulled out his handkerchief. "'Ere ya go, Roy," he offered, as he patted the man's back.

Once he caught his breath, Roy carried on. "Old Val, I've known her for years. She's another desperate bitch. She hates you, Cyril. She reckons you've given her the slip for too many years. The only problem is she had this hold over me. She knew I killed Rose. The sly bitch came to visit me one night after the pub was closed, after some information on someone. I can't remember exactly who. She thought she heard

462

someone talking in the garden, and the nosy cow took cover and listened." He stopped and chuckled. "But it was only me talking to Rose as I buried her. You know, a final few words. I honestly thought I was banged to rights, but the slippery cow said one day she would call in a favour. Well, of course, years later, she did, as you saw on the recording. When she came to me that night and told me what she wanted me to do, I thought it would be easy. She knew how much I hated the Carters, and she wanted her pound of flesh as well. I mentioned that Keffa had left his gun, hoping she would nick him for possession of a firearm, but no, she wanted blood, and I really mean blood. She wanted Adam Carter shot and Keffa to take the blame. Oh, and what a laugh! She wanted Johnnie set up for child pornography. I knew Johnnie liked kids, my Audrey for example, and well, what better way for him to go down for being a paedophile. My bucket list was therefore complete. And the icing on the fucking cake was her up there." A sudden high-pitched giggle escaped his lips, sending Cyril into a sense of horror.

Sampson indicated to the two coppers that they should go up to the flat.

Cyril knew he had to continue to get as much out of Roy as he could, just in case he clammed up when the detective interviewed him.

"Who, Roy?"

Roy slowly slurped his drink and sighed. "Jean River. 'Course, no one knew about me and her. That was her dirty little secret, but I weren't daft enough to think she really liked me. She just used me. I knew she clocked me, when I was leaving Adam's flat and she was going in. By the time I'd almost arrived home, I noticed her tailing me, the devious cow. She never admitted it, but she started asking questions about who's who and what's what. I was a bit pissed and stupidly told her about the rift between Keffa and Adam. I was thinking maybe she kinda liked the idea that I was as dangerous as her taste in men. I probably told her too much about the business between Keffa and Adam, but fuck it, what did I have to lose? Then she left, as she always did. She soon returned though, wanting something, a place to stay, or money. So, anyway, she's up there. I gave her what she loved most — a little bit of opium."

Cyril wanted to get back to Campbell and find out exactly her role in all of this.

"So, Campbell, the sly bitch, made you take that flash thingamajig and got ya to put it onto Johnnie's computer?"

"You've no idea about computers have ya, Mr Reardon?"

"Nope, not a fucking Jack and Danny. But how did ya manage to get into Johnnie's house with that great bitch there? She's vicious, that one."

Roy sat up straighter, his chest filling out with pride, as he projected a self-assured smile. He was there in front of Cyril Reardon having a decent conversation. Never before had he ever been privy to sit at his table, and now all eyes were on him, like he was the one for the first time in charge.

"That, Mr Reardon, was a piece of piss. His bitch was one of my pups. She loved me, she did, and my Rose took her out of spite. Anyway, Agro was all over me, making a fuss, while I downloaded all that shit onto Johnnie's computer."

Cyril asked one last question before he handed Roy over to Sampson. "And Adam Carter? I guess you had a good enough reason to blow his head off, eh?"

464

"Oh yeah, for shagging my little Lacey, the dirty fucking scumbag. He got it right between the eyes. I couldn't believe I was such a good shot, eh!"

Cyril stood up and held out his hand for Roy to shake. "You weren't no coward, Roy. You were a very brave man."

Roy was chuffed to bits, as he shook Cyril's hand and smiled, and then he looked over at Sampson, who almost jumped when their eyes met.

"It's all right, detective, I'll come quietly and—"

Before he could finish, the two police officers came hurtling down the stairs. "Gov, we have a dead body up there."

Roy stood up from the table and made his way towards the inspector. "I guess that's everyone accounted for now."

He held his hands out for the handcuffs, and as one of the police officers moved forwards to snap them on Roy's wrists, Sampson stopped him. "No, you don't. I will drive Roy to the station myself. He doesn't need restraining. Call forensics and get the body removed."

He nodded at Kelly. "Thank you. I owe you one."

Kelly winked and replied, "I might call it in, one day."

As Roy followed Sampson out to the car, Cyril tapped him on the shoulder. There was one thing he was desperate to know. "Er, Roy, was I on your bucket list? I mean I never caused you any pain, did I?"

"You, Mr Reardon, no, you never did. You were always a respectful man."

With a look of satisfaction in Sampson's direction, he said, "Take care of him, will ya, son?"

"You have my word, mate," he replied, as he opened the car door for Roy to climb in.

The drive back to the house was done in silence. Not only had they a lot on their minds but they were also preoccupied with their own thoughts, all shocked by the confession. That was until Cyril spoke up. "What are we gonna tell the kids? Gawd, blimey, their mother's dead. Jesus, I know I couldn't stand the woman, but even so. I also know that the kids are still angry for her leaving them, but when they find out she's been murdered, what then?"

Kelly swallowed hard, as she relived events she wished she could bury for good. Her past, she decided was just that: it was best to leave it at that. Some people, she knew, needed counselling for what they had been through, but she hadn't gone down that route. However, her young siblings, she thought, might need professional help. She wouldn't interfere, but she would be there for Malik and his sisters, should the need arise.

Valerie Campbell's decision to leave hospital before she was formerly discharged was based on fear. She was in shit up to her neck, once the police knew she'd gone to Roy and called in a favour by getting him to execute Adam Carter and to set up his brother Johnnie to place child porn on his computer. *That was a good euphemism for blackmail, if there ever was one*, she thought. So, of course, she'd had to leave the hospital: she was a lame duck, otherwise.

CHAPTER TWENTY-THREE

Six weeks later

The cold weather was creeping into their bones, as they huddled together by the grave. The reporters and inquisitive onlookers begrudgingly parted, as Kelly walked with her arm linked with Cyril's towards the graveside to join her brother. The family had decided on a swift burial for their mother. They had ruled out a service in church because Jean had never taken them to one. The sooner she was in the ground the better. It was bad enough having to attend a burial service. But Malik felt it only right that he took the three girls to say goodbye. Sassy refused to go at first, for she genuinely hated Jean, but she changed her mind at the last minute, knowing that this occasion wasn't about her; it was, for the greatest part, being there for her family. The coffin being lowered into that hole meant nothing to her. Star and Tilly didn't say much and only time would tell if their mother's death would affect them.

A gentle hand rubbed Malik's shoulder and all eyes were on them. He slowly turned and smiled at Kelly. "Thanks for coming, sis."

"I'm only here for you and the girls and always will be."

He nodded and clutched her hand. "And me, too."

Tilly stepped back, and, as always, eased her hand into Cyril's. They had a special bond, ever since the first cupcake she'd made for him.

An unexpected rogue reporter had stupidly decided to get a close-up of Kelly and barged his way through, almost knocking her down the hole, but as soon as it happened, a huge arm grabbed the scrawny camera-laden man and threw him to the ground.

"Fuck off, you bonehead," growled Keffa, with a menacing tone to his deep voice. He had only been released a few days before. The CPS dropped the charges, and he couldn't be charged with a lesser allegation, not since the serious issue with the superintendent would make the case a circus. The press would have had a field day with that kind of priceless information if it was leaked.

Malik held Kelly's arm to stop her from tumbling and instantly turned to see the man's flailing legs and arms on the ground. Malik's eyes glared, and within a flash, he pulled the man from the ground and cracked him hard across the forehead. "Now do one, before I fucking bury ya. Have some fucking respect!" He then shoved the reporter away.

Geoff Sampson stepped in to intervene. "Keep a lid on it. There are too many other reporters wanting to take a shot, and how the hell am I gonna protect you, if you're plastered all over the papers?"

"Okay, okay," conceded Malik, his eyes still flashing with anger.

The detective then turned to the reporter. "Move away, sir, before I nick you for trying to push Miss Raven over." In the ensuing staredown, the overeager young man got the message.

The priest continued, once the mumbling in the crowd ceased. There were no roses to throw in the grave and no eulogy read by a family member or by any friends. As the crowd began to leave, and the few faces that remained were recognisable, Cyril mumbled under his breath, "Either I'm going fucking senile, or there's a ghost standing over there."

Frank stared in Cyril's direction. "Jesus, that can't be, can it? I thought he was fucking dead."

Blakey witnessed who they were staring at and gasped, "Are you fucking kidding me? He ain't a ghost, surely?"

Malik looked over to the person they were talking about, to see a man in his late sixties. He was tall and fit-looking, with shoulders like a lintel, and dressed in a long blue Crombie. Malik could guess he was a Face in his day because he wore that expression of a hardman, so typical of villains. The tall gentleman was just staring at the grave, as if in some kind of a trance. Then he pulled out a handkerchief and wiped his eyes.

"Cyril, are ya gonna say something to him?" asked Frank.

"Yeah, of course I am. I thought the old bastard was dead, that's all."

They all watched as the man holding a white rose stepped forward and dropped it on the coffin. Then, as if he'd snapped out of his dreamlike state, he looked over and nodded at Cyril.

Star unexpectedly skipped away from Malik and went straight over to the man. In her innocence, she looked up at his face, her blonde curls falling over her eyes, as she asked, "Did you know my Mummy?"

The man crouched down, and his eyes lit up, as he stroked her cheek. "Why, yes, I did."

He walked with Star around the grave to find himself confronted with the gawping entourage. As soon as his tear-stained face turned into a smile, Malik knew who he was.

"Marcus River?" he enquired.

Marcus nodded at the young man, and in a gruff voice, he replied, "Yes, and you are?"

All the hate Malik had for his mother and his grandparents for abandoning him seemed to dissipate as quickly as the cirrus clouds above them. He'd always assumed that he would blast his grandfather with angry words and accusations for leaving them to rot in hell, if he ever had the opportunity to do so. Paradoxically, when he was in a more enlightened frame of mind, he would dream that his father or Marcus would come to his rescue, to save them all from their mother. For some odd reason, he looked up to the man, impressed by his size and vigour.

"I'm your grandson!" he stated simply.

"Gawd, blimey, Marcus!" exclaimed Cyril. "We all thought you'd passed away. I mean, you fucking disappeared and left the cottage to Jean."

Marcus looked at the girls, one by one. "No, as ya can see, I didn't die. After my Tilly left this world, I couldn't bear to live in that house anymore, so I took off to Spain. I never knew where Jean was, so I paid a private detective to find her. Two years, it took me. I wanted her to have the cottage."

"Did you know about us, Marcus?" asked Malik, determined to know whether or not he would love or hate the man.

His blank expression said it all: he didn't have a clue.

"I'm afraid, your mother had many secrets, so many, that I never knew what was true and what was not. But I'm pleased to meet you, er ..."

"It's Malik, well, Malakai. And this is Saskia, Sassy for short."

Marcus smiled at the confused look on Sassy's face. "Well, look at you, Saskia. Cor, you're a right stunner, eh." He didn't shake her hand but hugged her tightly, running his hands down her long wild mane of hair.

"Cor, fucking 'ell. Are you me gramps, then?"

Marcus gave a deep chortle, and his otherwise sad face lit up. "Oh, me girl, you're definitely a chip off the old block, I reckon."

His eyes then turned back to Malik. It was obvious to Cyril what Marcus was thinking, just by his bitter expression.

Cyril put his arm around Malik's shoulder. "You've no need to worry. He's a good kid, Marcus. He's been bringing up his sisters on his own and he's not like—"

Malik knew then what the issue was and jumped in. "No, I'm not like him. I may look like Eddie, but me and Kel," he nodded towards Kelly, "we ain't him in any way, Marcus, if that's what you're worried about."

The tightness in the face and shoulders immediately relaxed, and a fat tear left his eyes, as Marcus pulled Malik close and hugged him tightly. "Oh, I'm sorry, son. No one could be like him." As he looked over his shoulder, he winked at Kelly. "No one's born as evil as he was."

Tilly watched the dynamics and had a concern of her own. Marcus River was going to muscle in and take her family away. "Mr River, I've got me own grandad, you know." She squeezed Cyril's hand and leaned into his side. "I, er …"

471

Marcus laughed again, but this time it was at the hesitation in Tilly's voice and the sweet but determined expression on the youngster's face. He crouched down and ruffled her black curls. "And a fine one he is, too. So, what's your name?"

She smiled, and her dimples deepened. "Chantilly, but everyone calls me Tilly."

Another tear fell, as he thought of his dear old wife and how she had dimples and black curls. He looked back at Malik.

"Yes, you have four of us and me sister, Kelly, from another muvver."

A cold wind blew and encircled them. Cyril didn't want to hang about.

"Let's get over to the pub. We can talk there. Marcus, you can jump in with me, me ol' son. We've a lot to catch up on."

Marcus turned to Frank and Blakey. "Has he learnt to fucking drive yet?"

All the men laughed. "That'll be the bloody day," grinned Frank.

Malik and Kelly held back and watched as the others headed to the awaiting limousines and Cyril's Bentley.

"Well, sis, it's me and you now against the world." He watched as Star slipped her hand into Keffa's and as Tilly's hand gripped Cyril's. His heart melted. His wild Sassy was skipping alongside Marcus, looking up at him in adoration. Kelly looked over at Keffa wistfully, knowing that he had said something similar some time ago, when there was every prospect of a promising long-term relationship.

"Now, that's a sight, eh? I feel like a weight has been lifted. I've got so much family now. Just look at that! What more could I ask for?"

Kelly linked his arm with hers. "What about a girlfriend, Malik? Now, that would be the icing on the cake."

Malik turned towards her, and suddenly his face became very serious. "I'm seeing someone, sis. She's a bit older than me, but she's really lovely. I dunno what it is about her, but she makes me laugh. I invited her to come to the pub."

"Then, we'd best not keep her waiting, babe."

"You go on, Kelly. There's something I need to do first."

Kelly nodded and quickened her pace to join the others.

Kimi's grave was absolutely beautiful. The statue of an angel sat proudly over the headstone, and the fresh flowers filled the stone vase around which tiny winter pansies covered the freshly laid earth.

"I hope you are at peace now. Fly high with the angels. You, of all people, deserve your wings," he whispered sorrowfully. Then, unexpectedly, circling around him was a red butterfly which eventually settled on his right arm. It was extraordinary because it was quite the wrong time of year to see any of these beautiful creatures, let alone an unusual red one. He smiled through teary eyes. "Ah, Kimama, you will always be in my thoughts."

Malik's conscience and his loyalty and admiration for a friend were prime motivators in sorting out Kimi's burial arrangements. He just couldn't live with himself any longer, knowing her body was lying unidentified somewhere in a mortuary. Respecting the special part she had played in his life, he resolved to see that she was given the dignity

473

the lovely girl deserved. Sampson had proved his allegiance to the firm, and so Malik knew he could trust the detective to tell him the truth about Kimi. The body was released without question, and Malik saw to it that she was laid to rest beside her father.

Kelly's pub, The Cedar Arms, was packed to the rafters, with the exception of the reserved table, which had now been replaced with a larger one to include Malik and Sassy. They would have held the wake at Naomi's, but it was still being renovated after the fire. Malik mused over the amount of people present because in reality his mother had had no friends. They were all associates or acquaintances of Cyril's. It gave him a clear idea of the size of the firm and a sense of pride himself because he was treated with so much respect, a far cry from a year ago.

Cyril took his usual place and nodded to Blakey and Frank. "Cor, blimey, it only seems like yesterday we were burying Eddie Raven. And poor little Naomi, bless her heart."

Frank acknowledged this with a grim face. "Yeah, I remember it well. What a diabolical shame, eh? But the occasion had its better moments! Do ya remember when we let everyone believe that Kelly was the guv'nor, and when ol' Johnnie Carter walked in, he shit a brick?"

Just as he said those words, and right on cue, the crowd parted for Johnnie to walk over to Cyril's table. But this time he didn't have his swagger or cocky sneer. He bent down to Kelly and kissed her on the cheek. "All right, Kelly? Let me get you a drink."

Cyril watched and smiled. "How things have changed, eh? It may have been a joke back then, but it ain't now."

Marcus was preoccupied with catching up on Sassy's life. When he heard the change in Cyril's voice, he suddenly turned in his seat and stared. "Am I fucking seeing things or is that Carter?" he asked, to no one in particular.

Cyril waved his hand, gesturing for Marcus not to jump up and smash the life out of Johnnie. "A lot has changed, me ol' son, since you've been sunning yaself in Spain. Anyway, I'll fill you in later. Are ya back on the firm, then?"

Marcus looked around at his family and then back at Cyril. "Well, boss, it looks like you need some muscle."

Malik turned towards his grandfather and told him, "They have me in the firm now, Marcus. I can fight, ya know. I was born to fight."

Frank patted Malik's back. "Yeah, Marcus, this little fucker is favoured as the next Kent middleweight champion. He's only been invited to become a part of the Olympic squad to train for the Tokyo Olympics."

With a proud grin on his face and all thoughts of the Carter family now receding firmly to the back of his mind, Marcus said, "Ya know, son, I wanted to box for a living, professionally I mean, in my case, but I got kinda sidetracked."

Frank nudged Malik. "He was good an' all." He looked up at Marcus. "But Malik, here, is something special. I've never seen a boy fight like it."

Slightly embarrassed by the compliment, Malik tilted his head. "I guess I must take after you then, gramps, 'cos I wanna box for cash, not train with a squad for a medal. I'd still like to be recognised as the UK boxing champion, but I intend to earn real money."

"Oi, less of the gramps, it makes me sound old," he laughed. "Yeah, I reckon you'll do good, boy, and …" he paused and took a deep breath. "The truth is, I never was proud of my gal. I wanted to be, ya know, but she let me and you down, but as long as me legs can hold me up, I won't let ya down. I may not 'ave been proud of her, but I am of you, son." He grabbed Malik's hand and squeezed it.

A warm feeling engulfed Malik, as if those words from that man meant the world to him.

"So, who's training ya?"

With excitement and enthusiasm, Malik replied, "Only the best. Jack Vincent."

"Good lad. Well, I think I'll come along and give you a few tips of me own. I've got a special concoction, too. You won't like it, son, but it will build you up."

Blakey laughed. "And it gives ya the right shits."

Looking over at Kelly, who was now huddled in a dark corner, in earnest discussion with Keffa, Cyril felt a pang of sadness. The lads were getting excited talking sport, and in stark contrast, she looked a little lost among the mourners. He could see that Keffa was doing his best to fuss over her, although she remained somewhat stony-faced. He couldn't blame her, though.

"Kelly, when we leave here, can I take you somewhere special and just talk?" asked Keffa.

Her face was clearly marked with hurt, and he knew it.

"I guess so, Keffa, although where this will all end up, I'm really not sure, right now. You see, I did love you, and I know I didn't give you enough attention, but I just can't seem to get that vision of you and that horrible girl out of my head. It has made me sick, Keffa, fucking ill."

Her blank, cold expression felt like she was twisting a knife in his heart. He longed for her to look at him the way she used to – to giggle and act like the kid she was when he first met her. But he knew he had literally screwed things up to the point where he wouldn't blame her, if she didn't forgive him. Knowing her so well and how highly she valued honesty and sincerity, he wouldn't be surprised if she brought what they had to an end.

He nodded and lowered his head. "Kel, I'm gonna go and stay away for a while. I can see you hate me, and you've a new family to consider, but one day, I hope you will feel differently about me. Inside, you've a big heart, and it's taken a bashing by so many people and even by me. Betrayal is a sin, and I've let you down big style, I know that. I've shown weakness, and I can't forgive myself, so I don't expect you to. But when your emotions subside, and you've time to think things over, would you do just one thing for me?"

Kelly looked up at Keffa's face, unsure what he was getting at. But she could see the earnestness in his eyes – she knew he was really suffering. *Well, so he should*, she thought bitterly.

Keffa guessed what was going through her mind and decided to continue with what he needed to say before he bottled it. It had taken him days to go over everything in his head, and he was unsure if he would get another opportunity to say his piece.

"Look, as I've just said, I've shown weakness, I know that. But I'm only human. People make mistakes, even with those we love. I'm not going to make excuses for myself. I've treated you like shit. If I could turn the clock back to when I fucked up our relationship, don't you

477

think I would? All I'm saying is, please don't make hasty decisions about me. We've been through so much together. I've been there for you, when you needed me. I've shown you loyalty in the past. Yes, I've made a stupid mistake. But, should that one error of judgement wipe out the good life we've had so far, and should it destroy a possible future together?"

Keffa had made his pitch. Now the ball was very much in Kelly's court.

With that, he turned and walked through the crowded pub and was gone. Cyril noticed a tear trickle down Kelly's face, and he would have gone over to console her, but he knew she needed this private moment. Perhaps the new family would help to clear her head. She needed time to look at her relationship with Keffa afresh. He would wait a few days before talking to her about it. For now, he wanted to welcome his dear old friend Marcus. There was so much to catch up on, although watching him, it was as if Marcus had never left, what with that familiar twinkle in his eyes. Jean may have left him shadowed with disappointment, but she also left him a family to take charge of.

Kelly wiped her eyes and joined the others at their table. She was intrigued by Marcus. Malik did resemble him in some ways but so did Sassy. His large frame, huge hands, and hard face didn't match his soft eyes. The banter between the men showed her that he was a dear friend who had been a big part of their lives. She choked back another tear, thinking about how much he must have loved his wife to up sticks and go away when she died; it was all because he couldn't bear to live in that cottage without her. Her thoughts then returned to her and Keffa. Decisions, decisions. Perhaps she wasn't put on this Earth to have the kind of wonderful relationship which Marcus and his Tilly had enjoyed. She thought back to Keffa. If only.

As they sat chit-chatting, Kelly watched Malik's face suddenly light up. She followed his gaze and observed the woman standing by the bar, and her heart did a somersault: she couldn't believe who she was seeing.

Malik excused himself and rose to leave, eager to meet his girlfriend, but before he went, he whispered to Kelly, "There's someone I want you to meet."

It was the first time she'd seen Malik so excited, and she was amused by his exuberance, which lit up his eyes and turned that slight grin into a beaming smile. She had to admit her brother was a looker.

Kelly held in her own excitement. "I can't wait," she replied, with an upbeat tone to her voice.

Penelope was dressed in a beautiful black lace dress, her hair piled up in large curls with just a dusting of make-up, and she stood like the tall and elegant woman she was.

As Malik and Kelly approached, Penelope's eyes widened, and her mouth opened. *No, it can't be*, she thought. It was so much to take in. Her mind flashed back to the night she'd questioned Malik about him being like his father. At the time, she couldn't fathom what it was about his eyes and complexion which had initially made such an impression on her. But she knew now. There, before her, stood Kelly Raven's brother. And furthermore, Malik, like Kelly, would never stand for any shit aimed at friends and family. Loyalty was key. Instead of embracing Malik, she held out her arms to hug Kelly. Both enclasped each other not as strangers but as friends. Malik stood bemused, and as Kelly pulled away, she shook her head.

"Well, blow me, Penny McAllen, I wondered if I would ever see you again. We're still mates, ain't we?"

Penny giggled because it was a private joke. "Yeah, Churchy, we're mates."

"You know each other, then?" beamed Malik.

Kelly nodded. "Oh, yes. Penny taught me how to survive. If it wasn't for her, I may have died years ago."

"What?"

"Oh nothing, Malik, she was a good friend to me. It was a short relationship but a meaningful one."

Penny looked from one to the other. "Crikey, you *are* two peas in a pod." Instantly, she felt embarrassed. She was dating Kelly's brother, and Kelly would know that she was a bit older, and with Kelly's reputation, she didn't want to cause a problem. Her face said it all.

"Penny, what's up?"

Looking at Malik and then lowering her gaze, she answered hesitantly, "I know there's an age gap but——"

Kelly laughed. "No buts, Pen. If you make each other happy, then so be it. Besides, I don't wanna be fighting off any silly tart who goes after me brother. I know you, Penny. You are straight up, and after what you went through, losing ya mum and dad like that, you deserve a bit of happiness."

Malik had no idea what Kelly was talking about. Unexpectedly, Penny gasped, "Oh my God, Kelly, it was *you*, wasn't it?" Penny's skin was covered in goosebumps, she began to shake, and her face turned pale.

Kelly smiled. "Yes, Pen, it was me. I heard about your lovely parents in that awful fire, how you ended up homeless, and I always said one day I would pay you back for what you did for me, that day at school."

Penny put her hands to her mouth, unable to take it all in. Since the visit from the solicitor, she'd wondered who'd given her the beautiful hair salon with the flat above it. After the house fire, in which she managed to escape, but her parents burned to death, she was left homeless. The council stuck her in a hostel, until, out of the blue, a solicitor turned up with the keys to a business and a home. He wouldn't say who he was representing, but it was all above board. She vowed that whoever had given her this gift, she would make it a success and hoped that one day she would meet her saviour. "How can I ever repay you?"

Kelly shrugged her shoulders. "Ya already did, Pen, just by being you. Anyway, what's with this dodgy posh accent? Where's the old Penny?"

Penny laughed now, reverting to type. "I'm a boss now, ya know. I've got two salons, and I like to swan about with me airs and graces. Fuck me, the clients love it! Those rich, snooty birds pay a fucking fortune for a quick trim and colour. But, really, they like a good gossip. So, now, me salons are full of the toffee-nosed Londoners who splash their cash like it's going outta fashion. I managed to buy that house in Otford with a small mortgage. I've got a lingerie range, and guess what? I've called it Bluey's."

Kelly blushed. "Bluey, eh?"

"Yes, Kelly, I just like the name. It kinda stuck in me head."

Malik chuckled at the way Penelope – no, Penny – had ditched her finery and was very down-to-earth, much like his sister, Kelly. But she couldn't compete with his younger sister, Sassy, as he just caught the tail end of her in the background swearing like a trooper and Marcus laughing with her. Then Malik rolled his eyes, as Sassy, being the prying cow she was, came over to them. "So, this looks really cosy! Who's this, then?" she asked, her voice in good humour.

Malik turned to Penny. "Well, Pen, I suppose you'd better meet the rest of me family. Me two youngest sisters have gone home, but this here is Sassy, and yes, it's Sassy by name and Sassy by nature."

"Nice to meet ya, Pen."

Penny watched the dynamics and was so glad she'd accepted that first dinner date with Malik. If she'd let her misguided concerns about him being like Eddie get in the way of her heart, she wouldn't be here today. He treated her like a princess, and that was all she wanted, ever since he stood in her garden telling her to go inside and keep warm.

Malik was relieved that Sassy was polite and didn't show him up – at least on this occasion, anyway. Maybe she was growing up at last. Her pretty smile was new, so perhaps burying their mother had taken away any fears she held, or conceivably, she'd managed to release the anger that had been stored for so long in her mind. He had a sudden urge to hug her, but instead, he gently punched her on the arm, to which she gave him a grin that said, *I love you, too.*

Sampson was standing at the end of the bar, when his phone rang. It was the commissioner. Weaving his way through the crowd he went outside, away from the noise. Cyril clocked him, and swiftly followed. He was hoping for some good news, to put his anxious mind at rest.

By the time he reached Sampson, the call was over.

"I've got to go, Cyril. We've just had a lead that Valerie Campbell has a place in Cornwall and an arrest is going to be made any minute now. Armed officers have the house surrounded. By the sounds of things, they've pulled out all the stops for this one. I'm not surprised, though. The commissioner wants her head on a block." His smile was full of joy and relief. "Finally, eh? Well, that's one woman who would plead for the death penalty because can you imagine what she will go through inside a women's prison? I wouldn't want to walk in her shoes. Anyway, I best be off. I'm looking forward to interviewing her. I will savour every fucking moment," winked Sampson.

Cyril shook his hand. "I can go back and enjoy me pint now, knowing that justice will be served."

As Sampson walked away, Cyril pulled from his coat a letter and read it one last time.

Cyril Reardon,

Now I am just like you, a lawbreaker, I will be coming – and when you least expect it. I will take you down. I may not have the arresting powers as before, but there is more than one way to skin a cat.

Yours

Ms Campbell

He screwed it up and tossed it in the bin.

As tough and as brutal as Cyril was, that note had shaken him. Valerie Campbell had been the bane of his life. Knowing what she was capable of had left him uneasy, not for himself, but for his new-found family. She was dangerous as a superintendent, but then she'd had to abide by the rules. Now, however, all bets were off: she was a desperate woman on the run, and there were no rules. Still, as far as

483

he was aware, he was safe for the moment and so were his greatly enlarged family. He sighed, relaxed his shoulders, and headed back to his friends.

CHAPTER TWENTY-FOUR

Kelly stared at the result for what seemed like forever. She then left the bathroom and sat down on her bed. "Fuck, fuck, fuck!" she said aloud. She'd wondered if that little Caribbean adventure might bring with it unforeseen consequences. Well it had, for both of them. She would, at one time, have been shouting from the rooftops, but recent events had put paid to that feeling of ecstasy, for sure. What was that saying? Act in haste, repent at leisure. That was it. Yes, but at the time, she and Keffa were having a blast. They were totally in love, almost in each other's pockets. They'd thought they were made for each other. But reality had now set in, as she sat there staring at the cross clearly visible indicating she was pregnant. She didn't know how she should feel. The time alone should be spent going over her future.

But she couldn't go there just yet. She needed to look back, if she was to make a future work for herself and her little one to be. And Keffa? Up until the Caribbean trip, they'd put off going away together because they were busy with the business. Was that how they'd *both* seen it, though? No! She was deluding herself. She'd been the one who had kept putting off times to be with him to focus on her immediate priority: the business. She'd wanted the adulation, the feeling of achievement. It had never been about the money. Christ, she'd shed loads to fill Selhurst Park.

She thought back to that time after she'd set up Ruth in her former home. In his hand there was an envelope. He'd asked her to open it. Inside were two tickets to the Caribbean. She recalled his words and smiled grimly. He'd said something like, "Me and you, babe, two weeks, just us, no business, no running around saving the world, just time out, please."

Well, they never went on that holiday, did they? Then, there were all those cancelled date nights. What was all that about? She knew why, really. She was just trying to anaesthetise herself from her own guilty conscience. And always, there would be Keffa, with his concerned look on his face saying, "Don't worry, Kelly, you go and do what you have to do. Our dinner can wait." How many times had he said those words?

So now to the present. Her heart sank. The time away from him had done her some good, in so far as she knew she loved him, and it was a stark reminder that she was as much to blame for the deterioration of their relationship as he was. The problem was she had always believed in the perfect partner. But there was one big black cloud hovering over them: the fucking barmaid at the Mitcham Mint. That vision of her boyfriend and the slapper was still driving her up the bleeding wall. It wasn't him, that aggressive shag. He wasn't like that, was he? It dawned on her, of course, it was like watching a stranger because that wasn't the man who gently laid her on the bed and carefully massaged her bare skin, taking his time, and showing how much he loved every inch of her body. Because that was it. He did love her. That shag was just that: a shag. She had neglected him and what should she expect – a man running around after her, answering to her every whim, or being thrown aside when it suited her? No, that was not what she wanted. No, she needed Keffa – for it to be back to the way things were. He and her together, as a family.

She stared at the pregnancy test once more before she picked up her bag and left her beautiful home in Farnborough Park to return to Peckham – to her man. She just hoped he would still be there waiting for her and he'd not moved on like many handsome men would. He was a good person and had loved her from the day they met when she was fifteen. A feisty kid ready to take him on and fronting him out in his posh apartment. He could have had her killed, but he never did; he was intrigued at first, but as she grew into a woman, she was the only one for him.

Well, she needed to sort things out, now, before the relationship became irrevocably damaged.

The drive was spent with tears helplessly falling down her cheeks. How could she have turned her back on him? Although she'd ensured his release from prison, her manner had been unequivocally cold. He didn't deserve it. The traffic piled up as she reached Peckham, her first proper home, where she changed from a scared young girl into a confident woman, taken off the streets by Rudy and Lippy. The cars came to a standstill, and to the side, she looked at the house where she'd been loved. She could almost visualise her dog, Legend, on the doorstep, but he'd died along with a piece of her heart. Dear Lippy, the woman she loved so much, with her purple weave and skintight shorts and a deep laugh, she envisaged her busy in the kitchen. The huge cooking pot with her delicious curry bubbling away was just one of many memorable moments living in that home. Then her mind went to Rudy with his animated laugh and puppet-like moves. A lump lodged in her throat. She had neglected them too. She'd been so busy trying to make money and keep the business going, she really had lost sight of what was important in her life and especially those who meant so much to her. Showing everyone that she could run her business alone, what had it all been for? She needed to make things right. A car hooted and made her jump. There, ahead, she saw a perfect parking space, fifty metres from the house. Reaching her old home, she smiled at the familiar cracked concrete step, still a bit of an eyesore, pulled out the bunch of keys from her pocket, hesitated, and nervously swallowed. Would they mind her just popping in, almost out of the blue? She hadn't been near or by for months and her visits were getting less and less frequent. Did she still have the right to retain her keys and let herself in?

Nevertheless, she turned the key in the lock and stepped inside. She could visualise Legend hurtling down the stairs slobbering all over her. A tear pricked her eyes. Her beloved dog – the house didn't seem the same. Then she heard voices and an unmistakable laugh. It was Rudy and her dear friend Ditto.

Almost by magic, Kelly settled herself into her old home; it was as if she'd never left, just like old times. The smell of newly made curry hit her, as she entered the hallway, and she knew that Lippy was cooking. Then she recognised another voice, a deep distinctive tone: it was Keffa. She was surprised, as she'd not seen his car parked outside.

Suddenly, the room went quiet, and they turned to face her.

Ditto jumped from his seat at once. "Bluey, it's Bluey!" He hugged her tightly like a brother. Then, Rudy jumped up. He hadn't aged. Still as bouncy as ever, the only change was that his dreadlocks were so long now. "Look at me lickle chil'," he laughed delightedly, as he, in turn, hugged her.

Keffa stood up and gave her a compassionate smile, but, all the same, he seemed uneasy and almost teary eyed. "I'll go, Kelly. You wanna spend time with ya family."

488

Stifling the urge not to cry herself, she held her hand up. "No, Keffa. I'm going to spend time with my family, but, please, stay, er, that is, if you want to."

She thought she saw his bottom lip quiver, and so she did what came naturally, and she threw herself into his arms before he acted less than the big man he was.

"I'm so sorry, Kelly, I didn't mean——"

"Shush, it's over with. I was a fool, I was wrong. Let's just move on, eh?"

He held her away with a deep frown etched across his brow. "Move on?"

She nodded, her eyes shining with tears. "Yeah, together, Keffa. Let's just face the world as one, like we've done before. I may have a big family, but you are my man, and things will change, I promise."

The reconnection was cut short, as Lippy walked into the room.

"Well, if it ain't me lickle Bluey! Ah, chil', lets me take a good look at ya." She pulled Kelly away and into the light, turning her from side to side. With a look of concern on her face, she gently said, "Sweet pea, is there something you need to tell us?" Then, gently, she patted Kelly's stomach.

The three men took a few seconds to take it all in.

"Kelly, are you, I mean——"

A slow smile spread across her face. "Keffa, I know I've taken on a whole new family, but I guess it's just gonna get bigger, with a new addition on the way."

The high-pitched squeal made Kelly jump. Lippy was jumping and clapping, as if she'd just won the lottery. Kelly laughed. It was so good to see Lippy a picture of health, after her brain tumour scare just over a year ago.

Keffa pulled her close. "I think we've a babysitter, when you go back to work, babe."

Kelly shook her head. "I've someone to take over. I'm spending time with my family. All of them. Malik knows the ropes. I trust that kid more than I trust myself."

Keffa grinned. "He's a chip off the old block and a diamond of a man."

"He is, Keffa, and like me, he doesn't take after our father."

"No, Kelly, no one does. We can now live a life without secrets."

She looked down at her tiny bump and smiled. "Yes, no more cruel secrets and no more wicked lies."

492

Printed in Great Britain
by Amazon